Angela's Hope

By Leah Banicki

Angela's Hope
by Leah Banicki
Copyright © 2013 Leah Banicki

Book 2 of Wildflower Series

https://www.facebook.com/Leah.Banicki.Novelist

Acknowledgements –

To the many people who helped and supported me through this long road of healing and writing.

Pat , Leslie & Patty

LLPP – we make a great support team. I pray that God will bless our efforts for years to come.

To my family for their patience and care while I wrote and healed, I pray that you will be rewarded for all that you have done for me.

Most of all I thank God who has loved me despite my weakness and flaws. His loving hand has held me through so many dark nights. His love endures forever.

Part 1

Prologue - Angela Fahey
May 2nd 1848- Oregon Trail

Angela could taste blood in her mouth. She had just fallen into a ravine and she was badly injured, she knew that. The night was pitch black and moonless. There was a sore spot on her tongue but that was the least of her worries. She was sure she had sprained or broken her arm before she had fallen. Now it was tangled in a heap with the rest of her.

There was something scratching her face whenever she tried to move her head. The deep throbbing in her leg was the most concerning to her. She had called out for help a minute ago.

Had it been a minute? She wondered.

Would anyone come searching for her? She was only a maid after all. If her employer, Andrew Temple, had any say she would be out here all night. The fear of it all crept from her belly and traveled through her; a ferocious fear that crept like a demon up her spine. Would she survive the night?

Pain pushed all thoughts from her head for a few minutes as she prayed while the pain was soaring through her body. Some thin object had pierced her shoulder in the fall.

A stick? She wondered.

"Lord, please help me…" Angela whispered into the dark night. She felt a moment of peace wash over her. Somehow she knew God was with her. It was confusing and overwhelming, feeling peace and pain battling within her for purchase. She wanted the peace to win.

She gathered her strength every few minutes and yelled out for help. Angela felt foolish. She knew the wagon train was far off. She would have no clue if anyone would be out in the black night who could hear her. She prayed that her voice would carry.

She had tried to sit up and pain shot through her legs and arms and she screamed out involuntarily. She cried for several minutes as the pain overwhelmed her. She did not yell out for a while, but instead just prayed and held herself together. She took deep breaths and listened to the night sounds around her as she waited.

She heard the faintest human sound above the rasp of her labored breathing, her chest and ribs were bruised and she kept having moments of panic. She was certain though, she heard something.

"Hello," A voice called out. It was far away but if she could hear them, then perhaps they could hear her. She would try and yell again through her hoarse throat.

"Please help me!" Angela yelled out three times than stopped to breathe. It was getting harder and harder to project her voice. In her fall her body had taken a beating. She hadn't eaten since the morning of the day before. It was probably after midnight by now, a new day.

"Keep yelling!" The voice was closer.

Some momentary hope urged Angela to yell again and again. Her voice caught several times in a near sob.

"She's here." A familiar voice said. It was either Lucas or Russell.

She thanked God over and over in her mind but had no more energy to speak aloud.

There were three gunshots fired into the air. She could see a few lanterns above her and a few minutes passed as more people gathered near.

"We are coming to get you, Red." Clive's voice said, soothingly. His was the voice that sent her over the edge, emotionally. She began to sob in pain, relief and a few unknown feelings. He was the closest thing to a father she had left. He was a beautiful old soul that had become her protector. They all had come to save her. Her weary joy overflowed, as did her tears.

The men climbing down the ravine loosened some debris, some clods of dirt and a few broken branches fell on her or near her, as the men tried to get to her safely. The falling stuff mattered little to her but men were yelling and scrambling to keep her safe, all trying their hardest to do no more harm.

Her sobs had quieted. She felt faint and weak as she waited. She listened to the men around her and realized how surreal it all was. They were coming for her – A nobody, a servant. Her own stepfather had basically thrown her away like trash. Then, just today, her employer had done the same. Why were these men risking their lives for her?

Clive and a man she didn't know were near her. They both had lanterns and she enjoyed the warmth of the light after her terror in the pitch-blackness for hours. They seemed to be examining the situation. Clive was talking but it sounded far away to her. Like he was talking under water.

Clive grabbed at the bush that was next to her and hacked away at it then tried to remove some of the brambles from her hair.

The other guy removed a large rock from her right ankle. Angela screamed once the pressure was removed and the men decided it was time to just pick her up and get it over with. Angela tried to be brave but the pain of movement was too much. Clive spoke words to calm her and she leaned against him.

Only a few hours ago she had accepted that she would probably die soon. God had other plans.

❊ ❊ ❊ ❊ ❊

Andrew Temple
May 4th 1848 - Fort Kearney

Andrew Temple was a desperate young man, his guts eating away with what he had to finally admit to himself as guilt. He had suffered two days at the hand of his own crew, men he paid, all giving him glares and disrespect. It had finally broken through his hard-hearted wall. A young girl was nearly killed and it was *his fault*. He kept replaying the day of the accident over and over.

All the scouts he had been riding with had been complaining. The whole wagon train had been very annoyed by the lack of available firewood. He had a certain amount of pride that their stores of dry firewood and kindling were more than enough to last through a barren section. He had servants out gathering daily. He took a certain pride in his outfit. Three wagons and a cookie was one of the best set-ups in the whole train of more than a hundred wagons. At twenty-five he felt like the best man, and he liked that feeling.

When his one servant girl, a red-headed skinny thing, had come back from a gathering run of several hours with such a small offering he knew that was to be expected. He knew everyone was struggling to find firewood. He didn't know why he had yelled at her, he wished over and over to relive that ten minutes. He sent the girl out into the night for no good reason. Andrew pushed off the pleading of his other servant, Reggie, and his whimpering wife, telling him that the dark night wasn't safe. He allowed a lantern to be sent to the girl, but he knew the oil hadn't been filled. Every detail was replaying in his mind. He didn't want to ask himself why he had done it.

His wife, Corinne, had begged him with tears in her eyes. She rarely asked anything of him anymore. She had been avoiding him for weeks. He was happier for it. He only married her to appease a sense of duty to her father. He was not in the market for a child bride and he let her know it often. The only thing that said they were married was the paper in his wagon. Corinne was an inconvenience and part of him was pleased every time he could make her unhappy. Overworking her

6

servant, Angela, was always a thorn between them but finally the threats had worked and Corinne and Angela's friendship was under control. Seeing Corinne's tears the night of the accident at first had made him smug. Now they just reminded him of all his mistakes.

The girl had been gone for hours. Reggie and Corinne had stayed up and paced around while waiting for her to return. He thought they were being dramatic and had gone to bed. He awoke to the sounds of yelling and horses. He dressed quickly and joined the other men on horseback.

The news of a girl calling for help out in the darkness made his blood run cold. For a moment he felt the first inkling of what he had done. He pushed it away quickly and put his wall of pride back up.

The men were going to form a search party and started to ask him some rather pointed questions about why his servant was out in the dark, moonless night. This area was dangerous and there had been many warnings about staying close to the fires because of wild animals.

In his own pride and sense of protecting his reputation he had bold-faced lied. He called the girl silly or something like it. The next few seconds were a blur. He saw his crew, the Blake brothers and Reggie and even the gruff cookie, they all looked at him with shock. It was their disappointed looks that had distracted him enough that he never saw his childish wife flying at him in a rage. She screamed at him like a wild creature.

He held her off for a minute but she got one solid slap across his cheek. He couldn't believe his first response had been to hit her back. He pulled a fist back to shut her up.

Her screaming about him being a hateful liar was embarrassing and his face stung from the ferocity of her hand clapping against his unsuspecting skin. Clive Quackenbush, a man he respected highly, was behind him and grabbed his fist before he had struck his wife in front of so many people. Once the rage left him he realized the magnitude of this moment. Not sure he had ever felt lower, his mind flew back a few years and remembered the same kind of feeling once before. Shame started again coursing through his veins like a poison.

His weeping wife was pulled away and comforted, then he joined the other men on horseback to search through the night. It was hours before the girl was found. The state of her brokenness only added to his pile of self-loathing. He was done with any smugness or pride. He knew he was a wretch. A horrible wretch!

The girl was found at the bottom of a rocky ravine, tangled in brambles, with broken bones; bleeding and scabbed from head to toe. The men had yelled for everyone with a lantern to gather so they could get to her safely. It had taken some doing to get her unraveled from the mess of thorns and bushes that had caught her from her tumble.

Andrew felt physically ill when he saw her. A mix of all the shame, guilt and abhorrence for what he had done came at him like a crashing wave. He willed himself to not vomit.

He could see there was actually a stick coming out of her shoulder! It had penetrated her skin and was sticking out like she had been on the losing end of a knife fight. He didn't want to look anymore and forced himself to walk away from the scene. His respected friends, Lucas and Clive, took charge of getting the girl wrapped into a warm blanket. She moaned several times while the men lifted her broken body up to Lucas on his horse.

There was nothing for them to do but everyone agreed they needed to get her back to Corinne. His wife had a gift for healing, some knowledge of medicine and would care for the girl. But Andrew had little hope. He knew with her injuries that infection would probably finish her off within a few days. He was a graduate of veterinarian medicine, after all. He knew that if she had been an animal and this badly injured… Andrew pushed away the rest of the thought.

His head was full as the next days passed. He heard the girl's cries from across the camp as the wagon rolled with her in it. The word infection was on everyone's lips. Corinne was doing her best and had to do several torturous procedures to remove more debris from the girl's wounds. His stomach flopped with every new realization of what he had done.

He had several voices in his head competing for attention. The voice of shame and self-loathing was the loudest. Telling him every day he had been prideful and evil to this servant girl and also his wife. The other voices were his parents. It had been over three years since he had said goodbye to them.

He was still feeling the anger bubbling up from inside about how they just left him behind.

Ok, I was a young man and studying at the University. I had barely gone home to Kentucky at all during my school breaks. Andrew chastised himself. Knowing his anger had been misplaced at his parents.

There had just been so many issues at home. He battled his own mind most days. His Christian upbringing had taught him against the things he was doing.

His mother had always warned him that he was like his grandfather, always angry about everything. She worked and prayed with him growing up telling him to go to God when his angry tendencies took over. He had accepted the Lord when he was young. He knew he was a sinner and many times he went to God for help when his temper would rise to the surface. He couldn't explain sometimes how much he wanted to just yell or lash out for no reason.

He would pick fights at school. Then, when he went home his parents would punish and then pray with him.

He had gotten the strap a few times in his life but his father had never been harsh with him. The few times he had deserved it and he knew it. His mother had told him so many stories about her father, how his anger had been constantly bubbling under the surface. He had hit her and her mother sometimes, but the worst was the yelling and the insults, all the time. His mother was sweet and gentle and she would say over and over how she married a man as different from her father as she could find. It was a constant conversation between his parents and him. 'Go to God to control your anger.'

By fifteen years old Andrew Temple had a better temperament. He was a close friend then with the preacher's son and he had been a great example. It was only when he applied for college at Harvard that the anger started creeping back in. He did not get accepted and he was devastated. Everyone was talking about him and he was humiliated. A friend of his parents, John Harpole, had written a letter to the board of Harvard and magically the acceptance was received, but now his heart was hard again. He prayed about it often but nothing calmed his anger. He shut his parents out and sulked until it was time to leave for school. School was not hard for him and, because of that, he had plenty of free time, he made some new friends.

His mother was constantly writing letters, reminding him to attend a church and keep his heart humble to God. He responded like he knew she wanted him too. Saying all the right words but his church attendance was dodgy. Instead, he spent weekends with his friends. That was how his anger issues reached the boiling point. It still blurred in his mind. *It was the girl's fault.* He would tell himself but he knew. His conscience knew.

While in his second year of college he had spent a weekend at a friend house, a very wealthy family who threw magnificent parties. He enjoyed the flowing champagne and the attention from all the pretty girls. They liked his southern accent and they constantly told him he was charming. He had been accepted into this world of the wealthy and influential of the community. He was a Harvard student and his father, a wealthy ranch owner. He lost sight of his own morality when, in a moment of too much champagne and young stupidity, he took advantage of a maid in his friend's home after a party.

He barely even remembered it and a few months went by before the consequences snuck up on him. The maid was claiming to be pregnant and had told them that he was the culprit. The family was furious and was threatening to go to the Harvard board and turn him in. Andrew was in trouble and had no idea how to get out. His friends were talking behind his back and rumors were spreading. He was confronted with his sins and afraid for his standing as a student at Harvard.

How dare the girl turn him in! She had been a flirt every time he stayed there. How dare she, a mere servant, try to ruin his reputation? He wanted to lie and claim he had nothing to do with it but he knew he couldn't do that. There was a part of him that was ready to face the consequences. He had written the letter to his parents confessing several times and then burned each attempt. Somehow he had to get out of this, and then suddenly it was over. He received a letter from his friend's home. The maid had lost the child and they would not be addressing the issue again. But he was no longer welcome in their home and they proceeded to lecture him on his morality. He read the letter over and over, feeling relief over the release from the troubled situation but then anger at being lectured. After all, it was only a servant girl. If he had made that mistake with one of the young ladies at the party he would probably been forced to marry her. His friend had been his roommate at the university and had promptly moved out. He spent the rest of the year alone and it wasn't good for him. His friends avoided him and his grades dropped a little. Not enough to be kicked out but his pride manifested once more.

His guilt and shame issues were never dealt with and the next year his parents left for the West. They visited him before they left and seeing them so happy to be leaving him behind, he felt more alone. They wanted him to join them after completing college and he knew he would. He didn't want to go but he would, and he resented it.

It was all wrapped up inside him like a hot ball of pain and now he rode his horse alone, on the Oregon Trail, a graduate of Harvard, in a marriage to a girl he resented and had never even kissed. His actions, all came together as a hammer to his brain. What had he done?

He was heading to Fort Kearney to fix it, he had to fix it. There was no way out unless he could find a way to save her. He kept seeing that blanket covered in Angela's blood and he thought now of that child he had conceived a few years ago. He never thought of that child, ever. The maid had been pregnant, she had lost the child. He could not even remember the maid's name. She was a brunette, he remembered fuzzily. But now the maid from his past and Angela bleeding in the ravine merged together to show him the man he truly was.

He needed help and he pulled into the fort just as the sun was beginning to rise. He spoke with the man running the Hudson Bay store. He bought supplies and spoke with him about his situation, keeping it simple.

He was led to a cabin of a Captain Henry Sparks. The Captain was eating his breakfast when Andrew knocked on the wooden door. A pleasant lady answered and when he was invited in, no questions asked, he was surprised. These folks were very trusting.

"I was told you might be able to help me. I have a girl in my wagon outfit that has been injured badly. She has been cared for the best we can but she needs to heal and rest and I fear the journey and jostling of the wagon would finish the young woman." Andrew realized he was calling this servant a woman. He had never thought of her as anything but a servant, one step above trash until today. "I truly fear the journey will kill her."

The woman gasped and she looked to her husband, wordlessly they made a decision and the man spoke quickly.

"Absolutely, bring her to us. We will care for her."

The woman next to him nodded.

Andrew provided them with passage money for her, after she was healed and some money for their care of her. They tried to refuse but his desperation to do the right thing had urged them to finally accept all he offered.

Andrew rode back to the wagon outfit relieved in a way but also dreading the confrontation with his wife. His face still bore the scratches from her attack from a few nights before. Her friendship with Angela had been a sore spot between them and he had threatened Corinne many times that he would leave Angela behind if she even spoke to her maid. He wondered now why he had ever cared. But, he knew why, he had lost his closest friends and he envied his wife for having her own friend. He was angry over her happiness. He had done everything in his power to split them apart. Now he would tell his wife they would be leaving her friend behind.

Andrew's surprise over his wife's acceptance was brief. He thought she would be pouty and mean to him, and he would have deserved it. Instead, she accepted it bravely and he left them alone to prepare.

Angela was delivered safely into the household of the Captain and his wife Edith. He thanked them one last time and left his wife alone with them. Corinne needed to know that Angela was in a safe place in order to feel comfortable. Andrew knew from his conversation with the Sparks that they were good people. There had been a cross on the wall and a bible on the table. They were like his parents. His mother would have called them brothers and sisters in Christ.

His heart was hurting as he walked back to the wagon train. There weren't many people around, for everyone was excited to resupply at the fort or refill water stocks at the creek nearby.

Andrew ran into Clive Quackenbush when he was near his wagon outfit. Clive waved a hello but stopped in his tracks when he saw the young man's face.

"Something troublin' ya?" Clive said in his easy mannered way.

Andrew's throat was thick with emotion and he was at a breaking point. His guilt and shame had piled so high on his shoulders he wanted to crawl into a hole.

"Yessir," was all the Andrew could manage. He couldn't believe that Clive even cared to speak to him. He had been the one who stopped his fist from hitting Corinne. Clive and Corrine were friends. He treated her like a treasured daughter.

He must despise me. Andrew thought.

"You wanna talk about it Andrew?" Clive asked with a concerned look crossing his weathered face.

"I am certain you have other things to do." Andrew said, with his internal bitterness creeping forward. He didn't want to be judged by this man. Clive was the most respected man on this wagon train. Andrew wanted to find a hiding place for a while.

"Can't think of a thing to do that would be more important than talking to you right now." Clive said and put his arm on Andrew's shoulder.

Feeling Clive touch his shoulder was the moment of release. It was all he needed to allow his pain out. Clive was a willing person to listen, a good person.

"Clive, I am a wretch." Andrew blurted out, his throat hoarse with pain.

"As I am too, Andrew." Clive said. He could sense that Andrew needed to share. Clive took him by the arm and led them both over to a shady tree. They both sat and Andrew lost his composure.

"I nearly got her killed." Andrew exclaimed.

"You didn't do it on purpose." Clive answered.

"Yessir, I did." Andrew confessed. He began to weep.

Clive shook his head and said a prayer for the young man. He had had many talks with God about this fellow, his treatment of his young wife and Angela being the main reasons for most of the prayers. He had seen many a young fellow like him in his days. Full of something that made them lash out and treat people rotten.

He listened as Andrew spilled his story about his grandfather, his parents and even the maid he misused in his college days. His heart was broken and Clive let him talk. When a man faced up to his sins no matter if he was twenty-five or fifty he felt like a fool. He didn't want to give Andrew any reason not to trust him.

12

"God forgives even those things." Clive said simply after all the tears were done and stories shared.

"I don't deserve it." Andrew said quietly.

"None of us do." Clive said simply.

Clive and Andrew prayed together under that tree. Andrew confessed his anger to God and received the forgiveness he needed. Clive prayed for the young man who struggled with anger and hoped the journey to healing would be fast for everyone involved. The men talked for a while longer. Clive shared some bible verses that had helped him through some hard times. Clive encouraged him to keep a journal to help him through the tough days. They talked about Corinne and Clive encouraged him to give her plenty of space and that God could work on her heart to forgive him, too. Andrew cried a few more times during that talk when he thought about all the people that were hurting because of his actions.

Clive was grateful to see Andrew in that broken state. Sometimes that was how the healing started. The wall had to break down to be rebuilt. Clive knew the man would struggle with anger again but he was one step closer to working through it.

They split up later with a promise from Andrew to talk to Clive whenever he was struggling. Andrew could not put Angela back together again, or unsay all the hurtful words he had said since the journey had started to his wife. But he had a peace in his heart, undeserved, but by the grace of God he would try to be better. Only God could help him.

Chapter 1 – Angela Fahey
May 4th 1848

Angela was tucked in, snug as a bug, according to Edith Sparks, her new caretaker. Angela spent a few hours with her closest friend in the world, Corinne Temple, and it distracted her from the pain that rolled through her body unmercifully. The pain in her heart was just as terrible. The Sparks were wonderful people. Henry was a jovial sort with a friendly smile and a mustache that smiled too. He loved to tell funny stories and even though it hurt to laugh, it was good for Angela to have these last fleeting moments with her friend as good memories to hold on to. Corinne had finally left with many tears and Angela was tucked into her bed. She had several more visitors from the wagon train who left her notes and gifts but it was over too soon and they were all gone. Angela was alone in pain and talking to God.

Had it only been a few days since she fell into that ravine, breaking bones and tearing flesh on branches and brambles as she went. The darkness of that night still lingered with her, and the sounds of the night terrifying her mind in dreams and waking thoughts. She wanted to shake away the fear, the perpetual fear of being left alone. It seemed to be her lot in life. Now here she was, only weeks into the Oregon Trail and her journey ended because of a fool.

The building she was in was the cozy and comfortable cabin of Captain Sparks. He was in charge of the men at arms at Fort Kearney. His loving wife was a sort of mother for everyone in the fort. They had only had one child who had died of scarlet fever years ago and they hadn't had any more children. They were in their early forties and ready to be caretakers for the 'poor sweet girl'. Edith and Henry had gladly allowed their lives to be flipped asunder to make room for this wounded girl. Edith's heart was full of love in an instant. Her longing to be a mother again filled her soul with purpose to have a new charge.

Angela's hot tears were a permanent fixture for several hours. Angela had bouts of crying jags that would make her whole body hurt. Edith Sparks was there to be supportive, as much as a stranger could be. There was a stack of fresh handkerchiefs on a nearby table for Angela to use and plenty of hot tea to sip when her crying would slow down enough to breathe. Angela felt like a child when she started hiccupping for a while. This kind of grief was never attractive, but she had to get through all the phases of it.

Angela had a lot of emotions to get through in that first hard night.

"It will be just one step easier tomorrow dear. I know." Edith Sparks patted a comforting hand on Angela's and spoke soothing accolades. It helped better than having no one. Angela so desperately wanted her mother to be near her. The faded memory of her face but that soothing presence still remembered, it lingered like a bitter pill.

"I feel like every good thing is always taken away from me." Angela said to Edith. A sob threatened to come out again but she swallowed it down, making her throat ache.

"I knew a hard life before I met my dear husband, I have known many who lived to see so much heartbreak. All my younger brothers died on the ship that brought my family to America, my father was so angry that I, a mere slip of a girl lived when his boys, what he called 'his future' all perished on that horrible stinking ship that brought us here. My mother and I ran away from my father just a year after we came here to America. I begged in the streets and my mother sewed and worked at a hotel for low pay, cleaning rooms to save enough for us to leave the city. It was a horrible struggle." Edith shared, knowing the things she saw in the young woman's eyes before her told their own story of loss and heartbreak.

"I know you are broken child, but you are not beaten. God will heal you, and mend your heart. I feel it in my bones. Like me, you have hope still. It burns behind those green eyes of yours." Edith dared a kiss on Angela's forehead and felt the girl begin a soft sob again, her emotions so raw and open.

Lord, please bless this child. Calm her heart and heal her pain. Edith prayed and held the girl's hand through the night.

❅ ❅ ❅ ❅ ❅

Angela woke several times when her pain increased. Edith would wake and give feverfew and sips of a foul-tasting tea to Angela and then helped her shift positions if need be. Her seeping wound on her shoulder would bleed if she moved too quickly or shift the wrong way. The bruise on her thigh ached the worst. Sleep was fitful when even the slightest movement would touch the bone deep bruise.

"Your fever is gone child." Edith said the first morning after Angela woke. Edith smiled just the tiniest bit. She knew how difficult this day would be.

"Has the wagon train left yet?" Angela asked. It was torture knowing her best friend was rolling away. The feeling of her heart ripping from her chest was renewed, but she refused to cry. She held it in and took a deep breath.

"They pulled out at first light. I have a letter for you that was delivered by a young lad named Reggie. I think it is from Corinne. You want it now, or would you like to read it later?" Edith showed her the letter on the table.

"Later is better. I can look forward to it for when I really need it." Angela dabbed a stray tear but felt stronger than last night. Her prayers had never ended. "This is the day that the Lord has made. Just yesterday I was in such misery in the jostling wagon. I knew I would die if I stayed in it. How could I have healed in such a place? I will rejoice in having a safe place to heal with kind souls who will care for me. Thank you Edith, for helping me through the night." Angela moved her head just the slightest bit and smiled so warmly at Edith that the woman's heart melted.

"God has a plan for you child, I am so blessed that I get to be part of it." Edith scurried away to get a breakfast prepared and left Angela to her thoughts.

The day had been hard but the two women battled through it together. Angela fought the tears and pain, and Edith was by her side constantly throughout the day. Her hands always there when Angela needed them, to comfort or to help her move positions. Angela held herself together as well as she could. Let the tears fall when they had to and dried them when the crying jag was over. Angela finally asked for the letter from her friend. It was sitting on the mantle of the small fireplace in her room. The pain was in so many parts of her that she wasn't sure how she would ever sleep. The letter would work as a distraction.

Edith brought her a stack of fresh handkerchiefs earlier and she knew she would be using them. She handed her the letter and let her have some alone time, Angela knew she would be hovering close by.

> Dear Angela,
> I was remembering that day just weeks ago, a good and terrible day it was, when my husband separated us. We snuck into the wagon and arranged everything and whispered. I wanted you to feel safe and protected, though we know better now that there is no perfect plan for that, especially on a dangerous road.
> I do not want to lie to you or myself. I feared for your life, nearly certain the jarring wagon ride and the dirty trail would finish you. I cannot be angry at Andrew for leaving you behind, and it was good of him to find you a place. Writing these words hurts me, waves of anger and perhaps some bitterness fills me so fully to prevent me to even thank that man for anything. I am in constant prayer trying to forgive him. God is going to have to really help

16

me for I want to loathe him, but my mother taught me better.

When my father left for the West I was never truly angry with him, not the anger I have now in my heart for Andrew. I was sad when my father left, and sad that my mother had died. This sadness I feel tonight is something so different. Already I feel so separated from you. This feels like a knife to my heart. I dearly want you as my sister. That is the truth.

So I will make it as official as I can in this letter. You are my family and until we are back together I will be only a part of myself. Just as I am with my father, missing a link that holds me together.

I will lean on God as I pray you will too. We will need the Lord's guidance through each of the hard days at first. I know your pain must be nearly unbearable. I am praying for the Sparks to take good care of you.

I feel I must truly set aside all thoughts of your injuries, somehow – if I ever could – and focus instead on the words I must say.

You must accept my financial help. I cannot accept a refusal or a repay of the funds. Both my parents were fortunate and money has never been a burden to me. I was told hundreds of times from a young age that generosity was the responsibility of those who have been blessed. God allowed us to stay blessed because our family was always being generous with those in need.

My father loved talking about bible stories where people would get a double blessing after good deeds. I wish my bible wasn't buried so deep in the crates and I could find the verses. Trust me, I just spent a few minutes digging around, I made a terrible mess to clean up. I am laughing at myself, even as I have tears in my eyes over my loss of you on the rest of this long road. I dread the fact that you must cross without me, once you heal. It digs at my stomach and makes it hurt sharply.

Please set aside your thoughts about the charity of money. Consider it a gift from someone who loves you as family. You need to be blessed. Your turn to be a blessing will be in God's timing. There is no shame in a fresh start. If anyone has ever deserved it, my friend, it is you.

I will be praying daily for you.
Sincerely,

Corinne

* * * * *

Life on a fort was one of structure and a few surprises. Though for six weeks Angela had little experience outside the four walls of her room. She heard stories of a few Indian skirmishes miles away from the fort. She also benefitted from the supplies that came in from the East. Fresh fish and game was prevalent and Edith and Henry Sparks kept Angela well fed. The broken bone in her arm had set nicely and her movements were becoming less stiff. It had been much easier for her to sleep and the healing in her heart was mending too.

Many long hours of talking with Edith and Henry Sparks had helped her empty her thoughts about the numerous hurts done to her. Her forgiveness was a growing thing, but also a daily one. Henry's big mustache matched his wit and his heart. He made plenty of room for Angela as part of the family immediately.

"There are some days the reminder is so close to me of how much Andrew Temple hated me. How could he have done such a thing? To send me out when it wasn't safe. But he also did it to punish Corinne, because she cared for me. I cannot understand it. What had I done but be a servant, to fetch and carry, and gather firewood? He disliked my friendship to Corinne, my better according to station and propriety. I had been drilled so often to know my place. Perhaps this really is my punishment. I have known worse. Horror stories at the work house led us all to believe that acting above your station only led to starvation." Angela saw Edith nod. Her own experience as a child on the street had taught her that.

"Angela, you may never know why he acted in that way. The only true way to forgive is to let it go. Knowing you cannot know why, perhaps ever." Henry said, his dessert on the table was untouched. He was glad to see Angela at the table but he could tell the chair was causing the young girl discomfort. He glanced to his wife and they wordlessly communicated that they needed to move her.

"I agree, and tell my heart so every day... Many times." Angela said with a tired voice. They had an invalid chair they borrowed from the fort infirmary that was made of walnut and had three wheels to get her around the house easily.

"You are doing so well, Angie, God is healing you inside and out." Edith said and stood to help Henry get Angela wheeled safely back to her bed.

"You both take such good care of me. I hope you know how much it means, more than the care; also the listening. I know I am a burden but I pray every day for God to bless you for all you have done

18

for me." Angela said with full sincerity. Finding kindness after many years of struggle and abuse was humbling and awe-inspiring.

❊ ❊ ❊ ❊ ❊

Watching the men do their formation drills had become a favorite part of her day, even if it was a distraction for the men. The invalid girl in their midst was a sweet breeze in a barren land for them. Angela's health was improving and her coloring had recently switched from the pale sickly to a pinker healthy glow. Many young soldiers took notice and thought of many ways to visit the Captain's home after the first week of Angela being allowed outdoors.

She was now considered the Fort pet. After week two of being outside her confinement she had several new friends who were constantly buzzing around her. Edith kept a close watch and Henry gave many verbal warnings to keep the young soldiers at their posts. He insisted that the young woman remain safe and untouched in every way. There was no need for the warnings though. Those soldiers would have protected her with their lives.

Chapter 2 - Angela
July 1848

It was time to start walking again. Angela woke determined to do more than stand. Two weeks ago she had tried to walk but the deep bruise on her leg was not ready for her body weight. She had felt the trickle of fear run up her spine that maybe she wouldn't heal properly and be unable to walk again. It was only fear. She prayed, then confessed her fears at breakfast to Edith and Henry. After her nap later in the day there was a card on the nightstand in Edith's bold handwriting.

As I wait on the Lord, with good courage, He will strengthen my heart. - Psalm 27:14

It was just the thing she needed to bolster her patience. God had not left her behind. He was with her through every moment, especially the painful ones, He saw her through them. Angela said a prayer of thanks and then called for some help into the invalid chair. Once she was in she could push the wheels around and move through the house somewhat effectively, but the wheels were forever catching on things. Eventually Henry dragged most of the rugs out of the place for the small bits were always getting pulled into the wheels and snagging. It was never fun trying to get the little strings unraveled from the stubborn wheels.

A few weeks later she tried standing with a chair nearby to hold onto. Now she wanted some greater momentum. The breeze through the window in her room was warm and dry and as she lay in bed she could see no clouds through the windowpane.

"Edith, I am ready when you are." Angela called. She was patient and within a few minutes she could hear Edith's distinct steps across the hard wood floor. Angela had her covers pulled back and was sitting up waiting for Edith to help her get dressed. Her left arm had been broken and was healing but the help to get tricky clothing on was still needed. Even after nine weeks. Edith suspected that her healing was going to be jumping forward in huge leaps soon. Angela was grateful for less pain and better sleep at night. For anything else she was willing to wait and see. All she had to do was remember the pain of that one day jostling in a wagon after her accident to be thankful for healing even if it was slow.

Edith and Angela made quick work of getting her dressed. It always warmed Angela's heart to hear Edith humming softly under her breath as she did any work at all. It was so quiet and barely there. A shy song but it added a moment of joy to Angela's morning, being so close to her and hearing her soft whispery humming. *Just another thing to look forward to today,* she thought. *That and walking!*

"I want to get outside today. Seems a lovely summer's day." Angela's voice was chipper as she ate her ham and eggs. Henry had slaughtered a pig just two days before and all enjoyed the fresh meat, the cafeteria would be sharing some of the fresh pork with the men today and everyone was buzzing about it around the small town. Venison was much more common, pork was luxury to the soldiers of the fort.

"I could see us getting out for a bit today. After morning exercises the main courtyard would be ideal to try out a few steps. It's open and flat and there is a pleasant breeze. I am sure you want to get out of this hot house. I have been meaning to put in a summer kitchen for Edith. Perhaps I should do that this year." Henry said and grabbed one of the women's fans that were on a nearby stand. He spent more time near the home while Angela was there. He could lift her better than Edith. "Edith, now that I know how hot your kitchen gets in the summer, even now in the cool morning it's hot as *hades* in here."

Edith hushed him from talking about such places with a chuckle. "Well, a summer kitchen is something I do dream about, perhaps a nice place just in the back of the house with a nice awning. A small cook stove would work just fine. I even saw in one magazine how some women use a mesh screen around the place to keep out bugs. But a simple awning would be a delicious start." Edith grabbed at any empty dishes on the table and was softly humming again. She plunked the dishes in the wash water and then wiped at a few with a wet rag.

Henry left to check on his soldiers and keep them drilling. He had a new training officer and liked to keep an eye on how his new man did things.

❀ ❀ ❀ ❀ ❀

A few hours later Angela was in the courtyard where the soldiers usually did their marching drills and morning exercises. The ground was even and the breeze was nicer out in the open instead of the hot kitchen. Henry and Edith were very supportive and as soon as they got her invalid chair in place Henry made her wait so he could get her a chair to lean on.

"No need for you to fall when a chair could steady ya." Henry said practically.

Angela nodded and waited patiently for him to come back with a sturdy kitchen chair. He placed it next to the invalid chair and held out an arm. It was time. With a few wobbly movements trying to get out of the wiggly chair she was standing. Once she felt secure on her feet Henry brought the chair closer. She used the chair back to balance and put her weight on the uninjured leg. One step down, she could feel the muscle weakness in her good leg even from just all the lying about. Soon she got brave and swung the other leg forward and put her full weight on it alone. The bruised muscle did protest but it was bearable. She let go of the chair leg and Henry took a few steps closer. She looked at Edith and was almost certain that her caretaker wasn't breathing.

"It's okay, it hurts but it is manageable." Angela said.

With her arms free she stepped back to her stronger leg then before she lost her nerve she took five steps as normally as she could without thinking. She was surprised to hear the whole place erupt in cheers as the mess hall doors opened and the fort men made their presence known.

Henry moved the chair over to her and she gladly took a seat. Her legs were wobbly from her first attempt. All the soldiers ran over and did three cheers for their favorite fort pet.

"I see you have made a few friends here at Fort Kearney" Edith said while chuckling.

Angela was stunned. She was used to a lifestyle in the background. Being invisible was part of her job in her former life. People being nice to her and actually being concerned for her welfare was something that Corinne did but not many others. She had only started feeling welcome with some folks on the wagon train, the Grant family and Clive Quackenbush. Now she had all these other souls that were not only noticing her but actively helping her. She was profoundly moved.

"Thanks everyone." Angela said with a meek voice, sounding lame in her own ears.

"Alright men, back to your grub. There are duties to be done." Henry used his Captain voice and got the men to scoot back into the building. Angela loved hearing the two sides of Henry Sparks.

Chapter 3

Dear Angela,

We are arriving at a fort tomorrow and I wanted to get word to you. My heart is still broken. I know yours must be too. When word came that we could send letter by post I knew I had to write. I thought I would have so much to say but I find myself stumbling for words. I miss you. But I missed you when you were traveling with me, Andrew's cruelty eats at me and daily I have to work at forgiving him. I am so glad he is away most days.

The days have been better; the Grants and Clive have been watching over me. I have such guilt about leaving you behind. I should have stayed. I wonder every few days if perhaps I shouldn't turn around and go back for you. I do not know what the right thing to do is.

My dearest friend, forgive me. I should have fought Andrew harder that night. I should have stayed in Independence, Missouri with you and never left with Andrew. We could have stayed behind and written to my father that Andrew was cruel and he would have found a way to come for me and we would be safe. I think of a thousand ways that this situation could be reversed and they hurt my heart daily.

I pray that your body is healing. That God will ease your pain and help you forget that horrible night. I wish so much that it had never happened or happened to me instead.

Chelsea and Brody both send their love and Brody told me to send a hug to you. We all will be waiting for you in Oregon.

Sincerely,

Corinne

Angela read the letter and cried over her friend's pain. She had wondered how Corinne was fairing and said a quick prayer for her, for her to let the pain go and not carry any guilt about leaving her behind. She knew God could comfort her friend. The Grants and Clive would talk her through the separation. Angela could write but it would take so long for her word to reach Oregon territory. Most likely her letter would never reach Corinne. The West was still hard to reach and the post was not very consistent. She would just pray.

✿ ✿ ✿ ✿ ✿

September 1st, 1848

Angela was helping Edith in the garden. Her arms and legs covered in sweat but she felt good to be at work. She got tired some days but every day was a little better. It was her sixteenth birthday today! Edith had a treat planned for later and the soldiers were teasing her all week about her needing to be kissed at her birthday party. She would just laugh and blush.

Angela saw the stores of potatoes and carrots they had hoed out of the garden that morning and felt good for her help in it. She felt useful and that was a excellent feeling.

Edith braided Angela's hair in a fancy twisted braid with bright white ribbons. It was the fanciest her hair had ever been and Angela smiled in the mirror. The evening was planned out for a dinner in the main hall. A few of the men played instruments and agreed to put together a small musical in honor of Angela's day. Edith made three cakes to have enough for everyone. Edith only allowed Angela to help with the frosting of the cake. So Angela sat in the kitchen and kept Edith company in the afternoon.

The dinner and musical evening was perfect. Angela was asked by several of the soldiers to dance when the music was playing but she declined. It was still a little painful to walk. She knew that dancing would only irritate her poor leg even more. The soldiers all took it well when she explained. Soon the food was served and everyone was making a fuss over her. Edith and Henry stayed with her all evening watching to make sure she didn't get worn out with the activity, but Angela seemed fine.

The time came and a few gifts were brought out. There was no fancy wrapping to be had out here in the wilds of Missouri but several soldiers had little gifts for her.

"Treasures!" Angela declared over them. Several young men had quite a talent for whittling. One made her a horse and another made a cute little dog standing at attention.

From Henry and Edith she got a few gifts as well. The first was a stack of soft cotton handkerchiefs, all of them with dark green initials in the corner. AH.

The next gift was a leather bound journal. On the front page was a summer daisy pressed into wax paper. The bright white and yellow standing out against the paper was beautiful.

"So you can take a piece of this summer with you. As I will in my heart." Edith said with tears in her eyes. "By next summer I know you will be gone from me but I will never forget you."

Angela accepted the gift and the embrace from the woman who had done so much giving to her. Bittersweet tears mingled for both women. Henry handed her the last gift from a small box.

It was a silver pendant watch with white mother of pearl behind the watch hands. Angela gasped at them when she realized it was the first piece of jewelry she had ever owned.

"You don't know what you both mean to me." Angela said with a tight throat.

"You say it with your eyes, lass." Henry said and patted the girl's shoulder.

Edith laughed though she still had tears in her eyes. "Ya do, Angie dear. No one can know ya without seeing it. You probably don't even know you do it. But you show love with every look."

Angela was overwhelmed and speechless. She just accepted the gifts and love with a humble heart.

❊ ❊ ❊ ❊ ❊

The next day Angela was up early and excited to help Edith in the garden again. The work was making her stronger. She needed to be stronger for what lay ahead. She couldn't do the work standing all day, at some point she pulled a crate out and sat while working until she got stiff and sore. But she knew with every day that passed she would eventually get her full strength back.

She was counting down now. She would be leaving in six or seven months, give or take. She had discussed it with the Sparks family at length and they would strike a deal with a nice Christian family that was coming through. If they had no takers in the first train that went through there would be others. Western expansion was on the rise and every newspaper was talking about it. Every time the post would come by, the newspapers were pored over for news, even if they were old by weeks or months. It was treasured out in the wilderness. Though several families now lived near the fort. A few weary souls gave up the Oregon Trail and squatted near enough to the fort and built sod homes. Anyone that applied for land was usually granted the right to build and farm the land, but it was a dangerous business. There were lots of wild animals and this place was the hunting grounds for several different tribes of Indians. The fort was there to keep the Indians from warring as its main existence. The Indians traded with them at the Hudson Bay store and it had a pony express post and a telegraph office now but it was not any type of society. Having

25

neighbors was exciting to Edith but she had little hope of any kind of town life.

Angela and Edith spoke wistfully of the Sparks moving west when Henry retired from his post at the fort. They had grown close and Angela felt a small bit of sadness at leaving them behind.

"I have heard of a lovely Valley in Oregon." Angela hinted with a few sly winks.

"I feel suddenly drawn to know all about this Oregon. We shall send for more news on it. I have friends in Illinois that would gladly send me any paper or pamphlets I asked for." Edith said and winked back, her hands busy cleaning the caked-on dirt from the potatoes, carrots and other vegetables.

Edith grabbed a few potatoes for their dinner that night. Fried potatoes would go lovely with the roasted venison. She was teaching Angela all she could about cooking and survival. She felt a motherly affection for the girl and her heart ached already over the thought of losing her. She would not pressure to girl to stay, though. Her prayers were thorough about it and she felt truly that the child's path was to go west. Edith knew that Angela's brother was there, and somehow they were meant to meet again. Edith prayed for the young man, only knowing his name and the tidbits from Angela, but somehow her heart ached for them to re-unite.

After supper Angela pulled out pen and paper and worked a bit more on the letter to Corinne. She had been crafting it for weeks. Wanting it just right. Angela claimed her penmanship had been better when she was younger but she was working on it daily. Edith was encouraging her to keep writing and reading.

"You are a smart gal. It will come back to ya darling. I only learned to read as a near adult. I felt so lost and ignorant as a child trying to survive in a world that I couldn't fully participate." Edith shared more about her life. The stories gave Angela a deeper respect and love for this woman. God was showing her in small ways that good people can break free of hard upbringings.

❀ ❀ ❀ ❀ ❀

It was over a month later that the post came through saying they were heading west with parcels and letters, they had several mules and bragged that there was now several post offices at other forts, they would get fresh horses and mules and continue all the way to Oregon then to California. They were charging extra, but Angela finally had a letter for Corinne that she was proud of, the cost was worth every penny.

Chapter 4
October, 1848

Dearest Corinne,

    I miss you my darling friend. My time spent with the Sparks family has been a time of healing and joy. It reminds me of days long ago with my mother and brother, the feeling of family and belonging brings warmth to my heart. Edith Sparks is taking perfect care of me as my wounds heal. I have to admit my heart took its time to heal though. My prayers were troubled many nights after you left, with the wonderings of why it happened this way. I can say now that I forgive Andrew for his part in my pain. I wish him well but hope for your sake that he made good with his promise to be annulled from you. I pray in my heart for you to find a good husband someday that will cherish you. I guess I pray that for me, too.

    I yearn to be my old self but am taking it slow. I am walking well and the wound on my shoulder has healed completely. The area that was the worst was the bruising on my leg. I suppose more time will see how that will heal.

    Thank you again for your generous support and your farewell letter. Your entreaty to accept your charity warmed my heart and has created in me a sense of independence. I feel that you were right to address me so boldly. As God has called us all to help those in need. I do suppose in your shoes I would have done the same. My only job in this situation is to accept your monetary help with humility and thank the Lord for providing me with a way out of servitude. I feel at ease in my heart to stop fighting your gift and to pass it on by being a friend to you and then eventually, finding my brother and helping him. I pray that my information is still good and I can find him. It is nearly time for me to go. Edith has been teaching me how to be a proper wife. Baking, sewing and we talk always of how to care for babies. She is such a blessing. She will be sad when I leave in the spring. Henry Sparks is always squeezing my shoulders as he walks by us womenfolk. He calls me 'Red' like Sean did when I was young. I somehow wish the Sparks family were coming with me.

I will write again soon.
Sincerely,

Angie Fahey

❀ ❀ ❀ ❀ ❀

It was weeks past and a message came from a western fort. The town was buzzing with excitement and the breakfast dishes were cleared quickly and Edith and Angela were cleaned up and out the door to the post office in the Hudson Bay store. There were a few soldiers there too, waiting to see if they too had received letters or if there was any news. Everyone was always so starved for news.

When it was finally their turn, Edith and Angela were handed several letters and they ran off eager to read on the front porch.

Edith had her own news from a friend back east and Angela had two letters; one in the flowing hand of her friend, Corinne and one in a different hand. A bold stroke that looked like it was from a man.

The top was dated June 2nd. 1848, Angela wondered how far Corinne had traveled by June. She also wondered where she would be come June of 1849. She started the letter with a feeling of tenseness. The thought of the travel was not as much about adventure to her anymore, but more about survival now.

Dearest Angela,

I have so many thoughts jumbled in my head to pour out on my page. I will just be out with my news first and then it shall be said, to ease the torture in my mind. Andrew Temple died a week ago of cholera. The group of scouts he rode with are gone except for one. They were infected by a pool of brackish water they all drank from in the midst of a treacherous area full of drought and barrenness. His suffering was intense and will stay with me all my days.

I know not how to impress upon you the pain I have in sharing this. My mind is mixed up about my husband in so many ways. I pray daily that God will work in our hearts, both you and I, to heal any bitterness or anger at what he had done.

I feel the separation from you acutely. It keeps my thoughts busy as I cross the miles.

The dark of night creeps into my wagon and honestly the tears blur my eyes. I will write more letters and send when a post is available. You are not forgotten.

Sincerely,

Corinne Harpole Temple

There was more than one gasp that escaped from Angela's lip as she read that first letter. She opened the other letter still stunned from the words she had read.

To Angela Fahey,

I do a lot of correspondence with my sons and for business. But I rarely have the chance to send a letter to someone that is not my own family. This is truly a rare occasion.

I am a God fearing man and have long kept you in my prayers, Miss Fahey. Somehow God has put a burden on my heart when it comes to you and your dear friend Corinne. I sort of feel the need to care for you as I would my own daughters and granddaughters. I can't recall the verse just now, but I recall a verse or two admonishing us to care for the widows and orphans. That love covers a multitude of sins. I have had my fair share of sins. So perhaps this is God allowing me to make up for them since I have prayed so many days of my life for God to give me tasks worthy of his forgiveness. I know better now, I cannot earn God's love any more than I could tame the wind. It's a gift and I accept it as such. But child, I do wish to treat you as family. I pray you cling to hope, and through your healing you grow and learn more about how much God wants to love you.

The world may be full of wicked sinners, but there are those of us that try to do our best to take care of one another. Seems to me the Captain and his wife that you were left with were those types of folks. My prayer for you is a speedy healing. Corinne tells me about your brother and how you long to re-unite. I will be praying for him too. Somehow, girlie, you are now my family, and as such, so is he.

I will talk briefly of an encounter I had with Andrew, not to cause you pain but to hopefully help

your heart to heal. I have shed a tear for you and for
him. Seems a strange thing to say but I can honestly
say his death was hard on me. He was a broken and
angry young man, his conscience about his treatment of
you did bring him to me more than once in the weeks
before his death. He stayed away from the wagon train
as much as possible. People treated him differently
after the rumors started about how he had acted with
his servant.

I know he went to God often for forgiveness.
The day you were left at the fort he was desperate and
frantic, after securing you a safe place he was finally
able to confess all to me and then finally to God. He
was a troubled man but he did feel shame for what he
had done.

I know it doesn't undo your blood on the
ground, your broken bones and bruises. I fight my own
feelings of regret for how I should have intervened
somehow. But I hope the vision I can leave with you, a
broken man, praying for God's forgiveness can be an
encouragement for you, and a balm to your heart.

You need not write back to me, but I do expect
to see your healthy red cheeks and green eyes again
within a year or so. Corinne will not be content unless
you are safe in her keeping for a spell.

Clive Quackenbush

Angela was lost to tears for a few hours. She read and re-read
these letters, talked and hugged Edith more times than she could
count. She felt a wash of emotional confusion that overwhelmed her.
The man who had sent her to her death had perished. She tried to clear
her thoughts and pray for peace but her mind kept going back to
everything she had ever thought of him. The multitudes of prayers she
prayed that God would help her forgive him. She had felt many times
that she had put it past forgiveness in her mind to then relive the pain
and hurt and have to forgive him again.

Now he was dead. She reminded herself. She had to let it truly
sink in. It was the only way that perhaps her mind can truly let it go,
forever.

Clive's words sunk in over the next few days and Angela was
glad that Andrew had finally realized the error of his attitude to herself
and his own wife. It was a wicked shame that someone had to nearly
die for him to come to that realization.

Angela also came to terms with the fact that she would never be able to confront Andrew. Her forgiveness would have to be completely within herself. Andrew would never have an opportunity to apologize. In a way it helped her to forgive him more. She began to focus on praying for his family and that they would be comforted in their mourning.

It was with teary eyes and a calmed heart that she finally wrote back to Corinne.

❄ ❄ ❄ ❄

December 1st 1848

Dearest Corinne,

I received your bundle of letters. I have been at a loss for a few days at what to think or say. I am sorry for what Andrew went through. His death must have been difficult, I know what cholera is and its horrors are well known. I am glad to know in my heart that he knew God and has a place in heaven. My tears lately have been for poor Andrew and his young life gone. I had such hard feelings for him for a short time after being hurt, remembering how alone I was in the dark of that ravine due to his irresponsible actions. He was young and a bit foolish with you and me, but it is a shame for his life to be snuffed out.

I am glad the Grant family is with you. I look forward to seeing them again, as well as Clive. Can you send salutations to dear Mr. Quackenbush for me? I do dearly miss his teasing, and his wisdom. He helped me through many lonely moments when I was not allowed to talk with you along the trail.

I received a packet of mail from Boston for the both of us. In it was another letter from Sean. He is in California territory now with his friend Old Willie. I am uncertain if he is involved with the gold that has been found in that territory. Everyone is buzzing about it in Fort Kearney. Any man with a strong back is threatening to leave his military post in the spring and head off to the west. The correspondence is saying that gold is just lying about the ground and you have to just go pick it up, it is so plentiful. I fear that many men will be pulled into a lie.

Maybe I have seen too much pain in my young life but I do not believe in silly stories anymore. Wisdom says that these are false hopes. I have to work hard at believing in people. I have known too many liars.

I am getting stronger every day and dreaming of being with you again my friend.

Sincerely,
Angie Fahey

Chapter 5

March 28th 1849

Henry Sparks burst through the front door with a spring in his step. Angela and Edith were playing checkers at the table. Angela had won the previous game and Edith was competitive enough to challenge Angela to a rematch. They both looked up from the game as Henry grunted out of his coat.

"You seem to be back from your rounds early." Edith said with a grin. Henry bent and kissed his wife on the cheek.

"Got news." He said and sat with emphasis in the empty chair. He raised an eyebrow to see who would ask for the news first. He was enjoying himself.

"I'll bite." Angela said finally after a minute of watching his eyes travel humorously between the two women. "What's the news?" Angela said sarcastically.

They all laughed.

"A small wagon train is a few days out. A scout had been riding ahead to see how well the store was stocked. Already have a few running out of supplies." Henry Sparks shook his head at the stupidity of some.

"Well, with the talk of gold spreading like a brush fire the fools will be out in the multitudes." Edith said and moved a checker thoughtfully.

Angela's heart jumped at the thought. It has been nearly a year of her life spent here waiting. She has been walking and exercising all through the winter to be ready for the journey. Now the days were drawing close. She would be back on the open road soon. *Lord willing…* She thought.

She dreaded the harsh weather and conditions, but knowing her life would no longer be on hold was what kept her working so hard.

"It scares and excites me." Angela finally shared after she made a move on the checkerboard herself.

Edith took a checker piece and jumped over two of Angela's pieces.

"I can tell you are distracted." Edith smirked and grabbed Angela's hand and gave it a squeeze.

"I am." Angela admitted and rolled a checker piece under her fingers nervously. She kept her eyes lowered because she felt slightly ashamed of herself.

"You can talk when you are ready child." Edith said in a motherly voice.

"You nervous going by yourself?" Henry asked. "You know we will find a good God fearing family to take you." Henry put his hand on her shoulder and gave her one of his squeezes.

"Yes and no." Angela said and wiped a tear. "I know God has a hold of me and will get me across somehow. I just have that last little remnant of fear. I need to let God talk me out of it." Angela felt better having confessed her fear.

"I wish we could take you ourselves, my child. I have filed my papers to retire from the military, but cannot go until I have a replacement." Henry rubbed his hand over his jaw; it was his way to think. "That could take a year or more."

"I do not want you both to worry over me. I just had a moment of being scared of the open road again. I know it's foolish. There is nothing that can happen to me out there that couldn't happen here." Angela knew that the Sparks were going to miss her. They spoke often of how much nicer it would be if they could have taken her to Oregon. "We are all going to have to learn to trust God and His timing on this."

"There is lots of wisdom in those pretty green eyes of yours." Edith said then took a checker and moved closer to a piece of Angela's. Angela was no longer distracted and jumped over two of Edith's pieces and laughed victoriously.

❉ ❉ ❉ ❉ ❉

It was two weeks of wagon trains pulling in and out before they found the right family to escort Angela. A family named the Brannigans, a nice Christian family. The husband and wife had heard through the grapevine, mostly spread from the general store about a young woman that was looking for safe passage. The Brannigans were expecting another child and the mother could really use an extra set of hands to keep her three children safe on the rigorous trail.

The wagon train was stopping a few days at the fort to make a few repairs on several wagons and to wait out some wet weather. The mud was hard on the wagons.

They ended up staying near the fort for a week for the mud to dry up. It gave the Sparks and Brannigans plenty of time to get to know each other. The husband was of strong stock but treated his wife kindly. Henry even took some time to talk to people with the wagon train to see how they treated others. There were only good reports from everyone. The Brannigans were respected and everyone seemed to be on board with accepting Angela as a new wagon train member.

Edith and Henry supplied the Brannigans extra food from their own cellar and they fed the whole lot of them several nights that week while they stayed nearby. Edith kept declaring how much she loved having so many children running through the cabin and in the back yard. All the children loved Edith's extra sweets and treats and gave her hugs around her waist.

The day finally came when it was time to leave. Angela had sturdy clothes and her own tent packed away in the wagon. She would pull it out every night and sleep next to the family. They had a large wagon and several pack mules and a cow for fresh milk.

Edith had baked for days to load the Brannigans food stores with biscuits and bread, enough for a week of meals. Angela had worked hard with her, soaking up all the last minute words of wisdom and love from Edith. She would miss her dearly. Angela wanted to talk about them coming to Oregon again but somehow she didn't want to pressure them. They had mentioned before that they were praying about it. She would learn to trust God and put it in His hands. Edith and Henry Sparks had their own life and journey. She had to allow them to be on it and not force her will on the situation. It was hard to let the thought go but she was able to in the end.

As she was grabbing her last satchel to leave she gave both Edith and Henry each a warm hug and wiped away a few tears that bid their way down her pale cheeks.

"Thank you for all the love. When I write, and I will often, I was wondering if I might have your permission to call you Mama and Papa Sparks?" Angela said through a lump in her throat.

This question brought out about a few more tears and hugs all around again. They all agreed that her request was a good one. Mama and Papa Sparks walked Angela to the waiting wagon train.

They held hands and prayed with the Brannigan family to have a safe and blessed trip. That everyone would draw close to the Lord as they all crossed this blessed country.

Angela began her long walk with a good family's protection and she kept her eyes forward. The Oregon Trail was her road again.

Part 2

Chapter 6 – Willamette Valley

September 22, 1849

She wanted to kiss the ground. Instead her eyes scanned the horizon along with everyone around her. The family she traveled with was nearby but the wagon was not moving anymore. Angie Fahey pushed her bonnet off her head and tried to scan through the crowd to the front for one friendly face. It was several minutes of searching but she surprised herself with the yell that came out of her own throat when she saw her dearest friend.

"Corinne!!" Angie yelled and found herself running on her weary legs. They protested with burning pain and a bone-weariness but she pushed it away.

Her arms wrapped around her friends shoulders and they laughed and cried together. It was a momentous occasion for Angie and her mind thought it would never be so. Her prayers and dreams had come to fruition.

"Oh, you don't know how much I prayed for you Angie. I know what you went through." Corinne wiped away Angie's tears as they looked each other over. Corinne looked happy and healthy with her rosy complexion and dark brown hair.

"You look radiant, my friend." Angie said and gave her a glance down from her face to her shoes. It stopped on the way back up to the wedding band on Corinne's left hand. "You are married!"

Corinne nodded happily.

Angie hugged her again and then added. "I beg you, find me a chair, and bath and then tell me all. You smell like a floral garden as always, making me more and more aware that I do not." They shared a laugh as Angie led Corinne back to the wagon where she introduced the Brannigan family to her friend. The Brannigans were eager to be on their way but polite to Corinne and spoke only praise about her comrade Angela.

"She was a dear girl and a pleasure to travel with. My bairns will be sad to not have her sweet hugs every morn." Mrs. Brannigan said before she left with her children in tow, her husband giving her eager looks to be about their own business.

Corinne took Angela back to the party of people waiting for her. After Corinne's father made his presence known and introductions and hugs given by Angie they gathered luggage and headed back to their group and wagon waiting in the fields nearby. A feast was prepared and families from the arriving wagons were fed and helped. There was a boardinghouse in town for those without shelter and barns for animals to be fed and cared for.

"Angie, meet my husband, Lucas Grant." Corinne announced. Angie smiled and embraced the familiar man before her.

"Oh Lucas, I somehow knew you would turn out well." Angie teased him about how she secretly knew that he had an eye for her friend. "You were always nearby. Thank you for making my Cori so glowingly happy." Angela's praise made Lucas blush the tiniest amount, which continued the teasing from others nearby.

"Where's my redhead girl?" She heard the man's voice before she saw him.

"Clive!" Angie peaked around Lucas and saw the man with a heart of gold. His peppered hair cut shorter than he kept in on the trail last year, he wore a vest and tie and she was taken aback by his cleanliness. "You look like a city merchant, Clive." She laughed and saw him curtsy in his comedic way.

"You scared me last year, my girl. We were all afraid for ya. I can't say how warm my heart is today to see you alive and well. Though you are mite skinny girl. Corinne better feed you good to get the red back in your cheeks instead of it all bein' in your hair." Clive looked upon her with some emotion. She could tell he was happy to see her.

"I shall be glad for some love and care for a few days, but mostly a roof over my head and the ground staying firm beneath my feet. I am so weary of the traveling. I have walked through two pairs of good shoes." Angie confessed. Clive sat her down and planted a well meant kiss on the top of her red head.

Everyone that loved and cared for the girl watched her eat heartily with a caring eye. All with memories of a year gone by of worries and regret for the girl's past troubles. All secretly praying for her life to now be one of safety and healing.

❀ ❀ ❀ ❀ ❀

Angela Fahey awakened in a strange room; the outer wall with the curtained windows had smooth logs that were a warm light brown with white chinking to keep out the breeze. The inner walls were nicely decorated with shelves and books. Angela smiled to see a few bottles of plant oils on the shelf. The smell of lavender and other scents drifted through the room as she slept that night.

Angela reached above her head with a long stretch and a yawn of one who was still weary after a long journey. She padded around on her bare feet and noticed her blisters were still burning persistently. She had walked her fair share of miles these last months. She could not expect to feel perfect in a day.

She did another long stretch and grabbed a fresh dress from her satchel she had dropped by the door the night before. She dressed in a simple green cotton dress and brushed out her long red hair and braided it hastily, listening to her own stomach as it growled for attention. Angela opened the door with the smallest hint of a creaking sound and was instantly bombarded by a young blond boy. Angela searched her brain and remembered his name. She had met him last night.

"Good morning Cooper," Angela said quietly. She accepted his brief hug around her middle. She was not sure what time it was so she wanted to err on the side of quiet in case others were still sleeping. The light coming through the window persuaded her to hope it was still morning.

"It's not morning anymore, Miss Fahey. It's nearly lunchtime and I am going fishing with Dolly after lunch and I wanted to see if you would come. Dolly is an Indian girl. A real one!" Cooper's face was alight with pride.

"A real Indian girl. I met her last night. She is very nice." Angela said, watching Cooper nod. He was seven years old, and had enough enthusiasm to spare.

"Yup," He said and bolted away to have his own adventure.

Angela saw her closest friend sitting in a chair near the fireplace. Cori Grant's long brown hair was neatly done in a long braid down her back. Just seeing her made Angela grateful for surviving the long trail. She was the closest thing to a sister she had ever had.

"Hi Cori," Angela joined her in an empty chair by the fireplace. "Sorry I slept so late. Cooper informed me it is nearly lunch time." Angela was still talking quietly. She was a guest in Lucas and Cori's home, she felt so strange and out of place, not sure how to act.

"No worries Angie, we all felt exhausted after arriving. A few days rest and you will be bouncing around like your normal self, I promise. We have dinner tonight with my father and Marie. She will feed us like royalty. I am still working on my cooking skills. It will be a while before I can match her prowess. Though as busy as I have been with the harvest and building a botany greenhouse and lab we eat from Marie's kitchen often. Marie has been a Godsend." Cori squinted her face in a focused look of concentration and bent over her needlework.

"Are you darning stockings, Cori?" Angie laughed, actually feeling joy bubble up inside her. The feeling was pleasant. It did not happen near enough.

"Yes, and you are only allowed to laugh once dear friend. Any needlework I do is extremely tedious but it must be done. All of my winter stockings are a mess of holes and the weather will be getting colder soon. I hate for my toes to stick out of my stockings. It annoys me to no end." Cori's face was still squinted in concentration as she spoke and her fingers furiously tore at the knotted thread that refused to do her bidding. Angela worked very hard to keep her laughter on the inside.

"I would be glad to help. I am pretty skilled at needlework as you know." Angela held her hands out to take the mess of thread and stockings off of Cori's hands.

"NO!" Corinne says forcefully. Angela jumped in her seat, her coppery eyebrows high in surprise.

"You are no one's servant, you are my guest and you are resting from a six month journey. There is no way you are lifting a finger in my house!" Corinne was firm. She smirked a little at Angela to calm her frightful look but she wasn't budging from her decision.

"Well, may I borrow your kitchen then? I shall recover from your bold statements while eating. I am not sure if I can wait for lunch." Angela asked.

"I have a plate made up for you. Some bread and cheese and we had some oranges Clive brought from California. They taste so delicious, like tasting sunshine. Even at my Aunt's fancy house in Boston the fruit did not taste this good." Corinne dumped the mending mess into the chair and they walked together to the kitchen.

"I am sorry to say I do not miss your Aunt much." Angela confessed. She accepted the plate and they sat together to visit at the oak table.

"I will only admit to a few people that I do not miss her much either. She tortured you and the other servants much more than she did me but I am grateful to have escaped. I do not know how her and my sweet mother could have been sisters." Corinne kept her hands busy by cutting up a few apples as she talked.

The girls prayed a blessing over the food then it was devoured quickly by Angela until she came to the orange, after taking her time peeling it she ate the slices slowly, savoring every juicy morsel.

"You are right, that is a heaven-inspired fruit." She washed the sticky juice from her fingers at the nearby washbasin.

"Are you still tired?" Corinne asked, her concern about Angela was very endearing. Angela squeezed her hand.

"I have a little energy. Did you want to take stroll?" Angie asked.

"No, I have a surprise for you but I don't want to overwhelm you. I do not know when the right time will be so perhaps now will be the best." Corinne seemed at a loss for words so Angela let her pause to find them.

"I have a trunk full of your mother's possessions." Corinne finally blurted out. Angela felt her heart start a wild pumping inside her chest, pain and love and other unknown emotions flooded her.

"That's not possible…" Angela said in a voice that was barely a whisper. She held her breath for a moment.

"When my Aunt agreed that you would be my ladies maid for the Oregon Trail, I began writing a series of letters. First to a lawyer who was handling my father's money held in trust for me. I put him on the trail of your stepfather, Stanley Lankarski." Corinne watched her friends face. Angela looked shocked but she seemed stable enough for Corinne to keep talking.

"My lawyer found him quickly and before we left I had my lawyer working on your behalf to get your mother's affects and any property for you and your brother. Because your brother is in places unknown the items were sent to you. You will be pleasantly surprised to know that you are a woman of independent means." Corinne smiled. There was much more to talk about but this was a start. Corinne had a horrifying fear after the trunk arrived a few months ago that Angela wouldn't survive the trip and… Corinne settled her thoughts, the worst-case scenario did not happen.

Chapter 7

The trunk was larger than Angela had expected. She imagined it to be something small, a few books, maybe a drawn portrait or two.

"I am not sure I am ready for this." Angela said. A few tears escaped her green eyes and down her face. "What good can come of revisiting all that pain again?"

Angela felt like a haze was drifting into her brain trying to shut out the past. Her walls of protection were usually down when she was with Corinne, her closest friend. She didn't want to go into how much it really hurt to lose her father and mother so close together, then the work orphanage was a horrific nightmare that stole her brother away too.

Angela stared at the trunk; it had a dark green patch of leather on the top with Fahey stamped into it. There were gold leaf details along the edges, brown leather along the sides and a handle on each side with decorative carvings pressed into the metal. It was the trunk belonging to an affluent family, one that had money and choices. How could people with these kinds of choices end up with two children going from a beautiful neighborhood to a dirty and poorly maintained work orphanage, a thieving establishment that stole money from the orphans as they got older and worked outside the orphanage?

"You can take your time Angela, we do not have to do anything today. I just wanted you to know it was here. I have looked through some things to make sure everything was there as the lawyer requested, you will have to sign a few papers to send back, your brother will, as well if we are able to locate him. But nothing has to be done today. There are a few drawings and diaries that you may treasure." Corinne had her hand running up and down Angela's back to comfort her.

Corinne had lost her own mother in the last few years and knew that that kind of pain didn't have a time limit. One moment you were fine, the next you could be devastated like the pain was a fresh bleeding wound. Though time passing makes things easier in some aspects, there were ways that a close death could change you profoundly. Corinne knew that the pain of what Angela and her brother went through was catastrophic to them. They were both used and abused by people they should have been able to trust. Thrust into a situation that no child should have to face.

"I shouldn't be afraid Cori, I know that in my head." Angela wiped a few tears away almost angrily. She didn't like to be this weak.

It made her feel out of control. Why was she always more real around Corinne?

"I just need to tell my heart to stop being afraid. Help me open it Corinne. I may need some help to get started." Angela plopped down to her knees, swiping a handkerchief , a gift from Mama Sparks, on the tears that were in a non-stop cycle. She faced toward the treasured and dreaded trunk, knowing that her real family, the love they shared was inside somehow, that could not be stolen by anyone.

The trunk opened with a creak of wood and a crackle of worn leather. The inside had a few planks of cedar and the smell was unmistakable. Angela could see the trunk was full to the brim, several bound books, items wrapped in canvas, four small wooden boxes, some larger items wrapped in parchment paper underneath. This was treasure, Angela's heart nearly burst with the overwhelming bittersweet pain.

"Oh Lord, please help me." Angela whispered. Her fingers ached to touch but her heart longed to run away from the memories. Her family's hopes and dreams were all tucked away in a trunk.

Corinne sat next to her but let her have time to process. She was there to cry or cheer with her, whatever friend duty was required in this kind of trying moment.

Angela reached in and grabbed the first item on top, a wrapped object. The white canvas unwrapped easily and fell into Angela's lap.

The frame stared at her for a few moments before her brain could register what she was seeing. Angela saw her mother first; the drawing caught the sparkle in her eye. Angela could see how much she looked like her mother as she had grown older. The next was her father and his face triggered a pain through her stomach that was an unexplained agony of resemblance. Sean was so young, his face a smaller version of her father and she was in her mother's lap with her mother's arm wrapped around her side.

Oh to have that arm touch her now… was a beautiful tragic thought. Angela just stared with her mouth covered by one hand. Her teeth wanting to bite down to keep herself from crying out or screaming or maybe laughing in a hysterical way. There was nothing like this, mourning, and it had a tangible feeling about it that no one could grasp unless you had felt it yourself. It was like a person that came to visit and brought gifts that hurt you and blessed you at the same time. It carried both memories of sweetness and heartbreak. Capturing moments of your life but constantly reminding you it could never happen again. Those moments could never exist again on God's green earth.

Angela let go of her face and traced the drawing against the glass with her finger, it was as close to an embrace that she will ever get anymore with everyone in the picture, save one. Sean was hopefully still in this realm, alive and kicking up trouble, Angela mused.

"You have a beautiful family." Corinne sniffed. Angela looked over to see tears in her friend's eyes. They cried together and embraced for a minute, the frame between them.

"Thank you Cori, I miss them. Thanks for telling me about this. I will get through it all. This is enough for today. I think I can handle the past in manageable pieces. All at once, may just do me in." Angela sniffed and blew her nose with her handkerchief.

The girls stood up and stretched their arms. Corinne decided that a visit to the barn would be in order. Perhaps a ride around the property would do them some good.

"Cori, I will try and ride but I am not as good a rider as you. These huge beasts still frighten me a little, though after the Oregon Trail I am not as afraid anymore." Angela walked with Corinne to the barn and she was introduced to a gentle horse that was grey and white. Angela patted the mare on the nose to make friends and was helped into a pair of Corinne's boots then up into the saddle. They both laughed when Angela nearly fell over the other side on the first try.

"I guess my muscles are a little weak from the journey still. Let's hope the horse goes slowly or I may have a few fresh bruises on my backside." Angela laughed as she got settled in the saddle.

"You already have bruises on your backside?" Corinne laughed and gasped.

"Well yes, of course?" Angela nodded.

"Whatever from, Angie?" Corinne's eyebrows shot up in shock.

"Well Barlow Pass was such an easy road, flat as a flapjack and easy as a Sunday stroll." Angela gave Corinne a look that spoke of heavy sarcasm.

"I found Barlow Pass impossibly difficult, a horror of steep inclines, rocky obstacles and strenuous to the extreme. It nearly killed me and my horse Clover here a few times. I shall not question you further about it." Corinne laughed to commiserate with Angela's own journey as she had made the trip just the year before. Angela's injuries during a tragic fall had prevented Angela from finishing the journey with Corinne.

"Yes some of those rocky obstacles were a bit much for me. I was put in charge of three children and keeping them from falling off the cliff's edges was a nightmare. I think they took delight in testing the laws of nature to see how many ways they could nearly die in my presence. I loved the family I was with well enough but the children seriously lacked discipline. The mother had three children and they were all under six years of age, she could birth them but had no backbone to raise them. She will be lucky if the oldest boy does not become an outlaw by the age of sixteen." Angela laughed as she shared.

They headed out on horseback to see the lay of the land. Several fields of lavender had been harvested but a few remained to be harvested by the end of the week.

Angela gasped several times as the fields of lavender spread out before them and overwhelmed her with sights and smells.

"It actually smells purple, Cori." Angela smiled and tried to take in the beauty. The heavy scent of lavender made her head light, she could taste it a little.

"I thought so, too. When I asked for lavender fields from Lucas, I had no idea what I would get. I can imagine God using my valley to paint Heaven as one of the most beautiful places to see. It makes me so happy, seeing my dream come true. Now all we must do the hard work of capturing the flower." Corinne grinned beautifully and Angela enjoyed seeing her closest friend so happy.

❀ ❀ ❀ ❀ ❀

The girls enjoyed their morning in the sun and Corinne took Angela all around Grant's Grove. The trees were small but Angela was impressed by the amount of trees they had planted. It would be magnificent with the almond blossoms when the trees grew larger. Angela could see it in her mind. Corinne explained that next year they wanted to begin an olive grove. There was so much to do and Angela could see a bright future for the new Grant couple.

"We have need for more orchards than we can grow but we are starting. We will be trying to make contact with other growers to buy their harvests. We are not sure if the almonds can survive the climate here. We have a few ideas. Clive is very helpful and we talk to other farmers for input. Just telling Clive of having of the potential for olive oil and almond oils in a few years has helped spread the word among the other growers. We already have orders and the trees are still infants." Corinne said as she rode.

"I do not think infants is the proper term, Cori." Angela teased.

"Oh hush, they are my little infants and don't you say another word. I sing to them often and call them my little babies. They like it." Corinne said and nodded emphatically. She was not to be discouraged.

The land spread out and the mountain views were a healing balm to Angela's rumpled spirit. The weariness was easing out of her as the day progressed.

❀ ❀ ❀ ❀ ❀

Lunch was a hurried and loud affair with harvesters in from the edges of the field. Some piled into Corinne's kitchen and snacked on the loaves of bread and cold chicken. There were homemade pickles and pies loaded up. The ones that couldn't fit inside huddled outside, picnic tables were carried around from the back of the cabin. The men carried the food as Corinne passed it to them, the tables outside were loaded down.

"Cori, I am so impressed at how well your cooking has improved." Angela praised her friend.

"Oh, I can take no credit. Chelsea Grant brought the bread and chicken last night, I pay Chelsea to keep me supplied on harvest days. Marie made the pies and the amazing briny pickles and she stubbornly refuses to be paid. But somehow a few bushels of fruit just find their way to her front stoop, frequently." Cori's laughter tripped through the room. "Today is abnormal for me, usually I am busier, and I want to make sure you are rested. Tomorrow I am back in my greenhouse planning and plotting for my lab. I have so much to get done before the snow flies. I must have everything in working order." Corinne took a few plates that needed refilling.

"Oh my, you are a busy gal." Angela saw more men approaching. There was a need for more tables.

Corinne pointed to a few men who had arrived about more tables that were near the greenhouse. It was a few hundred yards away but the men were happy to do it.

"We all are thinking of how to improve this process for next year." Corinne went back inside for more food as the tables arrived.

"Harvest time is not the only thing to worry about too. I have lists upon lists. It is rewarding work though." Corinne said.

"I remember that Lucas went to school for agriculture, right?" Angela asked. She was drawing from a memory from sitting near the campfire on the trail.

"He gets excited about irrigation and soil, I get excited about my next shipment of seeds and lab equipment." Corinne smiled. Angela and Corinne stood talking and watched the men eat their lunch.

"I would love to see your lab soon. I am certain it will be full of wonders." Angela was pleased to see Corinne's excitement.

"Still waiting for some supplies to arrive from London, there are always new methods and breakthroughs in science and discovery in the plant world. I am so proud to be a part of it." Cori's face was beaming.

She could not see Corinne slaving away in a kitchen if herbs or her medicinal oils had a pull on her. Even in Boston under her Aunt's iron rule Corinne had to be dragged away from the Boston greenhouses nearly every day. Corinne had her strengths and she would stick to them, it was the way it should be.

"Will you be ok on your own tomorrow if I need to be away?" Corinne looked worried for a minute.

"I will be just fine, I have to go through my bags and mends some dresses. I may even fit in a nap or two if my body calls for it." Angela smiled.

Angela was already planning on visiting with Marie soon, to see if she needed help with her pies tomorrow. It would keep her from being a nuisance or underfoot.

❀ ❀ ❀ ❀ ❀

"Seeing my Angela girl safe and sound is like a song from heaven." Clive's jovial voice broke through the crowd talking and eating. Everyone grew quiet for a moment then a few cheers and jeers for Clive sounded out. His tall lean body walked in the room and always caused a stir. He was just that kind of character. His dark hair now more peppered with white since Angela saw him last year. She remembered a shave and a haircut that Corinne and her had given to him on the trail. It was one of the better memories for Angela of her first attempt of the Oregon Trail.

"I have been waiting to get to hug you proper Mr. Quackenbush." Angela jumped from the table when he got closer and planted a bear hug around his shoulders. She held on for more than a few moments and he let her. He didn't mind the affection and he had a special place in his heart for both young ladies he met last year on the trail. His eyes could see Angie moved toward him well, he would be watching her for any remaining injury as all of them would be that cared for her. Angela had a caretaker spirit and she hadn't had too many people trying to take care of her in her younger days. He knew of several folks that would gladly help in the protection of this girl- almost woman.

"Girl you smell like a breath of spring. I can tell you've been socializin' with Cori Grant and all her flowerizin' of everything. Her supreme mission is making everyone smell like a tulip, or perhaps a romp in a flower meadow." He winked at Corinne and picked up Angela for an extra squeeze before he set her down. Angela loved how Clive had his voices, sometimes he sounded like he was from the south, other times he could sound like the educated city man. Clive was a rare breed.

"I came to announce that Corinne had a shipment arrive at the store today from California. I saw cargo from Russia, China and

Australia. Also the town Doctor wanted to have a chat with ya as well. My other reason is obvious as I came to get another peek at my girl, Red. I will not be satisfied to leave unless I get at least three healthy blushes from ya girl. It does my heart good to see that kind of color on a fair cheeked maiden, I may be past my sixtieth year but it does remind me so of my first fair bride. She had a darker red than you but her face was nigh as fair." Clive held his hat to his heart and dramatically closed his eyes. He had a flair for speeches.

"I will do my best to give you as many blushes as you need Clive. I have missed your charms. You do me good, too. I hope to talk with you soon about getting mail off to California. I will try to locate my brother." Angela welcomed Clive over to the table with a gesture and they all enjoyed talking with the great man. His sense of humor, his patience and experience made him a rare find. He was a true gift to anyone who knew him.

❀ ❀ ❀ ❀ ❀

"Oregon City has grown so fast Angie. It seems a new business goes up every week. We now have an Apothecary, a Doctor and a gentleman named Gomer Hines is starting up a newspaper. The town constable is trying to get a paid sheriff position as an option passed by the town council. All in all it's a growing town. I don't love the politics or the politicians, as I have had a few run-ins with town councilmen. They have played me false over a spurned romance but that has calmed some. I haven't filled you in on the young Sidney Prince who fell desperately in love with me on the trail." Corinne made a few faces and made Angie laughed as they traveled along the main road.

"Sidney was a sweet young lad who turned sour when I tried to refuse his advances." Corinne was a fast talker when she was excited. Angela was trying to pay close attention to learn everyone's name that she didn't already know.

"Sidney?" Angela said with a question in her voice.

"Yes, he joined the wagon train after Andrew…" Corinne faltered a moment.

"Keep going." Angela urged. She knew Corinne was going to feel awkward about talking about Andrew. Angela had many a mile to let Andrew's mistakes go. She was fine for today. She wanted to focus on the future.

Corinne continued, "Well Sidney had a boyish crush. And I was not interested. He had the town council deny Lucas's right to get a land claim. I was willing to marry Lucas and leave town if we needed to but it all worked out in the end when Andrew's parents deeded their land to us." Cori saw the shadow pass over Angie's face. She should

47

have written a letter about Andrew's parents to Angela, she felt a fool for bringing up the issue now. Angie didn't need to hear about anything to do with Andrew ever, after what he had done. She explained quickly how Andrew's parents helped Lucas and her with acquiring the land by gifting it to her before they moved off to California. Corinne apologized for reminding her of Andrew.

"You did nothing wrong Cori, dear. Your first husband, Andrew, was a part of your life, a rather unpleasant part, I might add. His parents had no idea what he had done and the foolish way he got me injured. The fact that something good came from them is a sweet reminder how God works out the good. I have forgiven him and accepted that we have all moved on." Angie's speech sounded completely levelheaded and adult. Though her voice only faltered a little.

Not everything is as easy as words make them to be. Corinne had a smile and a few misty tears threatening to fall.

"I had the Sparks taking good care of me, and now you and I are together again, and my journey west was not halted forever. You have found true love with Lucas and *that* makes my heart happy. Your dream is coming true. I may actually find my brother and get to share a few memories with him, too. I think we have both come a long way." Angie smiled and looked around and her heart was in her throat. Her thoughts dwelled on the memories of the night she fell into a ravine, her body a broken mangled mess. That night was like a dark tent hovering over her, threatening to snuff out her light forever.

She shook off the memory and looked at the Willamette River that was nearby. Jammed with logs and working men on a few rafts and men with longs sticks that had an amazing talent for balancing. They pushed the logs along to the mills ahead, the big hulking buildings on the river's edge.

The town was busily working on this fall weekday, getting everything done. The talk of the town this time of year was about the mountain snows. When would they start? When would they get snowed in? When would the gap fill in and leave them all without land routes for certain supplies? Butting off routes to families and trappers who dared to live outside the comfort of even a small town. On their own, surviving off the land had its peace and quiet, but animals, accidents and sickness had no limit in this rough land.

Corinne and Angie stopped by Clive's office to take a peek at her cargo. The wagon would be there shortly, Cori and Angie made it to town a lot quicker than Lucas could in the wagon. Corinne felt a small twinge of guilt for leaving her husband to drive the wagon without her, but she wanted to have as much time with Angie today as possible. She felt an odd kinship with Angela that surpassed a common friendship or acquaintance. They were family now. If Angie was a year younger she would have begged her father to adopt her, but at seventeen Angie would probably feel a bit silly being adopted. She survived the Oregon Trail and she was of marriageable age. Corinne's secret wish for them to truly be sisters was just not meant to be. Lucas and Russell Grant had no more brothers that needed marrying off.

Silly me. Cori thought to herself. *Still having impossible wishes.*

The cargo at Clive's store was piled behind the building in the loading zone. Corinne had an overwhelming urge to break open the crates on the spot but Clive had just done the inventory of each one earlier in the day and taken great care to repack and close each crate. She wasn't about to make more work for him and his son, the clerk.

Clive paced around the dock waiting for his son, J.Q. to fill him in on a few store needs. Cori and Angie waited patiently for him to conduct his business and enjoyed the warm fall air.

For September it still felt like summer. Though the talk of mountain snows was a topic on everyone's lips. People do love to speculate on weather. It was part of the human journey, in life the wind will blow, the rain and snow must fall.

Several minutes passed and Lucas appeared with the wagon and a sturdy hand from Cori's father's ranch. Corinne couldn't remember the lad's name but she gave a friendly nod as he headed in her direction. He knew she was in charge in this moment. He didn't seem to be bothered taking orders from a woman.

"If you can get the biggest crates along the edges and then get the smaller crates packed tightly in the middle perhaps we can eliminate as much breakage and jostling as possible." He grinned and nodded sincerely.

"I have some old quilts to pack between them that will help, Cori. Just get them back to me next time you are in town. We will reuse them for your fragile orders. You and your tiny glass bottles, chile'." Clive chimed in. His mustache twitched in the corners of his mouth as he teased. He was very proud of his Cori. Her smarts and skills made everyone proud.

"Angie, I was hoping to have a chat with you. I have been thinking about your plan to find your brother and I have a few thoughts on the matter." Clive waved her and Corinne inside as the men began their loading. Corinne ran over and planted a kiss on Lucas's cheek to thank him properly for all his hard work. He rewarded her by grabbing her off the dock and with a spin kissed her on the mouth and then plopped her back on the dock where she had been. Her blush stained her cheeks and she wordlessly followed Clive and Angie inside the Hudson Bay store.

"I am glad to see you both like each other." Angie laughed nervously. She was happy for her friend, just getting used to the displays of affection would take a little time. Angie was certain she blushed more than Cori did.

"We do, I felt a bit guilty by not riding with him in the wagon. But he is so understanding, I have my Angie back." Cori gave Angie a sideways hug as they neared Clive's office.

"I have spoken at length about your brother with Corinne, Angie, and have a few ideas to toss at ya." Clive held out chairs for Cori and Angie and then plopped down himself. The dark wood table that filled a corner of the room had a few papers on it but there was still a little open space. Clive clasped his weathered hands together in front of him.

"I hear your brother is in California, most likely place will be in San Francisco. I have a Hudson Bay store there that is managed by my grandson, Gabe and his wife. They are just newly married and have a 'young un on the way." He smiled warmly at the thought. "I can forward some information about your brother Sean and see if he cannot pass the word along that you are looking, but I have another thought too." Clive took a moment and looked Angie in the eyes.

"What would you think of going to San Francisco and working at the store under my son's protection?" Clive started. He watched her face show a little bit of surprise but no fear. "You have a great way about you and…you would get paid for the work and you can talk to every customer that comes through. It would give you a great chance to ask questions and be closer to the area where your brother was last seen. I will be in California territory every month or so for business. We can keep tabs and if you want to take a break and come back here you can with no pressure. I just have a feeling that people will see you and try and help you more if you are there. Cori said there was a drawing of him, I know a few people who are good at scribbling and drawin' that could make up a few posters for you." Clive finished, his eyebrow up and hoping he hadn't upset her.

"California…"Angie said softly. Her own mind had wondered if she would end up there. Her heart sped up a bit at the thought. He was there. Perhaps she should be too. "I will pray on it Clive. Is there a certain time of year that would be better for me to go?" Angie suddenly looked younger than her sixteen years. She was a girl confused and still a bit weary from her last adventure.

"There is no rush my child'." Clive took her hand. "California will wait for you."

Chapter 8

The wagon was loaded down with all the crates from Clive's mercantile. Corinne led Angela through town to the post office where Corinne had letters. The postmaster allowed her to retrieve her father's mail as well. Angela was quiet and Corinne let her dwell on her own thoughts.

Corinne had to fight her own feelings about Angela potentially leaving. A certain selfish emotion rose up inside of her. *How can she leave when I only just got her back?* Corinne would try to act like an adult but she had a desire to grab Angela possessively and yell out, *mine!*

Corinne stepped into the town doctor's office and was greeted by Persephone Williams, the Doctor's wife.

"Hello Persephone, you are looking lovely today. I heard Doc Tyler was wanting to speak with me." Corinne grinned and enjoyed the friendly smile of the doctor's wife. Her navy dress was snug across the middle promising the town would have a new member soon.

"He stepped away awhile ago, there was another accident at the lumber mill. I am hoping it's not too serious. He mentioned to me that he wanted to know about some of your suppliers. He has heard you know your way around getting your hands on some hard to reach medicines. He would be grateful to share your connections." Persephone ran a hand through her dark blond hair that was loose in the back. Corinne could see a pin was nearly falling out.

"Let me, dear." Corinne reached up and secured the wispy hair and the pin. Persephone's hair was again neat and tidy and no one would know the wiser.

Persephone giggled nervously, she wasn't a silly woman but she did have a charming giggle when she was jumpy.

"The doctor had an order for more oils from you too." Persephone said after she recovered from her embarrassment.

"I am glad to help. I am heading to the apothecary to see what Mr. Higgins has to offer." Corinne said and waved, Angela waved wordlessly and followed behind her friend.

"She seems nice." Angela tried to make conversation. She still felt shy about meeting people, sometimes she slipped back into the servant role she had grown so comfortable with. It was easier than being rejected, in her opinion.

"She is, she usually does the midwife duties with her husband, this is her first child and will be on the other side of the birthing process." Corinne said with a wistful smile.

"Are you wanting to have children with Lucas?" Angela asked boldly.

"I would welcome it. We are just letting God's timing prevail. But the thought does give me a smile or two." Corinne shared.

Corinne and Angela stepped into the new apothecary shop and were lost inside for nearly an hour. Corinne became the teacher and talked about all the remedies with abandon. This reminded Angela of the few times she accompanied Corinne to the Boston greenhouses when she was a servant in Corinne's Aunt's household. She would be so giddy about every plant growing. She spoke lovingly to the plants like children.

They escaped the shop finally and found their way home on the wagon. Angela had a few purchases and put them away in her room and Corinne sat by the window and read her letters.

To my Dearest Niece Corinne,

I am glad to have received your telegrams and letters declaring yourself to be fit and well after the long ordeal you undertook to survive the overland passage. It gives me fevers remembering how worried I was over your person all those long days after you left Boston. I was shocked and amazed to hear about the death of your young husband, Andrew Temple, surely he was handsome and charming and did not have a feeble or sickly look about him. It is a sad shame that he had to die of such a horrible thing as Cholera. My own dear city of Boston just these past few weeks has started its own fight with a dreadful outbreak of that same malady.

The newspapers aren't saying where the outbreak started but I am certain it is the unwashed vermin down by the docks that started it all. If people would just take better care to be respectable they would live longer, I am certain of it. I have already taken precautions and not allowed my servants to shop in unsavory parts of town for any produce. I am afraid we have already had trouble. One of the scullery maids was feeling poorly today and we are all nervous.

I have thought about leaving here and going to my home in the country but I do not want to leave, the newspapers recommend people to stay near their homes.

I daresay I am a nervous wreck. I suddenly miss you more for you always know what to do around sickness. You are very levelheaded like my dear sister, Lily. I never knew two sisters less alike than her and I, but I felt her presence when I had you staying with me, dear girl.

I missed you from the moment you left my 12th street home. My son, Arnold, rarely visits from Kentucky and his girl, Megan, is very much like you from her letters. She is all about her books and drawing. I gave her your address to write you. She sent me a charcoal drawing that took me back to my youth when I grew up near the mountains. I was never meant for that life though. I do love living in the hustle and bustle of Boston. I do miss your Uncle Herbert as he was such a dear husband and took such amazing care of me.

I have been thinking about remarrying, a dear chap you met a few times while in Boston. Horatio Wilson was a close friend of Herbert, and his wife died several years ago, as well. I do believe we would suit and I would find it very pleasant having someone take care of me again. He is quite wealthy and I am sure he is not marrying me for my money. Our fortunes would combine well.

I was shocked when I heard of your marriage to a Mr. Lucas Grant so soon after being widowed but have to admit I am glad you have someone to take care of you, too. You are a frail little thing and I would dislike for you to be harmed out in the wilds of Oregon country. I do hope he is refined and your father approved the match. Your father's taste does tend to lean more toward a slightly rougher lot, being a ranch owner. But his business acumen, I am told, is spot-on.

Your news of your ladies maid, Angela, was the biggest boggle, I must say. You shared her history with me and at first my heart was hardened to the idea of a ladies maid having a story that unbelievable. That she had wealthy parents and then an unscrupulous man stealing everything from two small children. It is a sad tale. I am glad to hear her fortune has been returned to her. She was a sweet hard-working girl who did befriend you and despite my warnings, you saw her character. Perhaps I am too quick to judge and have ideas about people that are un-Christian. I believe I have learned a valuable lesson. I shall endeavor to judge people less often, I have begun devoting more thought to the poor and those that are less fortunate.

I was listening, my dear, whenever you would get flustered with me. You would speak eloquently about all men being equal. I may not have always acted on it Corinne, but I did hear you. Little by little I feel you have burrowed your way into my old heart.

I do hope you know how much I love and miss you. When Angela arrives safe to your home please send her my love and best wishes. Give your father a slug in the arm and wish him much joy in his new marriage. Tell Angela I am praying for her brother Sean and will pass along any correspondence.

I do above all else long to be more like my dear sister Lily, who always thought about the less fortunate. She was such a good mother and passed along those amazing gifts she had to you. I look forward to hearing about your own children. I do hope someday to have a namesake.

I send many felicitations of joy your way.

Very Sincerely

Auntie Rose Capron

Corinne read through and wiped away a few tears. She had no idea how to handle all the things her Aunt shared. It was a gift to hear from her Aunt and to know that her "old heart" indeed could still grow was astounding. Auntie had been the 'General' when Corinne was there and she wondered what amazing things had transpired to help her Aunt grow in such a short amount of time.

She read the parts to Angela that pertained to her and they discussed her Aunt for a while. Angela had mixed feelings. Her experience as a maid hadn't been good, but it led her to her closest and dearest friendship. She was now close to being re-united with her brother, Lord willing, because of her becoming a maid in the Capron house in Boston.

"I accept her best wishes with a heart full of forgiveness." Angela said when the words finally came to her. "I know the world she came to be part of, sees servants as a lower class. You are a rare person that can see past that." Angela reached a hand to her friend and with a loving pat on the shoulder she stood up.

"I need to rest a bit." Angela yawned and then headed to her room. A cat nap was required.

"I will wake you after a bit. Rest well." Corinne said and smiled at her friend's back as she walked away. It was so good to have her safe and sound. Corinne said a prayer of thanks to the Lord for the safety of her friend. She was more than thankful.

She looked back to her lap and saw that another letter was in her stack addressed to Corinne so she opened it as well.

Dear Cousin Corinne,

I heard from Grandmother Capron about your move to the West and must say I am fascinated. My father is as well. He talks all the time about heading west. He has had an offer for his farmland from a neighbor and is seriously considering moving to California, tales of the fertile land is whetting his appetite, even my mother is not against the idea, but she is nervous that I will not find a decent husband in such a rough and wild place. I personally do not care for finding a husband. I long to go to Europe and study painting, but my parents will not allow it. Instead I must focus on learning how to be a proper wife.

I heard from Grandmother that you are in Oregon City and you are married and you have started your own greenhouses and plan on running a business alongside your husband. I feel emboldened to ask to come stay with you and your husband for a while when my family eventually does move west, I suspect it to be within the year. I would love the opportunity to paint and harness my passion for art if just through books but in an environment that would allow me to be a woman with ideas. Not just a prize up for bid by any marriageable suitor my parents deem worthy.

If I have offended you in any way I do beg your pardon, but somehow as my seventeenth birthday draws near I feel a real fear of being shackled to marriage when I long for another life first.

This letter may be all for naught if my parents stay in Kentucky or ship me to Boston for a season with Grandmother Capron. I just know that she would consider my painting and drawing a distraction from my focus of husband hunting. All my prayers are set upon finding a way to be free to do my art and choose my own life.

Please pray about it.
Sincerely,

Cousin Megan Capron

❀ ❀ ❀ ❀ ❀

Corinne wasn't sure what to think. She was definitely against Megan going to stay with Rose Capron after her own experience. The grip her Aunt had on her young life was still having an effect on Corinne. Corinne would read the letter to her husband later and they could pray over it together. She had met Megan a few times when they were young on family gatherings but she didn't know her well. It was a big decision.

That evening the dinner at the Harpole Ranch house was a festive one. Marie had a wonderful spread prepared and Cooper had painted a banner that was hung about the large fireplace. They had a large gleaming table that Corinne's father had ordered with extra leaves to extend. Dolly was staying with them and was helping Marie with dinner.

"I hope you have been able to rest." Dolly said to Angela as they both were setting the table.

"Yes, today has been good. I had a nap a little while ago." Angela said. Corinne had told her all about how Dolly had come from her Indian village to learn from Corinne. "Your English is very good. Corinne told me all about you. I look forward to being your friend." Angela said simply. She wanted to get to know this girl with the kind brown eyes and the beautiful black hair.

"Chelsea is a good teacher. I knew a few words from my mother. But have lost some since her death." Dolly said with no sadness. But Angela felt it for her.

"My mother was gone when I was young, I am sorry." Angela said sincerely.

"I have learned from Chelsea the word orphan in white man's tongue. In my tribe I was told that they were my new family; as the Harpole and Grants are to me now. I have many mothers now. It is better for me to accept the larger family than to feel the pain of so much loss." Dolly said. Her eyes lit up as she looked around the room. Angela could see she loved her Oregon family very much. It sparked something inside Angie's heart to see Dolly loved and accepted here.

"Thank you Dolly." Angela felt silly thanking the girl for her speech. Her throat locked up for a moment so she left the "thank you" unexplained, but Dolly looked into her teary eyes and Angela knew the girl knew what she meant.

John Harpole called everyone together and they prayed quickly before the meal was served.

"I have a short speech prepared for the guest of honor." John Harpole said as the food was being brought to the table. Once everyone including Marie was seated he started.

"Corinne has been telling me about Angela since the day she arrived in Oregon. She has been telling everyone about this amazing and strong girl that has survived so much to be here. You are welcome to our home, to our land and into our hearts. Angela Fahey, you are now family. Welcome to Oregon." John Harpole said and everyone around the table cheered.

All Angela could do was smile and cry at such a heart-warming welcome. Once her tears cleared and she recovered her voice, she stood.

"I have never felt more loved. I just know that God has gone before me and given me a new place to call home. Thank you for allowing me to be part of your world." Angela felt so strange and unworthy. She enjoyed the meal but spent the rest of the evening in awe and quiet. Everything was changing so quickly, she didn't know who she was in this new life yet.

As she walked back with Corinne and Lucas in the moonlight she finally spoke freely.

"I feel so overwhelmed." Angela admitted.

"I know dear." Corinne said simply. "You have been a servant for a long time. You are a new creature now. You will find out who Angela the woman is soon enough."

"That sounds reasonable." Angela smiled at her friend who had grasped the situation so quickly.

"I am glad you are here with us, Angela." Lucas said. "You have all the space and time you need to heal and rest. Our valley is good for those things."

Lucas grabbed his wife's hand and squeezed it. Corinne smiled from her husband to her friend as they walked along.

Angela looked up at the night sky and could see the bright stars and the edge of the mountains were shining in the light of the moon. It sunk into her that she was finally home.

❊ ❊ ❊ ❊ ❊

The next day was a relaxing one for Angela and Corinne. Angela woke up early when she heard Lucas and Corinne in the kitchen making breakfast. They both had morning plans and Angela was glad she was going to have some time to go through her trunk in the quiet house after they left.

Corinne promised to join her for lunch and then spend the afternoon with her.

Angela ate breakfast with Corinne and Lucas and then waved them off. She gulped down her fresh milk and cleaned off her dishes. She knew Corinne didn't want her cleaning up but she did it anyway. She smiled as she thought about the trunk across the room waiting to be explored.

A few minutes later she was sitting on the floor and heard the creaking of the trunk as she opened it. She looked at the picture again that lay on top. She soaked it up, memorizing the faces. She would put this in her room today. She felt stronger, like she could handle seeing it now. The reminder of their faces did not hurt as much today.

She unwrapped a few more things. A few lace doilies of her mother's, a few hand towels, all things that Angela could easily see in her future home and it was a way to have her mother with her. Angela let the tears fall as she made her way through a few more special mementos. Her father's pipe made her pause a few minutes as she held it in her hands. The scent of pipe tobacco lingered on it and it brought fresh emotions. Today Angela wasn't afraid of the memories; instead she let them wash over her.

She got through a few layers of wrapped items when she found her mother's journal. That was the place she stopped for the day. The leather bound book was dated 1821 on the front page. She flipped through the pages and saw that the book was nearly full. Angela realized she had found enough treasure for the day. She wrapped up a few things and placed them back into the trunk, lovingly. A few things set apart in her mind about who should have the items. She already felt the pipe would go to her brother, Sean. She had a memory of her father's gold pocket-watch and had the faintest memory of seeing it in this trunk long ago. The more she touched the trunk the more her memory was recalling it. Angela was thrilled with the journal in hand and would get the picture up in her room. The other items could be discovered in their own time. Angela was thankful for what she had found. It was a healing balm to her. A reconnection to who she really was.

She sat on the cushioned chair by the fireplace with her feet up on a little stool. She was lost in her mother's words for a few hours.

❀ ❀ ❀ ❀ ❀

"Hello, my friend." Corinne said in a sing-song voice as she entered the cabin. The morning had passed by in a flash and she was refreshed by the walk to and from the greenhouse.

Angela closed the journal in her hand and stood to full height and gave a good stretch.

"I found my mother's journal, well more of a diary, really. She was just a girl when she got it from her grandfather as a birthday gift." Angela said, smiling happily.

"Oh, that is wonderful." Corinne reached over and laid a hand on the leather book that Angela held out. She closed her eyes a moment. "I can imagine that is such a blessing to you. Having her words…"

"So happy for you." Corinne said sincerely, her voice thick with emotion.

"Thank you so much Corinne. This really is more than I ever thought I would have of my parents." Angela felt the weight of the gift all at once. Corinne had done this for her. The letters she wrote and effort she made actually was giving her parents back to her. "I hope you know…" Angela's voice cracked. She couldn't say anymore through the lump in her throat.

"I know." Corinne said and gave her friend a hug.

They both laughed and wiped away a few tears a minute later. Corinne got up and made three plates for lunch.

"The harvest crew isn't coming?" Angela asked.

"Marie wanted them to come to her place today. Today is the last day we have the crew. There are other farmers who need them now that their crops are dry. The rain gave us the advantage last week." Corinne stated.

Angela didn't fully understand the workings of a farm or harvests but she knew she would learn a lot living here. Corinne had a way of passing along her knowledge without even trying.

"Is Lucas stopping by then?" Angela asked.

"He should be by soon. He is pretty predictable. He loves to stick to a daily pattern. He is very good for me." Corinne said with a smile.

Lucas arrived a few minutes later and washed in the basin in the kitchen. He was talkative about the harvest and how much work had been done. He was heading out with Russell later in the day to see to the progress of the saplings they planted earlier in the year. He ate with efficiency and gave his wife a kiss before he bounded out the door again.

"You both seem to be enjoying the place." Angela stated.

"Yes, we are proud of what we are building." Corinne blushed a little when she said it. "I hope the affection doesn't bother you."

"No, silly." Angela smiled and laughed at Corinne's embarrassment. "You are newlyweds. I just hope I am not imposing in any way." Angela had been concerned about living with them so soon after they were married. The cabin is a large one but Angela wondered if a long-term stay would eventually cause problems.

"We have prayed about it often, Angie, do not be concerned. We are all adults and can communicate with each other. There is nothing that God cannot help us through." Corinne wanted to be sure that Angela knew that she was welcome. "This cabin has plenty of room and you are more than welcome."

"I want to make sure you both have privacy when you need it. I know that married couples need space and time to talk out issues and things. I know I would be able to stay with John and Marie for a day or two here and there should you need some time alone." Angela offered. She had been thinking about options too.

"My father and Marie have already made that suggestion to us for when it was needed." Corinne cleaned up the lunch dishes as they were talking.

"I am glad. I was worrying a little bit about the long term effect my stay could have here." Angela said with relief in her voice.

"Stop your fussing. There is nothing to worry about." Corinne dried her wet hands on a towel and then pointed at the jackets at the front door. "Let's walk off lunch and go see how Marie is fairing. She doesn't want my help today but I can be support from the sidelines at least. If anything we can try and be underfoot." Corinne said with a giggle.

Angela enjoyed seeing her friend so relaxed and light hearted. Last year on the Oregon Trail it had been stressful and difficult dealing with her first husband, Andrew, who had laid down his own set of rules on Corinne. Now to see her in this new way was a full turn around. Corinne was happy in her new life. It did good things to Angela's heart to see it.

The September breeze had the smallest hint of a chill to it but the sun was still warm enough to feel like summer was trying to hang on. Corinne and Angela enjoyed the in-between weather and were pointing out the bits of color showing up on the mountainside in the distance. It was a lovely valley and was restorative to Angela every day she was there.

Marie was finished serving the harvesters and was elbow deep in wash water when the girls arrived. Corinne hung her coat on the hooks by the door and then sauntered over to Marie, scooped up a finger full of bubbles and deposited them playfully on Marie's cute little nose.

"No fair!" Marie exclaimed and they all heard Cooper hooting with laughter from across the room. She wiped at the bubbles with her shoulder and gave Corinne a non-malicious glare.

"Couldn't resist." Corinne said and scooped up her stepbrother Cooper.

"I think you are just showing off for your friend." Marie stated and gave Angela a wink.

"She and I have always been a little silly together. I am glad she hasn't grown out of it." Angela said with a smile and sat next to Corinne and Cooper at the dining table.

"I never stoop to silliness. I don't know what you are talking about." Corinne said and got a few more healthy belly laughs out of Cooper.

Cooper was a bundle of energy and ran back over to help his Mama dry dishes a minute after tussling with his 'sister'. They had a growing relationship that was a happy one. Corinne had been an only child and was really happy with the new arrangement.

Corinne and Angela stayed and chatted with Marie for more than an hour. They made plans for the week that included shopping and maybe a trip to the ocean before the winter snows flew for Angela.

"You must see the coast!" Marie exclaimed. They talked about the waves and the surf.

Angela had been to the east coast beaches a few times with her mother and brother but not been recreationally allowed to do so since. The thought had appeal.

The girls left with thoughts on pleasant things when they took a turn around the property. Corinne took her to the pastures and they got a good look at the horses getting broken by some rough lads with ropes. The girls both gave each other knowing smiles when a few rustlers gave them a nod or attention at all. John Harpole ran a clean ranch and the cowboys were respectful. But that didn't mean that they didn't look a little at two pretty young ladies in their midst. Corinne and Angela would admit to being flattered at the attention only when pressed.

Corinne was a good tour guide and they wandered into her greenhouse eventually. It was nowhere near the size of the enormous greenhouses in Boston but it was a pretty house of glass that was warm and moist inside. The plants were green and there were flowers blooming and other plants in early growth stages.

Angela did not recognize many plants but that was not her specialty, Corinne named a few things and Angie just tried to keep up with her happy friend. Corinne was in her world again, just like at the Apothecary Shoppe.

After being shown around Angie was beginning to tire, her fatigue from the journey suddenly catching up to her. Corinne walked Angela back to the cabin just fifty steps away from the greenhouse by a stone path Lucas had just set up the month before. During the rainy season the ground could get quite muddy between these buildings. The flat stones would keep their feet from tracking so much mud into the house.

Angela was glad to catch a nap before dinner, Corinne made a quick visit to her father's home next door and Marie sent a dinner basket loaded with goodies for them.

Corinne woke Angela up and told her dinner was ready an hour later. Angela walked out to see Chelsea and Russell Grant at the door shrugging off their jackets. Chelsea let out a pleasant laugh and ran to hug her friend with her free arm. Her other arm held a baby girl.

Angela gave her old friend a hug then gave her attention to the pretty blue-eyed girl with sandy brown hair.

"She looks like Russell and Lucas..." Angela said and touched the baby's cheek. Babies' skin was always like satin.

"Yes, she has the Grant look to her. They all take after their pretty mama." Chelsea said and gave her girl a kiss.

"I do not like being called 'pretty'" Lucas laughed and his brother grunted in agreement.

Lucas was handing plates to Corinne who was setting them on the dinner table.

"Well your mother was very pretty and so are her boys." Chelsea laughed at the men's protests. "Angela, I hope you are recovering from the trip well. It took me a few weeks to feel like myself again, but I also was pregnant at the time." Chelsea shrugged.

Corinne took the baby for a few moments while everyone got settled around the table.

"You eat first Chelsea, I will take care of Sarah." Corinne cooed and made faces at the sweet girl.

Everyone enjoyed the meal and chatted away. Lucas and Russell both tried to include Angela in the conversation by asking about her trip. Angela spoke with her shy voice at first but felt more comfortable speaking as the meal progressed. Even the Brannigans' family she traveled with had treated her like a servant, though she paid her own way. She wasn't used to being treated like an equal yet. It might take a long while.

Once the meal was done and everyone, including Corinne, had partaken, Chelsea served up several slices of apple pie. Lucas went to the stove and percolated some coffee and passed out mugs.

"This batch of coffee is a good one." Corinne stated after a few sips.

"Clive has been buying the coffee beans himself and learning to roast them. I swear that man must know how to do everything." Lucas laughed. "His first batch last month was a bit darker but this batch is very smooth tasting. He has mastered a new craft."

"He has nine lives, like a cat." Corinne said with a smile. She loved Clive like a grandfather.

"He makes the rest of us mortals look like we are sitting around doing nothing." Chelsea stated. "My grandfather needs a challenge at all times. I think it is about time he married again. Perhaps he would stay still for a few days with a wife to keep him company."

"He may be shy of another wife dearest. He has been widowed twice." Russell said with a nod.

"Tis' true. But a woman would be good for him." Chelsea stated. They all laughed but agreed that it would be interesting for Clive to have a new wife someday.

The rest of the evening passed along well. Chelsea and Angela were able to get reacquainted and their friendship was easily rekindled from their days spent together on the trail. Chelsea was very easy to get along with and made Angela feel like an equal.

Russell and Chelsea left after dusk to retrieve their son Brody from his Grandpapa Clive.

"Those two together are sure to be stirring up trouble if I let 'em loose for too long." Chelsea laughed and waved.

"I'll be by early to help build that bridge." Russell told Lucas. Lucas gave his brother a friendly pat on the back before he was gone.

Angela watched the cozy scene with a peaceful set in her heart. These were such good people, all accepting of her and each other. This was a place she could call home.

Lucas and Corinne talked with Angela until she grew fatigued. She was eager to have more energy but went to bed with a peace in her heart. Oregon was proving to be good for her. Tomorrow she planned to write to Edith Sparks and tell her all about her new home.

❈ ❈ ❈ ❈

The next few days were full of everyday tasks that Angela watched but rarely participated in. Corinne was certainly opinionated about Angela being a guest and would not allow her to lift a finger. It was fine for the first few days but as Angela's strength was growing her desire to have a task grew too.

Angela started sending Corinne off to her greenhouse and lab without her. Angela was beginning to get a feel for the land around her and she was getting fond of visiting with Marie and Cooper. Cooper was an excellent fishing buddy. Angela felt several times that since Corinne was as dear as a sister to her that she had a solid claim of Cooper as a second little brother.

They took a few turns around the property together and Cooper showed her all the places that had stories.

"This was where I caught a toad as big as my head." He exclaimed over a place on the trickling creek.

"This was where I saw a coyote." He said from behind the barn.

"He was probably trying to get to the barn animals." Angela said with a sense of mystery. Angela would always try and sound amazed with his every declaration. Her own childhood had been cut short and she was enjoying seeing the joy of this young lad. It made her heart a bit lighter. For the first time in a long while she had thoughts of motherhood. The idea of that "someday" was getting easier to see.

Marie and Angela became close over the next few weeks, as Angela's stay continued. Marie was a lot like Edith in Angela's mind, very sweet and full of motherly advice. Marie had dimples, blond curls and always a pleasant word to say. It was very refreshing to be around her. She sang old folk songs while she cooked and whistled prettily. Marie let Angela help in the kitchen and they would work and talk for hours. Angela was learning to crochet when she left the Spark's home. She saw that Marie had a basket full of yarn near the rocking chair by the fireplace. It didn't take long before Marie and Angela were sitting and crocheting together. Angela was still slow but learning a lot from Marie's patient instructions.

Chapter 9

A few weeks had passed and another round of harvesters were coming for lunch. Corinne buckled under Angela's protest and allowed her to help serve the men. They worked together at plating up the prepared food as the minutes ticked closer to the crew's arrival.

"I have been reading some of my mother's journal. Her words about Ireland are so romantic and tragic. My parents would not abide by the way many of the wealthy folks were treating the peasants. It seems that two times my parent's home nearly caught afire." Angie shared at the lunch table.

"Oh my, was it an uprising?" Corinne asked as she had heard many stories on the long trip from Boston to Oregon, so many people from so many places. She had heard of uprising in Ireland.

"It was one of my father's cousins who wanted the land and was angry when my father inherited. I guess that is why he eventually sold, perhaps just a chance to start again in America. I remember my mother saying my father was too soft-hearted to be a Baron. Perhaps I come by my gentleness honestly." Angie said with a smallest hint of a smile. The picture of her father was becoming a warm memory again. Somehow she had been angry with him for dying, it was irrational she knew, but she had had many lonely and dark days in the workhouse. Some days anger was its own battle to fight against, along with the starvation and abuse.

"I like knowing that he had a generous heart." She added a minute later.

"That seems a good quality to inherit, Angie." Corinne smiled and finished filling the plates with the warm bread and hot stew that Marie had just delivered.

"Will you do the honors?" Corinne asked and pointed to the bell just outside the door. The long table outside was ready for the stampede of the men helping with the lavender harvest.

Angela approached the bell and gave the rope a good pull then kept it going. The bell was loud and hurt her ears so she ran back into the house and laughed.

"Ha, Angie, it doesn't bite." Corinne giggled a bit then put her to helping get the plates passed out as they arrived. After a few got their plates some of the young men started whistling at the pretty redhead serving their dinner.

"None of that, young man." Lucas Grant strolled up and gave the man a cuff to the back of the head. The men all laughed and the situation was lightened.

"Miss Fahey is a lady and is to be respected. No tom foolery with this woman, she is under my protection." Lucas gave poor Angie a wink and the young man apologized respectfully.

Angie blushed through her mortification.

"That did not take long." Corinne stated as she kept handing Angie plates of food. "I knew she would catch someone's eye. We women are a rare thing to see out here, an unmarried woman, and a beautiful one is a valuable find."

"I know I am seventeen but I have no desire for a husband right now. I wish to find my brother first." Angie stated loudly a bit bolder after her embarrassment.

"No worries on my account, Angie. I have no wish to marry you off right away. I want you to be able to have some freedom before you settle down. You need a chance to dream a little first." Corinne said warmly. She was such a dreamer and the thought gave Angie pause.

"I think I should go to California, Corinne. Will you despise me if I leave you again?" Angie asked after the last plate was handed out. They sat inside and ate at the small table. The men had to have their own space where the pressure of table manners was less needed.

"I would never deny or question your need to connect with your brother. I am excited to think there is a hope of meeting him, myself. It is strange to think of him already as a part of my family. My prayer is that you bring him here to meet us." Corinne took Angie's hand across the wooden table. Her eyes did not lie. It calmed Angie's fears. She felt pulled in several directions. Clive had lit a flame of hope in her chest.

"I have had my own thoughts creep into my heart. Mostly fear and a selfish desire to keep you close. But I know your need to try and find Sean. Just know we are here for you, if you do not feel safe just know we would come for you, and you always have a place to come back to." Corinne said as her voice broke a little from emotion. "You should go Angie. Clive's family will care for you. I will be praying for you sister-friend."

They spent a good moment hugging and then got back to work. They were being watched and making a spectacle of themselves. They laughed as a few of the men were teasing them.

They kept talking as they worked. Finding a rhythm of serving the harvesting crew.

"I need to talk with Clive more, and find out when I should prepare to go. I need more clothes for most of mine are rags now from the journey. Also I need to handle my affairs at the bank. I went through the lawyers documents today, they are very confusing in places." Angie became more talkative when her nerves got the better of her.

"Going to the bank is a good idea. You should know what you have and then you can plan for your future." Corinne said. Her heart hurt at the thought of her friend leaving, but she knew her friend needed to go for the chance of finding her lost brother. It was a sad thought to ponder but Corinne knew she must accept it and be supportive. Angela needed to know that it was okay to leave through more than her words, through her actions, as well. Corinne would pray for the strength to let Angela go. It was the right thing to do.

❊ ❊ ❊ ❊ ❊

"When would be a good time to go, Clive?" Angie asked, leaning against the counter at the mercantile.

"Well, my girl, I've been pondering that. My Grandson and his wife could handle you at any time. They got a nice place downtown with a three-story building, nice and sturdy, iffen I don't wanna crow too loudly. I built it myself a few years ago. San Fran is a nice port town and gettin' supplies there makes my life and business easier. Sutter's Fort isn't too far off an' now with the Gold Rush it will be hopping."

"I just know my brother is in California somewhere and my heart aches wanting to know he is safe, I just want to see him." Angie saw the sparkle in Clive's eye. He was such a sweet and spunky man. He was truly a Godsend.

"Well I will get a telegram Gabriel's way and we can figure out when the best time would be. I would get ready iffen I was you. In the next month it would be a good idea to get yerself out there. The crowds will be getting larger by the day as soon as the ships from the east arrive. That store will be jumpin'. I will go with ya and be helpin' with the store for a bit anyways. So you will have some company. I will get the word out about yer brother. We will find him my Angel girl." Clive gave her a pinch on the cheek.

Angela shared a hug and then found Corinne and Marie making a mess in the fabric section. It appeared that Marie may have purchased half the bolts of cloth for Angela's wardrobe.

"I am so excited Angie, look at all the warm tones. You are gonna turn some heads for sure and certain." Marie's blond curls were escaping her bonnet and her genuine warmth and caring had won over Angie completely, that and her fried chicken.

"You will try and remember to not spend too much. I only need the basics." Angie reminded her.

67

"I will spend as I wish child. No child o' mine is going off to San Francisco without looking like the lady she is." Marie gave her a parental look and that hushed her.

"I guess she told you." Corinne laughed and handed over a few bolts to get Angie's opinion.

"I still feel odd accepting a whole wardrobe for nothing." Angie was troubled, so many people being nice to her made her uneasy. There was such a strange thing having so many people start caring about you after so many years of having no one.

"John and I will take care of you darlin'. Just let us love on you. You are worth it, child." Marie gave her a wink but the words sunk in. Angie felt loved.

They left the store with a wagon full of supplies. A brand new steamer trunk to fill with clothes, two new pairs of shoes, a few fashionable bonnets and enough ribbons to make more fripperies than Angie had ever owned.

Chapter 10

Angela was pounding out a ball of dough. It had risen to a big puffy blob in the yellow ceramic bowl. She had just poured it out over the counter covered in flour. She enjoyed the feeling of her strong arms stretching and punching the dough. It was a good way to get your thoughts in order. Corinne had been working all morning in her lab. She was doing some complicated procedure with boiling devices. Angela didn't fully understand it but Corinne was sure excited about her harvest and what she could do with it.

Angela felt the smallest twinge of guilt about making the bread and starting a roast on the stove but she had been in Oregon for enough weeks to start being helpful. Corinne kept trying to come home after working and throwing together some kind of dinner after her long hours. Some nights Marie would bring things over but Corinne had begun to fuss about that too. Corinne did not like the idea of using help, at all. Angela had her own theories on it. Having been a servant for a long time she felt okay with her thoughts.

Having help doesn't make you a bad person. How you treat the help is other matter entirely. Angela felt like she was a burden in their house. Another mouth to feed when everyone else had a job, she had no labor to do. Every time she tried to help, Corinne would get her braids in a twist.

Angela felt bad about thinking that way about her dearest friend, but she was not enjoying her long days with nothing to do. She had decided and worked out some details with Marie early that morning when Corinne left. Corinne did not come back home during lunch because she and Lucas had things to do during the lunch hour.

Angela had trotted over to John and Marie Harpole's cabin right after sunrise. Marie was feeding her husband and son Cooper breakfast. Marie smiled broadly and welcomed her to the table.

"I know you were planning to make dinner for Lucas and Corinne but I want the honor." Angela had said. Marie nodded and smiled.

"You getting silly with boredom, huh?" Marie plopped a breakfast plate down before Angela could protest. "Dinner duties are yours. You know what you are making?"

"I was thinking some homemade rolls and a beef stew. There was fresh beef brought in last night, the root cellar is full of vegetables. I wandered in there yesterday out of curiosity. I cleared out the cobwebs and tidied a bit while I was in there. I just know Corinne wouldn't like that I did that but I had nothing else to do."

"You have been here long enough to start feeling like you need a task. I know some young men in the area have been asking about you." Marie teased.

"Not interested in that yet. I have something stirring in me. I will be heading out sometime soon to find my brother in California. But staying with Corinne and Lucas feels strange and foreign to me. I am not meant to be a woman of leisure." Angela shared.

"Well, seems to me that you and Corinne need to have an honest talk. She has a life that is a little bit different and for her and Lucas it works. She wants you to feel like family, but she is forgetting something in the desire to not have hired help. She needs the help. You see the need and want to bless her." Marie gave her husband a kiss as he headed out wordlessly. John Harpole gave a pat on the shoulder to Angela before he left. Cooper followed his dad with a skip in his step.

Marie sat down next to her and continued with her thoughts. "Corinne is young still, having wealth her whole life has put her in an interesting position. She cares for you like the sister she never had. She also has the drive and characteristics of her father. I see that stubborn determination in her looks all the time. Corinne can never know what it feels like be a servant, and has never known what it feels like to be poor. But she has told me more than once about how useless she felt when on the trail and her first husband would not allow her to be a help to those around her. She was willing and capable, yet denied the right to help her comrades. She is now trying to deny you the right to help because she thinks it will make you feel like a servant. But what it's really doing is making you feel like a burden." Marie said.

Angela nodded and sniffed, feeling a bit emotional about how Marie had laid it out exactly how she felt. Angela had a handkerchief in her pocket and dabbed at the stray tears.

"I have tried to talk with her but she has stayed pretty firm that I am a guest and not to do any helping." Angela said once her throat cleared of the emotional knot.

"Well, if you need to communicate with food that might get the conversation moving in a new direction. I will pray for you both. This is a new situation for both of you, I would call these growing pains." Marie leaned in next to Angela and pulled her up into a hug. It felt like a motherly hug and Angela let herself be held.

After the hug ended the women had spoken about household issues and Marie gathered a few fresh herbs and shared them with Angela for her stew.

Angela left Marie with many 'thank you's' and another motherly hug. Angela felt less like an orphan today. She was starting to feel like family here. The morning mist was burning off but the grass under her feet was crunchy with a frost. Autumn was all around her and she enjoyed the mountain splendor as she walked back to Grant's Grove.

She was finishing up with getting the bread rolls in the step top stove that was built in the kitchen. Angela had doubted Corinne had even used it. Angela had found several cobwebs inside. Angela thought about the Temple family who had built this cabin, Mrs. Temple must have really loved cooking. The kitchen was larger than most, with the fancy step top oven built next to the fireplace. Corinne had mentioned that Mrs. Temple liked cooking for the work-hands often.

Angela took a deep breath and tried to think generous thoughts about the Temple family, praying for their new life and hoping they were blessed and happy. It wasn't always easy for her but forgiving their son for his actions was good for her soul.

It had to be forgiven often inside her, for that day bubbled up as a bad memory every time the ache in her leg came again. The nightmare returned of those hours in the dark ravine, bleeding and hurting. Listening to the bugs hover around her as she yelled for help and prayed throughout the night.

Angela shook off the memory of that dark day and continued with the happy work of chopping vegetables, crushing the herbs and getting the big round pot and hanging it on the hook arm next to the fireplace. The fireplace had a great set of hot red coals that was producing a good heat. She salted the meat chunks and threw them into the round pots. She heard the meat sizzle on the hot pan a few minutes later. She added a little bit of beef lard and stirred the meat around in the pot with a wooden spoon as Edith Sparks had taught her. Getting a few brown edges on the pieces of meat. A few minutes later she added water, the vegetables and some herbs. She had the potatoes peeled, cut them into little chunks and dropped the chunks into the water by the handful. The smell of the meat sizzling had filled the room with a wonderful aroma. The first batch of rolls would be done in a few minutes but Angela kept her hands busy by using hot water and baking soda and scrubbed the counter down, clearing away any remnants of the food mess. She swept the floor free of flour and any vegetables that had escaped the countertop where she had worked.

She felt happy and fulfilled, pulling up a chair and resting. She continued watching the kitchen fire contentedly until the rolls were done. Then she put in another batch and saw that the stew was beginning to bubble, such a lovely feeling.

"I made that." Angela said to the empty room. She enjoyed her feeling of accomplishment for the rest of the afternoon.

"Smells amazing in here." Lucas said as he opened the front door a few minutes after six o'clock. He turned and watched Corinne come in behind him. Corinne looked surprised when she came in too.

"Hello Grants." Angela said with a bit of trepidation. She had the dining table set, the rolls placed in a basket and butter and jam set out. There were two pies sitting and cooling in the window. "Marie brought the pies, she makes peach pies like nothing else on earth." Angela was waiting for them to say something.

"Thank You Angela, this looks amazing." Lucas broke the awkward moment. He walked over to the washstand and washed his hands.

"You don't need to feed us, Angela." Corinne looked confused, almost hurt.

"I know, I wanted to do something nice for you both. For taking such good care of me." Angela said and approached her friend. She wanted this to go smoothly but was ready for the serious talk.

"I don't feel right about this." Corinne sat down in a chair and she teared up.

Angela sighed, knowing this was getting complicated faster than she expected.

"I know, but I had a good talk with Marie and I really need to communicate something to you." Angela took a deep breath and tried to ignore the look of pain on Corinne's face. She continued, "The way I feel about you crossed the servant-master relationship a long time ago. I want to consider you as a sister. I love you as family. You fear that I will forever feel like a servant to you, but I do not. Very simply, I wanted to make you dinner as a loving gesture, and to have a task. I stay in your home, like family and have capable hands and nothing to do." Angela said.

"But I want you to feel relaxed." Corinne said. Lucas sat next to his wife and held her hand.

"Did you feel relaxed when Andrew forbid you from helping on the trail?" Angela wanted to pull the words back when she saw the look of horror cross Corinne's face. She burst into fresh tears.

Angela mouthed the words 'I'm sorry' to Lucas who then shook his head. He didn't seem upset at all. Just supportive and letting them have their talk. Angela felt a new respect for her friend's husband.

Corinne finally stopped crying and wiped away the tears. She took a few deep breaths before she spoke. "I am sorry Angela." She looked like she was going to tear up again but with a big swallow she held it back.

"You don't need to apologize, we just need to work out a life here. I feel awkward living with you and never being allowed to be helpful. Not as an obligation but as a way to say thank you." Angela finished her speech and held out the chair.

She smiled as Corinne settled in at the table and allowed Angela to do what she had planned. The meal went well and soon there was laughter around the table as they all enjoyed the meal together, as equals.

Angela let Corinne and Lucas do the cleaning up and headed off to her room. She wanted to leave them both alone tonight. She wanted some time to think to herself. She would be leaving soon. She wanted to go through her things a bit tonight and tomorrow; start to get serious about packing. She would be going to town tomorrow to talk with Clive about details. She wanted to have her head cleared of all her fears and doubts with a little quiet time and prayer that night.

❀ ❀ ❀ ❀ ❀

"We can leave on Monday. The steamship, *The Mariana*, is coming into port on Sunday and heading back out early Monday morning. You can stay at the hotel in town to get an early start if ya wish." Clive told her the next day at the store counter. The store was empty of customers and Clive just pulled up two stools for them to sit on.

"The hotel sounds like a good idea." Angela said in her small voice. Clive was watching her carefully.

"You will have your own bunk and it will take several days at least to get to our location. If the wind is mild it will shorter. If the wind is gusty it takes longer. These things vary." Clive said with a shrug.

Angela laughed at his easy way of acceptance. She had a hundred questions floating through her mind but suddenly felt shy of asking any.

"You look nervous, chile'." Clive stated with an eyebrow raised.

"Yessir." Angela said simply. "Not a big fan of boats."

"Me neither child. I prefer the ground under my feet. But this is the easiest and best way to get to California safely, this time of year." Clive was very matter of fact, it actually helped her fears.

"I can accept that. I appreciate that you will be with me." Angela finally said and saw the smile that spread across Clive's face. It was infectious and she smiled back.

"Would not have of dreamed of not taggin' along." Clive made a harrumph noise that was comical. Clive stood up and grabbed his stool and settled it behind the counter.

Angela assumed he had sat still for too long and needed to gad about the place. He straightened a few things then after he made a sharp whistle toward the back of the place. His son, Jedediah, everyone called JQ, popped out from the warehouse. He looked like Clive but for a few less gray hairs.

"This is Angela, they will be staying with your boy Gabe and his wife Amber." Clive said with a friendly introduction. "This is my firstborn JQ."

"Ah, that is fine. Amber will be glad for the company, that's for certain." JQ shook her hand with a firm handshake and a smile that matched his father's. "My wife will be glad to meet you when you come back to Oregon. She is busy this week canning and socializing with the church women." JQ shook his head at Clive.

"My kitchen was so hot yesterday my head nearly popped off. It smelled of stewed tomatoes, onions and peaches, it didn't combine well. I might invite myself to your place for supper tonight." JQ said animatedly.

"Not sure my stomach could handle that either." Clive said with a grimace.

"Mine turned the moment I got home last night. Still feeling a bit sour from the memory." JQ shared. His frown was exaggerated and Angela fought off the giggles.

Angela was already enjoying the banter between father and son.

"How is it possible you have a grandson old enough to be married?" Angela asked to see how they would both respond.

"Well, since you seem old enough to know about the birds and the bees, I figure you know how. But as my unusual vigor and handsome youthful appearance has fooled many onlookers I have had to explain this before." Clive lifted his hat and did a quick vain stroke of his salt and pepper locks before settling back on his head. "I had J.Q. when my bride and I were quite young. We moved out west and she was settled here and I set traps all up and down the coast while she manned the Hudson Bay store nearer to the coast. J.Q. and his brother were 8 and 10 when their ma passed on of yellow fever, some of the Indians had it and she was always checking on the families. She had such a loving heart. The boys and I made do for a while until we headed back east and settled in Indiana when I had remarried again. I got the itch to come west again and had a few job offers from the government to translate and communicate with some bureaucrats in

Washington. I also did some peace talkin' with a few tribes I was in good relations with.

We came back and resettled in the West and my sons help me now with the stores I have spread along the coast. I miss trappin' sometimes. It is a quiet, peaceful way to live. The forest being a mysterious thing to tame, but running my stores and keeping my family gainfully employed is always a challenge." Clive shared.

J.Q. Harrumphed. "Gainfully employed… We allow you to do what you want to do, which is to gallivant around like a stray dog." J.Q. winked at Angela and was rewarded with a smile.

"Stray dog." Clive huffed. He had no quippy comeback so he let it drop, he wasn't truly offended. Just amused that his son had him pegged.

Angela left after getting more details from Clive about the trip they would be taking in a few days. She felt confident that Clive knew what he was doing. She could trust him to keep her safe.

She had some goodbyes to say before she left, also some packing to do and had a few walks to take before she went away.. She wanted to take Oregon with her because she knew this was that closest thing to home she had had in way too long.

❀ ❀ ❀ ❀ ❀

The church was newly built and sturdy, the community pitched in together and built it as a schoolhouse for those on the outskirts of town. The rural community liked its location just on the edge of town. It was easier for the children to get there and the family thought the location for church services was a good one too. They didn't have to go all the way into town.

Angela enjoyed the preaching from the minister, Pastor Whittlan. He was witty and charming in his style and wasn't one to yell as he preached. Corinne and Lucas sat in the same row with the Chelsea and Russell. Brody was trying to make mischief but with so many family members in the row he wasn't allowed much trouble. He ended up in Angela's lap for at least half the service. He was a little squirmy at first but Angela was finally able to concentrate on the service.

The sermon was a one that was very practical about taking the time to lean on God and tell him your troubles. Angela felt compelled to spend more time in prayer and trusting God to guide her steps. She was enjoying the camaraderie of the small church and since she knew so many people already from the extended family of Corinne, she fit right in. She knew she was leaving the next day and had that twinge of regret that she would be halting the growth she had begun in this community.

With the service over and the young boy free from her lap, she stood and turned around to see Marie behind her. Marie gave her a wave from two rows back and Angela excused herself through the talking crowd to talk to Marie.

"I wanted to make sure I said goodbye." Angela said.

"I will miss your company, Angie." Marie said with sincerity in her voice.

"I do not know how long I shall be gone but I know I will be coming home." Angela stated. "You all have made my life vastly better and I cannot express how much you mean to me."

"My prayers will be daily for you and your brother." Marie promised. "I will write and pray. I have started an afghan for you and hope to give it to you when you return."

Angela was touched. "You have such a generous heart, Marie. Thank you."

Marie and Angela talked for a few more minutes about her trip and John came over and said "goodbye." Cooper gave her a hug around her middle and even squeezed out a few tears.

"I hope you will be back by the spring. I wanted to do more fishing. I catch the best fish in the summertime but the mud is good for catching worms in the spring." Cooper stated. He was frowning and it melted Angela's heart.

"I will miss you Cooper." Angela said and meant it.

"Okay, just bring me back some gold dust." He said seriously.

"Deal. I will try and get you some genuine gold dust."

✿ ✿ ✿ ✿ ✿

Corinne and Lucas helped her load up her two trunks and they all had dinner at the hotel downtown. It had a nice restaurant that served good food. Angela shared her hotel room that night with Corinne. Lucas rode back on horseback and left the buggy for Corinne at the stables next door.

Corinne tried to be brave and not cry about her closest friend leaving but she lost her composure once or twice.

"I won't stay away too long. I promise." Angela said when Corinne teared up near bedtime. "I have to try and find him. It's the right thing to do. He has money set aside for him. And he needs to know that I am here now." Angela didn't really need to explain but she felt sad about causing pain to her friend.

"I truly know this. I do not begrudge you the right to reunite with him." Corinne sniffed and held her handkerchief near her red nose. "I just pray you find him soon and bring him back to Oregon."

"I have no idea if he would want to come to Oregon. But I can sure try." Angela smiled to try and cheer her friend.

"Oh, I got this for you." Corinne said and handed her a wooden box with a cross on top.

"You have given me too much already, wardrobes and shoes and allowing me to live at your home." Angela protested.

"Oh hush. I ordered this months ago. Just open it." Corinne said with a smile returning to her lips.

"Alright." Angela shrugged and opened the lid with a squeak of new metal hinges.

The Bible had shining black leather and the gold letters on the bottom right corner spelled out. ANGELA FAHEY

"Clive told me about it then helped to place the order. Isn't it wonderful?" Corinne knew she was talking nervously but she could see that Angela liked it.

Angela felt the raised gold letters with her fingers and turned the pages. Corinne had filled in the first page.

This book is presented to Angela Fahey by Corinne Grant in November, the Year of Our Lord 1849.

"Corinne, it's stunning." Angela said breathlessly.

"You can fill in your family tree. Your legacy is ready to be written now." Corinne grabbed her friend's hand and held it fast.

"This reminds me of the hotel we stayed in…" Angela said. "In Independence, Missouri. When your husband Andrew was off preparing the wagons. We knew that change was near. We had a long road to travel but we had each other."

"We survived the separation, we can do it again." Corinne said bravely.

"I will write often." Angela kept promising.

"You know I will too." Corinne was equally sincere.

They thumbed through pages and Angela read a few of her favorite verses aloud before they both determined it was time to rest. The morning would arrive and Angela had to be up and ready before dawn.

Part 3

Chapter 11

The plank to get on the steamship was wet and muddy from many boots tromping across it. Angie could smell the scent of Clive's pipe tobacco clinging to him. His strong presence made her feel safe. He was in his trapping clothes, a tanned leather jacket and a sturdy wide-brimmed hat.

They stomped on wet feet to a very small room with six port rooms. Basically triple bunks with a thick curtain to pull closed for privacy. Clive announced that her bunk will be on top and he would be right below her for safety. Angie never would have guessed that these rooms were coed. The thought made Angie shiver a bit but she regained her composure and allowed her luggage to be settled up high next to her 'bed'. Angie was already thinking ahead on how in the world she would change her clothes in that small space.

"I made sure that Marie provided you with a dressing gown. You can get changed in the changing room before lights out." Clive's mouth had the smallest perceptible smirk as he read her thoughts so easily.

"You have a devilish humor, Mr. Quackenbush." Angie teased and accepted his look with a laugh.

"All the better to make you blush young lady." Clive helped her out of her heavy coat and hung it on a hook nearby. "Will you be warm enough?"

"Let's find a seat near a warm stove. This sweater is warm enough for now." Angela suggested.

They found a seat inside a sitting room with some windows at the far end. The chugging of the water wheel and the slapping of the water could be heard even in the middle of the vessel. Clive and Angie got settled in a comfortable pair of seats next to a warm sheet stove. Angie had a book and a lap blanket she brought from her luggage that she grabbed before they left the port room.

Corinne was very nice to share some of her book collection and Angie was lost in a dramatic story in no time. Clive settled into the warm chair and happily watched the people around them until the warm room and the swaying and chugging of the steamship lulled him to sleep. Clive woke from his nap and saw his young charge happily still reading by his side. Reserving this floor of the steamship had been expensive, but to have all this space and privacy was well worth the expense. The crush of people in some of the lower decks made the four-day journey cramped, smelly and tiresome. Clive figured that Angie had had enough bad journeys to last a lifetime. His goal was to make this her best adventure yet. His prayers were set on keeping her safe.

The days aboard went quickly with the books and meals served. Clive found himself surrounded nearly every evening after the first night of sharing stories of his travels. He told Angie all about how Corinne won over the Indians with her special oils. Then shared a story about snakebite canyon when he was trapped for three days in a sandstorm and only made it out alive when his horse found him. Angie and others were vocal and challenging the fact or fiction of his story but he swore to tell the truth. His claim, "The Truth is always more interesting than a made up story."

"I can understand that." Angie agreed. Her life already was a strange contradiction to itself. She has been born of a wealthy family, reduced to being a pauper and a servant, only then to have her fortune returned to her and now on the other side of the world having another adventure. "What will happen next for me Clive?" She asked him.

"Only good things Red, blessins and happiness fer you chile', iffen I could promise I would my girl." His words made Angie feel better.

❄ ❄ ❄ ❄ ❄

San Francisco, California Territory

The port of San Francisco was a nightmare. Getting in was a maze. The steamboat could only get so close for there were too many ships left abandoned right in the bay. The buzz around the steamboat was that the ships were left by the entire crews, every man for himself for the gold and fortune just lying about the ground.

Clive and Angela gave each other a look whenever people talked about the gold. They had their own thoughts about their doubts of the gold found being so plentiful for everyone just to pick it up off the ground.

The crew sent out a few longboats to shore and the passengers all had to unload the hard way, in small groups unloading their luggage and then had to crawl down the ladder. It was hard to do in skirts, Angela mused aloud to Clive as he waited below her in the longboat.

Her new boots did not like the chain ladder on the side of the ferry and it wanted to tangle and twist around her ankles between every step.

"I cannot see to fix it around my skirts!" Angela yelled over the sounds of the harbor. The wind was starting to pick up and the sway of the longboat underneath her did little to help.

"Try and hold it wide and still with your arms and lift your left foot…"

Angie pushed at the chain ladder and got the ladder to be a little more still and it stopped the twisting. She lifted her foot quickly and got another two rungs down before she got all twisted up again. Her red hair was escaping her bonnet but she got through the next few minutes with as much pride as she could. She watched three men scramble down the ladder with ease after her and she grumbled to herself about stupid skirts and petticoats.

A few minutes later the longboats reached the large dock. The boat was not quite tall enough to reach the high dock, so Angie was man-handled a bit to get herself up. After being lifted by the shoulders like an infant from a burly shouldered man she was plopped on the dock. She was glad to be on dry land, she would block the visual of herself playing the part of the ragdoll from her memory.

Clive had all her trunks loaded up on the dock and she waited patiently and watched the activity buzzing around her with amusement. It reminded her a bit of Independence, Missouri, when it was nearly time to leave for the Oregon Trail. She and Corinne were in a battle of wits with Corinne's first husband about their servant - master relationship. It seemed so silly now but then it was deadly serious. Mr. Temple's threat was to leave Angela behind. He made good on it later in the journey. Angie had to often push aside the remembrance of the night Mr. Temple forced her to search for firewood on a moon-less night with an empty oil-lantern. Angie could still remember the fear of stumbling around in the darkness, the animals around her fighting and the ravine that she fell into. She lay there for many endless hours of pain and confusion, some of it crying, some time spent begging God to just take her. Angela tossed her head to shake the memory from it. She grabbed a handkerchief from the inside of her sleeve and wiped a runaway tear that escaped, she blamed the wind.

"None of that now, Angie Fahey," Angie scolded herself. She had too much to be thankful for to be feeling sorry for herself about the past. She was in a better way now. That was all that mattered, God had gotten her through the worst of it.

❀ ❀ ❀ ❀ ❀

"Angela Fahey, meet Gabriel and Amber Quackenbush." Clive beamed from ear to ear as he gave his introductions. Gabriel gave Angie a firm but friendly handshake and a smile that he got from Clive. Amber was small in stature just like Angie and already well grown with child.

"I am so glad to have another woman around." Amber gave her hand a shake but it quickly turned into a hug. "Sorry, love, I am so glad to meet ya. Clive told us all about ye in his letters and I am so pleased to have an Ireland lass with me. I came over with my parents when I was a youngin' too." Amber's hair was a rich auburn, her eyes a soft brown. Her freckles and easy blush made Angela feel at ease.

"Clive is good at keeping secrets, he did not tell me there was an Irish lass waiting here. We shall have to punish him won't we Mrs. Quackenbush?" Angie gave Amber a wink. She felt an instant bond.

"Please call us Amber and Gabe. Quackenbush is quite a mouthful." Gabe said and grabbed Angie's trunks and gave them a strong heave up to the wagon box.

"Well Gramps, now I got two Irish gals with red hair in the house. I am outnumbered. What if the bairn is one too?" He laughed and Clive joined in. Their laugh was similar, as well. Angie gave Amber a look and they silently communicated their noticing how much alike the men were. The women climbed up into the wagon box and soon the wagon made its way down the bumpy road toward the mercantile.

Angie was surprised to see so many buildings. She expected this to be practically a wilderness with just a few ramshackle buildings thrown in to make a shantytown. It had a large bank and the mercantile that was three stories tall, a few empty buildings stood nearby with "for sale" signs up. The one next to the Hudson Bay store where they were standing, had a "sold" sign.

"We are to have some neighbors soon. My husband heard from the bank that a family wants to start a restaurant. I was dearly praying it wasn't another saloon. The bank was nervous as well. We have enjoyed our peaceful side of the street this year." Gabe told all this to Clive but Angie overheard and was grateful, too. A noisy saloon would not make a good neighbor.

"I do hope you enjoy your stay with us Angela. We have been praying so hard about how we can help you find your brother. We will get you settled in and get to work right way." Amber's sweet smile was friendly and warm. They were adding themselves to the ever-growing list of people that were genuinely kind and good-natured. Angie was hoping to shatter her ideas about people always wanting to hurt her. The more people showing their goodness, the more she could allow her walls down.

"I do hope that I am a help too. I know that your pregnancy will make it harder for you to run the store and take care of yourself properly. I hope there is a doctor in town." Angela said without thinking. In this part of the world there was no guarantees for any kind of medical help. She felt a bit foolish and reckless for even bringing it up.

"Well yes, but he is stretched pretty thin. We just keep our prayer that God will watch over us and keep us safe." Amber said. Her eyes had no fear in them. Angela was relieved.

"I helped a few women deliver babies when I was on the trail. There were no complications, I can help as much as I know how." Angie volunteered and saw Amber's large warm smile again.

❄ ❄ ❄ ❄ ❄

Angela's room was next to a large linen closet on the third floor. The young married couple was across the hallway. Angela felt bad that Gabe had to carry her trunks up the stairs so far but he seemed to handle it well with no huffing and puffing.

Angela set out two dresses quickly and hung them on the simple hooks on the wall. She wanted to get the wrinkles out of them soon. The dress she was wearing looked rumpled and already was showing white dots from the salty spray from being aboard the steamship deck for hours that morning.

She was relieved to see fresh water in the washbasin on a quaint little table by the door. It had a lovely mirror above it and she unpinned her hair. She brushed it into submission and pinned up the front. She let the back stay long and wavy. She was still a little young to be wearing it up. She got used to it on the trail for convenience, but Corinne was always reminding her that she was allowed to wear it down, she wasn't under the servants guidelines anymore.

She washed her face and hands thoroughly and dried off on the towel hanging off the edge of the table. She felt a little more like facing the world. It was still early in the day but so much had happened already. She would lunch with the Quackenbush family and perhaps nap this afternoon. She was travel weary but she put on a brave face before she left the room. She wanted to have Gabriel and Amber know how thankful she was for their hospitality.

She realized she had no need to feel strange around her new friends soon though. Gabe and Amber were friendly and very obliging to her. They made her feel welcome and she was laughing through lunch with all the stories and jokes told.

Gabe and Amber were teasing Clive a lot and he knew how to tease right back. Angela felt at ease immediately with the easy-going nature of the household. There was no formality at the table. Angela didn't participate much in the conversation yet but she was more than ready to join in the laughter.

❀ ❀ ❀ ❀ ❀

"Are you Mrs. Q's sister from Ireland?" Was the question of the day. Every customer that had been in the store before seemed to ask that same question.

"That would be quite an honor but I am just a friend of the family." Angie answered the customers as she helped them with their purchases.

"But you have the a bit of an accent." One gentleman teased a little about her lilting accent that persisted, even more so now that she was talking with Amber so much.

"Yes, I came over as a young girl with my parents and my brother, Sean." It was the perfect opportunity to mention how she was looking for him and his companion, Ol' Willie.

"Ol' Willie, I wonder iff'n that's Old William Shipley? I will ask around bout for ya, darlin'. I'll be back in a few weeks fer supplies. I will send word if I hear anything before then." The miner said.

I thanked the man and helped the next customer. After two days of learning the counter Angie was allowed to be at the front alone. Knowing the revolver was right below the counter was comforting. Gabe and Clive were nearby at the loading dock just twenty feet away. Even still, she saw someone peek their head around the corner every few minutes to keep a close eye on her.

Amber was downstairs and visiting often enough that Clive moved a rocking chair downstairs and set it next to the counter so at least Amber would sit while visiting with her newest friend.

Since she wanted as much face-to-face time with customers,, she spent as much time as she could downstairs. She figured it would give her more chances to ask about Old Willie and her brother.

They showed her around the store then the back storage room and even the loading dock in the back. She was told about the two other warehouses they had for large goods that Clive shipped off to his other stores. Angela was impressed with the grandness of the enterprise. There was more to running a store than she ever thought.

She caught on to running the counter quickly. It would take time to be able to answer customer questions but for now she could use the cash register easily. Clive left for a few hours and Amber stayed with Angela at the counter and they talked shop for a while. They had an easy camaraderie and worked well together. Gabe joined the girls again after dealing with a large order at the loading dock.

Clive bounded through the door and the small bell jingled with purpose.

"I purchased some land at the auction." Clive announced and held some paperwork in his hands. "Been wanting to make this store bigger and build it in brick."

Angie was sitting on a barrel during a slow moment. She had been listening to Gabe tell her all about how the political scene was in town. He thought statehood was going to be granted soon, especially now with the gold rush population reaching huge numbers. It was only going to get more and more populated as people keep arriving every week.

"That is a grand plan. Where you get the land? Near a wharf?" Amber asked, she was a good partner for Gabe and knew the business as well as her husband did.

"Yes'm, the new pier, and with plans for another just a few blocks south is planned. Getting away from the rowdy town square makes me feel safer. Sin and thievery in the streets and the politics is getting everyone stirred up." Clive said to his attentive audience.

Angela put canned goods on a shelf and listened as they plotted out the next few weeks.

"I have been wanting to build in brick for quite some time. I was talking to the town council and they have fears of the massive growth of this place. Fire and sickness is so easily spread when people get careless." Gabe said and Angela saw Clive nodding in agreement.

"We got the supplies, we can get started on a plan, just got to get some laborers and pay them well. Gold fever is hard to compete with, though when people get hungry they will have to come back to town to work. I cannot believe the gold is as easy to find as they say." Clive scratched his chin stubble and then flipped a small notepad open, grabbed a pencil stub out and did some figuring.

"I will come by tonight and we can do some thinking together. I have some loads coming in and the warehouse needs to be managed. I will come by for supper iffen that's alright with you Mrs. Quackenbush." Clive looked to Amber who laughed and nodded. He did a bow then with a spry move he pounced over to Angela and planted a quick kiss on the top of her head.

"Looking mighty pretty, Red." He squeezed her shoulders with a little shake that made her head bobble as she grinned.

Clive bounded out the door with his usual vim and vigor.

✷ ✷ ✷ ✷ ✷

The night was a windy one and the sounds of men outside kept Angie up for part of the night. Someone earlier in the day had found a few big nuggets and was shouting around town about his big find, there were cheers and jeers from the early morning crowd. It became a ritual for men to crow over their luck in the gold fields. They would go to the government building set up to test the quality and value of the gold then be given money to spend or take to the bank.

Word around town always spread quickly about the ones who spent their gold earnings in days with saloons and brothels charging extraordinary prices. A bathhouse visit, a meal at a hotel, and a night stay would cost a small fortune. Angela quickly grew to dislike the environment of this quickly growing city. It was a dark and dangerous place for a man, for a woman it felt lethal.

❊ ❊ ❊ ❊ ❊

The sound of booms and voices was the first thing Angie heard that morning while preparing the coffee. Amber was still suffering with morning sickness and the smell of coffee and flapjacks cooking did bad things to her. Angela quickly volunteered to do the breakfast cooking. After many protests from both Gabe and Amber, Angie put her foot down and insisted. Amber would get some extra sleep and avoided feeling ill and everyone got to eat before work. Angie found the chores soothing and the feeling of being helpful without being forced into servitude a pleasant new feeling.

Gabe went to his room for his jacket and then joined the women in discussion before he was going to go to work down stairs in the store.

"It does indeed sound like our new neighbors have arrived." Gabe's hair was dark brown and cropped short to his head. He had large brown eyes that were honest and he was medium tall with a strong build. He had a few features he shared with his father and grandfather but he tended to be more serious and stocky. He still could be a tease when he was in the mood for it, though.

"I was hopin' to make a welcome gift for them." Angie said, thinking through her favorite recipes in her head. Marie has taught her some new things while she stayed at Corinne's.

"Amber was too, perhaps this afternoon I can take over the counter duties and let you ladies make a mess in the kitchen together." Gabe gave her a friendly wink and Angie laughed at his jest.

"That sounds wonderful." Angie stated shyly.

That afternoon Amber and Angie had some lovely time together making a few pies from the fresh shipment of apples they just received. They were a little dry from the journey but a little soaking and some sugar perked up the flavor. Then with a secret smile, Amber

85

added a shot full of rum to the apples mixture and let it sit a while to soak up the flavor. Angie gasped in pretend astonishment.

"My Gram was always saying a shot of whiskey makes all baked goods better." Amber said with a wink.

"I was just reading my mother's journal and my Great-Grandfather's famous Irish sipping whiskey recipe is in there. I wonder if I am the last of the family to know it." Angie mused and smiled over the thought with her new friend. Soon they began rolling out the dough and cutting the strips for the top lattice the of the apple mixture. It gave her an idea but she set it aside to focus on her baking.

"I miss eggs so dearly. It would finish the crust so nicely to have an egg wash. I only know of a dozen or so live chickens in the area. So many have died due to neglect. I haven't seen an egg in months." Amber finished with the last pie and then held her back with her hand in a gesture of discomfort. Angie saw her discomfort and gave her a massage of her lower back muscles. Amber accepted the rub gratefully. She was so thankful for the helpful hands of a new friend.

"I have a memory of there being chickens somewhere on the manor house property. I just remember my brother Sean teasing a rooster once, just a fleeting memory. I was young when we left Ireland." Angie felt Amber's muscles relaxing under her hands. She hoped to be a blessing and a help more than anything else while she was here.

"I did ask my husband to build me a coop. I know Clive can get us some live chickens from Oregon. Gabe agreed but when I got pregnant he put the idea off. He doesn't want me having any more work to do." Amber made a face and sat back down in her rocking chair. Angie got both pies in the oven and set down in the chair next to her. They listened to the bells from the ships ringing on the harbor.

"Maybe your husband will let me get the chicken house started. I can get it built, I have seen several examples in the magazines downstairs, and I read through them when there are no customers. If Clive can get me some chickens to get started perhaps this town can have eggs again."

"Yes, but if you do the work I want you to make the profit. If you decide to move then we will buy the chicken house back from you; just like a proper business." Amber stated firmly.

"That sounds great. I will ask your husband to rent me some space in the yard."

"I will probably just ask for a three eggs per day as rent. That sounds fair and the rest you can sell for profit. No rental needed. Our new back yard has a nice high fence and nothing else. It is empty, flat and barren. Some chickens will liven up the place." Amber decided.

"I sure hope Gabe agrees to it." Angela thought.

✿ ✿ ✿ ✿ ✿

The pies were finished and cooling next to the second story open windows near the kitchen. Amber and Angie separated and put on their *"going visiting"* clothes. Then they took turns fussing with each other's hair until they both felt pretty.

They left a pie behind for dinner and headed down the stairs to pass by Gabe talking to customers. A few whistles for the ladies or the fresh baked pies were heard. Gabe gave his wife a quick kiss before both the women headed next door to meet the new neighbors.

The place was dusty but the family was already working hard on the cleanup. They looked to be a large family, with two grown sons and a daughter near Angie's age.

"Welcome neighbors." Amber said first. Angie felt a bit shy and stepped behind Amber for a brief moment, suddenly feeling anxious about meeting new people.

"I am Amber Quackenbush, My husband Gabe runs the Hudson Bay store next door."

"Hello." Several said simultaneously and they were welcomed into the door fully.

"I am Franny Henderson, my two boys Bradley and George, and my daughter Sheila." Angie looked around and saw them all smile and wave. "My husband Oscar is around somewhere, searching for my big pots last I heard." Franny said with a welcoming grin.

"You have a crew working hard for you I see. This is Angie, a friend of the family. She is helping us handle the store while I get slower and rounder." Amber laughed and held her belly.

"Looks like a healthy one already." Franny gave Amber a gentle handshake after she wiped the dust from her hands. She accepted the pies and said several thank yous to both Amber and Angie.

"I see you wearing a cross around your neck." Franny pointed to the small silver cross Amber was wearing as a necklace.

"Yes, my mothers." Amber's voice was small for a moment.

"Just letting you know there is a minister settling nearby. He was on the ship with us and plans to minister to the miners and families of San Francisco. His wife plays the violin well. They do enjoy singing spirituals if you like that sort of thing."

Amber smiled and gave a little clap. "That sounds wonderful, I miss having Sunday service. I do hope they stay and not get pulled away to the gold fields... So many do." Amber shared, knowing that having a new neighbor was a blessing. A Christian one was better than she had hoped.

"We are here to feed the miners and hoping to make some roots here. We heard people talking about this being the place for a fresh start. It was so difficult to keep a restaurant in New York. The gangs had control of all the goods coming in and out of our street. If you did not bribe the right person you did not get your goods. We decided when the Gold Rush was announced we would all start over. We get gold by feeding the miners." Franny settled herself down into a chair after she spoke and welcomed Amber and Angie to join her in the chairs that one of the young men cleaned off and brought over to them.

"Here you go, miss." A tall boy with a simple grin sat a chair next to Angie and gave her a wink. She blushed a little but tried to be only a little friendly, no need to encourage him. Even with his tall handsome looks Angie was not even interested in the slightest. Sometimes someone just doesn't strike your fancy.

"Bradley, go find your father. Tell him to come meet the neighbors."

The family got a makeshift table pulled together and everyone sat a little while for a friendly visit. They all shared where they were from and simple peasantries over the snacks Angie and Amber had brought. It seemed a good impression was made and the good neighbor feeling was shared. There was a comfortable start to good relations.

Chapter 12

The moment the ship was docked Ted Greaves grabbed his luggage and his father's trunk and headed in a separate direction from the only person he knew in this part of the world. He never wanted to see the man's face again, kin or not. His anger had been days at a boiling point and just being off the ship with that man was beginning to work within him to calm him. He was not the type of young man that would hurt anyone, intentionally, but the last few days had pushed him further into anger than he had ever been in his young life.

The young man awkwardly pulled the trunk along the way with his carpetbag settled on top. The mud was going to be a problem soon but he wanted away from the foul ship and the vision of his father being buried at sea just two days ago. His Uncle would be coming off the ship any minute and he wanted to be as far away from him as possible. That bridge was already burned and he wanted nothing to do with the man responsible for his father's death.

Ted looked down at his father's boots, now on his feet. Wondering how he was going to tell his mother and sisters. *How do you write that letter?* He asked himself.

'I arrived safe and sound, Ma. But dad died of scurvy. Yea Uncle Hank is fine too. Yep, he went ashore to get food and supplies and came back with the entire fruit ration gone. Ate it all himself and let Papa just die. His excuse was that Dad was just 'too far gone. Gotta feed the survivors he said.'

Ted had never felt such anger in his life, even when Hank convinced his dad months ago, that he was not a real man if he wasn't brave enough to make the trip to California territory. Hank laughed at Ted's mother when she called it a silly dream, Hank never did listen to women ever. That was probably why his wife actually divorced him.

"That and his philandering ways," Ted thought bitterly.

His uncle had finally pushed his very religious wife, Ted's Aunt Olivia, to go against everything she believed in and she divorced him. She moved into the old shanty on a friend's property and did not visit anyone but her sister. She wasn't allowed back at church because of the divorce. Somehow they let that cheating, no good snake back in every week, but not the woman brave enough to leave the philandering, abusive man.

The complication was that Hank and his Pa had married sisters. It was probably because of Hank's deep-seeded need to always be competitive. Pa was courting the prettiest girl in town. Hank soon swooped in on the equally pretty and younger sister.

Ted had so much venom in his heart this day he felt like he might just choke on it. He hailed a wagon and offered money to the guy for a lift to the nearest hotel. The guy laughed but took his money and loaded up the trunk into the wagon box.

"You will not find a good hotel, but we can drop you off where there are some tents they rent out." The man in the wagon had shared.

"Only a tent?" Ted grimaced but said nothing else.

Ted got into town and got a tent rental. There were 300 men on board the ship he was on and a few families and even a minister's family. Ted wanted to find out if the minister would be holding a service in town. Ted's mother was instrumental in teaching his sisters and himself how to live, and going to Sunday meetings was a big part of his upbringing. If there were no meetings they made one at their house. His ma was good at teaching them to be kind to everyone and to never judge others.

With his trunk and bags settled in a flimsy tent he set himself off to find any kind of vittles and see what he could do for work. He had no interest in digging for gold. Actually he was dead-set against it. He asked where he could get a few supplies and got directions to the local mercantile.

It was that moment he saw her. She was not just a beautiful girl; cause there were plenty of them back home in upstate New York. She was an angel, long red hair flowing down her back. A face that was sweet with compassion behind her eyes, a fair complexion. She was so near the image of his favorite departed sister. She had passed away years ago, but Ted always felt she was still with him. She died of a fever at four years old but they were kindred souls. His heart had been broken but now suddenly he felt just seeing this young fair maiden was like a visitation from her. Like the Lord above granted for a moment a vision of her as she would be now from heaven. As he saw her walking into the mercantile he was more than certain that he was destined to meet this girl.

The door of the store had a jingling bell and as he walked in the scent of pipe tobacco and fresh coffee combined nicely. It has been months since he had tasted coffee. The stocks of food aboard the ship had been poor. That trip had been the biggest mistake. Ted's head hurt just thinking about it.

"Greetings." A male voice said. Ted smiled and walked up to the counter. He gave a once over to the guy at the counter. He seemed friendly and genuine.

"Hello, just off the boat needin' a few things, also looking for some honest labor. Know of any places lookin'?" Ted gave a handshake when offered and was glad to have met someone friendly. The man renting out the tents had been mean and irritable.

"Gabe Quackenbush, have yourself a look around, as fer work, you can throw a rock and find it. Everyone left everything to go pick up gold from the ground. So many ships abandoned and work left undone. People are desperate for a pair of strong arms. You will have your pick of jobs. I could probably keep you busy a few day myself." Gabe said with a laugh.

"That is good news, I was hornswoggled to get out here and now that I am here I would rather do anything but get caught up in the gold fever I have heard of non-stop since we left port in New York more than five months ago." Ted grabbed a few items, a clean shirt, and a few canned goods. He nearly choked on some of the prices but realized out here there was not much for supply lines. "You know of a Sunday meeting in town at all?" Ted asked.

"Until today we haven't had a minister in town for several months. The last one ran off to find gold. But I heard there was a new one just off the boat today that is intending to stay in town and save the miners as they come in for supplies. I just spoke with him a bit ago, named Gideon. A proper name fer a minister." Gabe chuckled at his own humor, "Will have a tent set up in the square up the road."

"Well that's a relief. I was raised to count a good Sunday meeting as important as meat and potatoes." Ted stated with no nonsense about him.

Ted looked young just then and vulnerable to Gabe's eye. He saw a good young man in front of him. Old enough to be a man but still lost in the world a bit. Gabe wondered at how he got here. This was not a place for a good young man alone. It's too easy to get lost in the wilds of liquor, gambling, and loose women.

"Where you stayin' lad?" Gabe gave him an eye.

"In a dreadful tent across the street yonder." Ted pointed behind him in the direction of the tents he'd just left.

"Well fer a dollar a week I got me a place two doors down above the abandoned laundry. There are steps up to the place. The rent is affordable if you are willing to keep an eye on the place and clean up the place downstairs. They left in a hurry and with my wife expecting, I haven't felt a rush to clean it up. Sound good to you?" Gabe saw potential in this young lad.

"I will certainly be accepting such an offer. You can count on me, sir." Ted's eyes were wide and he wondered at how his luck could have changed so quickly. God was indeed looking out for him.

"Thank you Lord," Ted prayed in his head.

"I expect no gambling or bringing women up to your place unless it be your own mother or a wife." Gabe said with a serious look. He was practicing his parenting voice.

"Absolutely sir. Would you be needin' a deposit?" Ted ran a hand through his blond hair in need of a trim.

"No son, but I would be needing to know your full name to put in my papers." Gabe got out his notebook from his pocket.

"Ted, ugh… Thaddeus Greaves, sir."

"Good to meet ya Ted. I will ask around for some good work for ya. I know plenty who will be glad to get you more than enough work for any able-bodied man. Now get yourself your bags and whatever is yours before it gets stolen from your tent. I will get you set up when you get back."

Gabe watched the young man bound out the door with a grin feeling like he'd been part of something good. You never knew when you would meet someone that you might have that chance to be a blessing just in time to change their life. He had that feeling that this young man needed a guardian angel just now. Just a passing fancy really, but it stuck with Gabe all that day.

"You sure got a sweet smile just now husband o' mine." Amber stepped slowly down to the bottom step of the staircase. Her body moving a little slower everyday but still the glowing, sweet beauty he loved so dearly.

"Yes, just helping a fresh young lad straight off the boat. He wants nothing of gold mining and just had a feelin' about him. Gonna rent him the place over the laundry. He has agreed to clean up the place for the lower rent. Just somethin' about him. Was ponderin' how God can put people in yer life for a moment and it's our job to be a blessing." Gabe kissed his wife after he spoke.

"I love that you notice these things, Gabriel. The reason I married you, outside your good looks, was your big heart." Amber teased but stood to her tiptoes to plant a kiss on his cheek.

Chapter 13

Angela took over the counter duties with Clive while Amber and Gabe left with a young man over a rental property nearby. Clive and Angela talked over prospects on how to get word out about her brother. This place was a hodgepodge of people all with their own agenda. With gold on the brain and high expectations talking to strangers was sometimes like talking to a brick wall.

"I have a feeling this may be a long stay here in California." Angie said with a bit of a sigh.

"Yes'm." Clive quipped. "It very well could be. I have found family reunions don't always go as quick or as well as we'd like em' too."

"I understand that. I just wonder how I will pass the time. Gabe and Amber warn me a lot about never going out and how unsafe it is here. I think I am doing the right thing but what will I do with myself once I am no longer needed to run the counter? Amber is a determined woman. After she delivers I betcha she will be back on this counter with a baby slung around her shoulder. She is not the kind to sit still for too long. What'll I do? Do ye think we can actually find Sean?" Angela spilled out her emotional thoughts.

"That was a heap a questions, Red. I think for now you just keep praying and being yourself. You will find your purpose here." Clive gave her a pat on the shoulder affectionately.

"I am not Corinne with her brilliance, ye know. I am no miracle worker or brilliant businesswoman. I am really rather un-extraordinary." Angie finished lamely, not sure what else to say.

"Well I can see you been working real hard thinking up ways to belittle yerself. You feel better now that you spit all that garbage out?" Clive gave Angie a pointed look.

She shook her head 'no'.

"Well, I never asked you to be Corinne, did she?" Clive asked.

"She never would do that." Angie said protectively.

"Well then who did?"

"No one really." Angie wondered where all her emotions were coming from. It just hit her like a wave. *"What in the world is wrong with me?"*

"Looks to me that life has thrown a couple of hard things your way, right Red?" Clive grabbed Angie and gave her a sideways hug and let her nod against his chest. Her escaping tears landed on his soft flannel shirt.

"Ye know it to be true." Angie's voice a web of emotions, catching in her throat.

"You are no longer a servant, but you don't know what you are yet, do ye?" Clive asked, not really expecting an answer. "Seventeen is an interesting age, chile. Give yerself time to grow up a bit. Perhaps here you can learn all sorts of new things. Yer a smart gal. You will figure it out." s

After a few minutes alone in the store the door rang repeatedly with activity and the quiet embrace shared between Clive and Angie was interrupted. Angie wiped at her stray tears and helped a man purchase some staples for his hunt for gold, coffee, canned food, matches, a lantern, and a few extra shirts.

"Thank you sir, good luck." Angie sent the man in the direction of a man selling tents across town. Her directions were memorized but she had yet to travel outside more than one block since the first day.

After an hour Gabe and Amber came back to make plans for the evening. Seems like the big news is that tomorrow the first Sunday meeting in a year would be in the morning. The girls excitedly talked about clothes and things and even the men decided getting spiffed up might be in the order of the day.

Angie helped Amber with getting enough water upstairs. They had two barrels outdoors and a bucket to pull to the second story, Angela stood below and made sure the water bucket was as full as it needed to be before it was pulled. Gabe took over pulling the buckets up after the first few. Angela was glad of it. Amber took over heating the water on the stove as they filled the cast iron tub. Once the first barrel was empty Gabe and Angela took a few trips to the nearby water well and refilled the barrel. They laughed as they were both covered with the cold well water after the several trips back and forth.

The bath night was a success. Angela realized it was a lot easier to do the weekly bath in Oregon because getting the water to the second floor made things more complicated.

Angela and Amber sat by the fire and brushed their hair near the heat until it dried. Amber kept laughing when she felt the baby kicking. The two women enjoyed talking about the hope of the new church.

❖ ❖ ❖ ❖ ❖

The morning brought a heavy fog over the bay and the air was thick with moisture but there was no rain. The dark grey clouds and the fog combined to make it a dreary morning. The Quackenbush men led Amber and Angie across the muddy street to the hastily prepared tent that was a block away. It was in an open space between the bank and livery.

"There used to be a building here but it was so poorly kept the town council had it knocked down. Not sure who built the ramshackle mess, but glad to tear it down." Clive shared. He seemed invested as much here in San Francisco as he was in Oregon. Angie had to wonder at how much Clive had done in one lifetime.

The tent was stained canvas, with many patches holding it together. Angie wondered if a good rain would carry it away. *Is to be any hope for a dry service week after week?* She mused to herself.

There would need to be walls built, and soon. When they all got through the tent flap at the front they saw the Henderson's, their new neighbors, already at the front talking with a short man. There was a wobbly pedestal at the front as well and a few rows of benches. The wood on the benches looked new and not even sanded yet. They looked freshly built.

Clive, as the patriarch of the group, introduced them to the minister and his family. He was short and round with a patient smile. His wife was equally as warm and friendly. They had a son and a daughter both taller than them. It was a lovely boggle.

"I am Gideon Haimes, this is my wife Grace and my children, Gideon Junior and Naomi." He paused while everyone shook hands with everyone then he added as an afterthought. "They get their height from my grandparents. It obviously skipped over me." He laughed at his own joke with a chuckle and the ice was broken.

"We are all glad you are here no matter yer height. Some good preaching and singin' will do us all some good." Clive seemed to say the right thing to get everyone moving toward the benches. Angie watched a few more people wander through the tent flap before the time to start.

Being in the front row she got to sit quietly and get a decent view of all the introductions. An elderly gentleman in a string tie and black vest named Walter claimed he worked at the bank. The young man Angie saw in passing with Gabe and Amber the day before was named Ted. He turned and met Angie's eyes for the briefest second before he passed and found a seat behind the Quackenbush family. Gabe stood and gave the young man an invitation to lunch. Angie wondered about the look he gave her as he spoke with Gabe. He looked as if he knew her. But she certainly had no memory of him. Perhaps she was just being imaginative. It had happened before. Angie smiled as she cleared her mind of everything and watched Gideon Haimes take the pulpit.

They began the Sunday meeting with a prayer and then they all got to sing a few popular hymns. There were no hymnals yet,

Gideon claimed they were still packed away and next week there would be more music. It was grand to everyone even in its simplicity. Gideon's preaching about love, and loving your neighbors was a good one. The room had not more than twenty people but it felt friendly and like a small community, in only one service. Grace played the violin beautifully and she ended the service with a lovely song she said she made up herself. It was sweet and struck the hearts of many. It needed no words; it was just a sweet gift. To Angela it reminded her of an evening spent at the Grant's when Lucas would bring out his violin.

The service ended and everyone's mood was light and friendly. Angie talked again with Sheila Henderson and found out they were both just seventeen. Angie was hoping to make a friend. It was still a fresh new relationship but Angie hoped to cultivate it.

She heard from Amber that a new friend of Gabe's was coming for Sunday supper. Angela was a little nervous to meet someone new but tried to hide her feelings. She was sure that a friend of Gabe would be a nice person.

❈ ❈ ❈ ❈ ❈

"Hello Mr. Greaves, I am Angela Fahey." She was seated next to the young man she saw at the church service earlier. Angie and Amber had put together a stew the night before and fresh bread two days ago. The table was full with Clive and Ted joining them.

"I heard from Mr. Quackenbush that you were from Boston and you are looking for yer brother here in California territory." Ted spoke clearly and his face was genuinely interested in her answer. Angie still got nervous around strangers sometimes. Some people were so good at being dismissive to her. She was a servant for a long time. She felt invisible still.

"Yes, my brother Sean, he came to this area about a year ago… according to his letters. He may be hard to find but I am willing to stay in the area to find him." Angela saw that the young man was actually listening and she gave him a friendly smile. His hair was relatively short but had a tendency to curl. She had to admit she liked the look of him.

"I will be praying for you to be reunited iffen ya don't mind." Ted nodded at her and grabbed a piece of the sliced bread as the plate went around the table.

"I would be appreciating that. Prayers are always welcome." Angela nodded when he offered her the bread. He took a piece and placed it on the side of her plate then found the butter in a small china bowl and let her dip into it first.

"Thank you." Angie murmured and Ted just nodded.

"You settled in nicely at your new place there Ted?" Gabe asked Ted.

"Yessir, the place is fine. I need to come by the store tomorrow to get a few supplies. But I have a lot of work in town this week. It seems everyone is needin' a hand. Your grandfather Clive has got me working tomorrow makin' a shipment near Sutter's mill. I guess the area is springing up faster than anything. Looks to me like no one cares where they live, people just throw up a tent and get a pan in the stream. Seems awfully silly to my reckonin'. A hundred jobs to be had here in town and a thousand fools squatting in the dirt." Ted got the whole table laughing.

"No need to come to the store when yer so busy. After the meal we can get ye what ya need." Gabe gave Ted a wink and finished off his buttered bread.

"That would be a blessing." Ted said.

"Not a problem, ye seem a good young man and I am glad to help ye out. So many come and get lost in the 'gold fever'. It's good to see some wisdom in such a young lad." Gabe and Ted spend a little time in the store then they returned upstairs.

Everyone was noticing that for some reason Ted kept finding reasons to talk to Angela. He finally got brave and spoke honestly to her about why. Amber, Gabe and Clive kept giving each other looks and a few smirks.

"You Miss Fahey, I have no desire to be overtly friendly - I have some small shame to admit." Ted said as he watched her crocheting a baby sweater.

"Whatever have you to be ashamed about, Mr. Greaves?" Angela was a small bit concerned but for the friendly and lighthearted manner he had. Ted seemed like an easy-going lad. No malice in any of his looks.

"Oh nothing to be afeared of, just when I saw you the first time across the street a few days ago I thought you were the spirit of a dearly departed sister of mine." His eyes were honest and she saw that he was speaking truth.

"Well, I am truly sorry for your loss." Angela felt it sincerely. Too much loss in her own family had made her sensitive over other's losses.

"You seem a lot like her as far as I can see in such a short time. She was a 'little mother', we all called her for she cared for everyone around her. Even us older siblings felt her 'mothering' and her heart felt such compassion. I can see that in you as well." Ted said quietly.

"That is indeed a kind thing to say. She sounds like someone you loved very dearly." Angela could feel her emotions rise. She hated feeling so strongly but she knew no other way to be.

"She was, she died young of a fever. I always felt like she was with me somehow. After a terrible boat trip I saw you across the way and somehow thought maybe her spirit came with me. Or maybe it's just my fancy imagination again." Ted grabbed for the yarn that fell from her lap and placed it back where it needed to be.

"Well I am glad you are doing well after the journey. I have heard a few stories about the long trip around Cape Horn. The Oregon Trail was a hard one as well. Seems the way West is full of peril by land or by sea." Angie said and nodded but kept her eyes on her crocheting. She was enjoying talking with this new friend of Gabe's.

Ted was quiet for a bit just taking turns from talking with Gabe, Clive and the two women in the room. The company was friendly and he felt at home. He tried not to but many times that afternoon he caught himself watching Angela crochet. The sweet young woman was indeed a giving soul, a lot like his sister. But her friendship was already something he felt. He was thankful for meeting Gabe but somehow even more importantly he felt a strange feeling that Angela Fahey was going to be a dear friend.

He went home that night and spent a while in prayer over her and her desire to find her brother. It felt good to want to bless her. His heart was in earnest about her happiness.

✵ ✵ ✵ ✵ ✵

Angie was washing the evening dishes after supper. Amber was feeling slow and achy and Angie forced her to lie down. The night was quiet and Angie liked to look out the small window above the washtub and see the mist rolling in from the bay. The distance between the bay and town was enough that she could not see the water when it was foggy but the open sky was drawing her gaze. It would rain soon, she thought. The night air was getting chillier and she was glad to have a roof and warm clothes. She heard Gabe's heavy steps coming up the staircase and turned to give him a nod and reminded him to be quiet.

"There is a young man to see ya." Gabe said quietly. "Bradley Henderson" His mouth in a smothered grin.

"What in the world would he be doing wanting a visit this time o'day." Angela wondered. She dried her hand on a towel that was draped upon her shoulder. She took off the work apron and grabbed a shawl from a nearby peg.

Angie hopped down the steps with the bounce of energy even after a long day. Her curiosity about having a visitor was setting her brain abuzz but she was very surprised to see the tall young preacher's son with his Sunday best on. Angie suddenly felt a little self-conscious in her simple frock. It was clean but very simple. She had been helping

Amber all day with cleaning and packing some things for the move to the new building. It would still be a few weeks but getting a head start was wise in Amber's condition.

"Hello Miss Fahey." He was tall and his voice was even and pleasant. He had medium brown hair and his eyes seem to look a lot like his father's.

"Hello Mr. Henderson." Angie had never actually spoken to him but for a handshake and hello just a few days before, then just a nod at the Sunday meeting. Angela felt a bit awkward but wanted to be friendly.

"I know we haven't spoken much but I wanted to say hello and get to know ye' a bit. You can call me Bradley if ya wish."

"I thank you kindly." Angela was completely at a loss. Is it proper to speak someone's name so soon after knowing them?

My training as a maid is no help here. Ach. Why couldn't he have come during the day to the store? Then at least she would have had Gabe or Clive nearby to ask. Angela thought to herself.

They struggled through a few more stunted sentences before Bradley made his exit. She knew the store hours had passed so she locked the door behind her. Her steps were slow as she was thinking too much while taking the steps up to the home above the store.

"How is the young Mr. Henderson?" Gabe asked from the sink, his hands soapy and scrubbing a pan. His smile was nearly her undoing and she thought about laughing for a silly reason.

"I have no idea what that was about, Gabe. We had so little to say I am not sure what in the world he came by for." Angela shrugged her shoulders and gave Gabe a silly grin.

"I have an idea, Red." Gabe had adopted the nickname Clive has given her and it sounded good. It felt a bit like how family was.

"What are your thoughts then?" Angie grabbed a dry towel and dried the wet dishes in the wooden rack next to the washtub.

"He fancies ya." Gabe said simply and enjoyed watching the blush creep up her face. He chuckled a little and turned away to let her be mortified in peace.

After a few minutes of quiet Angie had the nerve to speak. "Not sure I want to be fancied just now."

Gabe gave her a slow nod. "You will know when the time is right. Perhaps a friend would not be a bad thing. Just let him know. Amber may be better at this than I, but just be yourself and be honest with any young man that wants more of a relationship than you do. We young men can actually get carried away when we see a pretty face. Just saying you want to be friends first can help if ye need to keep things simple." Gabe had a moment or two he wished for Amber or

Clive to save him. But seeing Angie smile and nod after listening made him feel better.

"I have no idea what I am doing. Perhaps my Ma would have told me all about how to handle young men. But I've been working as a maid or in a workhouse too long. I never expected to be able to go courtin'. Not sure I am ready for that." Angie looked up to Gabe and saw that he cared. She realized that he saw her as more than a girl to help out or a clerk for his store.

"Thanks for caring Gabe." Angela said above a whisper.

The words were simple but the look in her eyes nearly broke his heart. She was just a young girl that needed family and connection. He felt a sort of brotherly affection rise up in his chest. He would protect this young lady with everything in him. He knew Amber felt the same after she told him so many nights about how precious Angie was. Gabe finally saw it too.

"I am here for ya, Red." Gabe stated and they wordlessly finished the dishes. Amber woke from her rest and strolled out. She sat in the rocking chair after a bit and did some mending by the fireplace. The sun had gone down and the light of the fire drew everyone and the night passed calmly. Angie shared the silly visit with the young man with Amber and she agreed with Gabe. The womanly advice was the same. Any romantic notions can be dealt with usually with an honest plea for friendship.

Chapter 14

December 23rd 1849

Angela walked with Clive and Ted down the few streets to see the progress of the new building. Clive has commissioned the use of brick and iron beams for safety. He shared how many small earthquakes had hit and his desire was to have the business nearer to the new wharf that was almost completed. The square in the center of town was a hub of activity but also crime was heavy there. It was dangerous and riotous upon occasion and both Clive and Gabe were relieved that they would be moving further away from there.

"Gabe has been keeping me up to date on the politics. I have had my ear to the ground. Glad I grabbed up this property when I could get it." Clive stated.

Angela kept quiet and just let her eyes scan the streets around her. The wind was a bit gusty at moments and she watched some paper fly down the way and tumble along.

"Another two weeks the place should be finished. The crew of builders we have are good lads and they are paid well. So far the morale is good and no one has left for the gold fields. Though the cold and snow in the hills are a pretty good deterrent." Ted's voice was soothing and Angela smiled to herself just listening to him chat away with Clive.

"Your chicken house will go in the back, the east side of the building is the dock for unloading the large orders and behind the property to the north is the warehouse. It is nearly double the size of your current warehouse. You have some grand schemes Clive."

"I do, I have been talking about supply lines and the use of a steamer for transport." Clive continued on talking about Sacramento and lumber rights and the many intricacies of the running of his large-scale business.

Angela turned her focus inward even as they arrived and she was getting another tour. She was here a few days ago but she could see the outside structure was mostly finished. The inside had more work that needed doing but the roof was on. The rooms were full of supplies and it was pretty chaotic. Sawdust was everywhere.

The rain had been scarce and the street was mostly dry, which was rare for this time of year. Angela had not enjoyed the hours she had spent trying to save her boots from the ravages of the muddy streets.

Ted and Clive were talking animatedly about the plans and then Ted showed how he was planning to finish some of the living quarters and stairs that day.

"The supplies are here and I have an extra set of hands today." Ted grinned when he got praise from Clive. Somehow Clive was just that kind of soul. Everyone wanted on his good side.

Angela could see such strength of character in her new friend, Ted. She had hopes that her brother was like him, strong in his faith and a hard worker.

Angela stood idle for a few minutes to look up and down the street. Another brick building was rising just as fast. This was quickly becoming known as a brick row. Businesses setting themselves apart from the riffraff and there was lots of talk about the kinds of businesses that would be run here. A bank was moving, a doctor's clinic and a newspaper printing press were rumored. It was all speculation but Angela was pleased to see it growing daily.

There was a promised boardwalk and a park nearby according to Clive, but he hinted that those kinds of plans were always talked of but rarely followed through on. In a boomtown like this everyone was almost always focused on profit first and beautification last.

The front window of the store was a large piece of glass that impressed Angela.

The large yellow letters of QUACKENBUSH in an arch and then the metal roof hung the Hudson Bay sign that was at least ten feet in the air. It would be easy to see for anyone walking the street. Angela had a sense of how historic this time and place was. The whole country was talking about California and what was happening here.

There was a part of her that was amazed to be a piece of it, the history and the making of it, and another part of her was back in Oregon where she wanted to make it her true home.

Her heart was not into celebrating Michaelmas in two days but she knew she must get over her doldrums for Gabe and Amber. They had been so kind and Amber was enjoying planning her new life as a mother. There was something special about celebrating as a family. She had memories as a child about a yule log and feasting at the manor house. The glimpses were vague and distant but the faces she could see in her mind's eye were dear ones to her. Her brother was always a bit silly and she remembered he loved singing the songs around the fire with everyone. He had a lovely voice, Angie remembered.

Before the lunch hour Ted and Clive escorted Angela back to the old store and she took over counter duties while Gabe spent the rest of the day and evening making improvements on his new home.

❉ ❉ ❉ ❉ ❉

Dec 24th 1849

The morning was dawning and the gulls had not yet begun their calls for the day. The wharfs were beginning to liven up with a few ships going out but no one had arrived yet. The muscled men worked near the bay every day, cleaning, dealing with fish, ropes, cargos and sometimes, passengers. The docks were full of men busily working when they first heard the yelling. A loud ringing pierced the air and several men stopped their activity to glance up, their curiosity peaked. A sound rang out that did not belong to the early morning. Something different was about to happen. The bells ringing were usually only for celebrations or tragedy.

❉ ❉ ❉ ❉ ❉

Angela sat up in her bed, the loft where she slept had a low ceiling above her bed and she jumped from her bed in a crouched position but only missed hitting her head on the wall by less than an inch, she could actually feel her hair brushing against the wall.

Why am I awake? She asked herself in her head. *Was I having a dream?*

She could hear muffled voices coming from downstairs, and then stomping and the voices growing a bit louder. This could not be good. Angela's heart did a jump in her chest and in a frenzied rush she grabbed a gown and changed into it in a flash. Something was happening.

Gabe was at her door pounding not thirty seconds later.

"There is a fire burning a few streets away. We must get to safety. Dress warm and be downstairs in less than five minutes." Gabe's voice was rough and stressed. She could hear his feet descending the stairs with the creaking on the wood boards. In her mind flashed everyone she knew and cared about here in San Francisco and she realized the list had grown quickly. She tied a vest over her gown and grabbed her long grey wool coat, a scarf and bonnet. Angie took a glance over at her bag and trunk. She had a moment of relief wash over her the most of her family items were safe back in Oregon. She had her mother's journal and her portrait here. She grabbed her empty carpetbag, the journal and picture and shoved them inside.

She got her boots on and buttoned and grabbed the bag again and put a few necessity items in there, her bible, items from Corinne, and her letters. She thought quickly, grabbing a spare gown and a hairbrush.

"What do you need in an emergency?" She wondered for a moment. If the house burned what would I need to survive. She had learned from the trail to live with little to no comforts, so she knew if they could stay out of the path of the fire that she would be fine with food and shelter.

Her feet slid down the steps quickly and she saw the second floor was empty. Gabe had doused the coals in the fireplace and the house felt empty and cold. Angie could hear people outside and there was a racket of yelling and a persistent ringing bell. Angela could see nothing through the window above the water tub and decided to join everyone downstairs. She opened the door and quickly descended the stairs, a little too quickly and the heel of her boot slipped down a few steps before Angela caught herself on the railing. The motion wrenched her shoulder and her badly bruised leg from her injuries last year, it was throbbing a bit and she took the last few steps slowly and with a hint of a limp. Her heart was pounding in her chest and she felt a fool. Everyone was waiting at the bottom of the stairs and saw her slip.

"Are you hurt Angie?" Gabe asked. Amber had tears in her eyes and a worried look.

"No just foolish, I will be fine." Angie said. Her brain was in still a bit of a daze from waking up so abruptly. The throbbing in her leg was shoved to the back of her mind. But she had to work very hard not to continue her limping.

"I can get the ladies to safety. We need to help with the fire. If it jumps the streets, the whole city could burn." Clive said with no nonsense in his voice. The gasp from the women came involuntarily. There was nothing about this morning that felt right.

"Get them over to the new building and get them out of the way. Clive, I will have Ted help you transport all our important belongings over by wagon."

"Sounds good. Ladies, please come with me." Clive grabbed the arms of Amber and Angie gently and began his escort. Outside the morning was still dark and a few streets away the glow could be seen. People were all running about in a frenzy and Angela was afraid, truly afraid. The smell of smoke was already thick in the air. The wind came in cold gusts around her, with no hint of moisture. It has been several days since rain.

"Clive, please don't worry about us. I can get Amber and I to the new building. We will be fine. Please make sure Gabe and Ted stay safe." Angie could hear the strange sound of her own voice. It sounded high and squeaky to her ears. Her red hair whipped around her back in the wind and lashed at her eyes. She pushed the unruly waves away for them only to return with no respect for her wishes.

"No, darling, I will get you safe and sound. If at any point you see the fire come more than two streets away go to the water. You will be safe on the rocks." Clive's long strides were hard to keep up with but the women did manage it well enough.

The brick building had a roof and outer walls now but not much more than floors, the stairs nearly finished inside and no counter or furniture to speak of. There were tools lying about everywhere. Clive found matches and a lantern and grabbed a few wooden crates from outside and set them near the front windows. The two girls took the cue and sat on them wordlessly.

"I want you to remain calm." Clive was looking at Amber, she nodded but stayed quiet.

"Angela, please help her stay calm. I will be back shortly with the wagon. I will be bringing over clothes and some food." Clive was speaking to them but his eyes were far off, thinking and planning what had to be done.

Clive gave them both a hug around the shoulders and left them alone in an empty brick building.

The scene from the new glass window was grim and dark. This part of town was new development only just recently sold. A few other buildings were up but not many lived here yet.

"I am scared Angie." Amber finally spoke. Her voice sounded small and weary. She was taking deep and slow breaths. Her hands splayed out across her grown belly. She would be giving birth in a month or so.

Not today though, Lord please. Angie thought in a plea to God to keep her friend calm and safe.

Angie took a hand and rubbed across Amber's shoulders, she saw Amber close her eyes and accept the comforting gesture. Angela stood over her that way for the next hour as they watched out the window.

❀ ❀ ❀ ❀ ❀

Ted and Clive quickly loaded up the wagon with a few trunks and some canned goods from the store. Clive had grabbed the trunk of clothes from Angela's room and felt himself sigh with relief when it was loaded into the wagon. She didn't need to lose anymore. With the heavy smoke in the air he felt the fear rise up in his own chest. The city was in mayhem. This is what happened when there was no structure. A city was adding a few thousand people a week and they wondered what would happen. This was what happens. Clive pushed his logical brain to the back and brought out his practical self-back to the front.

His arms and legs were burning with the strain of running up and down the stairs and loading the wagon. This is a young man's game and his body was feeling old this morning. He would not admit it now though. He would have another day, Lord willin', to sit in a rocking chair to consider how old he was. The horses were jittery and ready to get further from the ruckus a few streets away. Clive realized that he had been praying nearly every minute. Knowing his family was in danger was a pain throbbing in his head and his gut. He would be glad to see this day through with no harm to come to anyone.

His grandson Gabe was part of the new Vigilance committee and probably helping fight the fire at this moment. Clive sent out more prayers as he worked that early morning.

✿ ✿ ✿ ✿ ✿

The first load of goods was all unloaded and Ted and Clive got Angela and Amber set up with a few blankets. Clive wished somehow the woodstove had been hooked up and able to work properly. Instead it was still sitting in it's crate, shoved into a corner with twenty other crates full of supplies to be rummaged through this week.

"Blast!" Clive muttered as he hit his head on a support beam. Wandering around in the dark was not a good plan. Clive gave up on the idea of setting up the stove.

"Clive I am going to see if I can help get the fire out, I am hoping something is organized." Ted's voice carried through the dark room.

"Wait up, I will join ya." Clive yelled.

✿ ✿ ✿ ✿ ✿

Angela watched as Ted unloaded the wagon wordlessly. Seeing him strain under the weight of the heavy trunks. His forehead has a pinched look of stress that seemed to be a common look for the morning.

"You stay safe, Miss Fahey." Ted said to Angela while he waited for Clive to come back from some expedition he made to the back storage area.

"Ted... please... don't get hurt." Angela felt her emotions rise just thinking about the briefest chance of him in danger. This young man was starting to become important in her estimation.

"I will help put it out Miss. No need to get too close." Ted felt awkward and at a loss of what to say. This young woman was showing care and concern for his well-being. That did something to his insides, a feeling in his chest to protect and ease her fears. It was an odd feeling

106

for such a morning but it would take some thinking on another day. After the danger had passed.

The men left quickly. Angela and Amber again waited as the morning got brighter with the sunrise. The sounds of the city around them continued to fuel the fire of concern growing over the men in the thick of danger.

It is so helpless sometimes to be a woman, Angela thought to herself. *Nothing left to do but watch and worry.* What could be happening in the square, the center of town where the fire began? *How will we know when we are safe?*

✢ ✢ ✢ ✢ ✢

Ted took the bucket and passed it along waiting a few seconds before the next one landed in his hands, the water sloshed over the edge no matter how much he tried to keep water inside. The wind whipped around him and it had a chill. The crush of bodies and the burning flames leaping from the building in front of him had him sweating. Men were yelling orders for hours on end. It had made for frayed nerves and sore throats. The smoke, dust and ash flying around the square caused him to choke. Every few minutes he had to take a moment to cough and try to catch his breath. He wondered how Gabe and Clive had fared.

Gabe was in charge of ordering the bucket brigade a street over. Ted heard rumors that had gone well. Clive was sent off to help somewhere else. Some men refused to help put out the fires, claiming they had to stay with their families down by the water.

Ted went over and over in his mind how he had left Amber and Angela. Angela was bravely taking charge over Amber, keeping her calm and comfortable. She really was an Angel. Even in her own fear she said prayers over the men as they left. It felt good knowing that someone was praying for him. So far from any of his close family, he sometimes wondered how God had allowed for him to be here, for him to be so far from any decent place.

Clive has lately been sharing about Oregon and how peaceful and fertile it was compared to the chaos and crime surrounding San Francisco. The Quackenbush family and Angela were the city's only redeeming joys, as well as the small church off of Broadway. They had only just begun to build. Ted had hopes that Broadway would remain untouched. Ted had a fleeting thought of his own small apartment and wondered if at some point today he would be passing buckets to douse flames coming through his own windows. Only time would tell.

Ted continued to help as the city fought to stay alive. Hundreds of buildings have been lost so far. All they could do was wait and work.

By four p.m. the flames had died down and many men were sifting through the ash to make sure no more fires could start back up. They pulled down a few buildings to stop the flow of the fire and in some cases it worked, others did not and the fire jumped across the street as the debris carried on the blustery wind coming across the city from the ocean side.

❄ ❄ ❄ ❄ ❄

The women's waiting was over as Gabe and Clive dragged their weary bodies to the new home. The brick building looked nothing like a home when it started, but Angela grew tired of waiting and had moved a few things around. Amber yelled at her to stop every time Angela had the hint of a limp but she was good at hiding her pain. She moved slowly and surely through the place getting things open and organized. The tools were neatly stacked where they would be easy to get to but less likely to be tripped on.

"The Lord be praised, you are home." Amber said as the men dragged themselves through the front door.

Angela and Amber asked about the fire and though their old home had not been destroyed the fire had been nearby and the smoke would be lingering and smoldering nearby for a while. There would be shifts of men to watch for sparks. Already the council was talking about the necessity of a fire brigade.

Angela nervously watched out the window. Neither of the men had seen Ted after he had separated from them to join a bucket line. Angela said prayers for him as she half-heartedly listened to the discussion from the Quackenbush family. Gabe was gathering his strength to finish the stairs and begin connecting the second floor to the first. The second floor's walls were finished but no furniture could find its way up there until the stairs were done. This was not how they wanted to move into the house and business, but at least for today and perhaps tomorrow, they needed to stay away from the smoldering area of the city.

Clive took it to task to move boxes and get the wood-stove for the first floor set up. With that done the family could stay warm in cots on the first floor at least. It was not ideal but they would stay healthy and warm. Amber was recovered from her excitement and explaining to Gabe how a sheet could be hung across the ceiling for the ladies to have privacy for the night.

Angela breathed a sigh of relief when she saw the ash and soot covered Ted heading toward the mercantile down the street. It was almost dusk and Angela's worry had nearly reached a fever pitch. She refrained from showing her true feelings according to her own imaginings but to Amber, Clive and Gabe they all wordlessly noticed then nodded to each other. There was something brewing in all their minds.

Ted was let in and received handshakes from the men and Amber gave his hair a friendly tousle, like a mother would. Black ash drifted from his head and everyone laughed.

Angela gave herself a task and got a towel damp from a bucket of water that Clive had recently hauled over. She handed the towel to Ted and she didn't trust her voice to stay even so she said nothing.

Ted said "Thank you," at a near whisper. It seemed they were both being shy and strained.

"I am glad you are safe. Did you hear of anyone getting hurt in the blaze?" Angela finally asked.

"News is so unruly today, rumors were flying around and I found it mostly untrue. I heard early rumors that the old mercantile was gone, others said that all the wharfs were burned." Ted wiped the grime away from his face as he talked. His face was black from the smoke and the towel swiped it away to the fresh-faced lad that Angela was growing to appreciate more and more.

"So was the fire not as bad as we thought?" Gabe asked, he was amused at watching the young people before him and their shy games but he was also curious about parts of the city he had not seen that day.

"I saw personally two saloons burned completely and the place where the hotel was is now flattened. There were no tents to be seen near the square and there had been hundreds just yesterday. I don't know where these men and families will be sleeping tonight." Ted took the chair that was offered him and a plate of warmed up stew.

Gabe had brought over some more things from the kitchen at the first mercantile. There were still leftovers from the night before the fire. For Angela, it reminded her a bit of life on the trail. Making do for today only had been the way of things. Having a roof over your head and steady meals had you spoiled when the hard days rolled back around.

Chapter 15

January 4th 1850

Angela was working the counter of the new brick building when she saw a familiar face come through the mercantile door.

"I think I may know where yer brother might be little darlin'." The miner was in a few weeks earlier and she had spoken about her brother and Ol' Willie. He had said then he would ask around. Angie's heart jumped in her chest to hear his words.

"I've been talking around about any one named Ol' Willie and everyone agrees that he's been travelin' around with a young man named Sean and matches the description ya gave me. The hard part is nailing them down. They aren't doing any mining. William Shipley is strongly vocal about being against any get-rich schemes. He has a cabin out past Sutter's mill and it's a hard place to get to without knowin' where yer going. They are always moving around checking their traps and hunting. I haven't seen 'em in town in over a year. They live off the land, I heard. They been selling their meat to miners and their pelts in other parts. I will keep asking around. I will tell others to get word to ye or your friend, Clive. Everyone wants to help ye out little missy." The miner was a fast talker and kept going on about how much everyone wanted to help her find her brother but her heart was a little down. She had a name at least but without being able to leave and investigate she felt a bit lost still. She had her journal out and wrote down all the details the miner had told her.

When he finally stopped Angela made sure to thank him for all the work he did to find out information for her. She had some news at least. Perhaps now she could use this info to ask more people that came in for clues to Sean's whereabouts.

She was thinking about her brother. Wondering if truly he was with the man William Shipley. Clive had sent out feelers but the area was in chaos. Getting information that was trustworthy was not easy.

❀ ❀ ❀ ❀ ❀

Angie had her hands covered in flour and scooped up the ball of baking soda biscuits and plopped it down on the table and smoothed the rolling pin over the dough. She got it to the right amount of thickness and cut out the biscuits with a metal cutter that she grabbed from a shelf above her head. She looked over the back yard and had a thought for the third morning in a row. She wanted to build a chicken coop. She had discussed it with Amber but she had not had the nerve to ask Gabe. She had some money set aside and thought it would be a blessing to the community. There were simply not enough eggs in town.

There were a few chicken coops behind a saloon across town but they sell their breakfast with eggs and salt pork for $5 a plate. People spoke of it often. The moment they got their gold strike they headed to the Painted Lady Saloon for a night with a pretty lady and eggs for breakfast. Gabe got offended when men spoke about such things down in the store but Angela knew that there was no help for it. With the influx of so many men without their families the morality code around town was seriously lacking. Angie heard from Amber that across town at The Painted Lady, the women strutted around topless on the upper level sometimes. Angie was indeed shocked to hear that could even be true but she had not seen it, and had no desire to. She had stayed in her safe little world above the mercantile. She had been to church on Sunday and a few walks with Clive or Gabe for safety. Otherwise she had stayed close to the store.

She got the biscuits cut and Amber set her free to go downstairs, the bell had been ringing from the front door of the store steadily for several minutes. The women thought that Gabe might need some help.

Angela bounced down the stairs and immediately got to work helping customers, mostly miners in for supplies, the rain had slowed down for a few days and miners were itching to get back out of the city. The riverbeds were what a lot of men spoke of when heading out. Panning in the stream was cold and wet work.

Angie had her first look at a small gold nugget, as one miner came in crowing of his find earlier in the week. He had a loaded revolver in his belt but he was headed to the bank next. Gabe gave a low whistle in appreciation of the glinting gold in the man's palm. Angela couldn't help but gasp at the sight of it. It had a strange effect on a person, truly. When you know something's value your brain reacts to the sight of it.

"It's surprising how heavy it is." Angela said after holding it for a moment. The man with a dirty beard and a grin accepted the nugget back and gave her a wink.

"It is a beautiful thing." The man left a few minutes later but the talk was buzzing around town. Every time someone found more than gold dust it got everyone stirred back up again.

The morning went quickly with lots of new men arriving every day. When it got nearer to lunchtime Angela got brave enough to ask her question.

"I was wondering if I could speak with ya Gabe about a business I been meaning to start." Angie said it quickly before she allowed her shy nature to turn her into a quiet coward.

"I am all ears my dear girl." Gabe smiled warmly and calmed her fears.

"I was hoping to rent some space in your yard to build a chicken coop." She watched him nod and he smiled again. He looked like Clive when he grinned like that.

"That sounds like a sensible business plan. Amber has wanted to do the same but I wouldn't allow it during her pregnancy. She just hates it when I pull the 'obey' word from our vows. But the doctor agreed with me on this one. " Gabe scratched his chin the way his grandfather did while thinking.

"Yes, she mentioned it to me as well. She was hoping to get eggs in trade for the space rental. Then if I leave to go back to Oregon we can negotiate a buyout." Angela blurted everything out so fast and her nerves were getting shaky again for some reason.

"That would be a good thing. I will get you a quote from Clive about how to get you a starter flock. Maybe ship them over from Oregon. I know there were some chickens out by Sutter's place." Gabe said thoughtfully.

"I have money for the startup. I have been thinking about this all week. I should have mentioned it earlier." Angie felt a bit foolish but she was getting excited.

"I am already looking forward to having eggs again for breakfast. I do enjoy baking soda biscuits just fine. But my wife sure does know how to make a fine cake when we have eggs around." Gabe gave her wink and rubbed his stomach comically. "I will get some lumber out back and ask Ted to help you get the coop built the way you like. He is quite handy, he is getting a reputation around town that he can fix anything."

"Can you please give me an invoice for the lumber? I have money down at the bank." Angela was all business for a moment. Not wanting charity for her little project.

Gabe hated taking money from her but he knew she wanted to be taken seriously. "How about we agree upon a price and I take it out of your pay a little bit every week. No need to take money out of your savings." Angela agreed and they shook hands. It was settled.

Chapter 16

January 15 1850

Angela was glad today that Ted was coming to help her build the chicken coop. She knew from Clive and Gabe that Ted was very handy and creative. She also found his company pleasant. He was nice to have around.

She knew that Clive was preparing to leave in a week for Oregon but he promised he would be back with her chickens. She wondered why he was spending so much time in California territory and had a suspicion that he was hovering near her to make sure she stayed safe. She could not ask him to stop. She would never tell him to stay away, never in a hundred years.

Ted Greaves arrived at noon on the dot and Angela had a lunch already prepared for them. She gave him his lunch and dragged him to the fenced area of the yard and they discussed chicken coop ideas over their sandwiches.

"I want a lot of room for them and a goodly number of nests. I will be wanting a healthy flock." Angela spoke between bites, her smile and excitement was infectious and Ted was more than happy to help her out.

Gabe was paying him for his time but he argued gently to Gabe that he would gladly help Angie for free. Gabe had given Ted a questioning look and was close to giving Ted a lecture about Angela. Gabe seemed to have changed his mind before he said anything. Ted was glad. He would honor any request of Gabe Quackenbush, but if he asked him to stay away from Angie he would be sad somehow, not sure he could have done it without a long talk.

"I helped my Ma with her chickens every time we moved. We had to start with a new coop and we always lost chickens in the move. We can build up a flock in no time." Ted finished his food and used a napkin to clean his face of any persistent crumbs.

"Thank you so much Mr. Greaves. I cannot thank you enough." Angela shared a grin that made his heart beat a bit faster.

"I think you should start callin' me Ted now." He raised an eyebrow and she laughed.

"That suits me fine as long as ya call me Angie."

"Perhaps someday soon I can call ye Red like Clive and Gabe do." Ted stood and watched a blush climb her neck attractively, filling her cheeks with color.

"Perhaps." She said softly. Ted decided to stop his teasing and get to work. They had a plan going and soon he was able to have a drawing for the exact thing she wanted. She had to leave after a while to go back to working at the counter but she checked in on him often and thanked him sweetly.

He got the pleasure of dining upstairs that evening and came by the next day and got the coop finished up with a wired fence around and a gateway to get in. He used a bit of left over lumber to build a bench big enough for two just outside the coop against the back of the building.

Chapter 17 - Corinne

January 1850, Willamette Valley

The house was empty and the lantern glowed yellow and the fire had grown dim. Corinne sat in the late day waiting for Lucas to return from an errand and she was deep in thought. Her friend had been gone for too long now. The room Angela had stayed in was empty and it dug at her a little every time she went by it.

She was missing her friend, again. The long wait for her to heal after the accident then waiting for her by wagon train and now this wait, weighed heavily. She was growing impatient. She wanted her friend back. She had prayed a lot about it but she felt awkward talking about it with Lucas.

He was her husband and she loved him. Would he understand the need she had for her friend that was like a sister to her? Perhaps he would think that he wasn't enough. She did not want Lucas to feel slighted, so she kept her impatience to herself.

She was getting better at mending socks and stockings and was pleased when she had the job complete. She added a log to the fire and poked the embers into action with the metal prods.

She spent a while staring at the fire, praying for her friend and that her brother was found soon. She wanted her friend to be happy but she also wanted her back. She felt selfish and foolish but she knew God would help her through the waiting time.

Lucas came home a short while later and he had a basket full with dinner from Chelsea and Russell's house. Corinne and Lucas enjoyed the dinner and Lucas filled her in on all the family news.

Brody had sent a drawn picture that Corinne gladly hung from a nail by the front door. She thought it was a tree and a bear. She would gladly thank the five year old when she saw him next.

Lucas and Corinne discussed their day, Corinne's had been in the greenhouse and lab. Lucas had been clearing out some brush and felled a few trees with Russell on a piece of the property they wanted ready for next year. The talk between them was easy and they enjoyed each other's company.

They shared a piece of cobbler that Chelsea had included in the basket.

"Lucas, I know I have asked you many times about the dinner situation. You truly do not mind that I pay Chelsea to cook for us?" Corinne felt that familiar guilt creeping into her heart. Perhaps her desires and dreams had made her a bad spouse.

"I will tell you, again and again if I must." Lucas set his fork down and his green eyes looked into Corinne's brown ones. "I knew your ambitions when I married you. Chelsea loves to do it and for now it works. I have my own thoughts about what happens when her family grows. I know Marie also helps out when Chelsea gets busy. The harvest season may need to be adjusted next year. God will find a way. We all just have to remain open to His will." Lucas took another bite.

"I sometimes feel so guilty." Corinne said with a frown.

"I do believe you had a cook growing up." Lucas said. He raised an an eyebrow.

"Well yes, and my Grandmother lived with us too. She would sometimes help my mom in the kitchen. Frequently, my grandmother and my mother were occupied in the gardens and my mom also helped the doctor sometimes at the fort when the militia needed care." Corinne said. She knew that he knew all this.

"So everyone was fed and the women had purpose and meaning. Was your mother often wallowing in guilt about her meals being cooked by someone else?" Lucas asked with just the tiniest hint of sarcasm.

"Well, no, she kept herself useful in her community." Corinne said.

"Well then, like mother, like daughter." Lucas stole the slice of cobbler that Corinne had left untouched on the plate and scooped a big bite while Corinne laughed.

"Point taken, leave me a bite, you fool." Corinne stabbed at the plate with her fork to get any portion she could before her husband stole the rest.

❀ ❀ ❀ ❀ ❀

Corinne watched Lucas and Russell working side by side in the mid-afternoon. They were close in age, Russell just two years his senior but they were not very competitive. Lucas told stories how their mother had been on them early to appreciate their siblings and had harsh punishment for disloyalty to the family. She would always talk about when her own brother had died when she was young and she always felt it keenly. A cohesive and loving family was her main focus in their upbringing and she focused on raising children filled with God's Wisdom.

Russell was quick to help out with any needs Lucas had and the same went the other way. Labor hands were scarce with the promise of gold only a state away. The flyers printed in town said men were gaining mass fortunes and it all was spreading around on waggling tongues. The 'gold widows' were gaining in numbers.

Corinne had finished hanging a few necessities, she was going to go into town tomorrow to see if she could ask Clive's son J.Q. for some news. She knew Clive would be back soon from California territory. Perhaps with a few letters too. Corinne also wanted to step into Doc's and have him look at a rash on her neck. It was something she was unfamiliar with and perhaps she needed better protection for her skin while making her oils. They were strong and the vapors could be causing issues to any exposed skin.

She would ask the doctor though, it was never a bad idea, Corinne was decent at emergency medicine on the trail but her day-to-day knowledge wasn't complete like a doctor's education, she was always the first to admit that.

She rode Clover slowly into town. Her furs were warm around her. She had received them from the Indians while on the Oregon Trail and they were handsome. Clive had taken the furs and did his magic on them. She was always complimented when she wore them into town.

Doctor Vincent Williams was in his office and he thought that maybe the rash was related to her work too. "Maybe you and your employees should wear protective clothing while near the distillation process." Dr. Williams suggested.

They talked and pondered the ideas. He recommended a few ointments that she could get at the apothecary and was told to wash the rash often.

Corinne and Persephone had a nice chat after the doctor's appointment. Little by little Corinne could see that Persephone was opening up. She knew that her shyness would probably fade over time once she got to know people in town. Corinne was hoping to be a closer friend eventually. She invited the doctor and his wife to the Spring Creek Church meeting for that Sunday. She knew that Lucas would be playing violin and someone would be singing. Persephone had said that the church in town was pretty with new stained glass windows. But she hadn't made any good friendship connections.

"You are more than welcome. We aren't anything fancy, but I do love the preacher and his wife. We are meeting in the schoolhouse for now. But we are talking about building a church near the creek." Corinne shared. She hoped she didn't sound like she was pressuring them.

Persephone and her husband said with a smile that they would consider it. Corinne grinned and left and few minutes later.

She was pleasantly surprised to see them at service that very Sunday. After the lovely service and music the Williams couple both proclaimed they enjoyed it very much. They even stayed after the service for the discussion about the opportunity to build a church the next spring. The thoughts were to expand the small cabin of the preacher and to build a church building closer to the main farm road, right near the creek. The church agreed to the budget and all voted "yes" to build. Within a week the members who could afford to pitch in supplied the money needed for the budget.

Corinne was learning to lean on God as she waited. She knew that with spring would come many good things.

❀ ❀ ❀ ❀ ❀

Angela Fahey

San Francisco

The stationery store was full of wonders, Angie thought. The fancy goods section kept her enthralled while waiting for the owner of the shop to help her and Clive. The fancy quills, pencils and many styles of paper goods filled the walls from floor to ceiling. The other wall was filled with ornamental inkwells and stationery cases, from the simple to the extravagant. Clive showed her one that was particularly lovely with polished wood and mother of pearl artfully decorating it. It was grand indeed.

"Clive Quackenbush, to what do I owe this grand visit, with a young lady I see. Those are rare in these parts." The elder man gave a bow and Angela felt a little self-conscious.

"Well Waverly, I am needin' your wood carving skills. I have a need for an advertisement for this young lady. We have thought it all out and had a friend draw this up, simple and neat." He handed the owner the paper.

Family member looking for Sean Fahey: last known address California territory in the Company of Ol' Willie. For more information: Seek Quakenbush Mercantile, San Francisco.

"Looks easy enough. How many copies you needing?" Waverly rubbed his jaw. His hands had the look of a wood worker, callused and cracked but capable.

"We can start with seventy-five. I will take a few up to Sacramento when they are finished. Maybe head to a few places around Sutter's and a few of the booming places." Clive kept his ear to the ground and always seemed to know what was happening.

Waverly quoted a price and Angela insisted on paying. Clive harrumphed but allowed her to pay. It chafed him in any way to allow a woman to pay for anything. It was just his way. He could imagine his Ma, God bless her soul, would have cuffed the back of his head just now had she been here.

Waverly told them to wait a few days and come back for the advertisements. Angela and Clive walked back to the mercantile, the town square was rebuilding quickly after the fire. The buildings were not as tall as they were but several have taken the advice of some and start building in brick and iron. It wasn't disaster-proof but it took a lot to burn down a brick house.

"I am so hopeful about my brother, Clive, I hope I haven't put all this effort into this and nothing comes of it. It feels like such a vague wish." Angie wrung her hands while walking through the muddy streets. "The thought of going back without him is worse. It would feel like giving up. I cannot do that, yet."

Clive kept her company all the way and reminded her of something before he left.

"I will be leaving tomorrow for Willamette Valley, I am taking Ted with me." Clive saw an odd look cross her face after mentioning Ted's name. He waited a moment before adding a little fuel to the fire. "I will send Ted by later to get any letters and such if you care to send some." Clive had the oddest smirk on his face and Angela couldn't help but notice.

"Stop yer teasing Clive."

"I know nothin' of your meaning, child." Clive tried to look innocent and failed.

Angela shook her head and walked into the new mercantile without a word. Clive just laughed and did a quickstep around to the warehouse chuckling the whole way. Young folks and their feelings, everyone else in the world saw it first before these two shy kids would do a thing about it. He and Gabe have started a pool in the warehouse to see how long it took before these young kids decided to start courting.

Angela found Amber at the counter, Gabe was next to her but her face was distressed.

"Are ya feeling poorly Amber?" Angela went to her quickly to see if there was anything to do. She rubbed a hand soothingly down Amber's back.

"Just achy and the baby keeps kicking me in all the wrong ways. I keep telling him that I am not amused." Amber sounded worn out and crabby.

"Him?" Gabe and Angela said together.

"Well, just a feeling I have had lately. It just slipped out. He or she will have to answer for a few things when it comes out." Amber allowed Gabe to rub her back slowly. She closed her eyes and winced.

"Another kick?" Angela asked.

"No just a squeezing cramp that has been off and on today." Amber took a few deep breaths then asked Angela to help her up the stairs. Gabe interrupted and volunteered to do it. Angela could see a little worried frown creased above his eyebrows.

Angie spent the afternoon at the counter with a tablet scribbling out a practice letter to Corinne, she would probably not have long to write out the letter tonight. Amber would need help with preparing dinner.

When the last customer was served and the store was closed Angela got a surprise with dinner already on the table.

"I thought for certain I would be making dinner." Angela grabbed a few bowls and set them on the table. The tablecloth was new and Angela was again impressed at how elegant the place was. So different from the rough interior of the mercantile they lived above just last month.

"Angela, I appreciate how much you help around here but I have no desire to make you feel like you are expected to make dinner." Gabe said sternly, Angie wasn't sure if she had upset him. Her stomach churned into a knot of worry in half a second.

"I didn't mean… I just thought since Amber wasn't feeling well. I do apologize." Angie didn't know what to say to make it right. When she was a servant everything was always her fault. Even if it wasn't, it was still was her fault. The consistent rule of a servant, just say you are sorry and it won't happen again.

"We aren't angry dear, just want you to know you aren't a servant here. We pay you for some extra help downstairs but you are under our care." Amber said from the rocking chair. She seemed content with a blanket on her lap and what looked to be a cup of tea at the side table.

"I know I am not a servant, I am sorry if I implied that you treated me as such." Angie stood with her head down, completely bewildered.

"Angela, you don't understand. We are not angry with you at all. Calm yourself." Gabe walked in front of Angela and lifted her chin. "We are trying to help you adapt to this new life of yours. You still are sometimes acting like a servant around here and we just decided to help you stop. You are so helpful and sweet but we also want to allow you some freedom to grow up a bit too."

Two fat tears slip down Angie's cheeks. "You aren't angry with me?" Her voice was small and pitiful.

"No, my dear girl. Come sit next to me. Let's talk about baby names until you calm yourself." Amber gave a nod in the direction of the chair next to her. Angie was handed a full bowl by Gabe and she took a few deep breaths and listened to Amber's ideas. She ate her stew and let the friendship calm her down.

Gabe delivered a bowl to his wife and had one for himself, then sat across from the women in a cushioned chair by the fire. He propped his feet up on an ottoman.

The women spoke of pleasant things and Amber seemed relaxed and more comfortable to Angela's eyes. She was relieved to see it.

After dinner Angela excused herself to write another letter to Corinne before Ted and Clive left tomorrow morning on the steamer. Angie's thoughts were distracted as she finished the letter and stared out the window into the darkening sky of dusk. The sun went down so early in January but Angela enjoyed hearing the water now that they lived so close to the new wharf. If the breeze was not so chilly she would leave her windows open but she thought she would catch a chill.

Her heart felt torn apart today. She was thinking about Sean and hoping for the best with the new plan of advertising to find him. Also whenever Clive left it felt strange, Corinne always claimed that Clive was her long lost Grandfather and now Angie wanted to claim the same. His heart had room for her too, it seemed. She was so thankful for the many good friends she had recently been blessed with. To think, it had not even been three months and she had grown close to so many people here in this city on the bay. Ted came to her mind and the thought of him leaving grieved her a bit, too. She was not exactly sure why but there was something about him. She let the thought go and sealed the finished letter.

❅ ❅ ❅ ❅ ❅

Ted came by after Angela has gone back into the sitting room. Everyone was cozy by the fire when they heard the bell from downstairs. Ted had a key and they could tell it was him from his light and quick steps up the staircase. He knocked and Gabe let him in.

Angela could not help but notice her face getting warm as she smiled at Ted. He seemed to be blushing to her too but it was probably just the chilled air on his cheeks. It was brisk outside today.

The visit was pleasant but short. Ted gladly accepted Angela's letter and promised to deliver it into Corinne's hand personally.

"You will certainly be treated well by her family. Her father lives next door and Marie, his wife, will certainly have you over for dinner." Angela said, her heart missing her Oregon family so much.

"That sounds wonderful. Clive has been telling me great things about Oregon. I have hopes of my own farm someday. Perhaps I can convince my mother to come west to start over. I am working hard and hope to save enough in the next few months to afford that very thing. With the Lord's help I can do it. Labor is paid well here. I will not miss this city much though, but for the few dear friends I have made and the small church. This city grows too fast to deal with the gangs and evil on the streets. I pray often you find your brother soon. So you can be home and safe back in Oregon." Ted said. It was the most he had ever said to her. Giving her more glimpses into his personality.

"I pray that every day." Angela said with a small smile.

"I will bring back letters from your friend in a few weeks, perhaps a bit more. Clive has some work set up for me, helping him with shipping supplies and also something in Portland, a small town that is growing in Oregon near Oregon City." Ted said. He felt privileged to have earned the trust of Clive. He was a well-respected man everywhere he went. Ted was very eager to see more of the west than just this city, having Clive as his guide was a lucky break.

"I look forward to hearing all about it. I do hope you enjoy your trip." Angela said sincerely. "I would love to know more about Portland. I do miss Oregon so very much." She knew she could have said more but her throat was growing tight with emotions. She didn't want to squeak while talking and give herself away.

Ted left shortly with well wishes and Clive stopped by to say "goodbye" and gave Gabe a slap on the back then they talked a little business.

122

Angela gave Clive a long hug before he left. She wiped away a few tears and Clive in his usually fashion cheered her up with kind words before he too had to go.

❊ ❊ ❊ ❊ ❊

Ted and Clive made quick time on the ship from San Francisco bay to Portland. The days aboard the steamship were spent talking and swapping stories. The town of Portland was a quaint port town. Clive told him about the founders and how they were connected to Oregon City, connecting the farmland and keeping trade routes running smoothly.

"It's how our country thrives," Clive shared enthusiastically. Ted had a hard time not jumping into his enthusiasm.

"I want to see if there are any buildings for sale to get another store started. Wanting to sell the San Francisco store to an interested party or maybe just hire on a manager that doesn't have a family. It's getting too rough for my grandson and his lovely wife." Clive continued.

"I agree, I fear for my own safety often. The fire still gives me nightmares, and the street gangs keep me up at nights. I live so near the square I can hear the brawls every few days!" Ted added. He also feared for someone else, a young lady that was occupying much of his thoughts of late.

They stayed at the boarding house near the wharf. The place was run by a husband and wife that had a lovely dinner each night for their boarders. Clive and Ted felt welcomed and enjoyed the company of the owners and guests. They were all entertained by Clive's stories and magnetic personality.

The next day they surveyed some land for sale and Clive on the impulse took the deal, there was already a general goods store in town but Clive had other ideas. With his connection in Sacramento, San Francisco and the expanding ports up the coast he knew that an imported goods store with access to China, Russia, and with the boats coming from the eastern coast of the US, he could provide this area with a variety of goods beyond just a general store. He was at the bank and paid for the land by mid-afternoon. Ted just followed around the older gentleman with awe.

They rented a few horses from the town stables and headed off to talk to a few folks that Clive heard spoken of in town. One man owned a lumber camp and another man who owned a wool mill.

They ended up staying at the lumberman's home and by morning an arrangement was made. Clive had worked out a deal that saved the lumber harvester time and energy by agreeing to purchase a certain amount of lumber each month. The miller also worked out a deal with Clive, having a few women in Oregon City who were experts with the raw wool. Clive was a superb businessman who had an uncanny ability to make everyone comfortable.

Clive seemed to live modestly, dressed is a simple suit on some occasions and like a trapper on others. He spoke like a trapper when he wanted too, mostly for humor's sake, but could be all business and proper when the situation called for it. He was a man's man that respected women more that anyone Ted had ever met. He was the first man Ted had ever really looked up to. He would like to be able to say his father was a great man, but he wasn't. The competition between his father and Uncle had made both the men fools. Ted's mother always hinted to Ted that he was stronger than any Greaves man. She had told him stories about the men in her own family. They had been practical and hard workers, like Ted was. Knowing a man like Clive Quackenbush made him proud.

As they traveled Clive shared how he had come to the west years before. He knew all the founders of the towns and had so many stories to share about the development. Ted adored the mountainous country with wide fertile valleys. It was heavenly. He was starting to imagine what a future would look like here.

The next day was spent down some lightly traveled roads connecting Portland to Oregon City. The roads were muddy and the route was winding. The terrain had lots of hills and rocks to move around but Ted could see that a wagon could make the trip, once they stopped at the top of an impressive mound and got a full view of the valley laid out. Mount Hood was enormous in the landscape.

"My home is heading toward Mount Hood.. We should be able to rest there in a few hours. I am ready for some rest. I don't usually spend such a long day in the saddle anymore. Last time I did was on the Oregon Trail. If I ever go back east again I will go by ship. The mountain pass and deserts are something I can remember just fine. I have no need to see 'em again." Clive said while absorbing the view.

"The ship was not a very pleasant one for me. I must say. But some of the horror stories of the trials on the trail were enough to make me decide to go by sea." Ted shared.

"Well, I know a few reputable folks in New York you can ask about how to get your family safely back in comfort. The Panama way is much quicker, as long as your kin wouldn't mind riding on donkeys for a day or two." Clive said.

"Your references would be appreciated. I fear that my father and his brother Hank were fool-hardy in their choice." Ted said, his tone dropping. Clive noticed Ted was feeling grim about something but would let him share in his own time.

"Usually you get what you pay for… save your money and take a more expensive vessel is always my best advice." Clive took another moment to soak in the valley and the snowy peaks of the mountains and then kicked his heels slightly and moved his mount forward. The thought of a warm bed and fireplace, hot food and great company was pushing him onward.

✵ ✵ ✵ ✵ ✵

Willamette Valley

"Dear Clive!" Corinne kissed Clive's cheek and Lucas reached forward through the door and gave Clive a clap on the shoulder.

"I knew if I didn't come today you would hear I had arrived and beat me with sticks" Clive declared, and Corinne nodded her agreement.

"Get yourselves in…" Corinne opened the door wide and allowed Clive and his guest in.

Lucas took care of the men's coats. Clive and the young man with him both had packages. Lucas took them and placed them on the table nearby.

"This here is a new friend, from upstate New York by way of San Francisco. Mr. Ted Greaves this is Corinne and Lucas Grant."

"Welcome Mr. Greaves." Lucas said and both he and Corinne shook his hand. "Please call us Corinne and Lucas. We hope you are enjoying our valley."

"Oh, yes, very much." Ted said shyly, it was hard for him to know what to say around new people but he would work on opening up.

"Ted has been a great worker for the mercantile and around town. I figured to drag him along with me. A strong back and company is never a thing I will turn down." Clive grinned.

Lucas led the way to the sitting room near the fireplace. The crackling fire was high and warm.

"You have a lovely place here Mrs… Mrs… I mean Corinne. Your cabin is much more impressive than I expected. San Francisco has so many haphazard buildings I nearly forgot about what a comfortable home looked like… please feel free to call me Ted." Ted said, trying to move past his discomfort.

"I am pleased that you like it. I have to give credit to the builders, we have added on but they had the fine taste and skill to build everything you see here. I was deeded the land." Corinne shared. "A sort of disjointed family connection. I would say." Corinne gave a look to her husband and he smiled conspiratorially.

125

"I have been told many stories about this place from Miss Fahey, she misses you both so very much. I heard from her that your father lives close by." Ted felt more at ease.

"Yes indeed, in the plot next to ours. We have our house on the far edge of our land and he on his. That way it keeps us closer and safer from predators." Corinne was talking with her hands as she spoke. It made him realize that Angela did that too. He could see why they were dear friends.

The talk lasted for a while, Clive jumping in and asking about the entire local happenings. Lucas and Clive talked about the future of Oregon Territory, whether it would become a state. It was hoped for by most. Some thought that perhaps it would be its own country, but few people wanted to be separate. The popular consensus was that the land between the Atlantic Ocean and the Pacific Ocean should be united.

Marie stopped by later with a basket full of dinner items and took her chance to hug Clive and meet the young Mr. Greaves. They were invited to dine with them the next night. Continuing the feeling of hospitality and kindness in Ted's mind.

After they ate Ted finally wanted Corinne to have her box from Angela. It had several letters and a small rectangular package wrapped in brown parchment.

"Oh, letters and a gift." Corinne exclaimed. She gingerly opened the package and saw a beautiful carved box. Inside was a matching carved pen and stationery with flowers drawn as the letterhead. She gasped and touched the paper tenderly.

"We found a fancy goods store in San Francisco. She could not resist getting this for you." Clive said with a grin. He was pleased to see her reaction and promised himself he would remember this moment and tell Angela all about it when he returned.

"I will have a letter or two to send back with you. So be sure to stop by again before you leave." Corinne made Clive promise.

It was not a hard one to keep. Clive and Ted had plenty of visits in with John and Marie, Russell and Chelsea and even twice more to the Grants before they traveled back south. Clive was able to get lots of business done and still seemed to have time to give Ted a grand tour of the Valley. They attended church with the Harpole's and Grants. All in all Ted felt like he had a good grasp of this budding community. Clive was good at his job and felt a hankering to give the boy a liking for Oregon. Just in case his inclinations about Ted and a certain redhead were true.

Corinne had asked Clive before they left if there was anything she should know about this attractive young man. She had pulled him aside.

"He has mentioned Angela several times. He seems to light up when we talked about her." Corinne was curious.

"There is nothing beyond the sparking, as I can say but they are both shy. They may need a nudge if they are ever to move past it." Clive stifled a laugh.

"Well, I like him. He seems a good Christian lad. If God sees fit to put them together I could see it as a match." Corinne nodded.

She handed several letters to Ted before they left to go back to Portland. "If you could deliver these to her yourself, I would be much obliged." Corinne smiled and gave Ted a warm hug and goodbye. Lucas was just as friendly and grabbed his handshake with both hands and told him he was welcome in their home at any time. He leaned in and whispered too.

"Oregon is a good place to settle. I would be glad to see you around here someday. God Bless ya." Lucas let him go and Corinne and Lucas followed them outside to see them off.

❀ ❀ ❀ ❀ ❀

San Francisco, California Territory

Ted delivered the letters to Angela the day after he arrived. The steamer had arrived at night. They decided all to stay on board and get off in the early morning.
Clive was ready to be about his business with Gabe. He had so many plans swarming in his head he was chomping at the bit to get with Gabe and discuss the move of the business.

Ted got his two bags to his room over the laundry, fit in a quick shave and cleanup and was out the door by nine a.m.

The mercantile was nearly ready to be opened and Ted saw the smile of Angela through the large window. She opened the door for him and she nearly leaned in to hug him, he thought. Perhaps it was wishful thinking.

"It is good to see you back safe and sound." Angela said, a pretty pink blush lit up her cheeks. "I thought I heard Clive in the back room with Gabe but I didn't want to disturb them. From what I could hear they were deep in business talk."

"Clive is a dynamo, he impressed me so much with all we did while we were gone. He has so many business ventures, I have no idea how he can keep them all straight." Ted said with enthusiasm. He had been tired but being in Angela's presence had him awake and a little jittery.

"I am sure we will hear all about it tonight at supper." Angela smiled. This was a pleasant side to Ted.

127

"You were right about Oregon." It was his turn to blush. Knowing what his thoughts implied to himself. "It seems like a good place to settle. The land is so beautiful and I was told by many how fertile the land is."

"I hoped you would like it." Angela said without thinking. It was a bit forward to be telling a young man where he should settle, especially if she wanted to live there herself. Her pink blush turned red. Angela could tell that Ted noticed.

It was an awkward minute until Ted reached into his jacket and retrieved the letters from Corinne.

"I should be off, I haven't eaten since last night. My need for some breakfast is great." Ted put his hands in his pockets and let his gaze follow the lines of Angela's face a moment before he had to will himself to leave.

"Oh no, stay right there." Angela with a quick turn was around the counter and running up the stairs. Her skirts swishing as she hopped up each step. Ted could not help but grin.

She was down just a minute later with a plate heaped with a few biscuits with jam, a few slices of bacon some potato hash.

"We only just ate less than an hour ago. If you don't mind leftovers you can save yourself a dollar. The restaurant prices are going up." Angie said practically.

"I don't mind at all." Ted said accepting the plate.

Angela patted the seat by the counter as an invitation. Ted gladly took it.

"You can keep me company while I get the store ready to open." Angela's sweet smile was Ted's near undoing. He had no idea how to think when he was around her but somehow he needed to figure out a way to… he didn't even know what he wanted to do. Well, perhaps he had a thought or two. Her pretty pink lips and green eyes were keeping his full attention.

"You eat your food Ted." Angela said when she saw he hadn't eaten a bite in several minutes.

"Yes'm" He said and stopped the staring. He was going to have to get a hold of himself. He ate his breakfast but was still able to watch Angela as she worked her way around the room tidying and nudging things into place. He decided that this was a fine way to spend a morning.

Clive and Gabe joined up with Angela and Ted. Angela gave Clive a quick hug and went back to her work. Clive gave Ted a questioning look.

"She fed me breakfast." Ted said lamely, trying to explain his presence. "Oh yes, I also delivered the letters."

Clive laughed and gave Ted a knowing look. Ted knew he wasn't fooling anyone. Clive gave a look to Angela who was busy with her counter duties. Clive raised an eyebrow to Ted and shook his head. Ted wasn't exactly sure what Clive had said with all his gesturing but he was pretty sure that he had failed at something in Clive's estimation.

Ted left after his breakfast plate was empty. He returned the plate to Amber who was upstairs.

"See you folks soon. I will be checking around for some work. God bless all." Ted waved.

They all said goodbye and both Gabe and Clive noticed that Angela watched from the window as the young man walked down the street.

"You go take a break, I will cover the counter dear. You go read your letters." Clive offered. Angela squealed the tiniest bit and ran up the stairs. After a brief moment talking to Amber she went to the balcony off the side off her room. It had a nice little chair and table.

She read the letter from Corinne:

Dearest Angie,

I am missing you again. I have been busy as a bee with my labs and plants. The oil production is started and the science is working the way it should. Producing clean and pure oil from my piles of lavender plants. Dolly has started staying with us sometimes and the missing you is easier when I have female company. Her English has improved greatly and she now insists on reading out loud from our bible after dinner every night. She has confessed a new belief in God but struggles with how it all goes together. We all help when we can but somehow we know that she has to find God in her way. She has the desire, I can tell, but her upbringing was so very different. But she talks about her Mother and Father having been believers in the white man's God. She is a strong young woman and knowing her has been a blessing. I hope she never leaves the area. She sometimes talks about how her tribe wants her to come back. I don't know how to feel about it.

We added on to the cabin on the North side, with a whole new section with two bedrooms, and a large room for feeding the harvesters. Lucas says our crowded cabin is going to burst if we have to repeat what we did last fall. The wing to the west that Andrew's parents built for us is finally the way it should be. It is three rooms, a bedroom, and a sitting room, both with a fireplace and a small kitchen with a wood stove. It

129

is connected to the house but offers complete privacy. Marie and I have decorated it. Lucas thinks it would be a great wing for a housekeeper. But I am adamant to have no servants. I know you understand my reasons.

Marie has a few dresses made for you when you return. She made me a darling new Sunday dress that is so fashionable. Lucas whistles every time I wear it.

I sent a reply back to my cousin Megan and they telegrammed to me that they set sail in April. They will be setting up their new home near Sacramento, California. Her father, Arnold Capron, wants to set up a large dairy operation there.

Lucas and I have told her to come and stay with us over the winter months if she wishes. I am not sure what kind of escape she is hoping for but I am always willing to help when it comes to family.

We had a lovely visit with the nice Mr. Greaves. Ted, as he allowed us to call him, seems a very good young man. He spoke very highly of you and was always mentioning you every time we had him over for dinner. Perhaps it was my active imagination but I do believe he mentioned settling here about a dozen times. Does that please you, friend? I would dearly like to know. I cannot keep from grinning, as I am here with more than a mild curiosity about how my dearest friend is making such good acquaintances. Please do tell if there is any news on that front. Before I burst with my own inquisitiveness.

I have also sent along another letter that came by post a few weeks ago. I was excited to see Edith Sparks printed on the outside. I do pray she has good news. They were both so very good to you. I pray a blessing on them often.

As always you are in my thoughts and prayers. Please come home to me soon.

Corinne Grant

Angela sighed and read over every word. Feeling her friend's teasing over Ted, she had nothing to share with her friend but in her hopes there was the hint of something there. She would have to explore it further on another day. She went to the other letter.

My darling girl,

God has blessed our fort with so many visitors over the last months. The spring was the busiest I had ever seen. My root cellar was near empty as I sold out of all I had set aside for sale. I tried ever so hard not to dip into our own food supply but I will say upon occasion I did sell to a few desperate folk that were running out of food stores. I do wonder how they were to survive the long journey having prepared so ill.

I have some news. It was near summer when a wagon train pulled through. It reminded me of the day we met you when the wagon boss came into town so early. A father and mother were killed along the trail, one to snake bite and the other to a bad water crossing. They had three children, orphaned and without transport. The train did not want the responsibility for them.

The oldest child a girl, Heidi, who is almost ten years old declares that they had no family at all back in Illinois. The wagon boss shared all the belongings with us and upon our agreement left the children with us. The two youngest, twins, a boy named Peter and his sister Fiona are so beautiful and sweet little darlings. They don't really understand the loss of their parents but they have warmed up to Henry and I. At first we didn't know what to do with them. Henry sent a post to his commanding officer in Illinois about the children. Since the children were considered orphans we were sent papers that signed us as having guardianship over them. If wished we could send them back to any city to an orphanage or we could adopt them.

It was not a hard decision for us to make. I had spent years praying for children, then more years allowing God to work within me to get past my childless state. I had such a joy in my heart when we had you to take care of; though you were nearly grown it was such a blessing to me. My tears were plentiful after you left, the house so quiet.

We have decided to adopt the children as our own if they all agreed to it. Heidi was not hard to convince but her sadness over losing her parents created a melancholy in her for a time. The good Lord is helping us all to see her through it. The young ones are a constant joy and challenge. God has supplied me, at 43 years old, with a family I never could have expected.

Henry and I have discussed the topic at length and prayed extensively. Upon Henry's next re-enlistment he will decline. With his savings we have decided to continue west. We have our hearts set on being near you, Angela. You are a daughter of my heart and I would love to raise my new family on a piece of land near you. We would love to teach the girls to grow things, and Peter to have a place to run and grow into a Godly man. I have a dream of a nice cabin with room for a big garden and a farm stand to sell my produce. I do so love that part. Seeing people buy what I grew, it is less about the money and more about the providing someone with good healthy food. I am rambling on and on. I miss our chats.

Henry will be done with his post in April 1851. We will be well prepared to head out to the great unknown. I pray we stay safe and see you again. Lord willing our paths will cross once more.

With much love,

Edith Sparks

Angela's heart was full at the thought of her dear caretakers finally having a family. Only God can take a tragedy like those orphaned children and turn it around. Angela spent much of her day praying for this dear girl Heidi, who like herself, had seen both of her parents die too young.

She went about her week, thinking and planning. Hoping somehow to share the news with Corinne soon. Being so far away was getting harder. Oregon was the place she wanted to be.

❈ ❈ ❈ ❈ ❈

She had a white handkerchief tied around her hair to protect it. The white wash was a bit runny and her arms and the front of her dress was splattered. A few of the young people volunteered to paint the fence and the storage shed next to the new church. Angie was in the back of the church chatting with Sheila Henderson and enjoying the camaraderie of just being silly for an afternoon. The wind had died down and the bay was calm. Gabe was running the store and Amber had enjoyed a few peaceful days.

When they announced the need for a fence and shed at the Sunday service a few men volunteered to build it. Not one minute later Bradley made the suggestion that the young people could perhaps paint the fence and shed and also plant a few trees around the new church building.

132

This morning Angie was up early and Gabe was happy to see her bouncy and up before dawn.

The fence was nearly done but Angela decided to wait a few minutes to see if the whitewash was evenly coated. Sheila left her alone to go help with the a tree planting. Bradley loaded a few tools into the shed next to Angela and then approached her.

"You actually watching paint dry?" Bradley asked with a chuckle. He hadn't come by since that awkward conversation several weeks ago.

"Yes, I am. How silly. I just wanted to make sure it dries evenly." Angela thought about saying more about being perfect like a good servant but stopped herself.

"I understand, I enjoy finishing a job well myself." Bradley held his hands behind his back a minute and tipped on his heels nervously. "I was wondering if you would like to go with me to the theatrical this weekend. It is the first one held at the new theatre, everyone is talking about it." Bradley forced himself to stop nervously talking.

"I have heard about that, Mr. Henderson, but I am nervous that the show will be inappropriate." Angela didn't trust the flyer. She had heard that several of the dance hall girls were cast in the play. They enjoyed parading on Kearney St. in nothing but their skivvies on most days. Angie had no interest in seeing *that* kind of show sitting next to Bradley Henderson.

"I hadn't thought of that." Bradley looked perplexed.

"I will be glad to in any other case Mr. Henderson, truly. Just the theatre is a little untested for me." Angie smiled to calm him down. In many ways she felt older than him. Even though he was nineteen to her seventeen.

"I understand, could I interest you in a dinner with my family some night this week?" Bradley rebounded well and his nerves were a bit calmer now, his voice had lost a bit of the tension.

"That sounds delightful, your mother's cooking is getting acclaim all over the city. Men constantly talk about spending their gold dust at the Henderson's family restaurant." Angie flattered him well and Bradley puffed his chest out unconsciously. Angie noticed and smiled to herself.

Bradley saw her smile and took it for flirting. Angela's pretty smile had done wonders for his confidence.

✿ ✿ ✿ ✿

Two days later Angela was dressed in her dark green print dress with her hair up and lovely.

The dinner was at six, they had a big table downstairs in the restaurant. The place was full but the big room in the back was for families or special parties.

"We got some beef in from Sacramento yesterday, so steaks for everyone." The father said loudly in his booming jovial voice.

Angela clapped with the family as the plates were handed out. She was seated next to Bradley on one side and Sheila on the other. She did try to talk with Sheila but she was rather quiet today. Her relationship with Sheila was not a developed one yet. No matter how hard Angela tried it just wouldn't get past small talk. Angie didn't want to force it and kept it light throughout the evening. Angela strived on being a pleasant dinner guest and hoped everyone enjoyed her company.

"Let us walk down to the big rocks and watch the ships. I will keep you away from the riffraff." Bradley offered his arm after dinner and his parents grinned and nodded. Angie wasn't sure if Gabe or Clive would like for her to be out after dark but Bradley was a strong strapping lad. Angie was sure she would be safe.

"Thanks for inviting me to dinner Mr. Henderson." Angie said while watching the moon as it reflected off the bay. The rocks were up ahead and the night was relatively still. She could hear the ruckus of the saloons a few streets over but they were not bad tonight.

"I wish you would call me Bradley." He said.

"As you wish." Angie paused. "Bradley." She said to appease him. He was friendly so she didn't want to offend.

"I love the sound of your voice, with your accent. It's very pretty Angela." Bradley took a firm hold of her hand as it was clasped around his arm. She felt a little uncomfortable with him holding her hand, even with her gloves on it felt intimate and forced. She also had a brief thought that he had not asked permission to call her Angela. His hand holding hers was now pushing her boundaries.

Would it be rude to pull away? She wondered.

"Thanks Bradley." Angie says a little stunted.

"I feel like we have finally a moment alone to talk. I have a lot I want to say to you." Bradley took the hand he was holding and gave the gloved hand a kiss.

"Bradley, perhaps this isn't the time but I hope you understand I don't feel ready for a romantic relationship." Angela blurted out before he said anything embarrassing.

"I don't understand." Bradley looks dumbfounded. "I have money and will be opening up a restaurant in Sacramento in a few months. I want to take you with me."

"You barely know me." Angie stammered.

"You are sweet and beautiful and we get along well." His face was calm.

"Three days ago we were barely acquainted. I am flattered by your attentions but I do not feel your declarations are appropriate." She stated, trying to keep annoyance out of her voice. Bradley shrugged, unaffected.

Angie started to wonder about his ability to understand complete sentences.

"I will give you more time, sweet Angela." He leaned to give her a peck on the cheek and infuriated her further. "I should have listened to my sister. She thinks you are too shy to get married."

"Married? I have no intentions of getting married to you." Angela could not help but raise her voice a little.

Bradley was not paying attention.

"Not yet my girl. I will give you the time you need." Bradley tucked her arm back into his arm and walked Angie back. She was so mad and confused she did not know what to say. He was not listening to her. When they arrived at the mercantile door Angie had to push him away when he tried to kiss her cheek again.

"You are such a sweet little thing." Bradley chuckled and patted her on the head. Suddenly Angie felt her temper rise up in her chest. She was more than angry. She went in, locked and bolted the door behind her in a huff. She wanted to stomp up the stairs but she controlled herself but did climb them two at a time. What she needed right now was a task, or someone to slap silly.

Gabe sent her a quick look from his cushioned chair by the fireplace and a half scared smile spread across his face.

"What has happened to you Red?" Gabe tried not to laugh but a small little cough sound escaped. "You look a bit bothered."

"I cannot say that I have ever been this dumbfounded in my life…" Angela swallowed and tried to think how she would word it. A crash happened in the next room and all words and anger were forgotten when Angie and Gabe found Amber holding onto the desk in her bedroom. There were books on the floor and the hem of ambers dress was wet and moisture was spreading across the floor.

"My water broke and I bumped the dresser." Amber's forehead was damp with sweat.

"No need to apologize. Let's get you ready. Let me clear the bed." Angela said, clear headed.

Angela grabbed all the linen from the bed and pulled out a rubber tarpeline they had ready for the occasion. Angie got the bed remade with the tarpeline under the sheet and then she helped Amber out of her wet gown and underthings and into a comfortable nightgown.

135

"You are all sweaty. Were you having any cramps yet today?" Angie asked. She saw a nod but Amber was holding her breath. Angie could tell her pains had started.

"I will help you into bed. Gabe went for the Doctor. If he cannot come Mrs. Henderson will be here. I am not leaving. I have done this before." Angie wasn't sure why she was talking so much but it made herself feel confident. Amber crawled into the bed with a little help and Angie propped her up with a few pillows. Angie lost all her confidence when she saw drops of blood on the sheets.

"Amber, I think you are bleeding a bit." Angie said calmly.

"I know. That is why I knocked over the books. One second later my water broke. I have been talking to God while you got the bed ready. This baby is moving inside me. He is okay. I know it."

Angela left Amber a second to get a pot of water boiling. She checked back every minute to make sure that nothing had changed.

"I am fine now. My cramps are not close together. We have time." Amber gave Angela a peaceful and weary smile.

Mrs. Henderson burst through the door without knocking. "I came to help."

"Good. Finish filling the pan and keep stoking the fire in the stove. There is fresh water in the pot on the counter." Angie said.

Amber piped in from the other room. "You keep checking on me every sixty seconds. Just get done what you need too." Amber's chuckling eased Angie's fears. Amber must be a calm person in a storm. She would make a good mother.

Mrs. Henderson got busy in the kitchen and Angie grabbed towels and a few baby blunts set off to the side. She found the sharp scissors and scooped some of the boiling water out with a ladle and washed the scissors well, she gasped as the steaming hot water scalded her hands lightly. It only hurt for a second and no harm was done.

Angie heard Amber moaning and joined her next to the bed to hold her hand.

"Are the pains getting worse?" Angie tried to say the right thing, but maybe there was no right thing in this moment.

"I am fine, love. I know this is the way of birthin'." Amber let her breath out and grinned when it was over. Angie was amazed at how Amber was trying to comfort her in this situation. Some women were truly extraordinary.

Chapter 18

The doctor arrived with Gabe after thirty minutes of more contractions. Amber was uncomfortable and Angie noticed that there was more blood on the bed.

When Doctor Frasier got her situated and gave her a cursory exam he also noticed the blood. He felt how strong the contractions were with his hand on her belly. He listened with his stethoscope and said the heartbeat was still strong from the baby.

After a few hours of contractions he had raised concerns that the child's heartbeat was fast, but Amber was nearly fully dilated. Gabe was sent away and the women were to take care of Amber.

The pushing began and it only took a few minutes for the head to come out. Angie kept a hold of Amber's hand and had been cheering her on during each phase of pushing. Amber was so small but grunting and fighting like a warrior to deliver her baby. Angie was so proud of her.

"Angela, I need you to do something for me." Doc Frasier got Angie's attention. "The baby is struggling, see around the neck. I think the cord is cutting off the airway. I need you to reach in and pull the cord loose, you may have to push the baby in a way to do this."

Angie was dumbstruck, not sure if she could do this thing he asked of her.

"Will this hurt Amber?" Angie questioned more in her head that but it was the first thing she could think to say.

"Yes, there will be discomfort. I need your small hands. It will hurt less and we need you to do this now." Mrs. Henderson handed Angie a warm damp towel and she cleaned her hands. Without thinking too much she reached around the child's head and felt the cord indeed starting to tighten around the baby's head, its little face bunched up and almost purple. Angie felt her heart latch on to some courage and she felt the small shoulder beneath her finger and gave the smallest push. The resistance was real and she could hear Amber yell out, her body was now fighting against Angie's intrusion. The baby moved back in the canal and gave Angie a little room to get a hold of the umbilical cord, she didn't want to pull it tight and choke the baby completely. Instead the slippery cord cooperated and was around the head and the child was out of danger. She had a moment of inspiration and instinctively she grabbed the child by the shoulders and hearing Amber pushing with the contraction Angie helped pull the child's shoulders out. Angie caught the baby and immediately gave the little boy to the doctor.

The body was moving a little, Angie thought. Amber was crying and Angie was holding her breath, her heart pounding in her ribs like a drum. She could not believe she had just done what she did.

The room was quiet but for the soft voice of Dr. Frasier hovering and murmuring to the young boy, so red and fragile on the bed. The room was warm and the ears of everyone straining to hear the sound of life, something, anything to say that this was a good delivery.

"Doctor, please!" Amber sobbed out finally.

Doctor Frasier turned his attention away for the briefest moment his face a wash in regret and pain.

"No, no, no!" Amber yelled in a wail and laid back to sob, her arms lay limp at the sides of her. Angie let out the painful breath she'd been holding and reached to comfort when the sound they have all waited for escaped the young boy's lungs. A crackly scream escaped again and you could feel the tension in the room lift and fly away. Instead of sobs, laughter resounded and a cheer rose up from inside the room.

Angie wiped at the tears of agony and joy that mingled against her cheek. The boy was quickly making up for lost time by shouting his protests about all the poking and prodding the doctor was doing.

"A healthy baby boy, Mrs. Quakenbush." The doctor announced and handed the baby to the mother swaddled in a clean blanket after he had been thoroughly washed and checked over.

As the women cooed and crowed over the child the doctor helped Amber through the rest of the process. Angie was in awe. Her heart didn't know how to handle the feelings. This moment was so overwhelming and intense it stole her ability to think. Her heart was raw as she watched Gabe enter and share the joy with his wife over their own firstborn child.

The only thing Angie could think at such a moment was, 'My cup runneth over.'

Angie stood in the corner and wept her overwhelmed tears and rejoiced and praised God in her own way for the miracle she had witnessed.

Mrs. Henderson did help Angie with cleaning up and getting mother and child ready with a clean bed. A small cradle was near the bed to retrieve for breastfeeding.

❈ ❈ ❈ ❈ ❈

Baby boy Silas Gabriel Quackenbush, Angela wrote the boy's name into her journal. She had written about his birth and how the experience made her feel. There was a pride in her heart knowing she had helped in the delivery. She realized with every birth she had seen that the miracle of life was not something little to her. It was an enormous blessing and responsibility that the Lord placed into the hands of every parent. She thought a little about Edith Sparks and how her and Henry were taking on the responsibility of the three orphaned children, then she thought of her own story. Her step-father had sold her and her brother to the workhouse to avoid the work of raising children not his own. Angela was certain when she delivered her children into the world she would never intend for them to struggle so much. Angela wrestled with her thoughts but came back to a thankful spirit of realizing how much God had helped her out of the workhouse and even returned her inheritance. If she could have written a note to heaven to tell her mama that she was going to be fine, Angela would have done so on the spot, instead she prayed for her sibling. Thinking how a mother would pray for her children to be safe, she prayed as her mother would, that Sean would be safe and that God would protect him from evil and harm.

Angela slept fitfully, waking with every noise in the house. The nights and days blurred a little as everyone adjusted to the little guy's schedule. Though Angela had no part in the feedings, the house was up together when Silas was upset. He had lungs and knew how to project, well. Angela covered many shifts on the counter but loved when she would get time to take care of Silas when one or the other parent needed to catch up on sleep. Amber had been slow to heal from her ordeal and had been weak for a few days. The doctor was concerned at first but by the fourth day her color perked back up in her cheeks and she claimed she was improving. Everyone was watching her carefully though.

Angela was on the counter duty waiting on a customer when Clive arrived and threw the door open. He let out a gusty laugh at her surprised look and scooped her up from behind the counter.

"How's my pretty Red today?" Clive gave her a bear hug and swung her around a bit and made her squeal. Angela grabbed her head to make sure her hair was secure when he plopped her down.

"I am good, you old fool." Angie proclaimed. Her cheeks burned bright when she saw Ted behind him. It looked like he meant to approach her for a handshake or a hug but stopped short awkwardly. Angie nearly sighed in exasperation. She wasn't sure what she wanted him to do but just waiting around for him to do something might just kill her, she decided in her head.

"Hello Ted." Angie's voice was low and she jumped when she realized there was a customer present. Clive stared at her awkward display of nerves in front of Ted. She ran quickly around the counter and got back to work. Ted stayed in the room and watched her work a few minutes leaving her in a perpetual state of blushing.

"Clive, you should get yourself upstairs." Angie warned after the customer left. "There is a Quackenbush you have not yet met." Clive let out a hoot and jumped up the stairs two at a time.

"The baby came?" Ted asked and leaned on the wood counter. Just a few inches away from Angie making her feel a bit self-conscious...

"Yes, five nights ago, a little boy, Silas. He is a dear one that can holler like a champ." Angie and Ted laughed together.

"Amber is well then?"

"Yes, she was weak at first but is stronger now." Angela could not look him in the eye just now, his gaze very intense on her.

"I have some letters from Corinne for ya. I stayed with her and Lucas a few days while Clive was off for a weekend trip while we were there. He said he had some errands to run to a few friends off yonder. I have found Clive to be quite a character, maybe the most interesting person I know." Ted smiled, clearly thinking about something.

"I appreciate the letters. How are Corrine and Lucas?"

"They are dandy, both kind and accommodating. Corinne gave me at tour of the place and Lucas gave me some help discerning where some good land was still available. I am looking for a place to settle once I have enough... A few miles outside of Oregon City is a nice area to raise some dairy cows or sheep I'm thinking. I love farming of any kind." Ted actually blushed when he realized how much he was sharing. "Sorry to carry on Miss, I mean, Angela. I should just give you your letters and get to unloading the chickens." He smiled attractively and corrected, "Your chickens."

"I would like my chickens but you can carry on all you like." Angela said with a shy smile.

"You are easy to talk to, sweet girl." Ted said before he swung the door open and the bell jangled right along with her skipping heartbeat.

Gabe bounded down the wooden staircase and joined her. He asked about Ted then joined him to unload the crates of chickens and feed. A short while passed and the chickens, a little weathered and scrawny, pranced around their new place, fifteen hens and a rooster. Angie was hoping the rooster would behave and not get everyone up too early. Any more sleep disruptions may just do everyone in.

Though Angela has been reading all about how to care for the chickens both Gabe and Ted gave their advice willingly. Angie was all ears and allowed for all the help she could get. Her hopes for a thriving egg business was born.

Sunday arrived after two weeks with the child and everyone was ready for a good Sunday meeting. Angela held the baby while Amber ate her breakfast. Gabe took the little one when Angela wanted to fuss with her hair after Silas's chubby little hands pulled on the front of her hair and sent it into disarray. She cared little for the fuss as he had wormed his way into her heart for certain. His perfect little lips and fingers and even his loud cries are all part of the miracle that was Silas.

The weather was windy and the family was bundled against the chill in the air as they walked the two blocks to the church. Once they arrived the Henderson's gave Angie a hearty wave. Bradley waved for her to come and sit by him, reminding her about the strange night by the water.

I have never dealt with Bradley, she said to herself. He needed to get a firm grasp of the truth. She was not interested, simple as that. She walked over.

"You are looking pretty today. I heard the youngin' has been keeping you all up late nights. My Ma came for a visit the other day. I know you been busy helping at the store but I look forward to seeing ya soon." Bradley was running away with his words again.

"I am sorry Bradley, I would like a chance to visit here soon. I will be sitting with the Quackenbush family but perhaps later today you can stop by. I need to have a word with you." She gave a quick smile to make her words sound less forced. His puppy dog grin said volumes to Angie that he did not understand her still. She would have to do better later. She would ask Amber and Gabe for advice.

"I will be glad to, my Angela." Bradley said sweetly.

Angela walked away before she caused a scene. *Was it right to be angry with someone during a church service?* Not everyone had the same set of smarts but she was starting to doubt that Bradley had any.

I am sorry, Lord, she prayed in her head. *That was not nice of me to think so poorly of Bradley.*

She had more to pray about on the subject but the service started and she forced herself to pay attention and sing along.

When the church service ended Bradley interrupted a conversation she had with the minister's wife to tell her he would be by at three that afternoon. Angela tried to keep her face neutral. The minister's wife chuckled a little when he was gone.

"He seems attentive." The pastor's wife said with a grin spread across her face.

"Yes, obnoxiously so." Angela said a little too quickly. She immediately felt guilty for saying such a negative comment but had no words to make it better.

"I can tell he is more interested than you are. I suggest that you break it to him gently."

"I told him I only wanted to be friends. Then he said he wanted to *marry* me and take me to Sacramento! I barely know him. I am sure he wasn't listening to me." It felt good to Angela to share with someone. Not sure if her advice would help but to have someone trustworthy to talk was nice at that moment.

"Well my only advice is to make sure he hears you." She was smiling and patted Angie's shoulder. It was a gesture of understanding.

✿ ✿ ✿ ✿ ✿

A knock on the door frightened everyone in the room. Gabe was napping in the chair and Amber was near to sleeping in her rocking chair with some yarn sitting in her lap, her hands had been still for quite a while.

Angela looked at the clock on the mantle to see 2:45. -- Bradley!

She stepped fast and light across the floor and opened it before he knocked again and woke up Silas.

"Shhh…" Angela said in a hushed tone and mouthed the words 'the baby is sleeping.'

Angela pointed for him to go back and down the stairs. Angela grabbed her coat and joined him.

When they were downstairs she led him out to the back fenced area. She needed to feed and check on the birds.

"We will need to keep our voices down but I am glad you came." Angela sat on the bench and gestured for Bradley to join her. He had been wearing a silly grin since he arrived. It was completely distracting Angela.

"I told my parents today. I was too excited to wait." Bradley blurted out.

"You have news?" Angela went along with it but was wording in her mind how she was going to be frank with him about her lack of feelings.

"About our engagement, Angela darling." Bradley grabbed her hands and kissed the top of each one.

"Our… Engagement?" Angela forced her voice to stay at a loud whisper. She wanted to yell all of a sudden. "You didn't tell you parents that we are engaged. Why would you lie like that?"

"Angela, I told you my intentions a few weeks ago. We have an understanding." Bradley's face was perfectly serious for a moment.

"I have an understanding that you are out of your wits!" Angela pulled her hands away from his and paced around the yard.

"I would agree, I lose my senses whenever I think of you, my pet." Bradley's voice was syrupy and he reached for her to pull her back to the spot on the bench next to him. She stayed out of reach. He frowned for a half-second.

"You have no right to call me darling, Angel, or my pet, Bradley. Let me speak clearly. I …am…nothing… more… than… a… friend…to…you…" Angela felt good for saying it but when she saw the silly incoherent grin on his face her hopes failed.

"I understand Angela, I have not proposed properly, but I will. I promise." He jumped up and grabbed her hands again, she failed to escape and he tried to hug her. She ducked in time and twisted away from him.

"I think you better leave, Mr. Henderson. You are taking advantage and I do not appreciate it." Angela was so mad she could scream.

"I will come back soon. I am sorry to be so forward today. I promise not to tell anyone else about our understanding until I have asked you properly." Bradley gave a wave and left Angela alone in the yard with her chickens. She threw her arms up in a shrug and fed the chickens. She told them all about Bradley.

"You just met him… Yes I know. He is a bit dim." She filled up the water contraption and spread feed around as the birds clucked and pecked at the ground near her feet.

"Do you always talk to your chickens?" A familiar voice said from the back doorway. "I came to see you but I saw I was not the first. Bradley Henderson passed me as he was leaving." Ted was leaning on the doorpost looking handsome in his black wool coat. His blond hair had been recently trimmed.

"Yes Bradley was here, being a nuisance." Angela threw a handful of seed on the ground harshly. Perhaps a little too harshly, she grimaced a little.

"One shouldn't pelt the chickens with the feed like that. They won't lay eggs if ya scare them." Ted's chuckle took her mind off Bradley's idiocy and she acted like she is about throw seed on Ted. He held his hands up in mock surrender.

"Thank you Ted, I will try and be gentle from now on." Angela said sarcastically. She was feeling more and more comfortable around Ted. He was the kind that listened. She appreciated that about him.

"Come, they have enough now. Come tell me if I need to teach young Bradley how to stop being a nuisance."

"Well I am not sure I should say. Is it gossip to share news about someone being foolish?" Angela had a frown for a moment to think on it.

"Well, is he being foolish in a way that can harm someone?" Ted asked.

"Well, no… maybe. I mean it's complicated. I am not sure to be honest. Perhaps I can tell you in confidence if you promise under threat of…"

"Death?" Ted filled in her pause.

"You know I wouldna' kill anyone…" Angela smiled and pretended a slug into his shoulder.

"Then how about I just say that I keep it to myself, but I will give you advice if you should tell someone else." Ted said thoughtfully, Angela nodded and decided to share. Ted was good listener anyway.

"Well, Bradley is interested in me, romantically." Angela said, realizing how bad of an idea this was instantly.

"That is not foolish at all." Ted said and grinned very slowly.

Angela swallowed hard and muttered. "It isn't?"

"No, I know a few folks wise enough to have that same issue?"

Angela felt a heat coarse through her and hit her stomach. She felt a strange ill sensation for just a moment.

She somehow forgot what she was saying then began to blurt out everything.

"Well, he, uh… he told me a few weeks ago when he asked me to dinner with his family that he wanted to take me to Sacramento. But I told him I only wanted him as a friend. But he wouldn't listen and then told me we were getting married. I said no again and asked him to take me home. Then today he said he told his parents we are engaged, and I told him he was out of his mind and asked him to leave. I think he is going to buy me a ring now." Angela blurted it all out in one breath.

"I see." Ted said quietly. Angela wasn't sure how the next moment actually happened but in a moment he reached out to her shoulder and he took one step and then she was in his arms. His kiss was warm with the breeze from the bay brushing past her, his arms around her shoulder and one hand in the hair at the back of her neck.

Then the kiss was over. Angela was briefly sad as she stepped forward toward him but then teetered back when her senses returned.

She stared at Ted who suddenly was wearing a look she had never seen. Was it happy, or passionate or perhaps a bit cocky?

"You look pleased." Angela said suddenly.

"I am." His grin made her stomach dance a jig again.

"So when did you decide to do that?" Angela asked boldly.

"Well, I've been thinking on it for a while now." Ted blushed and the cocky look faded a bit, replaced by the shy Ted she has seen a lot lately. "Did I scare ye off?" he asked, a hint of vulnerability was back in his voice, but he kept his eyes on Angela, not looking away.

"Do I look scared off?" Angela had a moment of triumph herself realizing he was nervous, about her.

"No, actually you are looking quite pleased yourself. I am thinking about kissing you again, now." Ted took a step forward but Angela held up her hands.

"Now wait Mr. Greaves." Angela gave him a questioning look. "I know you are a good young man, but I am not the kind of girl that goes around kissing a young man without knowing his intentions."

"Ah, it is back to Mr. Greaves." Ted took a nervous breath and then let it out slowly. "Come sit, Angie." He led her back to the bench she so recently sat on with Bradley Henderson. "I apologize for what I said just now. I guess I've been feeling rather foolish lately and today was me attempting to overcome..." He struggled a moment to find his thought.

"Yer nerves." This time Angie finished his sentence.

"Yes" His face was serious as he desperately tried to find what to say. "I am normally pretty quiet."

Angela nodded her agreement. "There is nothing wrong with that. You are quiet but not dim-witted." Angela smiled and liked the smile he returned.

"I don't know if my words make any sense but I will just say what I mean and hopefully you can understand."

"I am listening, Ted." The way Angela said his name gave him the courage to speak.

"I think you are special. Not just pretty or smart, but something different and wise and confusing and..." He paused again and just shrugged. "I just enjoy talking to you more than anyone I have ever met. I guess the kiss was just my way to get past the words I don't know how to say"

Angela was silent for a moment.

"Now have I scared you off?" Ted asked again. His hand on hers was feeling infinitely more intimate than it had while in Bradley's hand.

"No, ye haven't." Angela just stared in his eyes and let the moment be intense between them. This blond quiet young man was making a good impression without saying much at all.

They sat and watched the chickens for a few minutes without saying anything. Just letting the moment be quiet and wonderful on the outside while they both let the butterflies and nerves jump around on the inside.

"Just so you know I was listening about Bradley… I have a suggestion." Ted said to break the moment up. The nerves were getting strong again.

"Oh?" Angie laughed.

"Yes, tell Clive. If Bradley cannot get some sense from Clive then there is truly no hope for him…Oh and one more thing. You should not be alone with him anymore."

"You think so?" Angela lifted an eyebrow. Wondering suddenly if Ted was jealous of Bradley.

"Yes, anyone that optimistic scares me. Optimistic people are too capable of getting their way. I have my own foolish plans for courting you that would be very inconvenient if you were suddenly wed to him." Ted said with a laugh.

"I can see how that would be inconvenient." Angie laughed as he leaned in for another kiss, just a small promise; a peck really.

A throat clearing broke up the kiss almost before it began. The two young people both nearly jumped into the air when Clive strolled out into the backyard.

"Ted, you lost me five dollars." Clive said then chuckled and slapped his leg. "The chickens are looking healthy." He said to Angie. Ted and Angie were both recovering from the surprise of the interruption.

"Five dollars?" Ted said rubbing his hand over the back of his neck. His nerves were jumpy but he tried to hide it. His voice gave it away, though.

"Yes. I had you down for next month." Clive winked at Angela, whose blush was purple across her cheeks.

Ted and Angela looked at Clive then each other, a question between the two but they were clueless.

Clive decided to finish the tease and fill them in on the joke.

"The warehouse has been running a bet about when you two shy kids would finally get over yourselves and start courtin'. Gabe wins. He is one lucky…" Clive shook his head and laughed again when he saw that Ted had his face covered with his hand and Angela actually had her jaw dropped.

"We all saw you two sparkin' since November." Clive laughed again and gave a punch in the shoulder to Ted. "Headin' up to see everyone. You two coming up here in a minute?" His voice had the smallest amount of censure. Like they had been bad children and needed to behave themselves. Clive was gone a minute later.

"That was embarrassing." Angela decided to speak first.

"Not any more than me acting like a tongue-tied fool just a bit ago with you." Ted said, not quite as nervous now.

"You said just enough, Ted. I feel the same. There is something about you too." Angela took his arm and gave him a nudge. They walked upstairs together.

"Before we go up I would like to ask something, perhaps a bit belated." Ted took her hand in his.

Angela was silent and waiting, hoping her smile made him comfortable enough to keep speaking.

"Would you allow me the honor of courting you, Miss Fahey?" Ted said with all sincerity written on his face.

Angela could only nod, not trusting her voice just yet. They both arrived to the door with deep flushed cheeks.

❁ ❁ ❁ ❁ ❁

The talk around the table first started with a good dose of teasing. The young people blushed attractively and Amber had to get Gabe and Clive to stop or the blushing would have gone on all night.

"I swear you men love your teasin'." Amber said.

"They do, Mrs. Quackenbush but I do not mind so much. Being teased for courting is far better than being teased for doing something ridiculous or being bad at your work." Ted said with a little wisdom.

"True, young lad." Clive laughed. "Had a few of those moments myself as a lad. Took me a long time to live down a few things that happened around the school yard as a boy."

Everyone was curious but Clive shooed away their requests. He said he had to keep a few mysteries, otherwise he would run out of stories.

"I guess perhaps now would be a good time to get some advice." Angela said, she looked over at Ted, she was momentarily distracted by his blond curly hair but tried to shake it off. "Bradley Henderson is being a pest and I have tried all within my power to dissuade his advances but it has gone further than I know how to handle."

She explained how he had told his family they were engaged then ignored her completely.

"Some young men are lacking in the brains department, it cannot be helped sometimes." Clive said with a serious look on his face. "A pretty face makes them lose all listening skills. Bradley perhaps is lost in a land of delusion. He is like a moth and your lovely red hair, the flame."

Everyone laughed at Clive as he fluttered his eyelashes at Angela, like a lovesick puppy.

"I understand the sentiment." Ted said and laughed right along with everyone else.

"I may have to pay a visit to the Henderson's place tomorrow before they open for lunch. I will try and explain the confusion. I will pass along your feelings to him and his family if necessary. I can stand in the place of a guardian for you, dearie. No need for you to face the eager lad again, especially since he is blinded by love. Hopefully his brains return to him soon." Clive offered. Everyone agreed it would be the best situation.

"I do feel badly, I do not want to hurt anyone's feelings but..." Angela paused.

"Bradley has made a blunder, Angela. You need not concern yourself over hurting him when you have explained yourself clearly." Amber stated. She patted Angela's hand across the table.

"So who wants my cinnamon crumble bread?" Amber stood and grabbed a few plates. Every hand went up.

Angela joined in and Ted took all the plates from her and told her to sit. Angela grinned and blushed but did as she was told. Being courted by the right person made a big difference she realized. As Ted served her a fresh coffee and dessert and sat next to her, she felt a little silly and liked it.

❀ ❀ ❀ ❀ ❀

Clive returned from the Henderson's restaurant with a smile and whistling. Angela was at the counter with Amber. Silas was in a sling around the front of Amber. Playing with a bit of soft clean cloth that was tied in knots. He enjoyed chewing on it with his pink gums.

"So, were you able to talk to Bradley?" Angela couldn't wait to ask.

"Yes, it was not an easy task. I ended up talking to his mother and father as well. I was hoping to avoid it but there was nothing to be done for it." Clive sat down on a stool for a minute as a customer came in. Angela helped the customer find the items he was looking for and took his money. She was very curious about how the meeting with the Henderson family went but she was very professional, no one would have known but Clive that she was even the slightest bit distracted.

Once the bell on the door signaled the customer was gone Clive continued his story.

"Bradley was not convincible by me. It was only after I confirmed several times to his father and mother of your lack of affection were they able to change his mind. I explained that you liked him very much as a friend but felt nothing more than that."

Angela frowned but nodded. Her heart was sensitive to Bradley's feeling a little, but if he had only listened perhaps he wouldn't have let his heart get so carried away.

"Was he able to take it manfully?" Amber asked hopefully.

"No, I can say that the conversation ended with an embarrassing scene. I hope they will be able to calm Bradley down as the day progresses. I know you enjoy the Sunday service, but perhaps this Sunday you should commune with the Lord from home. I cannot say for certain that Bradley will not make a scene." Clive shook his head. Angela could tell he was reliving the scene in his mind. By the look on his face it must have been comical.

"I can stay home, I do not want to cause him further pain." Angela said.

"I will stay with you. We can study the word together. Silas was a bit loud last Sunday and kept interrupting the preaching. This way we can have a peaceful time and no one needs to get emotional or renew their undying affection in front of a crowd." Amber said with a little giggle on the end.

"I will pray that Bradley recovers quickly. There is no need to get so worked up over such a short acquaintance. Truly, we barely knew each other." Angela declared, remembering his glares being so awkward and fervent.

"You barely know Ted." Clive said with a grin.

"I haven't made a scene and announced that we are getting married either." Angela retorted.

"Very true." Clive conceded and gave her a bow. "Well. I am headed to the docks. I have shipments coming soon. Will be checking the warehouses as well. There are some things to be shipped to Oregon. If you wish to send any letters be sure to get them to me by Monday."

Angela nodded and gave Clive a kiss on the cheek.

"Thank you for helping with Bradley. I owe you another one." Angela said with sincerity.

Chapter 19 - Corinne

February 1850 – Willamette Valley, Oregon

Corinne was ecstatic to find a letter waiting for her in town.

JQ was standing at the counter with his wife and Corinne had never been formally introduced so she spent a moment getting to know JQ's wife.

"Pleased to meet you. I am Mrs. Grant and I would happy if you would call me Corinne. I have heard a lot about your son and daughter in-law. I am so pleased to finally get to meet you." Corinne smiled sweetly.

The woman was tall and well corseted around a bigger frame. She wore an elegant blue and white day dress that impressed Corinne immediately. Her eyes were large and had an elegant look to them but the woman's frown was making Corinne a little nervous until the woman lifted the corners of her mouth for a polite smile.

"Charmed." She said at first, a bit haughtily in Corinne's estimation. "I am Millicent Quackenbush." The woman slowly extended her hand and Corinne grabbed it with a delicate shake. "Clive has mentioned you several times when he has visited."

Corinne felt the conversation dragging and tried to keep her face into the perfect picture of politeness.

JQ must have felt the strained conversation so he jumped in. "Millie really enjoyed the Jasmine oil that Clive got from you so much she hired the apothecary to make her a special batch of perfume using it. I was told you made that yourself." He said with enthusiasm.

"Yes, Dolly, who works for me helped with the distillation. We actually harvested that jasmine while on the Oregon Trail. It was growing in abundance in a fertile valley after our train had survived a drought. The Jasmine pods were the perfect time for harvest. It felt like a gift from God at the time. I am so glad that you enjoy it." Corinne realized she had probably said more than Millie wanted to hear.

Millie raised her eyebrows with a show of a smidge of interest but said nothing. J.Q. smiled and stated, "Clive is always excited when he comes back with something new from your place. I just got a box from him. I think this package is from Russia." J.Q. smiled and it warmed Corinne's heart for she saw the same warmth and a few similarities to her dear friend Clive.

"You look so much like your father at times." Corinne blurted out and then felt foolish.

He laughed and nodded. "Well if my hair gets any greyer than I will look like his brother and not his son."

Corinne laughed and saw that Millie had turned and was beginning to walk away.

"It was a pleasure, Mrs. Quackenbush." Corinne was trying to make a good impression but felt that it wasn't going to be easy.

"Yes, dear, a pleasure." Millie said without turning around.

"My Millie has a hard coating but once you are through, it gets easier." J.Q. said once his wife was gone from the room.

Corinne smiled but kept her mouth shut. She nodded and waited while JQ looked for the package. He was back a minute later. She thanked him and met Lucas who was waiting near the wagon. He had picked up the tools he needed and she hoped he hadn't been waiting for long.

"I met JQ's wife today." She said as he helped her into the wagon.

"Oh, that is nice. I haven't had the pleasure." Lucas said. He smiled up at his wife and saw her frown.

"She was a little bristly but JQ says she warms up after a while." Corinne stated and shrugged her shoulders. "I was polite."

"That's all you can do." Lucas said as he climbed up on his side. He tucked her package under the seat to keep it from sliding.

When the wagon was home Lucas had Corinne go in out of the chilly wind that had picked up.

She went inside and got the fireplace started. The coals were still warm enough to stoke with a little kindling.

Corinne opened the small box first and saw Clive's handwriting.

"These are a Russian breed of almonds. They are said to be hardier in the cold than the United States variety. I had the instructions translated by a friend here in San Francisco. See you soon, Clive Q." She read it aloud.

Corinne went over the instructions and opened the linen sack of seeds. She dipped her hands in and felt the dry and hard husks as they rubbed against her hand and each other. She set the bag and instructions aside and got out the letter.

Dear Corinne,

Things are going well since Silas has been born. Had a few unfortunate mishaps with the chickens but they are laying eggs for me nicely. With the cost of feed so high I have to charge a lot for the eggs but people are gladly buying every single egg I have for sale on a daily basis.

Ted Greaves started courting me this week. I like him very much and look forward to getting to know more about him. I also had another young man from the local church that wants to court as well but he is under some misguided idea that we are already engaged. I have told him several times that I am not interested. He is a bit dim, but harmless.

This week I also got the posters made and will be looking for Sean outside San Francisco. Clive is heading out to several different locations to spread the word for me. There is a part of me that wants to give up and come back to Oregon and get away from the city life and the corruption that is plaguing this place.

All I have left is hope. I guess I had this vision that a few weeks in San Francisco that Sean would just stride into the mercantile and we would be reunited. Then we would go to Oregon and live near you. I am now seeing that as an unrealistic expectation. Thousands of people are arriving here and we are told that thousands more will be pouring in every month. I try to stay positive but sometimes I wonder if the darkness within this city will overcome anything decent and all people with good intentions and a soul will be snuffed out in the greed that glitters like the gold dust everyone pursues.

I say my prayers every night for this city, that souls will not lose their way. I see evidence of crime and corruption everywhere. I just look at the ground whenever I walk through the city, only during the day because I do not want to be considered brazen in any way. Because so many women here are prostitutes I cannot walk the streets without being called the foulest things, I have had men bring me gold dust to the counter at the mercantile for unspeakable requests.

I am praying daily that God will bring Sean to me safe and sound so we may leave this place together.

Angela

⁂ ⁂ ⁂ ⁂ ⁂

San Francisco – Ted Greaves

152

Ted spent several days working at the town square. The rebuilding of a firehouse needed strong backs to get the roof on before the rains made the place a mud pit again.

The pay was good but Ted didn't like the group of men he was working with. A lot of miners had been trickling out of the city, as the weather was getting warmer. It was fickle, though. The cold and rain had its way of sneaking in and making a miner's job near impossible. Some camps had stragglers come back to town to say that the ground was not cooperating or the runoff of melting snow was making the situation unbearable.

Ted found the gold miners that stayed behind as a poor labor force. Their minds were always on something else, and their mouths always complaining about how they wished they could be in the streams getting gold dust. It reminded him of his lazy uncle Hank, who always had excuses when it was time to get things done. He always wanted to be fishing or drinking.

Ted could work and have focus and get the job done, he could have meandering thoughts of his dreams, even perhaps a few thoughts of a certain lovely young lady that would keep his mind pleasantly occupied as he worked but he could control himself.

His employers were very satisfied with his work and he was always offered more jobs than he could reasonably do. He took the work he was led to, usually he accepted the work that sounded most interesting and had the best pay, but not always. If he felt led to a job that needed him, he was open to lesser pay if he knew the deed was something that would bless someone.

He had done a few jobs on the docks like that. Some businessmen had lost buildings in the fire and were scrambling to get back on their feet. Ted and a few other laborers helped one man use an abandoned ship that had been towed up to the dock. They stabilized it and with a few nights of hard work had turned it into a small restaurant on the dock. Certain parts of the boat made for a lovely dining room.

Ted was quite proud of helping on that project and looked forward to showing it off to his friends here in San Francisco but also he could see his mother and sister enjoying the storytelling of how he helped turn a ship into a dockside restaurant.

He finished his work for the week and got his pay. He hadn't been to see the Quackenbush clan in several days and he was hoping if he showed up at this hour he might be invited to supper.

He had money to buy a supper at the Henderson's restaurant if he needed to, but he really wanted the companionship. Now that the weather was getting warmer Clive had been talking about a special trip inland. He was hoping to discuss it at length if Clive was around.

Ted walked the streets. The drizzle had slowed and a mist hung in the air but the sun was trying to peek through the haze. The hint of warmer weather was tantalizing.

Ted felt a tug at his heart wondering how the green valleys of Oregon would bloom with the spring sun. How those rugged mountains would lose most of their snowy caps and the land would be fertile and lush, the rivers full of fish and the wild game abundant. His visit had planted a fertile hope in his own heart. He wanted to take his own place in the world, as his own man. He had a pretty good idea where he wanted that to be.

The far-side of San Francisco was bustling with business. The streets were active with wagons and people getting the last of their errands for the day. The newspaper, The San Francisco Chronicle, office was getting a new sign over the door. A man on a ladder did an interesting balancing act to get the sign hung just right. The bank was next door and across the street was the general store that Gabe Quackenbush ran. The new rule laid down by the town was being taken seriously. Buckets of water were in front of every building. After the big fire in December and several other near catastrophes made the council pass a new law, every building was to have a minimum of 6 buckets of water in front of the building. It wouldn't keep a raging inferno away but would speed up the dousing of a small fire before it spread.

Ted stopped at a water barrel and splashed his face. He patted his hair back, hoping he looked decent.

I should have stopped and changed out of my clothes. Ya fool! He thought to himself. In his foolishness he had walked over in his work clothes.

He saw Angela had seen him from across the street. She was waving at him through the window. She was wearing a light-colored dress; her red hair was long and heavy down her back. She had a ribbon in her hair. She looked like perfection to him. His chest swelled at the thought of being near her again. The store had a few customers inside. Gabe and Amber were helping the customers at the counter. Angela was fussing with a display by the window when he entered. The jingling bell was as light as his heart when he saw her.

❀ ❀ ❀ ❀ ❀

Angela was nervous and excited about seeing Ted again. She had watched him since he was halfway down the street. She admired

154

his long strides as he took in his surroundings. She felt an unusual flutter when she saw him splash water over himself.

"So sorry, I should have changed into better clothes but forgot until I got here." Ted said with a look of slight worry across his forehead.

"No harm done Ted. You look tidy enough." Angela consoled him. She hadn't realized she had taken his arm as he approached her. She didn't want to be too forward but also didn't want to pull away and make him feel like she didn't want to be near him.

Ted gave her a smile and glanced at her arm wrapped close to his elbow. He clasped her hand with his other arm for a moment in a gesture of protection. It calmed her right down.

Ted and Angela kept busy talking and Angela half-hearted tidied up a few shelves while Ted held her left arm. It was a funny way to work. Ted teased and Angela blushed and laughed as they strolled through the store. Gabe and Amber finished up with the last of the customers and they all did a quick round of cleaning, Amber had a sleepy Silas in a sling around the front of her. Angela let go of Ted and went to the back for the bucket and rag. She wiped down the wooden counter, used a little bit of oil to shine the wood to a gleaming polish. Ted took the broom away from Gabe with a laugh and set about sweeping the floor. He got the job done quickly but his eyes kept sweeping to the pretty lass at the counter. The place was tidied in short order.

Ted got his wish when he was invited to dinner. They were waiting for Clive to come from the warehouse when they heard a commotion across the street.

Angela turned and saw three men running from the bank, all in a half crouched position. She heard the crashing but the sound didn't register in her mind right away. Glass from the bank windows exploded outward. Finally she realized with certainty that the cracking sound was gunshots. Her body was pulled down just as she saw another window break and then the glass of the store window exploded next to her. The glass was everywhere. Angela felt the scream leave her throat. Amber, Ted, the baby, and Gabe were all with her in this chaos. Ted had thrown her down and landed on her. She heard Ted groan and hiss as he grabbed his leg. He'd been shot.

❀ ❀ ❀ ❀ ❀

She lay in a heap of bodies, glass grinding into her arms and her bad leg had taken a nasty thud on the floor. The ache of the deep bruise made her want to cry out as a panic filled her. In the split second since the world exploded around her she saw blood on Ted's leg and she couldn't see anything else. Where were Amber and Gabe? The baby?

"Ted is hurt!" Angela said weakly. Ted was draped over her side. Still protecting her.

"Amber, Gabe...!" Clive ran in from the back door, his boots pounding on the wooden boards.

"We are fine! Behind the counter." Gabe grunted. "I think Ted is hurt."

Everyone stayed on the ground. Not sure if it was safe to get up.

"There was a robbery across the street. Two men shot up the place. I think they ran off toward the square." Clive said and his voice rose in agitation. He was crouched low and Angela could tell Clive was closer because his boots were crunching on the shards of glass.

"I am ok." Ted said. His voice was thick.

"You are bleeding!" Amber stated emphatically.

"The bullet got me in the leg." Ted was trying to downplay. "It grazed me."

Clive was soon on the floor next to Ted and Angela. He grabbed the edge of Ted's pant leg and ripped it open about six inches about his right knee.

"It was a smidgen more than a graze but the bullet went through. The bullet is in the floor over there."

Angie sat up a little, her arms stinging from the glass embedded in a few spots. Her eyes followed Clive's pointed finger and she saw a silvery gleam. Her eyes went back to the blood on Ted's leg and it stayed there

.

❉ ❉ ❉ ❉ ❉

Angela was overwhelmed with feelings. There were layers of thoughts running through her brain. Wishing she was more like her friend Corinne, who could take care of Ted's wound. Angela tried to sit up after Clive had moved Ted. The throbbing ache from her old leg bruise was stealing her attention. Then she felt guilty when she was thinking about her pain when Ted had been shot.

I am such a fool. Angela thought to herself.

What if Ted gets an infection? He could die. Her mind went to the worst-case scenario. She felt so out of control.

I should be more like Corinne, she thought to herself. *Corinne would know how to take care of Ted's wound and keep him from getting an infection.* Clive's hand on her shoulder interrupted her thoughts.

"How are you Red? You are looking mighty pale." Clive asked as he helped Ted and Angela off the floor. Ted was already standing and leaning on Gabe. They were headed toward the door. A bench was out front. Gabe had mentioned it as a good place to get Ted cleaned up.

Clive lifted Angela from the glass-covered floor. As she put weight on her leg she cried out, and if Clive hadn't been holding her she realized she would have fallen. She gritted her teeth through the pain in her leg and stood. She sagged against Clive's side. She panted from the surprise pain.

"Were you shot Red?" Clive asked, his voice nearly yelling with his concern.

"No, no." Angela said quickly. "My leg, the old wound." She tried to let go of his arm and put her full weight on the offending leg. The pain was excruciating. She knew she needed help to walk. She willed herself not to cry out.

Amber must have been watching the exchange because she had a stool there and Clive was lowering her into it.

"Are you hurting anywhere else?" Clive asked.

"Just some scrapes and a few cuts from the glass, nothing too serious." Angela said weakly.

❅ ❅ ❅ ❅ ❅

The working doctor that was down the street was busy with a bank teller that had been shot. He referred them to take Ted to the hospital. No one was excited about the prospect but Ted was loaded into the wagon and rode through town slowly.

Clive and Amber tried to convince Angela to stay at home but she insisted she go along. She plunked money on the counter for a cane from the store's stock. Gabe and Clive knew they had lost the battle. Angela would go alone if they didn't take her along.

The hospital was a sprawling building on the west side of town. It was not anything impressive to look at but had a few doctors and nurses working. The place had partially burned and been rebuilt after the first fire but the haphazard rebuild made for a slightly functional place to take care of sick people.

Angela remembered the sprawling brick hospitals in Boston. The newspapers were always boasting of the miraculous lifesaving surgeries that doctors were doing. They still had to battle infection and disease with vigor but the shiny corridors and clean rooms seemed a better place to fight the battle than the thrown together building she was in now.

The doctor on the floor found a bed for Ted to sit on. He took a look at the wound and tisked.

157

"The bank shootings have done too much damage today. I heard one of the bank tellers is dead. Wait here, I will clean and stitch this up. You were lucky." The doctor left them all in the hallway.

"Well I guess getting stitched here is better than nothing." Ted said. Clive laughed but Angela was still pale. She wasn't amused by any of this situation.

"You are looking peaked, Red." Clive stated and harrumphed.

Without her permission Clive grabbed her by the waist and hoisted her up on the hospital bed next to Ted.

"Stop being ridiculous, Clive." Angela said, she was trying to hide the irritation in her voice, but she knew she had failed.

"I want the truth now, Red. How bad is your leg?" Clive's penetrating stare made her uncomfortable and she dropped her chin in defeat.

"The old deep bruise is very unhappy." Angela confessed.

She looked up at Ted and saw his concern. He didn't know anything about the accident. She hadn't even mentioned it to Amber or Gabe. She wasn't trying to hide it from them, but she didn't want to be a complainer. The training from her years as a servant were well ingrained, never complain, always be efficient work hard and stay hidden.

"You may need to be off it for a few days." Clive suggested.

"I know. I shouldn't have come. I am sorry I was so stubborn." Angela's voice was subservient and apologetic.

"I know you were worried for your friend, you do not need to be sorry. Your body has been through so much. You need to be careful of having setbacks is all." Clive grasped her hand. The sympathetic gesture was so kind that Angela let her emotions show a little. Two fat tears escaped down her cheek.

"I will take it easy, once I can get myself back to the store. Gabe will have to do without me for a day or two. I remember the ice trucks would come through the streets of Boston. A wrapped chunk of ice would feel so good on my leg right now." She grinned wistfully and she wiped away her two brave tears. "Well, it would feel good and terrible at the same time." She laughed a little.

The doctor came back with a scrub brush and a basin of water and a tray full of items. Angela climbed down when the doctor asked Ted to lie down to make it easier to clean and stitch the wound.

Clive found a chair down the hallway that wasn't in use and set it next to Ted. The doctor had swung the bed around to allow Angela to be on the opposite side.

"I am here for you, Ted." Angela held his hand through the next forty minutes. First the doctor had to remove pieces of fabric and glass that were still in the wound. The first real challenge that Angela had was when the scrub brush and basin of soapy water was put to use. She relived her own pain in the wagon when Corinne and Chelsea had clean her deep shoulder wound that way.

Ted's sandy blond hair was plastered to his head with sweat and he gritted his teeth. Angela gripped his hand in both of hers and kissed it several times to comfort him and also herself.

"Deep breaths Ted, you are doing good." Clive said in a soothing voice. He had a grip on Ted's shoulders to keep him steady. He also knew the pain of scrubbing an open wound.

Angela was given a damp cloth by the doctor and she wiped his face down. Ted's face was more relaxed when the cleaning was done. Angela kissed him gently. She knew it wasn't really the proper time, but she was overwhelmed and just wanted to comfort him any way she could.

"She might just be the best pain medicine on earth, hey Ted?" Clive said in jest.

"I wish I could bottle her up." Ted said, his voice was weak but his smile was big. He grabbed her shoulder and pulled her close again, wanting another one of her kisses.

"Ok, enough of that, I am going to start the stitching, I need you to be still." The doctor said but he was smirking. Even he was not immune to young love.

Ted kept his eyes on Angela through the stitching, he winced and took a few deep breaths but the pain wasn't as bad as the cleaning had been. Angela's green eyes kept him thinking of better things.

❁ ❁ ❁ ❁ ❁

Later that day the decision was made that Ted would be bunking with Clive in the boarding house two buildings over. He had a spare cot that Clive insisted on using. Ted was to get some rest and use crutches for a few days. The stitches would pull if he overdid it. Angela shared some lavender oil and Clive gingerly dripped it straight over Ted's wound and wrapped it. Only a few drops filled the room with the scent that had Angela missing her friend.

"With the good scrubbing the doctor gave the wound I am not as worried about infection, but it will help it heal. Your leg will have an ugly scar. But I don't suppose too many folks will ever see it, depends on how you do your swimming." Clive laughed and Ted did blush a little.

"Ted, you get some rest, I am going to get Angela over into Gabe and Amber's care. She needs to get off that leg and I think I see a few little pieces of glass still sticking out of her sleeve. I want Amber to get a good look at that. Angela may need a stitch or two as well." Clive

159

left Angela and Ted alone for a minute as he puttered around in his small kitchen, the door was open but the two were glad for a moment to talk alone.

"I am sorry that I cannot hold your hand while you are being taken care of." Ted said sincerely. He held her hand as much as he could today. He felt lucky that she allowed him the privilege.

"I will be okay. This pain is nothing I cannot handle." Angela said bravely. She smoothed his hair away from his forehead. "You promise me if you feel any inkling of a fever you will let Clive know. He isn't as skilled as my friend Corinne, but he knows a lot."

"I really enjoyed spending time with her and her family." Ted admitted.

"I am glad, I was hoping that Oregon made a good impression, as well as the folks there." Angela kissed his hand that she held again. Her heart was full of care for this young man. Today proved to her how much she felt.

"There are a few reasons that Oregon is becoming something I think of often. The reasons I work so hard, and save every nickel I make." Ted said while staring into those green eyes again.

"You do like farming then? For Oregon is good for that." Angela asked. It was time to start delving into the questions she had. He was a captive audience at the moment.

"I do, I enjoy the tempo of a farm, the seasons changing and the animals. My father and his pestering brother were always moving, thinking the next place would be better. But every place was good, I think somehow certain people feel the need to move about, my mother called it wanderlust. I want to settle down in one place, become part of a community." Ted shared.

"You are a good man Ted, I see how much stronger you are than your uncle and your father." Angela said. "I hope you understand I mean no disrespect to them. I pray for your mother and her loss. I know she will be so devastated at losing her husband. I remember when my father died. Though, I was young. My mother was so very sad. It was hard on her."

"My father was too easily influenced by my uncle, they had the strangest competitiveness. When my father started courting my mother his brother soon after was dating her sister. They were known as the prettiest girls in the county. I am hoping to save enough here to get us all a fresh start; my mother, my aunt too, and my sister Sophia. It is a strange feeling, knowing I am the man of the family now."

Angela could see a flash of pain cross Ted's forehead and she knew that he needed some rest.

"I should go, but you rest. If I cannot visit in the next day or so I will send a note. I will pray for your speedy healing." Angela kissed his hand one more time.

"Thank you, my Angel." Ted said as he watched her leave, she was leaning hard on the cane and her limp seemed quite pronounced, it caused him to worry about what had caused her original injury. He was tired, and the throbbing pain in his leg was becoming distracting. He was trying to put together the pieces of conversation between her and Clive. Something had happened to her, he was clueless to what exactly. But the words of Clive earlier, 'Your body has been through so much...' made him think. He hoped when Clive returned that he could get more information. The thought of Angela being hurt was not a pleasant one to dwell on. He knew he needed to rest so he spent some time in prayer. Remembering to pray for his family, for himself and a special prayer for Angela. Soon he found sleep, he woke often with the pain throbbing through him but he was able to find some rest. Talking with Clive would have to wait.

Chapter 20

Angela's day started bad and continued on with an equal unpleasantness as Amber set to work on Angela's arm. Her leg was throbbing progressively worse by the hour but when Amber began prying the pieces of glass from her arm she forgot about her leg for a little while. Silas wanted his mother's attention and Gabe was trying to keep the boisterous Silas out of the way. All in all it was a bit of chaos until Angela had her wounds cleaned and wrapped. Angela and Amber talked about Portland and its prospects the entire time. They heard plenty from Clive and they kept talking to keep Angela's mind occupied.

She was exhausted before the sun was setting. She gladly wrote a note for Ted and went to bed early. The day had done her in.

❈ ❈ ❈ ❈ ❈

The next day was a better one for Ted. The throbbing was easing to an ache with the occasional stabbing pain. It wasn't pleasant at all, but healing never really was. Clive wanted a look at the wound and to give it air.

Clive had a pair of thin linen pants he got from the laundry, who sold the left behind clothes for half pennies. Clive snipped one leg short so the wound would be allowed to get air.

"I will keep it warm in here, so you won't freeze yerself." Clive helped Ted out into the small sitting room, where a cushioned chair was waiting near the fire.

Ted got himself into the linen pants with a few interested moves and jumps. One always takes for granted being able to use your limbs in the way they were meant to. Clive and Ted laughed heartily at the silliness it took to get Ted into those pants,

The wrap was tinged a dark brown with dried blood. But had no telltale signs of green or yellow along the edges, which sometimes spelled out infection. Clive had a basin of water and used the water to loosen the bandage once it proved that it had stuck a little to the wound itself. It was slow and slightly painful but they got through it. Clive was encouraged once he saw the wound. It was puckered around the stitches but the redness was normal, no angry streaks or smell of any festering. Clive added more lavender to the site of the stitches but told Ted he should let it get air.

"It feels much better today than yesterday. It isn't throbbing as badly." Ted claimed.

"That's good, you want to stay by the fire?" Clive asked.

"Yes, please. You leaving to get some work done?" Ted asked.

"I am feeling like sticking around today. You want to play some checkers? I could pull up a table." Clive nodded to the folded table in the back corner.

"That would be grand. I warn you. I am pretty competitive at checkers." Ted laughed a little. He was pleased to get some time with Clive. He had some topics he wanted to discuss with this wise man who knew Angela so well.

"Challenge accepted. Let me make some sandwiches. Gabe brought a basket of goodies over this morning. Oh yes, Red sent a note. I will let you read it while I putter in the kitchen." Clive rustled around for a minute and brought the note.

Dear Ted,

I know the days are long when you are stuck in bed. The healing process is hard and I learned from experience that God was there for me every step of the way. A dear friend, Edith Sparks, shared this verse with me on my own healing journey. I share it with you today, so you can keep your hope in the only thing that is strong enough to help us overcome anything.

As I wait on the Lord, with good courage, He will strengthen my heart. - Psalm 27:14

I am doing well, this deep bruise is a pest sometimes and I have to remember my limits. I hope to see you soon.

Sincerely,

Angela Fahey

Ted read through the verse several times. Trying to put it to memory. He appreciated Angela's kind words and he was anticipating seeing her again soon. With them both hurt he would have to be patient and 'wait' as the verse said.

Clive got the table set up a few minutes later, he grabbed a chair from the bedroom and they had a plan formed for lunch and checkers.

Once they were both done eating the checkers match began. They were an equal match for skill and they both were quiet and focused during the first two games. Ted won the first and Clive the second. They both laughed when one would make a good or bad move. It was a fun way to spend the afternoon. After the first two games the pace slowed and Ted wanted to take the opportunity to ask some questions about Angela.

"I overheard you and Angela talking yesterday." Ted said as he moved a checker piece.

"I figured you might be wondering about that." Clive muttered as he thought out his next move.

"She was hurt before. She mentioned in her note today about someone named Edith Sparks. I never met her in Oregon, I have more questions than I can figure out." Ted said.

Clive was taking his time on his move, mostly because of his internal dilemma, would Angela want him to know all? If Ted was interested in courting the girl, knowing her history may help him understand her better if he knew her past. Angela wasn't secretive about it, but he also knew she would not talk about it much. It was still something she was sorting through. Forgiveness was an ongoing struggle when someone hurt a person intentionally.

Clive decided to give up on the move and sat back in his chair. He ran his work-roughened hands through his salt and pepper hair.

"Angela has suffered through some hard things, she is a special girl with a faith that boggles me sometimes." Clive shared.

Ted nodded and sat back, the game was forgotten, and he knew he was going to find out more about the girl that was filling his thoughts.

"Her father and mother died when she was young. Her mother remarried after her husband died. A few years later, her mother died in front of her, it was horrific. Angela's mom was pregnant and fell carrying a washtub down stairs. Angela was only a child at the time. Her new stepfather remarried weeks after his wife's death and sold Angela and her older brother Sean to a work orphanage."

Ted gasped and let his head drop. He would let the story sink in later. He wanted to hear the rest.

Clive went through how Sean ran away from the orphanage and then Angela was then sent to Corinne's Aunt's to work as a maid, but her pay was sent to the orphanage until Corinne pressed her Aunt to get Angela's pay to be given directly to Angela. Ted realized the deep relationship between Corinne and Angela was something that was rare.

Once Clive started telling Ted about Corinne's first husband he was beginning to feel a fire in the pit of his stomach. *This Andrew*

Temple character was sounding more and more like his uncle who manipulated and mistreated women. Ted thought to himself.

When the events involving the night of Angela's accident came around, Clive held nothing back. How Andrew had sent her into danger, then laughed it off later to everyone else. Like she had been a silly girl.

Clive stopped when he could see Ted's distress.

"I know how you feel, Ted, this was a dark time for me as well. My own anger and resentment were tested that day." Clive said and patted Ted's arm next to him.

"Why would someone do something like that? It is truly hateful." Ted asked. Shaking his head and feeling the full weight of how it must have been for Angela's friends, waiting and wondering through the night.

"Through God's grace someone heard her yells, she was so far from the wagon train. I have to believe that God carried her voice. When we found her she was so very broken." Clive's voice broke a moment from the memory of it.

"Corinne did the best she could to clean her wounds and set the broken bones. Even two days later when the infection was settin' in they had to scrub out the wound, like they did for you today. She had been pierced with rocks and tree branches as she had fallen. I was there with her while she was being scrubbed. I held her. We all thought we were losing her." Clive shared. The pain of the memory took him away for a minute. Ted let him have time to continue if he wanted to.

"Andrew, the perpetrator, was actually the one to find her sanctuary with the Spark family at Fort Kearney." Clive said.

"Oh really?" Ted said in disbelief.

"Yes, he was a man eatin' away by guilt. After he got her safely in place with them he came to me. It was a strange night that I haven't shared with anyone. Though I perhaps will with Angela and Corinne together someday. It may give their hearts a sense of peace." Clive scratched his chin, thinking on how to continue. "That young man was so filled with guilt and anger. He confessed all to me, his past, and his rage about everything. How his Ma had always taught him to go to God but he had failed to do so time and time again. That night I helped this bitter and angry young man confess to God. In a moment when I wanted to judge and hurt this person who had caused so much pain, I had to set aside my own anger and help him back to the Lord. It tested me. Watching that young man cry out to God. I so wanted to keep my anger. But yet I could not."

Ted was shocked and quiet, his own anger brewing inside, battling the Christian upbringing of allowing forgiveness to overcome anger.

"I know Angela will not want to talk about this much. She has overcome so much. She is still discovering who she is, not a servant anymore, but as a young woman. Her faith is growing and she is learning to trust again, but it is a fragile thing. I tell you because I can see the bond between the two of you is growing. I don't want you to be another thing she has to recover from." Clive finished by looking into Ted's eyes, challenging him to be a man, not just a boy with puppy love.

"I will endeavor to always protect her." Ted said sincerely. Clive believed him.

The conversation moved along to lighter subjects and several more games of checkers were played.

Ted wrote a note for Angela, he pondered the words for a long time. His feelings for her had changed in a day. She probably would not like his thoughts, thinking them to be pity, Ted wondered. But in his heart the story of her survival only made her more desirable to him. She was fragile, yes, but she was also strong. She was a young woman that God had plucked from disaster and saved. He felt the need to move their relationship further. He wanted the note to say things that perhaps he couldn't say in person.

Dear Angela,

I use the word "dear" because you are very dear to me. As you held my hand yesterday I felt your sympathy and compassion, it meant more to me than you can know. I don't always have the right words to say but I need to tell you how I feel.

I must say I was first drawn to you when I saw you from across the street. Your hair was the first thing I noticed, hanging down your back. You turned and I saw your green eyes. I was lost in them. I could not help it. But I know that physical beauty is nothing to base a lasting affection on, but I will admit that is how I felt upon meeting you. Since that day you have grown in my heart, your humility and strength confound me.

You have such a compassionate heart and a willingness to help anyone. Your patience with my shyness and fumbling is another trait I must admire about you, for without it, I fear I would still be admiring you from afar.

I want to completely be above board and honest in all our dealings. I have the deepest respect for you so I want you to know I did ask Clive about your leg, he has filled me in on your accident from last year. I want to comfort you by letting you know that my feelings for you will never be pity, for I know I would not want that either. It will take a decent amount of prayer and work with the Lord to forgive that man that hurt you so maliciously. I only wish I had been there to protect you, but I know that God was there and you were saved. I am so very thankful for that.

Within you is a woman I deeply admire, for your strength, your purity, your courage and your morality.

I know not how to make my feelings clearer at the moment but to say I care for you very much. I hope I have not shocked you with the affection I carry but ask that if you do not feel the same way you will let me know soon. For I fear my heart will carry me further if you do not dissuade me.

Sincerely Yours,

Thaddeus Greaves

Once the words were on paper the way he wanted, he wrote it out again on a piece of fine parchment. He wanted no smudges or smears. He was now glad for the hours his mother had spent on his penmanship, for their small town school did not focus much on it. His mother believed a good man could write a fine letter with a strong hand.

Ted went to bed but gave the note to Clive to be delivered. Clive didn't wait until morning but left before dusk to pay a visit to his grandson's home. He figured the note would give Angela something pleasant to think on during her healing process.

※ ※ ※ ※ ※

Angela received the note after Clive had been chatting with the adults quietly near the fireplace. Silas was nearly sleeping in his mother's arms and the conversation and her rocking was soothing enough to keep him calm. Silas's cheeks were flushed with sleepiness and they all knew, barring some kind of chaos, he would be asleep soon.

"Ted wrote this for you dear." Clive handed over the note; he enjoyed her deep scarlet blush.

"How is he doing?" Angela asked to keep her composure.

"Today he sat up for most of the day. He bested me at checkers several times, the rascal. Tomorrow I may challenge him again in the evening. I can expect he will be testing the boundaries of his stitches soon. He is not one to be idle for too long." Clive laughed.

"I understand that well enough." Angela sighed. "I am also tired of being so still. This bruise kept me from walking for too long. I do not want to give into the pain, yet I know I must give it rest."

"If it is only aggravated you should see improvement soon." Amber said with an encouraging smile.

Angela was eager to read the note from Ted but waited until Clive had left before she excused herself to her room to go over the letter.

She had to say the first time she read through it she blushed and was overwhelmed. She knew that Ted liked her; the stolen kisses had proven that. But to know how deeply he was feeling, and his reasons were beyond her hopes.

She was attracted to him from the earliest moments she had met him as well. She knew he was a young man of Godly character. According to everyone around her he was a hard worker and had integrity.

She read through the letter several more times. Each time she pondered over his chosen words. "You are very dear to me." The word dear was a sweet endearment that worked within Angela's heart as she thought of him. She wanted to be sure before she let her heart trip over that invisible line. But with how he "deeply admired" her she had to admit to herself that she felt the same way.

It had only been a few weeks of courting and he knew he would not stay in San Francisco forever so she wanted to be sure that he was not obligated to make any promises to her. But what she did know was that he was a good young man, and caring for him was not wrong. She would definitely not dissuade him from continuing his good intentions, if that is what he meant in their relationship. She did not see him as the type to think of women as anything but something to be cherished and protected. She would pray that God showed her his full character, if he was a young man to be trusted with her heart. She finally was able to sleep after prayers and lots of thoughts over the words on that slip of parchment.

❄ ❄ ❄ ❄ ❄

Ted was up and around within a few days. His stitches pulled and itched but he kept himself busy with light jobs that Clive found for him. Since he was educated and could read and handle numbers, he helped Clive with inventory of the mercantile and the warehouses.

While they were busy with counting of sacks of whole wheat kernels, the warehouse was buzzing with voices.

It seemed a fire had broken out on of the docks. The main bells weren't ringing but a small hand bell could be heard through the hubbub of activity.

Clive and Ted immediately joined the throng of men as they ran to the docks to help.

Ted winced as the stitches pulled and he had to slow to a jog, Clive ran ahead and told Ted to take his time.

As Ted saw the small blaze spread across the end of the dock he paused to see if he could help with a bucket brigade. He could not see any kind of organization but knew someone should get one started. He saw a good place to get water and grabbed a bucket full of scales lying near a fish cleaning station. He knelt to the edge of the dock and rinsed it into a semi clean state.

He yelled. "Bucket line!" It was loud enough for a few people to get a hint to join him. A few men found buckets, as were usually plentiful near the docks. Men started gathering near Ted and with a few course words yelled and some cooperation the line was started. More added to it and soon the fire was getting the water it needed to begin to get a sense of control in the situation.

Ted knelt and dipped, so many times. He knew he had ripped a stitch. An older man realized that Ted was bleeding and took over the position and did the kneeling and handed the full bucket to Ted. The system was working, the more men that joined or found more buckets the better it worked. The fire was out on one side and one building was not blazing so high. No one wanted to see the fire reach the city streets again.

After thirty minutes of concentrated efforts by over one hundred men the dock fire was out. There was a little damage to a few buildings that dared to attach to the dock but all could be repaired easily.

Ted and a few men stayed on to help clean up. Ted had no expectation of the situation being anything but a simple clean up but it got out of control so fast. Ted had no idea trouble had been looking for him.

Without a thought Ted felt himself being swung around by the shoulder. He saw the glimpse of his Uncle Hank, looking sweaty and disheveled. He was shocked at the discovery. It took Ted a moment to realize he was in a fight. A fist connected to his jaw with sloppy but painful force. Ted finally registered that his Uncle was really here, now. The last he had seen of this sad excuse for a relative had been before he left the boat, months ago.

"You thieving — —!" His Uncle cursed at him while he swung his fists around again.

Ted was not surprised to realize his Uncle was inebriated. *Probably why his punch hadn't landed as hard as it could have.*

"You need to get your facts straight, old man." Ted weaved away from his uncle's advances.

"You stole my money." His Uncle Hank yelled, he was making a scene but Ted didn't care.

"I took my father's portion and that was all. You killed him aboard that ship. You murdered him when you ate the last of the food. You let your own brother starve and die of scurvy." Ted said as he heard some men gasp; the docks were full of men that lived by a certain code. Aboard any vessel food hoarding or greed was a despicable act.

"He was too far gone, you know nothing you stupid boy." His Uncle Hank slurred through his words and swung at Ted slowly again and missed, it threw off his balance. By then Clive was at Ted's side.

"I think you need to sober up, sir." Clive said with more than a dash of sarcasm in his voice.

Hank cursed at Clive, too. A few men were gathering closer. Ted's Uncle was losing the respect of the crowd quickly.

Hank, in a final gesture, got a kick in and caught Ted on his bad leg right below his stitches. Ted yelled out but didn't fall thanks to Clive who was there and steadied him. Ted could tell another stitch was pulled and blood was soaking through his pant leg.

A few men were grumbling about helping the idiot get sobered and without much ado Ted's uncle was grabbed by four men. Two had his shoulders and two scooped up his legs and he was tossed off the edge of the dock. The water was shallow and he stood up sputtering and cursing everyone around him but he was aware enough that the crowd was against him, too. He had to head away from the dock and find a way to get back on land and away from the angry mob.

Ted and Clive walked slowly a few blocks as Ted explained the full story about how his uncle had been with the group to resupply the ship. The ship had allowed for every family group to send a representative to carry in supplies, fruit was very critical as everyone knew. Ted's father had been showing signs of scurvy and Ted had been concerned. Ted saw that his uncle had hoarded and eaten all the fruit by the time he had gotten back from the supply expedition. There was no other way to say it but that his selfishness had cost his father's life.

Clive was just as disgusted as Ted and did his best to soothe and console Ted but Clive knew there were some things that couldn't be explained away.

"All I know is that my mother has no idea that my father is dead, and I don't know how to tell her. I don't want to write that letter." Ted said as they rounded a corner, they were near the doctor's office. He would need a few extra stitches, they wordlessly walked there.

Finally Clive shared his wisdom. "I know you may have a hard time with it, but I would be glad to help you write that letter. Your mother should know. It will allow her the time to grieve and you do not want her to have hard feelings for you as well. The truth is always better than not knowing. We can pray for her mourning to be over sooner than later. Then she can rejoice in your homecoming whenever that will be. Instead of it being the long awaited bad news of death."

Ted thought it over and nodded.

"I will gladly accept your help and prayer over this." Ted frowned. "She begged him to stay home. Now they will have nothing. The farm payment was not up to date. She certainly will have lost it by the time I even get back. Both her and her sister are skilled at sewing and embroidery and they will be able to get by. But there is nothing good I have to write about besides the few friends I have made here. Otherwise I would consider this the worst place to be." Ted was frustrated.

"Let's get you patched back up. We can work on your letter and get it aboard a ship headed back east soon. She will know and you will breathe and sleep easier for it. I promise Ted." Clive helped Ted the next half block. Ted's limp was getting more pronounced as the pain increased. Ted would have a few more down days again.

Chapter 21

Clive washed his hands outside the doctor's office and took a moment to look up and down the dirty street. There was so much he despised about this place. He had never felt a place could be truly bad, only the people in it. The bay was lovely, and had it not been for the gold found last year at Sutter's mill this town would still be the small port village, with a Christian mission a few miles away and Sacramento being a close enough neighbor to allow for more supplies if necessary.

Once Ted was stitched back up they headed up the street. Ted said he was able to get around. "Just no more fights." Ted laughed.

Amber and Angela fussed over Ted once they heard about the fight and that he had to be re-stitched. Ted was put in the cushioned chair by the fire.

Ted and Angela spent some quality time together that night talking. They were feeling very comfortable around each other and the stories flowed. Ted shared about his family back East and Angela shared a lot about her relationship to Corinne and some of the early good memories of her family.

She read parts of the letter from Edith Sparks, he shared her joy in knowing a good man and woman were blessed with children who needed caring for.

The time was well spent. The two felt closer by the end of the night. Angela was thankful that Ted was able to open up to her. His feelings about the day's events with his uncle had bubbled out of him. She was so sad to hear about Ted's father, and had her own feelings about the despicable nature of his uncle but she kept them to herself mostly. She just wanted Ted to know that she was listening and she cared.

Angela was the one to sneak in a kiss before he left. Clive was waiting downstairs. Gabe and Amber seemed occupied with Silas so as Ted turned to make his way down the stairs Angela made her move. She knew it was forward but she was feeling affectionate and protective. He had been hurt and she wanted him to know she cared.

"By the way, I loved your letter." Angela said and took a step back. She knew that was what he needed to know, that his feelings were returned.

The weeks that followed were good for them. Ted worked long hours but he took every chance he could to spend any amount of time he could with her.

As his bank account grew he realized his time with her was growing shorter. His mother and sister would need him to come back. He knew what *he* wanted to do and he was praying that he was doing what God wanted him to do.

※ ※ ※ ※ ※

March 1850

Angela felt a little silly, she had asked for time away and in the early morning Clive came by the mercantile to pick Angela up. The night before Clive had come to dinner and whispered in her ear that "The malted barley is in." Her heart jumped in her chest but she tried not to show it.

Her and Clive had a secret. It was a dear-hearted and delicious one.

"I need to borrow Angela for the morning and afternoon, Gabe." Clive announced nonchalantly after dinner the night before. Everyone seemed to take it easily with no curiosity. Clive and Angela did enjoy an easy friendship. Perhaps they all thought it was about more pamphlets or going outside the city to ask miners about Sean.

Angela dressed in dark colors and her work shawl before she met up with Clive in the morning. Her heart raced with her secret and she enjoyed the feeling of being the tiniest bit sneaky.

"Yer face is glowing, child." Clive said with a grin. He was excited about their little project and had been working for months to get everything set up for today.

"Yes, I am enjoying myself. I feel a bit like a naughty child sneaking in the cupboard for a cookie." Angela gave Clive a daring wink and grabbed his arm as they started walking towards the outskirts of town.

"We have all the legal papers and the warehouse we bought is on the outskirts. After today we will hire a few more employees to get things underway but it is a slow earning venture. We will have to wait three years for any good results." Clive explained.

"I understand, I am particularly skilled at waiting." Angela felt the cool morning air on her cheeks and thought of the future. Where would she be in three years?

It took them nearly an hour to get to the warehouse in the southern outskirts of town. The road could barely be called that. Mostly miners and wagons traveled the roads with supplies heading to southern parts of California territory. The Pacific Ocean was west and the warehouse was rather nondescript. Snug against a hilly and rocky terrain behind. A sign in front said "Warehouse C" with a "Q & F" underneath.

"Q and F?" Angela asked as they near the front of the building.

"Quackenbush and Fahey of course." Clive gave her arm slight pinch and saw her blush.

"I cannot believe we are actually going to do this." Angela allowed herself to be escorted in and the light from the windows illuminated the operation.

"Are you sure this is legal?" Angela gave Clive a nervous glance.

Clive wordlessly escorted her to the sidewall where a framed paper hung on the wall. "We have a proper license for the distilling of liquor."

"Brian Murphy should be here anytime but I wanted to get a tour in before we got officially started."

"I can smell the barley already." Angela closed her eyes and tried to imagine her grandfather with his own building. Probably a smaller operation, in a shabby barn or even hidden in the woods.

"I discussed with Brian and he suggested we release an early version to whet people's appetites for the whiskey but to also get the word out. The completed product would be smoother but the initial product would definitely have a kick. That is the part that is the least legal. Certain laws declared that the distillation process needs to go a certain way. But since we are not a part of the union and California is only a territory we have time to use the license and make up our own rules." Clive explained as they walked.

Angela enjoyed seeing the operation with the large wooden casks and the huge stills. The stacks of crates full of the secret ingredients, barley, rye, and a few other things that her grandfather had been famous for. Her mother's journals spoke of people coming from miles and traders and merchants spending good money for a jug of his whiskey.

"This seems outside my normal, but somehow doing this makes me feel connected to my roots, the journals are all I have left of my Irish roots. Everyone is dead but for Sean and even he is hidden from me. This feels like I am doing something." Angela said as they finally sat on a bench by the front office. It was a sparse room with a large desk and a stack of papers on the top.

Angela and Clive both perked up when they heard a door open and shut and the sound of footsteps nearby. A large man walked over to the office area and his smile broke open as he saw Clive.

Angela took stock of the man Clive introduced as Brian Murphy. Large and burley with working man's hands, Angela was drawn to him and enjoyed his easy banter with Clive. He would be the general manager. He would be the only one that would know the recipe outside of Clive and Angela. Clive offered him the job from a mill in Oregon. Clive had heard rumors about his managerial style, and how he used to get in trouble with the law in Ireland for smuggling illegal liquor into Britain for his family when he was barely in his teens. He knew the ins and outs of a still, and how to be a hard worker and stay out of trouble once he moved to the United States.

"Let's get the ovens started. The first step is getting the Barley ready." Mr. Murphy said and they all nodded, a bit excited to see how it would all begin.

❄ ❄ ❄ ❄ ❄

The wet thud of flesh hitting flesh pulled Angela from her pleasant dreams. Once her mind was alert she could discern grunts and a few words spoken harshly. *Some things need not be repeated*, Angela thought after hearing some very colorful language. She sat up and felt her long braid pull against her neck, her long, thick hair was becoming a nuisance. She would have Amber trim a few inches off soon, the hair's weight was giving her headaches again.

She carefully eased across her bed to the window that faced the street. The thuds and grunting hadn't stopped and she cautiously peeked over the edge of the window, she did not want to be seen looking. Gabe and Clive had both warned her plenty about not getting caught up in the dark activities of San Francisco, as the gangs were becoming a dangerous and a heavy reality that she had to face. She didn't understand all the politics involved but she heard a lot of rumors. Certain people did not like other ethnicities being allowed within the city. Others wanted law and others a free space to govern themselves. There was a committee for dealing with fire control and others who disliked who was or wasn't being hired for the fire brigade. It was tangled mire of angry men with little outlet besides violence and alcohol, and very little law to protect the rest of the folks just trying to survive.

Angela never left the mercantile without accompaniment, ever.

As she peeked over the windowsill the men below were in a group of about twenty men, it was hard to determine in the darkness with only a few lanterns and torches held by the men on the outside of

175

the group. Angela saw many scruffy beards and dirty clothed men, three in the middle of the group seemed to be exacting some sort of punishment on one man who was on his knees. Angela was horrified to see the state of the beaten man, his face no longer a face but just a bloody mess. She pulled away from the window, her heart pounding, she had no thought but just to stop the beating. She ran in her nightclothes to Gabe and Amber's door and knocked softly.

"Gabe..." Angela whispered harshly.

"I am awake. I will be out in a moment." Gabe whispered back. Angela heard a bit of scuffling from the other side of the door.

"The man outside, they might kill him." Angela said savagely when Gabe appeared from his bedroom, haphazardly dressed, carrying a small wooden bat.

"I just saw myself. I will see what I can do to disperse the crowd. I do not want to bring a riotous crowd on this place but I cannot abide a murder on my front stoop." Gabe said and headed to the stairs. "Help me make noise and light. Perhaps they will be scared away if we open for business."

"Okay." Angela could see what he wanted and followed him down the stairs. They both stomped and made each step exaggerated. Angela grabbed a handful of matches and began to light every light source available. Gabe went to clanging on the woodstove and was rewarded with a protest through the walls from young Silas.

"It cannot be helped, perhaps he will help chase the men away." Gabe said with a shrug.

Angela tried to keep her attention on the task and not on the men outside but in a moment of weakness she glanced over her shoulder and saw some of the men dispersing from the area. The three men were still holding on to the one man but his arms were hanging limply at his side, it seemed the fight was gone from him. Angela said a prayer in her head for him as the fighter let his body fall to the ground. Two of the fighters fled, one stayed for just a moment and looked at Angela through the mercantile window, his face was dirty and one eye blackened, he met her gaze and his glare said volumes. Knowing she had been caught looking she snatched her gaze away in fear.

"He saw me." Angela stated flatly. Gabe walked over to her.

"I saw that." Gabe said slowly, his hand rested on Angela's shoulder as she took a few deep breaths to calm her beating heart.

"It probably means nothing, let's go see if we can help that poor man." Gabe headed to the front door, Angela stood in the doorway, almost afraid to go out on the street. It was still before dawn and without lanterns the street was black and menacing.

"Get me a lantern please, I cannot see." Gabe stated. Then another voice joined in with a groan. The sound of the beaten man brought Angela's fear back to the forefront, she nervously ran inside and grabbed two lanterns and was at Gabe's side in just under a minute.

The beaten man was lying on his side. Gabe was whispering to him, asking him questions. He was answering in whispers.

"Angela, go back inside and lock the mercantile doors. I will leave this man for just a minute to get the doctor as he is just two blocks away. I do not want you to come outside." Gabe's voice was firm. He watched as Angela obeyed his orders.

She watched Gabe leave one lantern next to the man in the street and he took one with him as he began to walk up the streets toward the doctor's residence. Angela prayed for him to be safe as that crowd of angry men were still out there. Angela just hoped that they would be far away now.

Angela spent several minutes near the door watching and waiting, her mind fluttering with fearful thoughts about what she was doing here. Her doubts and hopes mingled inside her.

Clive kept talking about how the city was in growing pains, to have so many show up in such a short amount of months would make any place a den of iniquity. It was interesting dinner discussion but so much more real when a man could be bleeding to death a few feet from her person. Would the men retaliate with Gabe's business for interfering with their fight?

Angela suddenly longed for the lavender fields at Grant's grove, and the pretty back bedroom and the mountains nearby. The peace of Corinne's home was suddenly very desirable. The politics of small town Oregon seemed so much less violent to the gritty, muddy city she now resided in.

* * * * *

Gabe was back with the doctor in a small wagon. Angela watched from the window as the doctor spent several minutes with his new patient, who was bleeding on the dirty, wet street. Angela could hear the man grunting with pain through the door, every sound that escaped him burrowed into her about the dangers of this city, making her question her choices again and again.

Gabe and the doctor were joined by a neighbor who heard the commotion and together they lifted the wounded man into the wagon. Angela was so saddened by the entire event, tired and sad, a few tears escaped as the wagon pulled away. What had the man done to deserve that kind of punishment?

Angela unlocked the door and Gabe walked in, a little damp from the early morning's misty rain.

177

"You can get some more sleep if you are wishin' to." Gabe asked quietly, she could tell he was listening for any noise from upstairs. There were no cries heard so it seemed that peace had settled back in the Quackenbush home.

"No thank you Gabe, it is only an hour from dawn, I can unload some supplies that came in last night. I need something to think on, my head is in a whirl."

Chapter 22 – Corinne
Willamette Valley Oregon

Since the harvest of her lavender had been processed and she had a fresh supply of lavender, Corinne found herself in town more often. She spoke with the apothecary frequently and was working with Dr. Williams, when she was needed. She helped with a few birthings and also as an extra hand when his wife wasn't enough. Corinne was beginning to feel like a part of the community and she was glad to be helping in whatever way she could. She was also excited when the apothecary came up with several ideas about oils that he had read about that were circulating in Europe.

Corinne also had made an agreement of the local natives who were willing to work with her. They shared their ideas with her and Dolly, who both had worked hard at not only befriending them, but also sharing their knowledge and love of nature. They loved to see her drawings and several members of the tribe would bring her samples of new things to try. She would pour through her journals and books and see if they had names in the botany books but sometimes would come to a loss. She would get busy with her drawing pencils and do her best to replicate them. Then, usually with some help from Clive if he was in town or his son J.Q., they would find a supplier or help her find the contact of a person specializing in the plants she didn't know.

The apothecary was beginning a list of requests for other oils that would be very helpful and easily procured from what was available nearby.

"Pine oil is so good for breathing and circulation, you see." He would explain.

"I have heard many applications of pine tea and such but the oil would be very strong, perhaps too strong at full strength. It could burn the skin at the level you are suggesting.

"Yes, but with clear instructions, one or two drops in a 1/4 of a carrier oil to be smeared on the chest could ease the discomfort of pneumonia, I read that a few drops in a foot bath can help increase circulation."

"I see your point. We would have to be very clear on its uses and perhaps only sell it under clear instructions to apothecaries and doctors." Corinne stated, she leaned her head up against her hand. She was tired and her head ached.

"More and more I feel the need to put all this knowledge in the hands of the people in an easier way to understand." Corinne said with a tired voice.

The apothecary agreed. Corinne headed home with a notepad full of notes and a head full of ideas.

❆ ❆ ❆ ❆ ❆

A chilly drizzle fell on Ted's shoulder as he left his building. He had a few hours before he was due at the docks for the job he was working for the next week. Unloading boats from the dock was a good paying job. Extra money for staying the week, 'good labor in this part of town was hard to come by' said all the business owners in town. He was well taken care of. He had set aside a fair nest egg for himself and enough to get passage home as well. Today he was going to tell Angela. His heart broke in his chest at the thought but it had to be done.

Some dogs barked angrily nearby and startled him on his quiet morning walk. Nights were dangerous in San Francisco but the mornings were mostly quiet. The industrious part of this boomtown was beginning to stretch and open doors. Preparing for the day, eating their breakfasts, chopping wood, but the sounds were good ones. The world was waking.

Ted walked past the docks and saw the water was peaceful on the bay. The light rain hadn't come with much wind but it was chilly. Ted grabbed a cap from his back pocket and pulled it onto his head. It had been his father's everyday hat, grey and green plaid, weathered but warm. It made him think of his Pa working the farm back home. He had worn this cap every morning in the harsh winters to the barn to milk the cows and feed the animals.

Once Ted had been old enough he gladly helped his Pa. His Uncle would stop by nearly every day to jaw with his dad over the kitchen table. Mother would complain at least once a week that Hank would eat up all their food with his asking for seconds and thirds over lunch every day. Pa was never one to confront his brother. Ted didn't have his father's issue. He was a fighter, not a brawler, in his mind there was a big difference. Ted was a fighter for justice. He didn't look for trouble like some men, who tried to prove they were strong or good with their fists. Ted believed in integrity and hated to see people being mistreated.

Ted walked passed a few businesses that had folks stirring inside, he waved at a few people that he had come to know. He passed the Quackenbush store and saw Gabriel shoving wood into the fireplace. Ted walked faster so he wouldn't be noticed. His heart was a little heavy and he didn't want to talk to anyone this morning.

He came to his destination and knowing it wouldn't be open yet he sat on a nearby bench that had a canopy overhead. The drizzle was starting to form raindrops and the plop of rain on the roads was comforting. It was twenty minutes of thinking and planning his conversation with Angela in his head before he heard the door behind him open and a small bell chimed the store was open for business.

It was an all-purpose store, less useful than a Hudson Bay store with staples for living, but you could find a variety of goods for just about any situation. It was a bargain hunter's store. Ted had been here many times in search of something, not sure exactly what until he found it two weeks ago. A gift for Angela, he had it held by the owner, a nice Irish man with a bushy beard and an easy laugh. He had thought of that silver bracelet a thousand times a day wondering if it was the right gift. Wondering if it truly would be silly to her or she would understand what it meant to him but also to her.

Mr. Kelly had his easy laugh ringing through the room before Ted had the door all the way open.

"Young Ted, have ya finally made up your mind about the purchase?" His bushy beard was red and brown and bobbed as he spoke. It always made Ted smile.

"Yes, got all my money saved for everything I needed to and can finally say 'yes.' Would you be having a box I could slip it into? Something simple but clean-looking?" Ted asked.

Mr. Kelly wordlessly rummaged through a shelf below the counter. A green wooden box was set before him and Ted nodded with a huge smile across his face. He couldn't help it. Suddenly knowing he was going to buy something for his sweetheart was filling his heart with a pride he couldn't contain.

He plunked down his money and Mr. Kelly gladly placed his purchase in the box neatly.

"May I ask who the lucky lady is?" Mr. Kelly gave Ted a wink and Ted was slightly ashamed of the blush creeping up his cheeks.

"Only if you keep it secret. I would never want her to be shamed by gossip." Ted said seriously.

"On my honor." Mr. Kelly said, his laughter filling the room again.

"Angela Fahey, from the Quakenbush store. " Ted said quietly, his face beaming again just thinking about his girl.

"You could nay have picked a better lady. Never met a sweeter tempered red head in all my liven' life." Mr. Kelly said, nodding and crossed his heart with his hand as a promise.

Ted was out of the store with a green box in his pocket and a skip to his step. His heart was a mixture of happy and sad. He had one more stop to make at the stationery shop and his deed would be done. The store was open and ready and with little fuss he had the owner cut some fancy paper to size of the inside of the box and then allowed Ted use a quill to write the note.

With all my love, Ted.

He knew the severity of the words and writing them down was a promise to him. In his heart he was promising to come back to her. If only he could express to her the words how he felt them when he spoke with her tonight.

He returned to his room and hid the box beneath the bed and under a floorboard. Just in case. The city was crawling with thieves. Ted let out a breath and said a prayer. He let his worries go and them with a start looked at his pocket watch. He gathered his work jacket and cap again and headed back into the rain. He had a full day of work to think on the words.

Lord please help me say them right. He prayed as he walked.

✿ ✿ ✿ ✿ ✿

The day had been a full one. Angela felt a mess of dirt and grime with more than a fair share of child spit up her. She had cleaned her chicken coop out in the morning and then taken Silas for the afternoon. She was hoping for a hot bath but knew with everyone's busy schedule for the day the best she could hope for was the bowl and pitcher method. She would have washed her hair had she been able to get Silas to sleep. He was not sick, hot, or hungry by Angela's reckoning. Just wanting to make his voice heard. He missed his ma and Angela was a poor replacement today. Some days they got on like peas and carrots, just not today. Angela hoped one day to have a house full of children, but knew full well, there would be days like this.

Angela grabbed Silas under the arms and plopped him on her hip. She began the old 'dance around and sing to the baby' system used since the dawn of time. Fast songs, slow songs, even songs she barely knew just to keep the bouncing going as she made up words to the beat.

She was singing a spiritual song when Amber and Gabriel came home from their errands. Silas squealed with delight and held up his pudgy arms for his mama. A grin spread across his red and tear covered face. A true miracle, Angela was amused at how fast his moods could switch.

"Was he nothing but trouble again?" Amber asked apologetically. Her face was in a pout as she accepted her son into her willing arms. Gabe was trying to help her untangle herself from a shawl as the baby was grasping at everything he could.

"He is quite attached to you, but every trip will make it easier. I am certain. All babies grow out of it eventually. So I am told." Angela remembered Edith Sparks and her lessons on child rearing. While

Angela had been bed-ridden she had read every housekeeping and mothering book Edith had.

"You spend a little time for you, Angela dearest. I know Ted asked to come to dinner. You can rest up then put on that new pretty dress we finished. That lace collar Clive gave you was stunning. Not sure what I want to do with the one waiting for me. It's so hard to decide." Amber held a sleepy child and sat in her rocker by the fire to warm up after being out in the damp and cold. Silas was nearly asleep.

The little rascal, Angela thought with no malice. *Babies are babies, no expectin' them to be perfect.*

Angela got a kettle going on the stove in the kitchen and then washed her hair in the warm water in the privacy of her room. After thirty minutes she felt refreshed and clean. She even brought out a small jar of scented cream and used it sparingly on her arms and hands. It smelled of citrus and something else. Angela couldn't name it. She thought of Corinne, knowing that she would know the moment the jar was opened. She would tell her how the flower or herb would be of benefit to her.

Her heart ached to see her friend again. So many months away now made Angela start to feel that empty feeling again. Like she had no real home. She had dreamt of Oregon for so long and she loved and cared for those families like they belonged to her. Yet she was here, chasing down something that may never come to pass. She had repeated 'just one more month' for so many months.

She still felt that urge to stick it out. For just a bit longer… Her talks with God had led her mind to peace on that so far. But she knew with all her heart that San Francisco was not her home. This was temporary.

Her new dress was spread across her bed, welcoming her to put it on, it had a belled skirt so she found the bell hooped slip and got that into place and with a few awkward movements got the dress over her head and she was thankful for the pearl buttons down the front of the dress. Making it easier to dress herself. The fabric was red, black and green plaid. The pearl buttons and lace collar brought out the tiny lines of cream that were weaved in sparingly. The affect was nice against Angela's fair skin and with a dash of powder on her cheeks Angela felt nearly ready to face the dinner with her beaux, *if he could be called that.* She added in her head. She wanted to think so.

She sat with Amber for a bit and once Gabe took the sleeping child to his own room Amber braided and did up Angela's hair. It was too fancy for just a weeknight dinner, Angela exclaimed but Amber hushed her and continued with her pins and fussing.

Angela made a few cups of tea and they settled into a nice easy conversation about nothing important. Dinner was cooling on the stove. A beef roast with potatoes and the bread had been baked fresh yesterday. The women were enjoying the moment of silence.

"What will I do when you go back home to Oregon?" Amber asked a while later after they had drifted in silence.

"I was just thinking on that today. Somehow I know I won't be here forever." Angela said. Not sure how to word her thoughts, she didn't want them to think she didn't love them like her own family; because she did.

"I know how you are feeling." Amber shared. "Gabriel and I are getting more and more uncomfortable in this city full of sin. Gabriel and Clive are talking about a new store in Portland, Oregon. Now that we have Silas to think on this place is looking more and more dangerous."

"Knowing you might be in Oregon someday does my heart good." Angela said, a misty tear in her eye. "I love your family." Angela's voice cracked a bit and she let her words drop. She didn't need to say anymore. She could tell Amber knew everything she meant to say. Angela willed her tears to stay back and after a few minutes of staring at the fire they finally obeyed.

❀ ❀ ❀ ❀ ❀

The steps on the stairs made Amber and Angela both jump with a start. They were both a bit warm and drowsy in their hour of leisure. Clive knocked softly then peeked in. He hadn't wanted to wake up the baby so the new system had been adopted. Ted came in after Clive and they both removed their boots and set them by the door.

"New dress, Red?" Clive whispered. He bent in half and kissed her cheek.

"Yes, and your lace collar. Thank you." She kissed his cheek back and he pretended a halfhearted swoon.

Gabe came from the bedroom with a bright-eyed boy in his arms. Silas seemed to have recovered completely from his fussy day to having a pleasant demeanor for the evening.

Silas went happily into his highchair and played contentedly with the few toys set on the ledge.

"You look lovely." Ted said quietly near Angela's ear when everyone else had left them alone to go into the dining room.

"Thanks, Amber got carried away with my hair though. I think she thought I was going to a ball." Angela smiled and felt the lovely warm feeling spreading through her. Ted made her feel peaceful and safe somehow.

"I would gladly take you to a ball, Milady." Ted bowed and then sat down next to her in a wooden chair he dragged close to her.

"Well, I would be honored kind sir." Angela said softly, enjoying the silly nothings.

Soon they were called to the table and dinner was a success, lots of laughs and sharing to be had.

After dinner the family sat in the living room and talked of business and city rumblings. Angela was distracted and lost in Ted's eyes for most of the conversation.

Clive made an announcement that saved them from a slow insanity.

"I think the rain has finally stopped. You kids get out and see fer yerselves."

Angela and Ted needed no more invitation and excused themselves.

"I don't want your dress to get muddy." Ted said concerned when they got to the street. The mud had been worse but it was pretty wet.

"It's dark fabric and easy to clean. That's why I picked it. I am no dainty flower." Angela said and grabbed his arm. They walked to the pier overlooking the bay.

Ted used his jacket to clear the water off a rock ledge and they sat watching the light fade into dusk.

"You have something to say." Angela said. She liked the feel of his arm tucked next her but his silence was interesting.

"Yes." Ted said nervously.

"Take yer' time." Angela said, grinning and hoping he would be able to talk soon. He was making her nervous.

Ted laughed, leaned and rested his head on her shoulder. The action melted her heart.

"I have some things to say, some good, some bad." Ted blurted out. Hating the way it sounded.

"Bad news first. That way we end on the good." Angela was trying to stay positive ignoring the jolt in her stomach.

"My time in San Francisco is coming to an end soon." Ted lifted his head and looked at the side of her face.

"I knew you would be heading back to your family." Angela said. Her voice was a little stiff.

"I have to go and make sure my mother and sisters are okay. I want to bring them west." Ted said simply. Hoping she understood his sense of duty.

"What happens if your mother wants to stay there?" Angela asked the first thought that popped into her head. She was getting left behind again.

"I have thought of that. I have saved enough to get her settled but I will be coming back. I have a very good reason to come back, ya know." Ted's voice had the hint of a smile.

Angela found enough bravery to look into his eyes. She was scared to see weakness there, or even lies; promises of something and then just another person to leave her.

"I have been working hard and planning a future. I just cannot finish the plan until I know my family is safe. My sense of honor cannot do anything else." Ted said seriously.

Angela finally let out a breath she'd been holding. It clicked into her brain what he was saying. It was the kind of man he was, one that takes care of his responsibilities. It made her love him more. It settled her heart and calmed her fears.

"I trust you Ted, I know your heart is honest and you will do what's right." Angela kissed him after she spoke.

Ted wiped tears from her cheek after her sweet kiss.

"We have a few weeks to talk and spend time together before I go. I am going by land. It will be faster. No wagons, but just heading back on horseback with a group of scouts that are friends with Clive. We are meeting up in Oregon City and leaving once the mountain passes are clear.

"I will pray you have a safe journey. The overland route is a hard one." Angela said softly. She didn't want her voice giving away as much emotion as she felt.

Ted stopped talking and looked into her green eyes for a long moment. Leaving her was going to be the hardest thing he had ever chosen to do.

"Ya know, watching my father die aboard that ship was difficult. I know I don't talk about it much but I couldn't understand how he had done it. How he had left my mother and two sisters behind when my Uncle Hank had pestered and prodded him for weeks about coming here. The funny part is that my uncle hadn't even paid his fair portion. At the last minute he had come up with some lame excuse why he was short the ship fare. My dad had taken the crop sale and sold all the cattle to pay our way. And also then pitched in some for Hank, I keep thinking over every word him and ma had before he left. How she cried and begged him not to go. Just like your eyes are doing to me now. Here you sit so brave trying to accept one more person leaving you behind. I cannot be a good man, no matter what I do. All I have wanted to tell you is how much I love you and all I can think about is my Ma stuck on our barely functioning farm back east and wondering if they will survive to the spring. Then I think about you and wondering how much a chance I will have earning your love if I leave you here." Ted's eyes got misty at the magnitude of the moment.

"You love me?" Angela said, wiping a tear but her face was no longer as sad.

"Desperately." Ted said and grabbed her cold hands.

"You don't have to earn my love anymore. You already have it, Thaddeus Greaves." Angela stated without blinking.

"How can you, knowing I have to leave. I hate to, but I have to." Ted said again. He couldn't believe that she could forgive him for that.

"My heart is growing stronger. I can thank God for that. I have said goodbye to many people. There has not been one person I have said goodbye to that I ever stopped loving." She paused and took a deep breath. "With every part of me I will pray and wait, Ted. Just as I pray and pray for my brother, and pray and wait to see the sister of my heart, Corinne. My love for them only grows. Just as it will for you. If you never wrote a word to me, and I never heard an utterance from those lips again I would still love you. Your honor and duty to your family only increases it. You are willing to face the harsh wilderness to be certain of their safety. To me, there is no higher charge than to take care of your family. Go with my blessings. I will write to you, and if you allow it so I will write to your mother. It is the least I could do after all, she made you. I am quite thankful to her for raising such an a honorable young man." Angela gave him a fierce hug and held on and let her tears fall over her cheeks and they spilled over his jacket.

"I have something for you." Ted said as she finally pulled away from the long embrace.

Angela smiled and just waited. Ted saw the tear stains on her cheek but she was smiling. He could not contain the love for this girl. She was everything to him.

He pulled out the green box and saw her grin get wider.

"A gift. Oh Ted."

He placed it in her hands and she quickly turned it and began to open it. The sky was starting to turn to dusk but the light behind them showed enough for her to see the silver bracelet.

She picked it up and sighed. "It's so lovely." She grabbed the note and saw his words. *With all my Love, Ted*

"Help me get it on." Angela admired the decorative chain and wanted to see it on her wrist.

Once it was on, she held it out to read the single word engraved on the silver oval centerpiece of the bracelet. ~ HOPE ~

"It is the perfect gift. I love it so much Ted." Angela hugged him again and he kissed her as she tried to sit back.

"I thought it was the perfect thing for us. Not just you but also for me. God has shown me much about myself since I came to

California. All I have is the hope for the future. God is helping me hang on to that hope as you do with your brother. I want you to remember to never give up on the Hope for us." Ted said and kissed her again.

"It is the perfect word for us. We will live on hope." She held his hand and leaned on his shoulder. They had said so much tonight. For now she wanted just to enjoy being near him. They walked back after a few more minutes. They spent the evening playing checkers and talking with the Quakenbush family.

Chapter 23 - Corinne

April 1850 – Willamette Valley

Corinne's first batch of lavender oil was a success. They had the labels attached, the logo of Grant's Grove at the top of each label made her so proud, surprisingly drawn by Lucas. It was a flowering tree. The brown bottles were filled and topped with a fancy dropper with a rubber tip. Corinne always appreciated it when a pharmacy included the droppers so she found an affordable way to do it. The Grants now had enough dropper bottles stored away for two years of sales. Corinne was pleased with her success and was working with Dolly over the last few weeks packing up the orders for her first batch. It was harder than she expected to get the organization down but with the help of Clive and her father, Corinne got her orders into a working system.

Lucas had a few men working with him constantly clearing ground for more planting. There was half the acreage left to plant but lots of rocks, bushes and small trees would have to be cleared. Lucas was always happiest when planning something for the fields. He was so excited about irrigation and how the land was so fertile and how they should handle crop rotation for the best product. Corinne felt they had an amazing partnership and their newlywed stage was going well. The first year had its adjustments, learning to accept each other's strengths and weaknesses was a challenge.

Corinne felt so lucky to have found a man that accepted her dream for something outside the normal role for a woman. Her strengths in the kitchen were fair to mediocre. She could make a few staples but Lucas was a good cook himself, and shared in the duties when Marie didn't drop off dinners. The short walk between the properties made this arrangement a little too easy. Corinne was nervous for a long while that Marie would feel used or under-appreciated, but soon she found out that Marie Harpole showed her love with food, and she took pride in taking care of her stepdaughter while she conquered the world.

Corinne and Dolly loaded up the last box of the day and headed out of the warehouse behind the greenhouse and into the rainy weather.

"Are you going to stay with Lucas and I tonight or ride over to Chelsea's?" Corinne asked Dolly.

"I think I will stay close by. The clouds over Mount Hood seem …" Dolly searched for the word in English. "Dangerous. Yes?"

189

Corinne couldn't tell if Dolly was asking or telling but her half Hopi Indian friend was picking up English well and with a glance to the east she indeed saw some dark clouds lingering.

"Good, let's get inside." Corinne grabbed her friend's hand and pulled her across the path to the Grant cabin. The lights inside were glowing in the window.

They wiped their feet on the rag rug at the entrance.

❄ ❄ ❄ ❄ ❄

Corinne had gone early to the doctor's office to take a look at her healing rash. She was going to stop by the post office to ask about mail from California territory too if she had time.

The doctor and his wife Persephone were so kind and they had a lovely chat before the examination and Dr. Williams said the balm had been working.

She was staying away from the sticky sap and things were clearing up fast.

"Doctor, I think it's silly but two different women have told me that they think I am pregnant." Corinne stated bluntly when she got brave enough.

"Do you have any symptoms?" He asked.

"Just tired, and my dresses are getting tighter across the chest, and it is tender there too." Corinne blushed. She had helped this man deliver two babies within the last year but she blushed over such silly things now. She felt foolish.

They discussed her monthly flow and the fact that she hadn't realized that she had missed her cycle for several weeks. The doctor supposed her to be several months pregnant. He gave her some good doctoral advice about being careful on horseback and overworking.

"I know your drive is like your father's, you will need to remember to eat consistently. No skipping meals just because you are busy." The doctor knew her too well.

She suddenly was at a loss for words. She thanked the doctor politely and said little to his wife but the perfunctory goodbyes.

She went through her errands in a fog. She had really felt Marie and Dolly were being silly when they claimed she was pregnant. She didn't give it any tangible thought. Now with the doctor's agreement she felt different. Her mind raced with ideas and thankfulness and a little bit of fear of the unknown.

She rode the buggy home then wondering where her husband might be, took a walk to her greenhouse to see if anyone knew where she could find him.

She had good luck for he was there. He was replacing the metal part of a spade and he looked up to her and smiled charmingly.

"Hello, husband." Corinne said simply.

"Hello, my lovely." Lucas replied. He saw her secret smile and took a longer look and smiled back in curiosity. He had playful eyes and his smile soon matched.

"Come for a walk with me if you have time." Corinne said. She saw him nod and set the tool down.

The wintery air was brisk but not cold enough for snow in the valley. The mountain passes were well covered but the valley had very little snowfall that stayed for long. Lucas and Corinne walked outside, hand in hand, for only a minute before Lucas broke the silence.

"Are you going to tell me? Or shall I guess?" Lucas swung her hand behind his back forcing her closer to him.

"I am trying to form the words to say it right." Corinne said quietly. With Lucas staring at her so intently, it was distracting.

She gathered her courage and blurted it out.

"You are going to be a father!" Corinne said loudly with a laugh at the end.

Lucas's free arm grabbed around her and he kissed her passionately then let out a whoop.

"My darling," Lucas kissed her and looked deep in her eyes and whooped again. He said so many words with those eyes of his.

"You are going to make a wonderful mother." Lucas said slowly and sincerely and the words brought tears to her eyes. She wasn't certain why.

Lucas wiped away her tears with his strong hand and they wordlessly walked to her parents. Lucas knew she would want to share the news.

❄ ❄ ❄ ❄ ❄

Marie shrieked and laughed with abandon when the news was shared. John Harpole gave his daughter a bear hug and had misty tears in his own eyes. Cooper made everyone laugh when he made his presence known.

"It better be a boy." He stated emphatically.

They all laughed.

"It will be what God made it to be." Marie told Cooper with a laugh. Her smile was huge and her dimples deep in her pretty cheeks.

Corinne and Lucas stayed late and ate supper with them, talking of all things to do with babies and family. It was only when Corinne schedule was brought up that Corinne felt her first bit of discomfort.

"I am glad the doctor has warned you about not over doing it. I think I can finally convince you of the housekeeper we so desperately need." Lucas stated lightheartedly.

Corinne's face dropped. Lucas noticed that look in her eyes. Her brick wall was going up.

"I do not want to hire help!" Corinne said with finality.

Marie saw the struggle and tried to add wisdom to the conversation. "Dear, I am so thankful for the help I get. I love to be in the kitchen but between feeding so many families and helping your father with management and helping with Cooper's school lessons, there is just not enough me to go around. Having help is nothing to be ashamed of."

"I know it is not a sin or anything…" Corinne was starting to feel defensive. She felt strongly about her convictions and didn't want to discuss it in front of her father and stepmother. "It leaves a sour taste in my mouth to even discuss it."

"Well darling, I know you told me of how your Aunt's household was run. But not everyone mistreats the people in their employ." Her father chimed in, adding to her humiliation.

Corinne was getting frustrated. How could she explain her feelings to them when they sounded foolish even to herself? But she did NOT want to budge. "I know how to cook, it just takes away time in the greenhouse and laboratory." She added and felt foolish. They all knew this.

"I think Corinne is getting upset. I will take her home so she can rest." Lucas said wisely. He hadn't meant to push her but he thought maybe her parents could help him in this long-standing disagreement between him and Corinne.

Corinne and Lucas said their goodbyes awkwardly and they were silent on the walk to their property. What had started as a beautiful day had ended with Corinne in anger and not even willing to speak to her husband.

The cabin was dark and cold when they opened the door and Lucas was quick to get a lantern lit and get the fireplace started, the night was too early to go to bed but Corinne wanted to be in a different room than her husband.

A few minutes later she sat on the bed she shared with her husband in the dark room, just pouting.

How dare he bring up the servant issue? Lucas knew she had repeatedly told him over and over how she despised the idea and would not do it.

The plan had been working so far because she got help from Marie and Chelsea upon occasion. They weren't servants and it worked out perfectly. Well, most times. Sometimes she could tell that certain days it was a burden on them but Corinne tried not to abuse them. They always said they were glad to help. *Why did Lucas insist on having his way?*

"You want some heat in here while you plot my demise?" Lucas asked from the doorway. It startled her and she gave him a glare. His sense of humor was usually charming, but she was in no mood for it.

Wordlessly he started a fire in the fireplace. Corinne felt awkward with him there and wished he would hurry up with the task so she could go back to her own thoughts.

When he was through he came and stood in front of her. Corinne willed herself to keep her eyes down and not look up at him no matter what.

He finally kneeled in front of her. He took a hand and brushed it along her cheek tenderly. She only glared at her husband.

"Don't try and charm me now, Lucas. I feel betrayed and don't want to talk to you right now." Corinne said flatly.

"Betrayed is a strong word." Lucas said calmly. She did not like arguing with him when he was calm.

"You know how I feel yet you brought it up in front of my father and Marie." Corinne sniffed and tears started flowing. "How dare you?" She said weakly.

Her composure was lost and though she knew she was overreacting she sobbed into her hands. Lucas tried to comfort her but she pushed him away. "Please leave me alone." She asked through her sobs.

Lucas nodded and left her as she asked. She lay on the bed and sobbed the night away.

❊ ❊ ❊ ❊ ❊

Corinne awoke with hairpins poking her head and she was still wearing her clothes from the night before. She had never even crawled under the covers. Lucas had not used the bed. The first thought she had was to be mad but the second thought had a little more reason. She had asked him to leave. Her head was aching from crying and she felt around her head with her hands and her hair must have looked a fright. Pins were falling out and she could feel snarls and clumps of hair that had escaped and tangled as she tossed and turned. She probably looked like she felt – dreadful.

She remembered the evening and felt a surge of her same feelings. But she wasn't sure how this could be resolved. She was allowed to have an opinion in her own house. She pulled the pins out the best she could and brushed out her brown hair. It probably looked

193

a little funny after sleeping in the pins but she tied it back with a ribbon and let it be. She changed into a different dress and left the wrinkled one on the bed. She would deal with it later when she had time.

She peaked out the door and saw Lucas setting in his cushioned chair by the fire.

Blast! She was hoping to avoid talking to him yet. She had no idea what to say.

"Good morning wife," Lucas said politely.

Corinne wanted to grimace but kept her composure. It's hard to deal with someone that remains calm through everything.

"Good morning Lucas." She replied.

"There's coffee for you." He said.

"Thanks." Corinne muttered. It smelled good but she didn't want to admit it.

She looked around the kitchen and realized there was nothing to eat. Usually Marie or Chelsea would bring a basket of bread or something by for them. She couldn't remember whose turn it was.

"Has Marie come by yet with anything for breakfast or lunch?" Corinne broke her silence.

"Yes, but I sent her away." Lucas said and took a big swig of coffee. He gave Corinne a look that said he was ready for the fight that was coming.

"You sent her away?" Corinne said slowly.

"Yes, I told her we appreciated her help but we can do our own cooking from now on. She has been a blessing but we have been taking advantage of her kindness." Lucas stated and sipped more of his coffee.

Corinne was deciding in that moment whether all her manners were going to be used for good or she was going to toss them out the window.

She took a few deep breaths and decided she was not going to even acknowledge the issue. He wanted to cook then he could go ahead and cook.

"Well, I wasn't hungry anyway, fine." Corinne poured her coffee and added a little bit of sugar. She noticed it was the last of it. The bag in the pantry was empty. She would need to go to the store and get more. The pantry was almost always empty. When Angela had been there she had disobeyed Corinne's wishes a few times and went to town with Marie and they stocked the larder with a few necessities. Corinne realized that if they were going to have anything to eat today it was going to be pathetic and barely palatable.

The next ten minutes were torture. Two people sharing a house sipping coffee in a silent standoff. Afterwards Corinne redid her hair in a simple bun and without a wave she murmured a pert 'goodbye' and left.

❆ ❆ ❆ ❆ ❆

By midday Corinne was tired and hungry. At first she pouted and barely spoke to anyone. She wasn't often in a bad mood so her few employees just took it in stride. She wanted to be emotional but she forced it down. She was feeling betrayed and hurt by her husband's actions.

It took her a few hours to get over her pouting, she moved on to thinking and plotting how in the world she was going to eat anything. Her kitchen wasn't stocked for any kind of meal. She let the thought go and realized that she would have to go to town. There was no other way. She prayed for the first time that day, just a short prayer that God would help her not be angry with her husband. She wasn't sure if she really meant it. But she wanted to stop feeling that pit in her stomach. After a little while she was praying again that God would help her husband see her point of view. That prayer felt better. She was letting go of her hurt a little bit and now was starting to actually work instead of staying focused on the issue with her husband.

She spent some time with Dolly on her plans for the lab. Dolly was so smart and diligent in her work that Corinne just left her alone to her work most days. She was always coming up with smart ideas and Corinne appreciated her more every day.. It was while talking with Dolly that an idea sprung up inside her that shocked her to the core.

She had no problem paying any of her staff. She had two people working in her greenhouse during the week. Dolly was in charge of her lab when she wasn't there and even had recently hired someone else to learn how to do some lab techniques so it could run all night if it was necessary for the oil that was being distilled.

She was more than willing to have employees, just not help in the house.

She excused herself to Dolly and took a walk to the barn. The available stable hand got her buggy hooked up within a few minutes but the entire time Corinne kept thinking about the many arguments she had had with Lucas about a housekeeper. She had been so resistant because of Angela, and probably her Aunt Rose who had treated her staff so poorly.

She told the stable boy she was headed to town and to please let Dolly and Lucas know if he came around.

Corinne prayed the entire way to town. She knew she had to make things right with her husband and the only way to do that was compromise. She had been stubborn and hadn't listened. She had ruined what should have been a beautiful night of celebration and turned it into an unnecessary rift. She knew Lucas, his easy temperament was very calm and forgiving, but it didn't mean she should abuse it. She had to make this right.

She made it to Clive's shop and knew he would know who to talk to about getting help.

She was glad to see Clive at the counter. He was only in town a few more days before he planned to go back to California.

"Hello sweet Darlin'," Clive said with a grin. He was talking with his son about inventory issues but gladly set aside the talk to see one of his 'girls'.

He took her to his office and sat her down. She fully explained her issue, the fight, the pregnancy and her temper tantrum.

Clive congratulated her on the pregnancy but he kept it mild. The tears in her eyes told him that she had more to say.

"I have been praying the whole way here. I need a housekeeper, Lucas has been begging me for so long but I was stubborn. I prayed today that God could find us someone that needs the job and will be blessed by it. I know the struggles Angela has had over being a servant. I don't want to make anyone feel lowly. Truly!" Corinne said sincerely.

"That is a good thing to pray for and I might know just the right person, but I want to share something with you." Clive handed her a clean handkerchief for her to dab at her tears. "Everyone on earth was made for a purpose. There are doers, builders, farmers, planners, managers and helpers. I see mothers live their lives with just as much purpose and drive as any company owner. Everyone has their strengths. To some, a housekeeping job means a comfortable living, a room and a family to take care of. To others it would be a burden they would resent. Angela was forced into servitude. That is very different than being given a job you have been searching for."

They seemed to be the right words and Clive could see the tension leaving Corinne's shoulders.

"You think you might know of someone, really?" Corinne asked.

"Just yesterday Pastor Whittlan came to me with a prayer request and news about the young lady who had stayed with him and his wife until last fall. Violet Griffin is her name. She is your age, but is an experienced cook. She is married but her husband left for the Gold Rush and she hasn't yet heard from him. I guess the small house they lived in together is falling apart and she is looking for work just like you are needing. She needs a roof and an income without her husband around. It is becoming a common problem. I could enquire if she is still available, I could bring her by if she is. From what I hear she is in desperate need. The pastor and his wife just took in two orphans and have no room. They gave rave reviews on her cooking and hardworking attitude. They said she was sweet as pie." Clive grinned.

"That will be lovely. Now I need to do some shopping. We have no food at the house to prepare and we have nothing to eat ready. I better get home and start something if we are to eat anything today."

❊ ❊ ❊ ❊ ❊

As Corinne walked into the front door she could tell Lucas was there. She heard a rustling around. Lucas peaked his head around from the hallway and gave his wife a wary smile. He was checking the emotional temperature. He seemed to feel safe to enter the room fully but didn't say anything, he just watched his wife calmly.

Corinne tried to give him a kind grin, then she shed herself of her coat and scarf. She had taken precautions with the weather being unpredictable and wet at short notice. She settled the packages of food to be prepared on the table then walked toward the middle of the room just a few feet away from her husband.

"I would like to apologize, Lucas." Corinne said. She was standing a few feet away from her husband and was hoping he would approach her soon. She wasn't sure if he was holding any anger or resentment inside from sleeping separate from her, or if her words had hurt him.

Lucas nodded but stayed where he stood, his arms at his sides. Waiting for her to continue. She thought.

"I went to bed angry, and I was stubborn and I didn't listen or compromise or any of the things I should have done." Corinne said. She could feel shame bubbling up from inside her. Lucas was so good to her. Why had she fought with him? It seemed so stupid to her now.

Lucas lifted his arms up as a signal and she ran the three steps toward him and buried her head against his chest, where it fit so perfectly.

"I forgive you, Cori. I am sorry if I was a bit stubborn today myself." Lucas admitted.

"No, you were right. I needed a shock to wake me up." Corinne said against his chest. Lucas held her away from him a second to look into her eyes.

"I love you Cori girl." Lucas said and wiped away a few tears that were making trails on her pale pink cheeks.

"I love you, and I went to town today to say I'm sorry in a special way." Corinne said. Her eyes had lost all the anger from the last

197

day and they were peaceful. "I talked to God and knew that I needed to compromise."

"Come let's sit." Lucas led her to the cushioned sofa by the warm fireplace. Corinne explained her visit to Clive.

"So he may be coming by with a housekeeper this evening for us to talk to?" Lucas asked after he let her talk.

"Yes, I bought a few things to throw together for a simple dinner. I should really get to work if we will eat before nightfall." Corinne said. She was nervous about the meeting but she knew she had done the right thing.

"Let's make supper together. It's partly my fault that we have nothing to eat." Lucas grinned and stood. When his wife stood he grabbed her in a passionate embrace. His kiss and long embrace said volumes that words couldn't say about how he felt about her. It was hard to argue but the compromise tasted sweet on Corinne's lips as her husband released her and they playfully went to their kitchen and prepared dinner together. It was healing to let the anger from the night before fall off her shoulders and escape the house. The tension between them was gone.

After dinner Corinne spent some quality time with a quill and parchment. She wrote a long letter to Angela. Fully describing her stubbornness and even apologized again for her actions and not allowing her to help around the house. It was a blessing to tell her friend about her pregnancy and to be honest about her flaws.

She read the letter to Lucas and he laughed over her descriptions of him.

"I am not a saint, Cori." Lucas said with a chuckle.

"Well, you are so patient with me. You seem saintly enough." Cori said from her seat on the arm of Lucas's chair. He reached around and gave her side a squeeze just to hear her squeal.

"We all have our vices and flaws dear. Perhaps mine is loving you to distraction." He said with a mischievous grin.

"How did I get so lucky?" Corinne set the letter on the nearby table and with a deft move she went from the arm of the chair to Lucas's lap. Lucas didn't seem to mind.

Chapter 24
Willamette Valley - Oregon

Violet Griffin's heart was light as she gathered her things. She looked to the ceiling where the leaks were clearly showing signs of mold and rot. It had been a few weeks of living here with the wind and weather wreaking havoc on the home she had shared with her husband, Eddie. She had been so desperate just a few hours ago. She had tried to move back in with Pastor Whittlan and his wife but they had just taken in two orphaned children and had no more room for her. Their house was a small one next to the Spring Creek Fellowship Church. It only had a small loft and two rooms. She knew they had been spreading the word about her predicament, people were praying for her.

The windstorm a few weeks back sent a tree through the roof. A few men from the church showed up to help remove the tree and patch the roof with a tarpeline but with so many men gone in the gold rush to California her home repairs were forgotten in a town that was in desperate need of more strong backed lads than they had.

Violet said a prayer of thanks again out loud as she packed. Clive Quackenbush, the owner of the local Hudson Bay store, and a member of her church had stopped by just minutes before. He had found a potential live-in housekeeper position.

"God's blessings always arrive in time." Violet said to the room. She began humming a spiritual song as she grabbed a worn brush and with the help of an old, slightly cracked mirror on the wall she unpinned, brushed and re-pinned her long blond hair into respectable form.

She grabbed the few books she owned and set them in the trunk by the door. She wanted everything to be easy to get to in case she got the job.

Clive was coming back for her in an hour so she wanted everything to be ready. She put all of Eddie's clothes and personal items in the food pantry, where they would stay dry and closed away from the wet weather that leaked in so many places. The leaky rooms were a mess, she had no idea how she would keep the floor boards from rotting if she wasn't here to empty the buckets when it rained but she was at the point of considering this house as a loss. The owner who had rented the land was off to California as well. She had tried to find him to pay the monthly fee and his home had been empty. Violet didn't know the right course of action and sought advice from the local sheriff. He told her that if the landlord wasn't collecting his rents she had the right to stay there until he told her to leave. The sheriff had been kind and told her that he would back her up if there were any trouble. He was also a member of Spring Creek Fellowship Church.

Violet owned three dresses. One was for Sunday meeting and the other two were getting threadbare but she had no complaints. She had a warm shawl and a nice work apron that covered her daily dresses. She had no need to be fancy anyways. Her husband Eddie had told her many times that she was his beauty and would be in a satin gown or a flour sack. Eddie had been sweet to her. He had started courting her only a year ago. He would come by wagon with several of the lumberjacks every Sunday for service. They all worked out on the edge of Mount Hood and the surrounding area, but they always made it to church on Sunday.

Violet stayed with the Pastor and his wife and she sometimes sang a hymn in front of the church. She loved to sing to God and though she had a shy temperament on most days at church she felt safe. Singing was her way to thank God for all He had done for her. Eddie was not shy about how her voice and her sweet spirit touched his heart. He may have been a tough lumberjack by profession but he had the heart of a gentleman. He had a Godly heart and won her over. Seven months ago they had been married.

She stayed home while he went off for days at a time to do his work. His boss at the lumber mill sent the men to different places to prospect for good timber. His crew would be back after a few days and Violet enjoyed every day they had together. Eddie wanted to save money so he could afford to get land and build his own little farm. Getting land in Oregon was affordable. But building a farm took startup money. Eddie had a plan. He thought that with Violet's skills at baking and cleaning she could help them save. Maybe she could work as a cook or housekeeper. Violet knew that would be good work for her. She had been doing that for the Pastor and wife. She loved being in the kitchen and taking care of a home was just part of her nature. She found pleasure in making things tidy. She had been doing a little business selling her bread to the lady at the boarding house in town for a little extra money, but it was just a start in her mind.

When the buzz around town about gold being discovered in California started it was all the men could talk about. She watched her new husband being pulled away with dreams like so many other men.

"He left four weeks ago today," she thought. She reminisced about Eddie with his kind heart and strong arms that had held her. He had sworn to protect her and stay with her. But the temptation was too strong. Even with his boss's promise of extra wages for staying, Eddie couldn't resist it. He left by steamer with his closest friends and thought, *the danger of winter and danger be hanged!* Her pleas for him to

stay fell on deaf ears. He knew in his heart, he told her, that this was going to get them to their dream.

He had forgotten about a few things in his haste to leave to make a fortune and speed up his plan toward a farm of their own. The first problem had come after Violet had realized he left her with no funds for food. She had a little saved from her bread sales. But her sales dropped off dramatically when the boarding house stopped buying bread from her. With so many men gone off to search for gold the boarding house was near to empty.

Then the storm had brought the tree through her roof. Violet was at a loss. This place was nothing to brag about, but she knew it was just the place where her and Eddie would make their start. Now it was a ramshackle cabin with a leaking roof and mold beginning to make it dangerous to live in.

Violet felt ready to say goodbye to the only home she had shared with her dear Eddie by the time she heard the wagon outside. The jingling harnesses were music to her ears.

Clive knocked politely and Violet opened the door and was grinning and ready. Her dark wool coat pulled close around her. Clive grabbed the bag from her hand.

With a glance around he could see she had been busy. A trunk was at the ready and there was nothing laid about anywhere. The place seemed to be packed away.

"Your belongings in the trunk?" Clive asked.

He watched the young blond girl nod. He put the bag in the back of the wagon and came back for the trunk.

"Mr. Quackenbush, we know not iffen I have the job yet?" Violet said. She didn't want him wasting his energy if she was just going to be back within a few hours.

"There is no need chile'. You will be sleeping under a solid roof from now on, whether you have the job or not." He said with his charming grin. "And call me Clive, Quackenbush is such a mouthful." Clive laughed as he heaved the trunk up on his shoulders. He deposited it into the back of the wagon.

Without a look back Violet climbed into the wagon and said a prayer of thanks. She was not afraid of change. In her short life God had shown her that sometimes blessings are found around the corner.

✿ ✿ ✿ ✿ ✿

An hour later she was sitting in a lovely home with Corinne and Lucas Grant. She had seen them both at the church. She had never spoken to them but they had a reputation of being Godly people.

She had seen their lavender fields during full bloom over the summer and fall. It had been one of the most beautiful sights she had ever seen.

"I do love baking and keeping house. I know how to cook, mostly hearty and simple meals but I love learning any type of cooking." Violet said with a hint of nervousness in her voice.

Corinne and Lucas had welcomed her in and they all sat around the cozy fire. She hadn't been truly warm since the tree had broken through her roof. She loved this lovely home around her now.

"We aren't picky about food, though Lucas does have a bit of a sweet tooth." Corinne shared with a smile.

"Is there a certain day you want laundry done, or certain food on certain days?" Violet asked. She was at a loss on how the interview was going. They weren't asking many questions of her.

"Well, I have no particular wants in that regard." Corinne looked to her husband for help.

"We just need someone to help us keep the place running so Corinne can do what she is gifted at, which is her greenhouse and botany lab." Lucas said.

"That seems to be a good definition of housekeeping." Clive said with a grin, finally inserting himself into the interview. It seemed that the young people were being a bit shy about this interview.

"I am glad for a chance to keep your table full and your house in order, Mr. and Mrs. Grant. I enjoy keeping my hands busy and I love to bake bread and set a good table. We could figure out how that best works together." Violet offered.

"Since I am new to this I think that sounds like a great plan." Corinne said. This young woman had a spark of goodness inside her. A joy within her heart and Corinne knew she would be good for them, and they would be good to her.

Within an hour the deal was struck. Lucas and Corinne gave her a tour of the house and she was delighted with the area that was wonderful, cozy and private they had set aside for her. *A whole wing of the cabin for her own use.* Violet would have never expected to so blessed.

She would start the next morning. They all took an evening stroll over to John and Marie's to introduce her to the family. Since the properties butted up against each other it was a convenient layout of land.

Once the introductions done and some supplies were shared for the next day's meals the plan was for Marie and Violet to go into town together to fill up on supplies for the Grant's nearly empty pantry. Violet already had ideas bursting in her head about how to bless her new 'family'. She believed strongly that God had brought her to this young industrious family for a reason. She laid her head to rest on a soft pillow in a warm room with the sound of snaps and pops of a low fire in the hearth in the room with her. Her prayers for Eddie were heartfelt, and also for the new people in her life. Clive, Lucas, Corinne, John, Marie and little Cooper, the names danced in her head.

She prayed for God to give her the strength and wisdom to do a good job and to be a blessing to her employer.

Chapter 25

April 1850 – San Francisco

A steam ferryboat chugged into the harbor of San Francisco bearing Clive and a few dozen boxes of goods for the store.

Clive enjoyed the smell of the sea air and the hint of the earthy spring behind it. The bay was calm as Clive watched the wharfs go by slowly as the boat chugged along. He could see the way the city was still growing, fast and dirty and overcrowded. It was not a place he wanted to leave his loved ones. He knew that soon the plan had to be to move his kin out. He felt at a loss of what to tell Angela, he kept praying that somehow her brother would appear and save him from a hard conversation. But he placed the worry in God's hands and let it melt away for the time being.

Clive let his mind wander to business and plans for Portland, Oregon, to fill his thoughts as the steamboat finished the journey to the southernmost wharf. He waited his turn in line to offload and was happy to see his grandson, Gabe, waving from the dock. He had a wagon ready. Clive was thankful for the small blessings, his family still safe and well.

He delivered the letters he had to all parties. Having a few for Gabe from his mother and also a few for Angela.

He heard Angela squeal with delight from her room as he enjoyed a cup of coffee with his Grandson and had his great-grandson Silas bouncing on his knee.

"My dear friend Corinne is pregnant." Angela declared to Amber who was crocheting. Amber gave her a big smile in response and welcomed her over to the chair.

"I am just so very happy for her." Angela declared as she plopped into the chair. She wiped away a wayward tear. "I cannot say what made me cry, perhaps gladness or missing her…" Angela said feeling a bit silly but still grinning.

"Probably a bit of both." Amber said wisely and smiled at her sweet friend. "It has been a long enough separation that you probably could use a visit." Amber suggested.

"I have been thinking on that a lot recently. Trying to know what the right thing to do is perplexing. I am praying constantly." Angela confessed.

"You will know the right time if you let God tell ya." Amber nodded and continued her crocheting. She had been praying a lot on that topic herself.

The conversation settled in on how Clive found the trip and how Silas was beginning to show signs of a very healthy crawling tendency.

"We will have to keep an even closer watch on him now." Amber said but they all knew the dangers of the fireplaces and other hazards around the home.

"A crawling baby can find trouble quicker than a dog can steal a sandwich." Clive said and gave Silas an extra bounce.

Clive stayed for lunch and helped Gabe with the unloading of all the goods into the warehouse in the afternoon.

✿ ✿ ✿ ✿ ✿

After five o'clock Ted arrived for a visit with Angie, they went to the back yard and Ted talked while Angela fed the chickens.

"I have one more job to do but then I have to leave. I need to go back east." Ted held his hands in front of him. His face lined with grief.

"I expected this." Angela said through a tight throat. The thought of Ted gone was painful.

"My mother and sister will need me to help them. I will help them sell the farm and get settled. Maybe they will agree with me to come west."

"But no promises, I know." Angela put her head down and felt that fear again. Every time she cared about someone they had to leave her behind.

"That is not what I am saying. I care about you. But I need to take care of my family. Doing the right thing here feels wrong on both sides. I don't want to leave you. Nor do I want to leave my mother alone with a farm she cannot run. I am not certain she knows her husband is dead. I took so long to write that letter, and I only was finally able to do it because of Clive." Ted held his head with his hands and sat down. He was trying to control his emotions. This wasn't easy.

"I know Ted, you have family, and they need to be the forefront of your thoughts. I promise I am not angry with you. Your integrity and values are the reason I love you." Angela confessed and then sat next to him.

Ted stared at her sweet face for a long minute. He felt the same love for her but didn't know if he could say the words, not before leaving. He had to deal with his family duties then he could come back west. Maybe then he could finish what he started with Angela, the sweetest girl on earth, in his eyes.

"You need to leave the city." Ted took her hand and caressed her cheek. It was all he could say instead of the words unsaid that burned in his throat.

"I know, and I will soon. This city is eating my insides. I now know how to love and hate a place at the same time. It is a cesspool of hate and wickedness. It holds people I love and morals I despise."

"Leave soon if you can Angie, I fear for your safety." Ted said before he kissed her. He lost his hands in her flowing hair and his resolve to leave California nearly left him.

"I need to find my real home soon. My heart needs a place of peace." Angela said as she pulled away.

"I will find you." Ted said. But the sadness in his eyes proved that he did not know if it would be so.

"I hope you do." Angela pulled him up and they walked back through the dark streets away from the bay.

Chapter 26

May 4th 1850

Angela slept through the first round of bells that rang through the early morning. Silas was crying and that finally broke through her consciousness. There was crashing in the next room and soon pounding on her door.

She sat up with all her nerves and the haze of sleep left her quickly.

"I'm awake!" Angela yelled out.

"Fire!" Gabriel yelled out.

Without a moment's thought she reacted and was dressed faster than she ever had in her life. She clasped the bracelet around her wrist and grabbed the box her letters from Oregon and Ted and her mother's diary and shoved them all in a bag. There was nothing else she could think of in the moment of panic. There was enough light coming through her window that filled her heart with a near paralyzing fear. The flames must be spreading fast to light up the city so well to cast such a light.

She opened her bedroom door and helped wordlessly. Amber's dress was unbuttoned in the back and Angie ran over and wordlessly buttoned her up. Amber had set Silas on the floor and he was crying. Angela scooped him up and with another hand was patting his back the way he liked. She grabbed up several of his favorite toys that were near the dark fireplace and shoved them into the bag she had slung over her shoulder. She grabbed a few blankets and the bread that was leftover. She was trying to think of anything they would need. Her brain was in a fog.

"I will get some clean nappies." Angela said quietly and carried the young boy and she let Gabriel and Amber make a plan.

She was back in the main room after just a minute and everyone seemed ready. She was glad that Clive and Ted were gone out of town on a job. They were safe. Angela felt her mind going faster than her feet as she followed Gabe and Amber out of the store. There were people yelling in the street. Gabe would get the women out of town. Gabe got the wagon hitched and ready in only minutes. Amber climbed into the back and Angela handed Silas to her. Angela climbed in and took the blankets and wrapped one around Amber and her son, she wrapped the other around herself.. The wind had a chill and with the fear in her heart it felt colder. She was so glad Ted was nowhere near this fire, but she longed for his arms around her. He was her safe place and he wasn't here.

The wagon creaked out of town and there was already a crowd of women and children already gathered. Gabriel delivered the wagon to the top of a hill and then jumped down. Amber was already emotional knowing he was going to go back, into danger.

Gabriel kissed Amber through her tears and they muttered sweet words to each other. Angela tried to give them privacy but her heart was at a loss to comfort her friends. Gabriel's comfort to his wife was short and he strolled away with determination. He broke into a jog shortly. Angela watched but noticed that Amber did not. She sobbed softly into the sleeping child's form she held.

The city was ablaze and the sky was orange and yellow. The hastily built wooden buildings were just kindling.

Why didn't people pay attention to the warnings? Angela wondered angrily.

The early morning passed and fear gripped the crowd that watched in horror as the city was engulfed in orange flame. The view was terrifying and Amber and Angela clung together praying and crying over the sight.

The news wasn't good. Every hour or so a young boy would run up the hill and share the news like a herald.

"The fire has jumped Washington Street!" The boy yelled hoarsely and the people watching and waiting let out an involuntary gasp. He coughed a few times and someone came forward and gave the boy water and washed the soot and grime from his face. He ran back to the burning city to help with the bucket lines.

There was no sleep for anyone that night as the roaring and crackling of the city kept them all in fear and doubt. This city felt doomed. It had grown too fast. The words floated around all morning and even when the sun came up the talk didn't end. The smoke rising from to the sky showed exactly how much had been destroyed.

The news came as people made it out of the city. One family had been trapped in a fallen building and another group of men had been caught in a tent shanty section that burned so quickly they had nowhere to go. There were hundreds of people with burns and scorched lungs. Outside the city became the refuge and people poured out as they were no longer able to stay. Their homes destroyed and hopelessness was spreading as the smoke billowed.

The hours dragged on and Silas woke and was fussing with being held. The girls did not want leave the wagon so they walked around it taking turns bouncing Silas to keep him entertained.

By eleven a.m. The blaze was under control. Gabe walked a slow exhausted step away from the burned city. His face blackened by the smoke and ash.

"Our street is safe. The brick buildings were saved. Such a terrible shame…" He stopped to cough. "So many buildings burned." Gabe kissed his wife and son, leaving streaks of soot on their faces.

"I am hoping the smoke won't be too bad in our home." Amber said.

There was so much damage from the fire Angela cried as they rode through the streets. On a few roads there was debris and Gabe jumped down and cleared out the planks of charred wood.

They were home and settling in within a few minutes.

The sad list grew by the hour as people were declared missing or dead from the morning's fire. The street where their mercantile had been was totally burned. The Henderson's restaurant now, was just rubble. Gabe heard from the head of household that they were taking their money from the bank and leaving San Francisco for good. Angela said a prayer for the Henderson family and prayed that they would find a better place. It took her a minute to realize that Ted's small apartment building was also gone.

Her heart jumped into her throat at the thought that he could have been like those men earlier who were unable to get out of the building before it burned down. She knew he had been sharing the apartment with Clive but she couldn't shake off the darkness and fear in her heart that day.

That night the girls worked hard at preparing as much food as they could and had Gabe deliver it to the town square. Word was spreading that many people had gathered there and a few large tents were sheltering hundreds of people.

Pastor Haines and his wife were asking all of those not affected by the fire to contribute whatever they could. After dusk Ted and Clive arrived back from their trip to a few mining camps to deliver goods.

They both seemed agitated and nervous as they came in and checked over everyone. They had heard the news and tried to get back quickly. They were supposed to be gone a few more days.

"I just left the wagon and supply load where it stands. Probably picked clean. I could not care less." Clive said as he brushed a hand over Amber's head and Angela's then he held Silas close, despite his wanting to be put down. He needed to hold him for a minute and let the fear of the worst drain from his mind.

Ted stood awkwardly next to Clive, not sure what to do. He wanted to hold Angela but he did not want to make a scene or make her uncomfortable.

Angela took care of the issue by stepping into his arms. "I am so glad you are safe." She said in a muffled voice against his chest. He was a good foot taller than her and rested his chin on her head.

There was no secret about how much they cared about each other. That night was spent in a spirit mixed with sadness and also thanksgiving. Being thankful for what they still had while mourning the ruin all around them.

❈ ❈ ❈ ❈ ❈

The week flew by, as Angela kept busy during her days to distract herself from the thoughts about how Ted would be gone soon.

The ship was setting sail in a few days. Ted had been attentive as possible every evening. Angela prepared her heart as much as she could but she still cried herself to sleep several times since he had given her the cherished bracelet. She wondered what their future would be. Would his mother want to stay put, would he come for her? She had such high hopes but didn't want to rely on them. Her hope felt so painful. Knowing that it would be more than a year before she could possibly see him, and that was the best case. What was she to do with herself?

She had a few ideas when her heart was quiet and her mind at peace, but the questions would come back every night as the doubts came.

Amber and Gabe had been busily preparing themselves for their own move. Knowing that they would be moving to Portland in the fall they did a few projects every weekend to prepare.

"I swear we have been moving about so much the last few years. I will be bald to be settled in one place." Amber declared one afternoon while feeding her son.

"I am ready to be settled myself. The unknown is hard on my heart." Angela said with her own sorrow weighing on her. "May I ask something?"

"Always, friend." Amber said sincerely.

"Last week when Ted gave me this bracelet I told him that I loved him." Angela sighed. "I know he is leaving. Should I apologize? Was that perhaps too much for him before leaving? I do not want him to feel obligated to come back for me if his family doesn't want him to. He really needs to think of them." Angela felt sincere in her love but was so confused.

"Never apologize for loving someone. But if you want him to know that he doesn't have to worry about you, you should find the words." Amber thought for a minute. "I know relationships are complicated enough when the people live near one another. Love is

210

harder than just the feelings, it takes work and compromise, and you are both young. You have time to let God show you the way. If it is meant to be, it will be."

Angela nodded allowing Amber's words to sink in. She wanted a chance to talk with Ted soon. She needed him to know her heart.

❀ ❀ ❀ ❀ ❀

On the other side of town Ted was having a similar issue. He had so many regrets about leaving Angela behind it was eating him up. There was no good answer. His Mother, Aunt and sister were all probably scraping by on nothing back east while he prospered here, but this darling young woman would be here without his protection for a year or longer.

He had an impulsive thought to marry the girl and take her with him but inside he knew that wasn't right. Their relationship was a budding one but her life was here. They were not ready to be married and he knew that God was telling him 'not yet' in his heart. He loved her, he knew he did and every day the feelings grew stronger but he knew what he had to do.

Though he spent the next two nights with her he never got the chance to talk with her seriously until the day he was to leave. The boat was departing at 11:30 a.m. He had only a small window of time but he was at the store before it opened and saw her there. Her eyes pink, probably from crying, but she was still so beautiful to him. She was sweeping the floor and Gabe was moving boxes around the room. Stocking shelves.

"May I steal her?" Ted asked as Gabe opened the door.

"You may. Don't go too far."

"Just the bench." Ted promised. Angela wordlessly took Ted's hand and they sat on the bench in front of the store.

Angela held the hand tightly with both her hands, like she would never let go.

"You are a good man, Ted." Angela said softly.

"You know I will come back for you." Ted said in earnest.

"I do have the sweetest hope that you will but I need you to know..." Angela swallowed hard. "If you cannot come back, I will not despise you. I know things don't always go the way we plan them. We have made no vows, and I do not want you to be held to any."

Ted sighed and kissed Angela sweetly. "I would promise you."

"I know you would, and that is enough for me. But if you have to choose between your family and me, you may come to regret one or the other." Angela said sensibly.

211

"I pray that you will not stop loving me." Ted said his worst fear aloud.

"I will not dearest Ted. But I ask one thing of you. If your feelings lessen or change, please let me know. A simple letter will suffice, you need not explain everything but to say you see no future with us, will be enough. I do not know what lies ahead. Only God knows." Angela's tears began to fall again. So many tears these last days.

"I …" Ted faltered. Not wanting to promise something so unthinkable. To promise to say goodbye forever is something he did not want to do.

"I love you Angela, the thought of leaving without saying those words is impossible to me. But I promise that if I feel God telling me that we are not meant to be together, though it would break my heart, I would tell you. But I pray that will never happen." Ted realized he had said the words aloud finally. Angela leaned against his chest. He kissed the top of her head.

"Can we promise to hold on to our hope? Trusting that God knows our future plans." Angela said finally and looked at his with her tear-filled green eyes.

"That I can do." Ted kissed her again quickly, knowing he was testing his fate with Gabe so near. "I promise to send a telegram once I am safe. So you'll know. I will also write. Though, we know how long letters take."

"Send them to Oregon, I don't think I will be here much longer." Angela nodded and placed her head against his chest again. Hearing his heartbeat was soothing, she wanted to remember his warmth and his heartbeat.

"I will, darling Angel." Ted said

"Please stay safe." Angela pleaded.

"Let me go say my "goodbyes" to Gabe and Amber. I want to hold you once more before I go." Ted said. Angela nodded and stayed on the bench. Ted walked into the mercantile, the bell dinged.

Angela could see the fog over the bay was dissipating and the sky was a clear blue. The gulls were soaring. She took deep slow breaths to remain calm, a part of here wanted to panic. Ted was going.

A few minutes later the, the bell dinged again and Angela stood up. She turned and looked at Ted, memorizing his face, his eyes and the way he looked at her. He took two strides and he held her tight and for a moment the intense rush was almost painful; his hand in her hair, his breath coming in gasps as he kissed her. She had never felt so overwhelmed. She never wanted it to end.

"Goodbye my love, for now." Ted said before their last kiss.

Angela could say nothing as she felt him let her go. He had to walk away, he turned and waved but then he didn't look back until he reached the corner where he had to turn. Angela waved then held her hands over her face. He would be on the boat within the hour. The day had come.

Angela took a seat on the bench she had recently shared with Ted and she sobbed into her hands. The long wait had begun.

Chapter 27 - Corinne

Willamette Valley Oregon

Corinne felt the exhaustion of pregnancy on some days and others she had boundless energy. Lucas was constantly checking on her. He always tried to make it seem like he was just being affectionate. But she knew he was there to make sure she wasn't overdoing her work. She decided to not be annoyed but to take it as a positive sign. He cared about her and the baby. It was endearing and sweet once she allowed herself to realize how lucky she was. These last few weeks had been good for her marriage.

The reality of marriage was more than she ever expected. The sweetness of the first bloom of love deepened into something else. It grew like the trees in the orchard. It started and seemed so important when it first sprouted. She felt like she and Lucas crossed into a new understanding of each other. She knew the areas that she needed to let God in, to help her be a better wife. And God showed her how much Lucas really cared for her with his every action. The way he accepted her dreams and goals, without question. Her work was a passion for her and he didn't demonize her for it. He had never made her feel anything but special. She didn't know many men who would have allowed her to be her true self. She knew many stories about strong-headed females from her previous life in Boston and even as a young woman in Kentucky. It was always told as a cautionary tale to young women, especially in her schooling. A woman's place was a docile and domestic one. That was her purpose on earth. Corinne's mother had taught her differently but she remembered how some women had treated her. She was spoken of harshly sometimes. The memories were faded but she remembered how her mother had cried a few tears over lost friendships or judgmental words. Corinne was thankful for her life, grateful to have a place to work and be herself without fear.

Lucas strode into her greenhouse; the place was warm in the spring sunshine. He looked to have a purpose more than just a normal visit.

"Hello beautiful." He kissed her cheek after he found her. The foliage of some plants was thick with blooms and the place was full of green and growing things. Corinne smiled and leaned against his chest. Her hands were covered with dirt. But the affection was nice.

"Your father just found me in the fields. There are rumors of a few wildcats in the area. Some farmers in the valley have reported farm

214

animals being attacked and the sounds of the mountain cats. Their calls could be heard through the night sky by several different families spread through the valley." Lucas shared the news with a hint of tension in his voice. His calm demeanor was not challenged very often.

"What should we do?" Corinne asked, a little concerned for her and her family's safety.

"We can take precautions. We have several rifles. I want one loaded by the door at all times. But the local farmers and ranchers, as well as all the hands and workers should be on the lookout. This is one of the reasons why your father built his house and barns at the edge of his property and then the house we live in so close to his. In the valley we are out in the open, but our buildings and fires, smoke and movement will hopefully detour dangerous predators, people or animals from coming too close." Lucas rubbed a hand across Corinne's lower back as he spoke. It was comforting and felt good. She was very achy and the motion calmed her fears just as much as his information. He planted a kiss near her temple and then spoke again. "Your father wants us to come to dinner tonight, Violet too. Would you mind going to tell her? I want to ride out to my brother's place and make sure they are sufficiently warned."

"I would be glad to.. I am going to send everyone home early. I am feeling tired and achy. I may catch a nap before dinner. Feel free to join me if you get home and cannot find me." Corinne said and gave him a kiss and a smile that made him smirk.

Lucas left and Corinne had a good talk with Dolly and the others that were in her lab. Everyone seemed as concerned as she about the talk of wildcats and wanted to get to a safe place.

"You go and rest, I will clean up here and head home within the hour. I am staying with Marie and John tonight so I do not have far to walk. I feel safe while the sun is out." Dolly stated. Corinne gave her friend a weary smile and nodded. She walked the stone path to her home. She found Violet in a back bedroom hanging curtains.

"Those are lovely. You did a superb job on making those." Corinne said sincerely. The dark blue print with sprigs of flowers matched the bedspread quilt with a homey charm. This was Angela's room and it gave a pang in her heart about how much she wished her friend were home.

"Thank you. It was a pleasure to do. I am glad I took a chance on the fabric. Sometimes fabric is so hard to come by that is unique and pretty." Violet said. Her smile was a constant. She just had a joy within her, no matter what the situation.

"You have excellent taste, I am glad you found it. I thank God for you and your help every day." Corinne said and surprised Violet with a hug.

Violet blushed but squeezed back for a moment before she was released. This new job felt like more than a job. It felt like the beginning of a new life.

"I feel the same way about being here." Violet said.

Corinne could feel her emotions rise. "Well enough of the weepy stuff. My emotions are all over the place these days. Crying over curtains is a sure sign that I need a nap."

Both of the young women laughed. Corinne told her quickly about the dinner invitation and the wildcat situation. Violet had only done a preliminary prep for dinner but nothing was cooking yet. She did have bread baked and would take it over when they went. Violet sent Corinne off to rest as she retreated to the sitting room for a quiet activity. She would do the mending while Corinne slept.

❀ ❀ ❀ ❀ ❀

Dinner at the Harpoles was a pleasant affair. The table was extended to fit everyone to its maximum.

"You should think about getting a larger table, John." Marie teased.

"Well, with more people joining our clan everyday it seems a wise idea." John gave his wife a wink.

"I made a coffee cake for dessert, any takers?" Marie stood up and asked. A resounding 'Aye' was heard all around with laughter and hands raised. Dolly and Violet both jumped up to help. Dolly grabbed plates and Violet refilled coffee cups for those that wanted some.

"Before we talk about wild creatures and other community news, I wanted to talk about something with you all." John stood and took the cake and cutting knife from his smiling wife. He pointed her to her seat and she kissed him on the cheek before she obeyed his lighthearted command. He served the cake to everyone then resumed his speech.

"I have a daughter, and now a son, that I adore. Now my daughter is expecting her own child and I am so proud. In all the change in the last six years of my life I never expected to be so blessed. To have loved and lost and then found love again, I know that God has a plan better than I could have ever plotted out for myself. Now I find myself at the brink of another change." John paused strategically and gave his wife a wink. "Marie and I are also expecting a child."

The entire place erupted in a cheer, the clapping and backslapping commenced. Corinne ran first to her father with an embrace and then to Marie. Her tears of joy were sincere.

"I cannot be happier for you!" Corinne said into Marie's ear. She knew her mother, Lily, in heaven would have rejoiced as well. She would have wanted John to be happy. Corinne's heart bubbled over with joy. She would have another sibling. She patted her own growing belly. It was only just starting to push at her clothing. She had given up corsets when she had left Boston, her natural shape was thin but she was enjoying the feel of her growing life as it made its presence known.

Cooper was next on Corinne's list of persons to hug. They had a little sister-brother chat. Corinne knelt down to look him in the eye.

"I am so excited to be a big sister again." Corinne said to Cooper. His eyes grew big.

"I'm excited, too, to be a brother. But I hope Papa doesn't forget about me when the baby comes." Cooper said. Corinne could tell he had his own doubts about how he fit.

"Our dad has a big heart. He can love you and me, and Marie, and he has love left over for lots of people. That's how God made us." Corinne said with a nod.

"It is?" Cooper asked.

"Yep, I never had a brother until I met you. I couldn't help but love you. You want to know what dad told me just the other day." Corinne asked, her heart bursting to share a moment with her step-brother.

"What did he say?" Cooper asked.

"He bragged about how strong you were, and how smart you are around the horses. He thinks you are going to be a great man someday." Corinne said. "That's how men say I love you."

Cooper's chest puffed out with the praise. "He really said all that stuff?"

"I would never lie to you Coop. He said all that and more." Corinne gave the boy another hug and his arms slipped around her neck and he squeezed her tight. She had to admit, she lost her heart to this little man a bit more every day.

The talk around the table got a bit more serious a few moments later. They discussed a strategy for how to remain safe. Everyone agreed that staying inside after dark was a necessity. John also discussed how he was looking into getting a dog.

"Those aren't as easy to find in the west as they used to be out east." Lucas stated.

"I know of a few people with pups. I am heading to Portland in a few days, there is an Aussie shepherd litter that I want to look at." John said.

"I'm going with you!" Cooper stated and then ran and jumped into his papa's lap.

"Yes, you are." John tussled Cooper's hair affectionately.

Once all the serious topics were discussed the group moved to the sitting room. Dolly and Cooper sat near the fire and played checkers. Corinne, Marie and Violet plotted out new dresses first for Corinne, who admitted that her clothing was getting snug, and then for Marie who knew her time for expansion would come.

John and Lucas spoke more of strategies for dealing with the wildcats, how to keep the livestock from danger and other topics.

It was well past dark when they left. Lucas had Corinne carry the lantern and he had his rifle. But the short trip between properties was uneventful. Violet stirred up the fire in the sitting room and Lucas stoked the fires in the other parts of the house. Corinne sat and chatted with Violet for a little while but soon succumbed to her tired body.

Tomorrow a trip to town was planned for the women in the morning to look for fabric for a new dress for Corinne.

❀ ❀ ❀ ❀ ❀

The shopping had gone well and Marie and Corinne had several new fabrics to get their pregnancy wardrobe started. Marie and Corinne snuck a few bolts in for new clothes for violet as well. Violet was a frugal girl and they knew she wouldn't spend money on herself.

After a little debate Violet was given permission to help Corinne start a collection of booties and sweaters for the baby, since Corinne's crocheting skills were non-existent. She had tried, she knew she probably could do it if she focused on it but somehow her mind would wonder off to thinking about other things and her loops would be a dismal mess. Corinne finally gave up and swore to leave the crocheting to others.

"Not everyone is good at everything." Marie said generously.

"It is good that way, God designed us to have our failures to keep us humble." Violet added wisely. She smiled and gave Corinne a wink. "Thank you for letting me help. I need practice as someday I will have my own babies to crochet for, Lord willing. Hopefully my husband will return soon and we can work on that." Violet blushed at the thought and then laughed.

"I am praying he does return soon, as well as Angela." Corinne said. She stretched her back and winced as the muscles in her back were stiff.

Violet was good at seeing Corinne's discomfort and with a gentle hand she rubbed in small circles on Corinne's lower back. Corinne sighed with the relief of it and thanked her a minute later.

"I need some rest." Corinne stated.

"As do I." Marie agreed. "Getting more tired every day.. I may just grab a catnap before I start supper."

"Let me do the cooking Marie. I can make enough for everyone." Violet volunteered.

"That is a lovely gesture Violet, they can come over to my house for dinner. We have shared their table often enough. It can be our turn to bless them." Corinne said. "I will help out after I sneak in a nap myself."

Violet gave Corinne a look that Lucas would have been proud of.

"I can set the table at least." Corinne harrumphed and laughed. "No heavy lifting, I promise."

"Deal!" Violet took her arm and a bag full of yarn. They waved at Marie and Violet got Corinne tucked into bed with an extra pillow for support.

Violet enjoyed the chance to entertain. She had a menu whipped up in no time and was excited to get to work.

She had sourdough bread pounded out that had been proofing on the counter since morning. She had a good sourdough start that her and Maria were sharing that Chelsea was now part of. A good sourdough took a while to develop and this batch that Violet developed was proving to be a family favorite. Tonight she was making a braided loaf and it would be dense and flavorful. She had a few dry herbs that she was pounding into the dough and it would go with the roasted lamb. She had a fire pit behind the cabin that she designed that Lucas built for her. It was big enough to roast a large pig, a lamb or even a rack of venison. It would come in handy during the harvest season. The wood had been burning and the coals were nice and hot. Violet got some help prepping the lamb on the pole this morning. It was wrapped and seasoned then rubbed down with oil. It was in the cool of the root cellar but she would need a hand to get it over the fire.

Violet walked over to the Harpole ranch and John was nearby. He and a ranch hand helped her get the lamb in the pit. The seasonings on the lamb and the rub had darkened, and the lamb was securely in place. The u-shape of the coals allowed them to use heat from both sides and she placed a large trough in-between to catch the drippings and not cause a grease fire. Violet was well satisfied. She promised the field hand that had helped that if he came by later she would have a plate made for him. He left with smiles and would certainly love joking with the other guys about his special treat. John Harpole stayed with Violet a while and they turned the meat a few times and chatted. He also wanted to make sure the scent of cooking meat wouldn't bring out the predators. He warned her to be safe. She took his advice to heart and took the rifle with her every time she went out to turn the spit.

Corinne was up after a few hours nap. She was feeling better and was enthusiastic over the scent of the cooking lamb. Lucas was home soon after and took over spit-turning duties. John Harpole and Cooper seemed to want in on the action and stools and chairs were taken out back and the men folk talked around the roasting lamb.

Dolly and Marie came by close to suppertime and Russell, Chelsea and their two little ones filled the house with life. Lucas had taken a quick ride to his brother's farm to invite them, once he helped Violet with the pit in the morning he knew her plans for lamb roasting. The more the merrier.

The party was a good one. Cooper was excited because he was leaving with his pa the next day to look at puppies. Corinne and Marie were not allowed to lift a finger so they both enjoyed the camaraderie of their friends and family. Dolly and Chelsea helped Violet get everything into place. The two loaves of herbed sourdough bread were cheered over as they came out of the oven. She generously buttered the tops and let them cool off. Some of the lamb drippings were scooped out of the large pan and Violet use them to fry up some potatoes from the root cellar.

Once the lamb was roasted and pulled from the pit, the family prayer was said and the meal was served. Violet had done a wonderful job and everyone left the table full and happy. The only arguments were playful, a few thought the sourdough bread being the best part of the meal; others thought the lamb had been the better. Violet blushed with the praised but loved it. She felt at home, the acceptance was certain.

Lucas and Russell did all the dishes, with little Cooper designated as the cleanliness inspector. Any dish not passing muster would be washed again.

At dusk the family gathered together. A prayer was said for all the loved ones not with them, Clive and Angela, families back east, and Violet's husband Eddie. Everyone went home early but satisfied and happy to have had great night together.

Chapter 28 – Angela

San Francisco – California Territory

The bell rang like every day for the many months she had worked the counter. The day was slow. There were no ship arrivals today and the warm weather had the masses digging or playing in the creek beds for any gold dust they could find. Angela looked up from her sorting to see a tall thin young man. Her heart stopped beating for a few seconds before she gasped and nearly lost her knees.

"Sean…" She whispered and grabbed her face. She knocked over a glass jar in her dash around the counter but caught it and had it back in place before she was finally able to embrace the only living family she had left.

"It is you, Angie girl." Sean said, sounding like a man. It tore through her – was that some long ago memory of her father's voice?

The thin man with wavy brown hair held his sister while his emotions showed unchecked in tears washing down his tan cheeks.

Gabe came down the stairs to see Angie and her brother reuniting, he said a prayer of thanks for the blessed event they had all been praying for.

"You two go out back and talk, I have the store." Gabe said once the two were paying attention.

"Thanks Gabe," Angela grabbed the hand of her brother's and dragged him to the back of the building. They could hang with the chickens and talk.

"You look like Papa." Angela said when they were alone again. She looked over every inch of him. He was tall. With green eyes like hers and he looked strong. Not the sickly beaten down boy she had last seen so many years ago at the workhouse.

"You look like mother." His voice cracked a little. He didn't quite know what to say.

"I hope you are healthy." Angela said. She hadn't let go of his hand. Wanting to be sure by touching him that he was real.

"Yes, Ol' Willie and I stay busy. I do a lot of hunting. I sell meat to the miners. The fools never think ahead and buy enough to eat." Sean laughed softly, Angela smiled after hearing it.

"I have seen that to be true, they come back into town in a pitiful state sometimes. I see Gold Fever hasn't taken ahold of you."

"No Ma'am. It's an honest day's work for an honest day's pay for me. There is no place for chasing gold when there is plenty of work to be had." Sean said. He felt this strongly.

"I know a few young men that agree with those words exactly." Angela thought of Ted and thought about how many miles were now between them. She came out of her stupor to talk again. "I have news for you. I have a bank account for you. Our inheritance from our parents has been returned to us. I have a trunk…"Angie tried to tell him more but Sean interrupted.

"I have no interest in any money. I am doing well. We had no estate that I ever knew of." Sean said with a deep frown.

"Mr. Lankarsky, our stepfather, was persuaded to release the will and accounts that were entrusted to us. It was done legally, I can tell you all about it if you would stay today. I know I would love to know about everything you have been doing. We have a lot to discuss." Angela's smile was so warm and ecstatic Sean had no choice but to smile back. He had mixed feelings about this reunion but he would hear her out. He had known about her for several weeks before he had worked up the nerve to come and see if the rumors were true.

"I will stay for today and tomorrow in town to catch up. My heart nearly sped out of my chest when an old friend of Willie's came by the cabin and told us about you being in San Fran looking for me. Since I heard about all the fires and gangs, Willie and I had decided to stay away. We like it better out in the wilds anyway. The land is being torn apart with all the digging". Sean shared, Angela sat on the bench and he joined her.

"I heard that people were using hoses and water to blast away at the side of hills, just tearing away at everything. Some people have no respect for maintaining the land. The committee in town cannot keep up with all the law breakers." Angela shared the rumors she had heard.

"I hate to see you here in this terrible place." Sean said, and felt it sincerely.

"You are not the only one. But I had to risk this place to see you. We are family." Angela hugged him again.

His mind was churning for any thoughts or words to say to her. This was a new reality to deal with. He had no idea what to do about it yet.

Sean listened to Angela talk for hours. She kept talking through a lunch that Gabe brought to them wrapped in parchment paper from Amber upstairs.

She talked about where she worked in Boston and meeting Corinne to the trip on the trail. Her experience had been so different than his. She shared briefly about how hurt she was after her fall in the ravine. She watched his own emotional response to the abuse at the hand of the young Mr. Temple who had sent her out into a moonless night.

It made his blood boil. He was annoyed at his own response. He hadn't cared for anyone in years, besides his mentor Willie. They had taken care of each other for all this time. He had been Sean's father, brother and friend through everything. Now this girl who was his true flesh and blood was stirring up feelings that he would rather forget. Sean decided he owed her a few days at least. She had sacrificed much to find him. So he continued to listen, but his heart was not in it. He wanted to run away.

❋ ❋ ❋ ❋ ❋

Angela was thrilled to introduce her brother to the Quackenbush family. They ate dinner at the large table and even Clive joined in. He spent several long minutes praising Angela about her fortitude and willing attitude. She was humbled by all the praise that the Quackenbush family lavished on her too. Everyone wanted Sean to know the kind of young woman his sister was, and how lucky they all were for having her there. Sean was quiet and a bit aloof but Angela figured he didn't like crowds. Once dinner was over she led him outside and they sat and looked over the bay from the second floor balcony. The sun was behind them and the bay was peaceful. Angela was running out of things to talk about and was worried that she was boring him.

"I hope you haven't tired of me yet." Angela said and laughed a little bit uncomfortably. She noticed Sean was quiet and trying to think of something to say. This was awkward.

"I am just a bit overwhelmed. I have to keep telling myself that you are here in California territory. I never thought to see you again. I felt so guilty for running away from the work orphanage years ago. Willie was the one who finally talked me out of my guilt for leaving you behind." Sean's face turned red. Angela looked away to process her own thoughts.

"I never blamed you, Sean." Angela said it above a whisper. "I know you suffered from beatings every day there, from the older boys. It was a terrible place." Angela remembered and felt hot tears slide down her chilled cheeks.

"For many years I blamed God, then Mother for marrying that horrible man. I was able to get past all that anger but I somehow set you aside. Like you had died with Mother and Father. Maybe I just wanted to stop feeling like I left you in that horrible place. So I convinced myself that you were gone and I was just writing letters to a ghost." Sean said it through a tight throat. It was hard to admit these things.

"I don't want you to feel this way. It was not God who put us there. It was our stepfather. God helped us out of that dreadful place." Angela reached for Sean's hand. He let her hold it but he still kept his eyes on the bay and the eastern sky. A few stars were starting to peak through the navy sky.

"I know that now, I have made my peace with God. It was a long road and a great mentor who helped me. I was so lost and hurt for so many years." Sean finally turned and gave a smile to his sister. They looked at each other for a long moment and got to know each other a little bit better.

It was an hour later that Sean excused himself and stayed at the boarding house down the street. It wasn't much more than a closet-sized room with a cot, but he refused to bunk with the Quackenbush's family. Angela assumed he wanted his own space to think so they didn't press him. He promised to return in the morning for another day to stay in town.

❀ ❀ ❀ ❀ ❀

Angela was trying really hard not to tap her foot with impatience. Her brother had said he would be there at nine a.m. And it was already after eleven. After an hour she started to fret, just a little bit. Knowing the dangers within the city, her brain could process several scenarios about how her brother could fall into some kind of peril. Angela had a brown paper envelope with *Sean Fahey* written across it, it held all the bank paperwork that Corinne had filed for him. The money was his. Angela was determined to convince him to take it.

After the clock on the wall past eleven her heart dropped, wondering if perhaps he had decided against seeing her again. The potential was unthinkable and she shook off the thought several times. *He is coming.* She told herself, again and again.

At 11:42 a footstep was on the stairs. Amber and Angela both looked up from their crocheting. Figuring it was Gabe. Angela breathed out a sigh of relief when Sean appeared, finally.

"Oh good. I was beginning to fret." Angela said as she laid aside her crocheting.

Sean wordlessly gave a nod to Amber and then spoke. "Want to talk on the balcony?" His voice was low and his words were stunted. Like he didn't want to say them.

"That would be fine." Angela said slowly, trying to see if his face would give anything away. He was almost grimacing.

Once they closed the outside down they sat at the small table and chairs that was there. Sean had pulled out a chair for her but kept standing. He just paced around for a minute.

Angela felt awkward and spoke. "I hope you aren't injured. You seem out of sorts."

Sean opened his mouth to speak and then closed it again. Angela pushed the envelope at him, at a loss of what to say to this man that seemed a stranger now to her.

"I don't want that!" Sean said emphatically.

"It's yours whether you want it or not." Angela said, her voice sounding meek in her own ears.

"I don't want any of this." Sean said and he shoved his hands in his pockets. He paced as Angela's heart dropped further into her gut.

"Are you worked up about the money or something else?" Angela finally asked once his pacing had driven her to distraction.

"Everything about this is wrong." Sean wasn't yelling but every word felt like weapons. "I don't have a family anymore."

Angela let the air escape slowly from her lungs. She had no words.

"I don't want you coming back over and over again and disrupting my life. I buried you and everyone from my past a long time ago." Sean was looking over her, almost like she wasn't there.

Angela wanted to say something, perhaps defend herself by saying she wasn't going to keep coming back if he didn't want her there. But the words were trapped in her throat. Just like the tears were locked inside her. She would not dare to let them out. Her years as a servant taught her to hide her emotion at all costs. She was using every ounce she had of her coping skills all at this moment in time.

Sean took the envelope, folded it and shoved it into his back pocket. Angela felt the smallest stirrings of hope, she felt the fool but she clung to it. She let Sean stew in his own thoughts.

Sean finally sat after he paced in the thick silence between them. Angela watched his face, not knowing him well enough to know what flashed across his eyes. She wondered quietly. She prayed while she watched him. She felt something inside her bloom and then a thought formed. *He doesn't want to see me. He wishes I had never come.*

The realization was felt inside her like a razor knife, it was worse than the pain of the dark ravine, as every word he had said washed over her. She was pondering deep in the meaning of every glance and look from the day before as he endured her talking. She knew what an ignoramus she was now. She felt glued to her chair. She actually felt her jaw go slack with the knowledge of what a fool she really was.

She had travelled from Boston to the west for him, and then away from the safety of loved ones to this dangerous city for him. And he did not want to see her, ever.

Sean sighed and placed his hands on the table. The gesture was lost on Angela. Was he trying to calm himself? Or find more ways to insult her?

"You need to leave California." Sean said finally. He looked into her eyes without an ounce of affection or compassion. "Go back to Oregon."

Sean stood straight again then he pulled a cap from his front pocket and placed it on his head. He was through the door and his steps could be heard going down the stairs. The jingling of the bell on the front door was a faraway noise. Angela sat and listened until all signs of her brother were gone.

❊ ❊ ❊ ❊

She had sat on that balcony and had been numb for more than an hour. The sounds of Amber and Gabe eating a meal had been heard. Amber peeked onto the balcony and asked if she needed company. Angela had just shaken her head 'no' without looking away from the eastern horizon.

The rejection was felt and the hardest thing to swallow. She hadn't asked to live with him. She had no plans for that, really. All she had wanted was the connection. He obviously didn't.

Her tears finally made it through the cold numb facade and once they did, the full flow of emotions rolled through her. Her only living family could not even spend a full day in her presence. She knew she could not embrace her parents again until she was called to heaven but he was here and she was here and… the full impact of his words and actions were not lost on her now. He didn't want her as a sister.

The thought echoed through her head for the next two days. She talked with Amber and Gabe about it a little. They tried to comfort her but she brushed it off her, like she was just unaffected.

After dinner that first night she said flatly. "I think I need to go back home."

"I agree that would be best. We will be following you soon after. I do hope you will come and stay with us upon occasion." Amber said to try and lighten her friend's mood. It was hard to watch a friend be in pain.

"You know I will gladly.' Angela tried to smile at Amber with her sad eyes.

The discussions were quickly switched to her return to Oregon. It was the only thing that would engage her besides Silas and his baby antics.

Clive and Gabe had made arrangements for her on the steamship heading to Oregon first; it was later going to Washington.

Angela listened with half her attention as they discussed politics and talk of the states and territories of the West. She read the newspapers and knew everything the men talked about, but she just couldn't find the energy to join in.

After two days of crying herself to sleep she felt a little better. She let Amber into her head a little bit and shared finally everything that Sean had said. Amber, being an empathetic soul cried with her. She held Angela's hand as they spoke of Oregon and hopeful things. There was nothing much to say when family hurts you.

Angela proclaimed, "God and I have gotten through a lot together. He will get me through this too." Her brave green eyes showed the wounds, but she knew she was not fully broken.

Amber and Gabe would be following her to Oregon within a few months. The store in Portland was coming together. They would be selling fancy goods. Clive was working with sellers on the east coast, Russia, China, Japan and India so far. The west was going to be settled and Clive knew that people would need more in their homes than just the basics. Portland was a growing town and the port a good one. Everyone was catering his vision and on board with the plan. The San Francisco store was going to get a new manager. A businessman in town wanted to partner with Clive and split the proceeds. The store name would stay the same so he would not lose the loyal customers.

Angela felt relief knowing that Amber and Gabe would be close by once she was back in Oregon. Just the thought of those mountains and being home made her heart feel lighter. She felt like her heart was thin as paper and on the edge of shredding but the word 'home' calmed her. She wouldn't think about the words her brother had said or the rejection now. She would just go home.

Four days after he told her to leave she followed his instructions. She was leaving San Francisco.

Chapter 29

The goodbyes were tearful between Amber and Angela. There were lots of hugs and promises of visits when they got to Oregon. Angela knew her face was blotchy with tears by the time it was her turn to climb aboard the steamboat.. The newest port had allowed for steamboats to get right up to the dock for easier boarding. Angela was thankful for the less humiliating mode of travel. Clive held her arm as they made their way through the crowd. The process was now known to her, she didn't have the need to see everything aboard like she had the first time she had been on a steamship. Her baggage was handled and her bunk was adequate. She leaned on Clive throughout that evening by the cast iron stove. The nights were cold on the water and the wind whipped around the steamboat as it chugged its way to Oregon. Clive kept her company and was his best amusing self to cheer her. But Angela knew he wasn't fooled by her pretend smile. Clive was no fool.

She had some bad dreams about the ship sinking, and a few dreams reliving the last day with her brother. Then in one dream it was Ted telling her he never wanted to see her again. She knew her emotions were in shambles and she kept praying and reading the bible Corinne gave her when she couldn't find sleep.

The days were slow on the rocking ocean and the slow steady numbness led to a lingering melancholy. She pushed the thoughts away as much as she could but they were persistent in creeping back in. She prayed and felt God's comfort in bits and pieces but she knew she had a lot of questions about what she had done wrong to make her brother want to push her away so emphatically. The answers didn't come but she knew they would with time. Her brother had been right about something. She needed to go home. Her friends and the mountains were calling her back.

❆ ❆ ❆ ❆ ❆

Corinne

Willamette Valley - Oregon

The day had been a tough one for Corinne. A farmer within a mile had had two sheep mauled and eaten the night before. Everyone was on edge and the men were considering keeping a night watch. Putting men on rooftops and lighting torches and lanterns. Every able-bodied man had been put to task on getting all animals to safety within barns or secured areas.

Corinne had sent all her employees home at lunchtime. She promised everyone the full day wage but just felt that everyone would be safer if no one traveled alone at dusk. The situation with the wildcats was feeling chaotic and dangerous.

John Harpole and Cooper stopped by her place to introduce their newest family member, Pepper. The puppy cheered up Corinne immediately.

"I got to name him." Cooper said proudly.

The small grey and black Aussie shepherd was a bundle of energy. He had one spot of brown over one eye but the rest was black, white and grey spots with speckles.

"He has to be house trained, Papa said, but we will get him trained up in a few days." Cooper said and sat down on the ground where the puppy romped beneath Corinne's feet.

"It might take more than a few days, but these are known to be pretty smart." Corinne said. Then she couldn't help but giggle as the puppy licked at her outstretched hands. She was sitting on a stool. Kneeling was getting a little too difficult, not the going down part, but the getting back up part. Her new day dress that Marie had made for her had given her more room to move, but it still didn't take away the achy and sore back.

"This little guy is such a cutie." Violet declared as she popped out the door.

"His name is Pepper." Cooper declared again.

"He looks like his name." Violet grinned and sat right on the ground to get a good look. Pepper was more than willing to pounce on the newcomer.

"How old is he?" Corinne asked.

"Almost nine weeks. Been weaned for weeks." John said. "I almost brought one home for you. But thought the better of it. If you will be wanting your own we could plan it better and get from a different family. Clive was talking about more Aussie owners last we spoke of it. I can't remember where he said they were."

John and Cooper left after a while, the puppy needed to take care of his business and would probably take a nap after all the excitement. Corinne and Violet waited for Lucas to come home in the quiet of the afternoon.

The evening was tense. Lucas went over the plan for the night. He was going to join with the men on the dusk watch. Other men had volunteered to watch throughout the night. If the cats were in the area they wanted to keep them away from homes and the livestock. The wildcats could stay in the mountains, but when they started

229

encroaching in closer to town the danger to human life and helpless livestock had everyone on edge.

Corinne was worried but kept quiet during dinner. Violet and Lucas tried to keep the conversation light. Violet reminded her that Clive had promised to be back on the next steamboat.. Clive always could cheer her up. When he came back from California territory he always had letters from Angela.

Lucas called Corinne to their room after dinner. Once he had her alone he held her close.

"I know you are worried, but I will stay high and safe. I am a good shot and there are lots of good hunters taking this situation seriously. We will catch these cats and take care of the danger. I will be home before midnight." Lucas held her head against his chest for a few minutes.

"I love you." Corinne said as he let go.

"And I you." Lucas kissed her warmly and let her go a minute later.

Corinne followed him out and waved as he headed over to the Harpole's ranch.

She was comforted knowing he wouldn't be far away. She said a prayer for him and felt a calm peace fill her. She had to let him be about his work.

Corinne sat with Violet. Violet was crocheting little white booties, and talking about her husband. How many nights she prayed for his safe return. She was waiting for a letter, since he had been gone she had only received one short one after he arrived to Sacramento, he said he was headed to a place near Sutter's mill named Nugget Creek.. It was a miner's camp. The information in the letter wasn't much to go on but she has read the letter so many times it was burned into her memory.

She wanted to keep Corinne calm so she kept talking about anything she could think of; last week's sermon at church, the coming child, and her own hopes for children.

As darkness fell Corinne felt fatigued but refused to go to her bed. So Violet stayed up with her and once Corinne fell asleep in the chair, Violet covered her and kept her company. Violet was too agitated to sleep. She spent some time in contemplation and talking to God, just praying for the men's safety and then for her husband who was so far away. He now had been gone longer than they had been together. It only hurt some days. She would try and cheer herself but thinking about their future and perhaps he would come back and they would have enough to start their own farm. But she tried not to dwell too much on those kinds of hopes. Mostly she just wanted him back and safe in her arms.

Violet felt silly, knowing her arms were good for cooking and cleaning, but not for safety. Men were known for their protection, but she was growing more and more dissatisfied with the protection her husband had given her. He had left her with so little to live on. Violet shook off her negative thoughts and then prayed for her to be able to let go of her hurt feelings. She let her mind dwell on forgiveness again and then said another prayer for her husband's safety.

The clock on the wall said it was 12:10 when the front door opened. Lucas looked tired but all in one piece.

He gently woke his wife and told her and Violet that the watch had been uneventful. Everyone in the valley was notified of what to do if a wildcat was spotted. If a cat was shot it was a different code. A certain number of shots in the air, he said.

Everyone was very tired. Violet helped Corinne into bed while Lucas locked up the cabin. He secured his rifle by the door and made sure every window was closed and secure.

Corinne was asleep when he got to the bedroom. Violet had laid out Corinne's robe nearby should she need to get up for any reason.

Violet must already be in her rooms. Lucas thought with a thankful heart. Having Violet here was such a blessing. He hoped that she was happy here.

Lucas said his prayers as he held his wife close. Her deep breathing assured him that she was getting a good rest. He fell asleep quickly.

❊ ❊ ❊ ❊ ❊

The sound was a crackling sound, like far off thunder. Corinne thought through a hazy, sleepy brain. Without opening her eyes she could tell her husband laid next to her, his warmth comforted her. She wanted to drift back into sleep but the pain in her lower back was pushing her toward wakefulness. She tried to will herself back into slumber. She tried to clear her mind of everything and just focused on breathing, in and out, slowly. She was unaware she finally fell back into a mild sleep.

Within a few minutes another sound woke her, fully. A cracking sound that pierced the air. Then a scream and another, not human, like a roaring thunderous scream. Then she heard a gunshot.. The hideous growling screech again pierced the air. It was close!

Corinne sat up straight in bed, fear pumping through her as her brain deciphered the sounds. The wildcats! They were near.

Lucas was fumbling next to her in the darkness. She heard the distinct sound of a match scratching across a matchbox. The lamp next to Lucas's side of the bed came to life. Corinne saw the weary look in Lucas's eyes, and also the fear.

"The wildcats, I think they were near, dear God." Corinne said. Her heart praying for her father's family, the men on watch, so many prayers in a split second.

"Cori..." Lucas looked at her and his eyes grew round in horror.

Corinne followed his eyes to her lap and saw the quilt soak through with blood. For a moment she was confused – had she been shot?

"Oh no, darling." Lucas grabbed her hand but she pulled it away so she could shove the blankets away. The proof was covering her.

"The baby!" Was all Corinne could say in a ragged whisper and then the onslaught of emotions forced her to reality. She had lost her child in the night.

She didn't know she was weeping against her husband's chest. She became aware of it after a few minutes. She felt out of control. The horror and the loss were too big to swallow so she just sobbed. It was all she could do.

❀ ❀ ❀ ❀ ❀

"Violet, can you stay with her?" Lucas asked in a ragged and harsh whisper. Corinne was shaking and holding her pillow. She was gulping and breathing trying to calm herself. It had only been a few minutes, right? Since the wild cats screaming and the gunshots, and the blood.

Corinne was still in bed. She didn't know if she should stay or move. The sticky warm blood on her legs was making her very uncomfortable but she felt frozen.

"Lucas, you cannot go out, it isn't safe." Corinne came out of her stupor to realize her husband meant to leave. There were dangers out there in the dark. "NO!" She yelled. She was nearly back to feeling out of control again.

"The shots signaling the all clear were sounded. I will check on the status of the danger first. Then go for Doc Williams. I promise I will not be long. Violet will get you to a spare bed and help you." Lucas kissed her hand.

"Please, please don't go. Lucas, I cannot lose you too." Corinne began a fresh round of weeping. She was overwhelmed with so much going through her mind and body, pain, and exhaustion and a deep, deep ache.

"Let me help you first then." Lucas helped Corinne to stand, she still was crying but the sobs had stopped.

Violet took charge and the gown was off in a second. Violet somehow had gotten warm water around and with quick hand had cleaned away some the blood. A fresh gown was over Corinne's head within a few minutes. She had towels down and the quilt pulled back in a guest bedroom. Corinne wordlessly allowed Lucas and Violet to tuck her in. Violet sat on the edge on the bed and stroked her hand as Lucas grabbed a rocking chair from their bedroom. He placed it near the bed and Violet stood up.

Lucas spoke to Violet in whispered tones; Corinne paid little attention, her mind on the bed in the other room. The scene was replaying over and over in her head. She had lost her child.

Violet was gone only a minute and back with a cup of tea that she sat on the side table.

"It's a little too hot." Violet said.

"Thank you." Corinne said in a whisper. She was numb.

Lucas kissed her forehead and said he loved her.

"I will be back very soon."

"I am so sorry Lucas." Corinne finally said.

"Hush now. You can rest. Violet is with you. She will take care of you." Lucas had a mist of unshed tears in his eyes and left quickly.

❀ ❀ ❀ ❀ ❀

Lucas grabbed the rifle at the door and closed it behind him. The pain in his chest was real. He had never hurt like this in his life. The deepest dark hot pain spread through his guts and wanted to split him into pieces.

The last hour was a blur, the shots, the screaming of the cats then the horror of Corinne, all that blood. He had to know if he was safe to go to town. His feet ran the distance to John Harpole's place.

Dear Lord, I will have to tell them. He dreaded even saying it, because saying it made it more real. This wasn't some sort of nightmare that he could wake from, tomorrow he would go to work in the fields and come home and his darling beloved would be there still growing with child. She would smile, be tired and he would rub her back.

The Harpole ranch was buzzing with activity. John had a rifle and a wagon pulled around in front of the barn. Two men were dragging a tarp across the front lawn.

"I heard the all clear shots." Lucas said, his voice sounding ragged to his own ears. Why was he talking about the wildcat when his world was falling apart?

"Yes, there were two females. I shot one, and Hank here shot the other." John looked tired but he was taking care of business. John looked at Lucas sharply then looked down at his hands.

Lucas saw on one of his hands there was blood, probably from the blankets. He had pulled the quilt from the bed and thrown it in the shed. He would burn it tomorrow.

"I. Uh.." Lucas felt at a loss. "Corinne woke up just an hour ago. We believe she lost the child." Lucas choked on the words.

He heard John and a few other gasps but only felt the hot pain in his guts again. He had said it. It was real.

"I need to go get the doc, but she made me promise to be safe. I had to make sure the wildcats were taken care of." Lucas said, his voice thick with emotions. He suddenly was so very weary.

"Let me go, I will get the Doc back here." John's head rancher Hank volunteered. "Go be with your wife."

"Thank you, Hank, I don't know what to say, I know you must be tired." Lucas didn't want to be a burden but he wanted to stay with his wife.

Hank just whistled and someone handed him a mount, Hank was galloping off before Lucas could protest anymore.

"How is she?" John asked huskily. He had tears running down his cheeks, in his own form of pain.

"Not good, weeping then quiet. There was so much blood, but she had the strength to stand." Lucas said softly. John looked as devastated as he himself felt. The sympathy was Lucas's undoing. "Oh, God." He choked out a coughing sob and John grabbed him. They cried together over the shared loss.

"Go back to her. I am here for anything you need. Tell Violet we will handle any meals. I will hire someone to do the cooking for all of us." John grabbed his handkerchief and wiped his face. His pain was still etched across his eyes. "I will come by in the morning. I am certain that Marie will want… dear lord Marie." John had his own news to share. Lucas now knew the dread of it. John embraced his son-in-law again and sent him off. This short interlude had bonded them closer than he realized possible.

Lucas ran back to the house to be at his wife's side. There were no right words to say but he would hold her.

✻ ✻ ✻ ✻ ✻

It was dawn when the doctor left. He had made sure she was safe from any danger of bleeding too much. He did confirm that she had lost the child. But he tried again and again to confirm to her that she was young and many women had miscarriages and were able to have children. Corinne was numb and just tried to agree with whatever the doctor told her.

He gave Corinne a few sleeping drops in her tea and soon she fell asleep.

The doctor gave instructions to Lucas and Violet. To be prepared for lots of tears and up and downs for the next few weeks. She will probably spot and bleed off and on for a few days but if she bleeds heavily to come for him immediately. Her body will have to adjust to the changes gradually.

"Her body will still think it is pregnant and she may feel very sad for a while. Just let her talk through it as much as possible." He instructed. Lucas thanked him as he left.

Lucas and Violet shared the daily duties, Marie came by later to sit and cry with her step-daughter. It was a long day for everyone.

The morning mist hung heavy as the steamship chugged along the Willamette River. Angela clung to the edge of the railing on the top deck next to Clive to watch the landscape as well as they could through the fog.

Angela's heart was still a bit numb after all she had gone through. There was a part of her that wished she had come back after Ted had left. That parting had been hard enough. But she knew she would always have wondered about her brother's safety. He would still be in her prayer's but in a different way. She knew she had to let him go. Almost like another death. It would be the only way she could not feel the pain as much. The rejection was there, in the pit of her stomach but she pushed it back down whenever it tried to surface.

With God she knew she could handle this pain. Piece by piece God would help her and He would put her back together.

It felt an eternity of gliding along the river before the whistle blew. They were porting!

Clive and Angela departed with trunks and bags and made quick time of finding a wagon. They first headed to the Mercantile. They dropped off a few packages to JQ, Clive gave a brief but good report to his son and they were off on the wagon to get Angela back home.

❋ ❋ ❋ ❋ ❋

The knock at the door surprised Violet who was pounding out bread dough on the counter. Her hand and apron a mess of flour but she did her best to wipe off the remnants on any clean part of her apron she could find as she made her way to the door. Violet smiled broadly as she saw Clive upon opening the door. He was such a nice man. She thought highly of him since he had found her this job with the Grant family. Beside Clive was a pretty gal in a dark green dress and a brown bonnet, there was a few red curls escaping the sides.

"Is Corinne home, or at her lab?" Clive asked. Violet gestured for them to come in.

"Well, Corinne is not seeing anyone right now. She is in bed." Violet felt bad for blurting it out but she hadn't prepared for visitors besides the doctor and family."

"In bed, is she ill?" The redhead spoke with concern and an urgent tone.

"Are you Angela?" Violet asked.

"Yes, Angela Fahey."

"I would think you would be allowed back then, you might be the one thing she needs to perk back up. She lost her child a few days ago and has been feeling low and poorly." Violet shared. All that she had heard from Corinne about Angela she knew that Corinne would not have kept the truth from her. She saw Angela's tears form. She wasted no time and with swift motions was out of her coat and bonnet in seconds.

"Go Red." Clive said, his voice low and sad.

Violet and Clive shared a cup of coffee as Angela left the room.

❀ ❀ ❀ ❀ ❀

Corinne was not tired anymore in a sleepy way but her body was exhausted. She had sent Lucas out that morning to get some work done. She was going to be fine, she had told him. She really just wanted some space to pray and think. Her bible was at her side. She had been browsing through it when she heard the knocking at the front door.

She was only mildly curious, guessing it to be Marie or Lucas asking Violet about her. Her father had stopped by three times yesterday. She felt cared for certainly but she knew the hardest part of this journey would be just facing the reality of it little by little.

The tiniest knock on her bedroom door was what surprised her.

"Who is it?" Corinne asked, she knew that Violet usually only knocked once and entered.

"Someone who has missed you."

Corinne heard the voice of her friend and then with the door open she saw her. It was the one unexpected thing that filled her heart with joy.

"Oh Angela!" Corinne cried against her friends embrace. Angela was sitting on the bed next to her they rocked and cried together.

"I am so sorry, Cori!" Angela said sincerely through her weepy voice.

"No, no, no, not today. Today is celebrating my sister returning." Corinne held her friend and they laughed and cried together for a long while.

❀ ❀ ❀ ❀ ❀

237

After a while Clive joined the girls and gave Corinne a fatherly hug. He had spoken at length with Violet and had even stopped outside and chatted with Lucas. Everyone was putting their bravest faces on and trying to be strong for Corinne.

Clive and Angela talked with Corinne about San Francisco and kept the topic light. Corinne was glad of it. She wanted a night to forget about the heaviness in her heart.

After a time Clive left to go visit with his granddaughter Chelsea and see the children. Corinne and Angela both sent their blessings.

Angela found Corinne a little changed. More mature perhaps. Corinne said the same to Angela.

"You mentioned in your latest letter about your courting with Ted Greaves." Corinne asked. Her enthusiasm was there but Angela could tell her friend was still weak.

"Yes, he is..." Angela smiled a bit and sighed. "He is wonderful."

She showed her the silver bracelet and told Corinne about him, and how he left just a few weeks before by ship back to New York State.

"He has promised to send a post when he arrives safe." Angela shared.

The next hours were spent in sharing, the good and the bad of the last months.

Corinne cried with Angela as she had shared the experience with her brother and his ultimate rejection, and Angela had cried with Corinne as she shared the recent loss of her pregnancy.

"I wondered a little about my coming west, one night in the dark on the steamship. It was originally to reunite with him. But I can say with my heart that you, Corinne, are my home. The sibling that has never betrayed me." Angela let the emotion take over and sobbed in her friend's lap. She let out a portion of the hurt and rejection in that moment they shared.

"I missed you so very much, but I think in time you will be glad to have seen a glimpse of him, even just to know he is safe." Corinne said as she stroked her friend's hair.

"I know that is true. Even if it had not gone so well as I had hoped. He looked like my father." Angela sat up and grabbed a handkerchief from the side table. She wiped off her tear-covered cheeks. "He sounded like him too. I remembered." Angela smiled weakly.

"We are a pitiful batch of emotions today. Considering we are having our own little reunion." Corinne said.

"Yes, but I know we will make it through this hard day, to face another, perhaps each day will get easier." Angela said. She clasped her friend's hand and it was a quiet moment for them to draw strength from each other.

"Are you in any pain?" Angela finally asked.

"A little, very sore in parts and mostly just exhausted." Corinne frowned a minute. "I still have this lingering guilt, like perhaps I worked too hard or had done something wrong." Corinne admitted. "But I have to say that God is helping me work through these feelings. Lucas has been good to me too. We will try again when it is time." Corinne let the tears fall a little more and her friend did her best to comfort her.

Over the next week Angela barely left her side. Corinne was up and moving around soon and they began taking short walks.

The spring air was damp and earthy and the breeze carried the girls around the property as they both grew stronger.

Dolly made many visits to make sure everything was being done the way things were supposed to be but Corinne felt like her work would have to wait as her body healed.

Corinne wanted to try a trip into town to see the Doctor instead of forcing him to keep coming to her. Dolly was well practiced at driving the team so she joined with Angela and Corinne.

Town was busy as Spring always was good for commerce. People needed supplies and to begin the annual time of rebirth. It was the season to begin things anew.

Doctor Williams was glad to see Corinne up and around. Angela and Dolly waited patiently for Corinne and stayed out in the front room and chatted with Persephone.

"I am looking forward to the new church building. I hear they are starting the building next week." Dolly said to the doctor's wife.

"Yes, I am so thankful to have come to the Spring Creek church. Corinne was wise to invite us. Perhaps she knew I was just too shy to fit in with the fancier church in town. I get so flustered with some of the elegant folks there. There are many city founders and important people. I always feel foolish." Persephone stated. Her and Dolly had spent some afternoons together after Sunday service. The Harpoles had invited the Williams to Sunday dinner several times.

"I am glad to be at my home church again. I have a lot of people to get reacquainted with." Angela said. She was behind on a lot of happenings within the community and felt a little out of touch.

"The valley will give you time to settle in." Dolly said and her sweet shy smile made Angela think that she would indeed find her place here again.

"That is poetic, Dolly, I like that." Persephone said. She gave Dolly a little nudge and Dolly surprised everyone with a laugh. Dolly was always such a quiet person, a busy bee, Cori called her. Her laughter was a rare blessing.

After Doc Williams let Corinne go with instructions and a promise from her to ease back into a routine the girls headed into town to visit with Clive if he was available.

The mercantile was bustling. The girls kept themselves busy looking through the shelves while JQ was helping customers. Corinne pointed out to Dolly and Angela that she could hear Clive's voice from the back rooms.

After several minutes the store cleared out of customers and JQ had a break. Corinne spoke with JQ and made sure he was re-introduced to Angela.

"I remember her well. I am glad you are safely back in Oregon, Miss." He said with sincerity.

"Well thank you, I am very happy to be home." Angela kept looking at Corinne who had made jokes at home about how much JQ looked like Clive. Corinne was acting silly and smiling a lot. Angela was trying not to laugh.

Mrs. Quackenbush came through the back door and when she saw the young ladies at the counter it appeared like she was thinking about turning around. JQ said "hello" to his wife and she sighed and walked toward the counter.

"Good to see you again Mrs. Quackenbush." Corinne said. "You are looking well." Corinne looked to her friends and was going to make introductions.

"I heard a rumor about you Mrs. Grant," She said, her voice was low.

"Ma'am?" Corinne said with surprise in her voice.

"Millie…" JQ said quietly and gave his wife a nudge with his elbow.

"I am sorry about your loss." Millie stated, almost grumbling.

"Thank you, Mrs. Quackenbush. I am recovering." Corinne said quietly, her smile and demeanor shifted. "I would like to introduce you to my friends. This is a dear friend, Dolly and this is Angela Fahey, she stayed with your son and daughter-in-law in California for many months."

"It is a pleasure to meet you." Angela and Dolly both said in their turn.

"I am sure you are looking forward to seeing your grandchild Silas. He is such a dear boy." Angela was trying to lighten the mood. Corinne's cheeks were a little flushed.

"Yes, child, I am. I will be just as glad when they are away from that city of sin. I have been vexed with Clive for this past year for sending them there. Wretched place." Millie said with more enthusiasm.

"They were not sent. It was a fine place until the Gold Rush started. They are wisely moving closer." JQ was obviously uncomfortable. "I read in a letter that you helped with the birthing Miss Fahey?" He smiled at the redhead.

"Well yes, but I would be happy if you called me Angela. It was my pleasure to be a help in any way." Angela said as she tried to understand the strange tension in the room.

Millie harrumphed and cleared her throat.

"Mrs. Grant, pardon my mentioning it, but as one Godly woman to another…" She leaned forward over the counter and looked at Corinne squarely in the eye. "Perhaps you would be wise to keep your focus on your husband and home and then perhaps God will be blessing you with an offspring."

Angela and Dolly gasped.

JQ yelled. "Millie!! You mind your own."

Corinne looked as if her face had been slapped. It turned a burnish red then changed to a ghastly pale.

"I …" Dolly said then stopped. "I think you mistake concern for slander, Ma'am. I thought it was God's job to instruct his flock."

Millie Quackenbush gasped but was gently guided away from the counter by her husband as Corinne and her friend left the mercantile. Corinne had a small bolt of cloth still in her hand when she left and Angela took it from her. Seeing the shocked tears still threatening to spill from Corinne's eyes.

"I will take it in." Angela said and ran back into the store. She placed the cloth on the counter. JQ was still in the back of the room having a heated discussion with his wife.

Dolly and Corinne were sitting on the bench. Corinne was pale and speechless. Dolly was speaking in low tones.

"You have said on many occasions that you feel that you are led by God to do his work. To make healing medicine and remedies for people is the calling you have on your heart." Dolly said with certainty in her voice.

Corinne nodded and the few tears escaped and ran a slow race down her cheeks. "Psalm 143:10 says Teach me to do thy will; for thou art my God: thy Spirit is good; lead me into the land of uprightness." Dolly wiped the tears from Corinne's cheek. "That women spoke not in any knowledge or wisdom but in fear and jealousy. I know not why she said that but her words mean nothing when you know what God has put in your heart."

241

Angela sat on the other side of Corinne and put a supportive arm around her shoulders.

"Dolly is right. You are a good woman, whether you tend a home or tend a greenhouse garden. God has given gifts to all his children. To you He has blessed with courage to face many obstacles." Angela felt so angry inside. She wanted so badly to go and speak with that malicious woman inside. But she knew her words would be nothing like the wise words that Dolly said. Angela fought a hard battle to keep her anger under control while her friend took deep breaths.

"I will be okay, friends. I should have expected this sooner. My mother faced down rumors when I was young. There will always be people who don't understand a woman who is a little different," Corinne said, her voice was shaking. "It was hurtful, though. I have had those same fears in the dark of night. Perhaps my miscarriage was some kind of punishment. But I know that is just a lie. Whether or not I am able to bear children is in God's hands and whether I stay home and bake bread or work in my lab and greenhouse matters little. I will honor God by the work of my hands and trust Him to take care of me."

Angela and Dolly both nodded as Corinne spoke. The bell on the mercantile door made all three girls jump in unison.

"I would like to beg your pardon Mrs. Grant." JQ's voice was heard and they all looked up from the bench in to his kind eyes. "My wife has strong opinions and I do beg your forgiveness. She gets carried away when she gets her ribbons in a twist about something. I do not agree nor condone her actions today."

Corinne stood and Dolly and Angela mirrored her action, a united front.

"Thank you JQ, do not worry yourself. Her words are already forgiven." Corinne looked frail and wounded but her friends were so proud of her.

"You are a good woman. I will be praying for you Mrs. Grant." JQ said with sadness in his voice.

"Please call me Corinne. There needs to be no formality between us. Your father is like family to me." Corinne took his hand and shook it in friendship.

"Let's go home girls." Corinne said with a tired voice.

"I will bring the wagon over. Stay here." Dolly said and with a quick step she ran across the street to where they had parked the wagon, near Doc Williams' office. Dolly's light blue dress fluttered behind her legs as she ran.

JQ went back indoors when a customer went in.

Angela stood with Corinne and let the moment be still. When the wagon was nearly around the corner Angela finally spoke. "You

242

are so forgiving. I am still angry with that woman. How dare she…"
Angela stopped when Corinne was turning pink in the cheeks again.

"I will be forgiving her again and again. I have to try and hope
it sticks." Corinne looked tired and pitiful for a second. It made Angela
angry again for the insensitivity of that woman. JQ was such a nice
man, what in the world could have upset her so much to lash out at
Corinne? Angela helped her friend into the wagon seat and pulled
herself up, she was praying as she moved.

Lord please bless my friend, and help me to let go of this anger.

❖ ❖ ❖ ❖

When the girls arrived at home Corinne wanted to take a nap
and Dolly and Angela sat at the dining room table to talk over what
had happened.

Violet was concerned when she saw Corinne looking so tired
and flushed.

She sat down and Angela spoke first. "Corinne is upset, but I
don't know what to do."

"Is she unwell, she was so happy this morning? She was very
happy to be getting a trip to town. Did she overdo it?" Violet asked.
She had a potato and a peeler in her hand and set them down with a
soft thud on the table.

"No, but a woman in town said something hurtful." Dolly said.
"I will not wish to say the woman's name but someone questioned
Corinne's work and blamed her loss of child on her not being a proper
Godly wife." Dolly stated flatly.

"No!" Violet held a hand over her mouth in astonishment.
"Who would ever do such a thing?"

The three women sat in a quiet circle. They all knew the pain
of harsh words. Without saying much they all agreed to pray for
Corinne and keep the story to themselves. After Violet went back to
finishing preparations for dinner Angela and Dolly had a short
discussion. They both decided that Angela should tell Lucas, so he
could talk to his wife but also be informed.

"The thing that worries me is something Mrs. Quackenbush
said before she insulted her." Angela said.

"About how she had heard a rumor?" Dolly said and Angela
nodded. They both feared the same thing. Wagging tongues were the
devil's playground even more so than idle hands.

❖ ❖ ❖ ❖

243

Lucas Grant stretched his stiff shoulders. He had been chopping wood for several hours. He had slept poorly the night before. He was more upset by the words of Mrs. Quackenbush than his wife was. The morning sun wasn't up when he got out of his bed, restless and irritable. He had been praying since he heard. Trying to keep his temper down. Lucas had a long fuse. It took a lot to get him riled up, verbally accusing his wife of not doing her Godly duty was more than he was willing to accept with a calm demeanor.

He did not know the proper course of action. If it had been a man who had made a comment to her he may have had harsh words or even challenged him. With an overzealous gossipy woman he had a new dilemma. He felt helpless. If Angela was right about the statement about rumors, there was nothing to be done. If the town's women wanted to spread gossip and rumor that was a prairie fire that was hard to snuff out.

Lucas grabbed his axe and spent another half hour taking his frustration out on the firewood.

At noon he saw Clive ride up to the cabin on his brown mare.

"Clive…" Lucas said in greeting. He swung his axe down and it landed solidly into the side of the stump. He left it there and walked toward his friend. Perhaps a talk with Clive would settle his nerves.

"Talk to me, Clive." Lucas said with a bit of pleading in his voice.

"Be glad to." Clive said. Lucas stood near his friend and Clive clapped the young man on the shoulders.

"I am at a loss." Lucas laid his hand open in a hopeless gesture. "How do you mend a wife?"

"Oh, that is a question us menfolk have been asking since Adam and Eve. Either we hurt or someone else does. Or they act foolish and we get to reap the consequences. I figured out a man's job of loving and protecting his wife to be a lifelong battle." Clive sighed. "I came on a mission from my son's abode. JQ is feeling mighty sorry about his wife's actions. I come bearing a small package for Corinne and you."

"Oh?"

"Yes, but I doubt if it will have many solutions to your particular problem. I have known Millicent for many years now. My son married a strong-willed woman. In many ways she has always been a firecracker but she does not have much of a sensitive side. Before my second wife, Martha, passed on, Millicent and Martha were in a tiff every other month. Martha was a lot like your wife and had a free spirit and constantly wanted to be at my side in the business part of my life. Millie would always be critical and Martha was not for listening to anyone question her motives or actions. After Martha passed away Millie calmed, this town was small and neighbors were hard to come by for long stretches especially in the winter months. I think JQ had spent a lot of breath trying to help her understand that not everyone agreed with her way of thinking. Lately I have noticed her wind is back up. She has a pack of ladies in town that have adopted her as their leader of sorts." Clive scratched his chin.

"It is not fair to label my wife as an ungodly woman…" Lucas was exasperated. No matter who was the leader, he wanted people to keep their mouths shut about his wife.

"I know Lucas. I cannot know what to say to make this better. Is Corinne very upset?" Clive was concerned about the rumor and gossip mill in town.

"Actually not as much as I am. I was taking out my frustration on some firewood." Lucas grimaced and stretched a stiff shoulder.

"Let's go in and talk to her. I will hand over the package and see what your wife has to say." Clive gave Lucas a nudge and they walked in.

Corinne and Violet were in the kitchen talking. Angela was reading by the fireplace.

"Greetings, women of the house." Clive said. He saw all smiles from the ladies and was pleased. He was expecting a much more dour scene.

"I come bearing a gift." Clive said and laid the package on the table.

The ladies gathered at the table. Lucas was washing at the basin down the hallway and came back into the room.

"I would just like to say before you open the package, Corinne, that I believe you are gifted woman of the Lord. I consider my life to be blessed since I have met you and your extended friends and family." Clive looked like he wanted to continue but Corinne cut him off.

"Clive, please sit down. You know I consider you family, as does everyone here. You need not make any speeches. I am fine." Corinne set her hand on his arm to settle him.

Clive sighed and wordlessly sat at the shiny oak table. The small package sat in the middle and everyone looked at it for a minute.

"After yesterday a gift is the least of your worries, Cori." Angela said and everyone chuckled.

"Very true. Let's see what the fuss is all about. Shall we?" Corinne smiled at her friends and winked at her husband who was trying very hard not to frown.

The dark wrapping came off easily and a small card slid out.

Corinne opened and read aloud.

"Dear Corinne Grant, I must begin with an apology. I was insensitive and overzealous in my speech with you yesterday afternoon. I now realize how my statements may have been received as insulting and I do beg pardon. I seek your forgiveness for my callous and unfeeling remarks. I do hope from this time forward you would consider me a friend. Mrs. Millicent Quackenbush." Corinne finished and let out a deep breath.

She set the note down and looked at the blue painted box sitting next to the card. It opened with a creak and Corinne pulled out a cloth. Embroidered on the front – God Bless All In This Home. The embroidery was done with a delicate hand and the floral pattern around it was in bold red, blue and yellow flowers.

"Well, I guess that is that." Corinne said and handed the embroidered cloth to Angela. "You think you can make a pillow or something with it?"

Angela nodded and set it on the table. She didn't want to say what she was thinking.

"I have had a day to think on what Millie said. In my quiet time and prayers yesterday and today I just felt at peace. I knew when I had this dream in my heart to grow flowers and make medicines from them that it would be nearly impossible. I leaned on God and gave my dream to Him. God has been so good to me, I found a man who loves and believes in me and we work this place together. I have my friend Angie, safe and home. I have a new friend and helper in Violet. She is a constant blessing to my home and she says often that this job is a blessing to her. If a few women in town want to idly talk about me behind my back and say untruths that is their sin not mine. I feel that God has a plan for me. I am not without my own flaws and sins but I believe that I am doing the work God made just for me. Her statement about losing my child is the part that stung and I forgive her for that part. It is my job to forgive too." Corinne stopped and wiped one tear that escaped down her cheek. "I wish to write her a note tomorrow of forgiveness and think of it never again."

Lucas kissed his wife on the cheek.

Everyone agreed that they would all move on.

"Well, I am glad to see your heart is growing stronger by the day, my flower girl." Clive stood up and accepted a hug from Corinne before he left.

"It is, Clive, I know that not everyone will understand what I am trying to do here. They don't have to. As long as I feel God is for me, I cannot falter." Corinne said and waved as he walked out.

"Angela, get out the checkerboard, I feel like whooping someone at checkers. Who is up first?" Corinne smiled and the room lit up with activity.

Chapter 31

Another week was enough rest and Corinne was ready to be back at her job, she wanted to do half days in her greenhouse and labs. In the afternoons she and Angela would take longs walks. Exploring the property and the woods. Corinne felt at ease with her friend back home. Angela was beginning to come back out of her shell again.

"I thought of this place as home but I am getting to know Oregon better now. I don't have the pull to find Sean anymore. There is a part of me that wonders if there was something else I could have said to make him want to have me in his life. But I have to let those thoughts go. There is a life to be lived here and now. Dwelling on the past will bring me no explanations." Angela said on afternoon. She was enjoying the game they had been playing all week, trying to find any flowers peaking up through the dried leaves from last fall. Corinne had a bag full of mushrooms that she declared as treasure.

"You need to hire more children to pick flowers for you. You know that this valley is full of treasures." Angela winked and Corinne laughed, remembering the children from the Oregon Trail. She had handed out half pennies and peppermint candies for flowers and mushrooms, the children nicknamed her the Plant Lady. It was a good memory from those hard days and she savored the memory of those sweet faces.

"Your idea has merit. I may put you to task and head to the schoolhouse and tell the children what to look for." Corinne winked at her friend and Angela clapped excitedly.

"Oh, really?" Angela grinned with sincerity. "That would be a delightful chore."

Corinne nodded and they planned and plotted for the rest of their walk.

The very next day Angela left when Corinne did in the early morning. Angela walked the mile and a half to the schoolhouse. It was on the edge of Corinne and Lucas's property, they had donated the land to the school and nearby was the new church. It was not painted yet but the outer walls were built. The Spring Creek Community Church sign was sitting next to the western most outer wall. The crisp black letters were bold and Angela was proud to be a member. This was her home, her church and perhaps someday her own children and Ted would be sitting next to her in that very building. It was a beautiful dream.

The schoolteacher was a man named Marshall Crispin. He was young, but he was doing a good job of teaching, according to the neighbors. Chelsea Grant said that Brody just loved him and his students were learning.

Angela found the schoolyard to be bustling with young bodies at play.

She saw Brody and he ran up to her. His red hair was darker than hers. He gave her a quick hug, not wanting his friend to tease him for hugging a 'girl'.

"You haven't started yet today?" Angela asked him.

"Nope, Mr. Crispin says we gotta run out our wiggles before we get started." Brody said. Angela brushed a hand through his hair and laughed.

"That is very wise of the teacher." Angela sent Brody off to play with his friends.

Angela knocked on the door of the school and was welcomed in by the teacher. Angela had met Mr. Crispin at a Sunday service but this was their first time speaking. He was polite and loved the idea. He said that she could share her proposition with the class.

Mr. Crispin rang a hand bell at the door a few minutes later and the students filed in. There were twenty-one students', ages in range of five years old to thirteen. The older boys, Mr. Crispin explained, were only attending school classes until it was warm enough to start plowing the fields. Mr. Crispin was proud that a few of his older boys continued on with their studies and reading even when they didn't have too.

Mr. Crispin introduced Angela and let her have the floor.

"Class, I am here today to offer you a chance to help out my dear friend, Mrs. Grant with plant collecting." Angela went on to explain how plants help to provide good medicine. She held up a small bottle of oil, and let everyone smell the floral jasmine scent. She explained a few local plants to look for and welcomed them to gather morel mushrooms as well. She held up a morel to show them what they looked like.

Angela could see that they all were excited.

"I will come by the school on Tuesdays and Fridays, everyone is allowed to bring a small bag full. Each bag will be rewarded with a half-penny for the student and also brings a half-penny to the school for new books and supplies. I want everyone to ask permission from your parents and make sure you never go into the woods alone." Angela made sure everyone nodded their agreement before she continued.

Angela then explained the best way to harvest plants. "You need to use a spade to loosen the dirt away from the roots because we

249

want the whole plant. Not just the tops that are sticking out of the ground." The children asked a few questions and Angela did her best to answer them all the best she could. She was enjoying the time and the sweet faces that were so excited at the prospect of earning extra money.

Mr. Crispin had a few questions just to clarify the simple rules. He was very thrilled with the extra money that would be coming in for books and supplies.

Angela left with a full heart and with a task to collect plants twice a week it gave her something fun to look forward to every week.

When she got back to Corinne working in her lab she shared the good news.

"Well, Plant Lady, you have a new crew of gatherers." Angela shared with an infectious grin. Dolly and Corinne both joined with Angela and she told them all about her morning and how excited the students were.

❊ ❊ ❊ ❊ ❊

July 18th 1850

Angela and Cooper were wrist deep under a pile of rocks and dead leaves in the woods. They had plans of doing some serious fishing. They needed bait. Cooper and Angela had worked hard on making a good fishing pole over the week. They were both proud of their efforts. Cooper and Angela were thick as thieves again.

As they finally got their bait gathered and they were near their secret fishing spot, the clouds rolled in and a summer thunderstorm rolled over the mountains. They were closer to Cooper's house so they ran for it.

Angela laughed as they both ran awkwardly with their fishing poles swinging about wildly.

Once Cooper was safely inside Angela promised him they would get their fishing in once the weather was improved. Cooper only pouted a little until his mother produced a towel and a piece of cake.

Angela passed on the cake, she saw a break in the heavy rain and she took her chance. She ran along the path back to the Grants.

She arrived soaked from head to toe but slightly exhilarated. Clive and Violet were visiting at the table. Violet was mending something and Clive was drinking coffee.

"Let me change and I will join you." Angela said and ran back to her room. She laid her wet clothes in the wicker basket, with a promise to herself to wring them out after her visit with Clive.

She found a dry shift and a comfortable day dress that buttoned up the front. Her hair was a wet mess so she just ran a brush through it and did a loose and sloppy braid.

Clive was still there, laughing and talking to Violet.. Clive looked up and smiled in her direction when she appeared around the corner.

"What brings you out in this fair weather?" Angela asked as she plopped into the chair next to Clive.

"Well, I have to admit it was fair when I arrived, but the clouds sure did come in fast." Clive declared.

Angela laughed and nodded. "Yes, Cooper and I had our fishing spot all picked out when the sky turned black on us."

Clive enjoyed hearing the playful tone in her voice.

"I have something for you!" Clive announced looking at Angela expectantly.

"Oh, what, pray tell, would it be?" She said back at him just as expectantly.

"A telegram." He said, enjoying watching her eye grow wide. "From New York."

Angela gasped without knowing it. Violet giggled for she knew how much Angela had wanted to get this very telegram.

Clive set it on the table to see how fast she would grab it, but was surprised when she paused.

"It is good news?" Angela said with worry in her voice.

"Just read the thing, Red." Clive said and laughed.

The white paper had only six words, but they made her face light up with joy.

Arrived safe my Angel. Love Ted

The reminder of Ted sent a mixture of emotions through Angela. She had missed him, but had found many ways to distract herself from thinking of him. Now with this telegram it made her miss him all the more. She did not know any more than those six words. Had he spoken to his mother? Would he be coming back? All these questions pressed at her.

There is a certain misery that waiting brings, knowing your happiness in on hold. It takes a level of patience and character to push it down. Angela strove every day to keep that misery at bay. She would rejoice over the simple pleasures that life brings and make plans, so many plans and write them out in her leather bound journal. The Sparks had no idea the thoughts and dreams that would flow on those cream colored pages.

Drawings and thoughts spread over the pages. Angela began finding a certain peace in dreaming on those pages. The journal would never think her silly or whimsical.

Chapter 32 - Angela

It really began as a fluttering thought, a lingering hope for the future. Angela thought so often of the things in her family's trunk, the things that still held part of their life with them. It wasn't much to cling too. Not like the warmth of an embrace or a soft spoken word, but these things created a vision over time. The weeks and months she was home in Oregon were filling her up with visions of a future here.

She kept it close to her. During her quiet days alone, sometimes she helped Violet with the bread baking, Violet was always making extras for those in need. Angela enjoyed the quiet girl's company. She spoke of joy and peace, though Angela could sometimes see pain lingering behind the girl's eyes. She was only one year her senior, many older folks would claim that one so young could not have faced enough hardship yet to have regrets. But Angela knew better. Violet had a joy that bubbled out of her but Angela could sense that there was more to this young woman. It was easy to bond with her as she was everything Angela wanted to be. Violet was a servant in Corinne's house but treated with decency and respect, and Violet enjoyed and thrived in the position. She took a pride in her work that made Angela take notice.

Angela had never felt like she had ever slacked in her duties, but she had never fully had a joy in her heart the way that Violet did. Angela would not allow herself to beat up on herself for her actions as a servant, she just knew in the future her attitude toward working at something would be changed having known Violet.

❈ ❈ ❈ ❈ ❈

The catalog sat before her, she traced her finger along the items she had been dreaming about, a lovely side table with a hook for a towel. She had seen the towels she wanted as well. The pitcher and washbowl in a second hand store downtown would look lovely sitting on this table. It had green ivy leaves painted on the lower part of the pitcher and matching leaves and sprigs of heather on the bowl. It would go into a nook in a hallway beautifully, perhaps with a mirror above it.

Angela had been pondering for weeks about how to keep it all. Where she would keep it but she knew she had to order these things.

She excused herself after breakfast. She helped Cooper with his early morning chores of filling the water barrels. It was hard work but was pleasant to see the young boy smile as she helped him. She

253

didn't always do it, she knew his father was trying to instill within him a desire to work hard and provide a service to his family. John Harpole was raising Cooper as he would his own flesh and blood and Angela respected that. She had far off memories of the chores she had done as a young girl, even being a baron's daughter, she helped her mother in the garden and there was memory of spreading feed for the chickens. Perhaps it is why she longed again for another chicken coop. She knew when Gabe and Amber came to Portland in the fall they had already agreed to bring the chickens here. She wanted a few chicks from her original batch to start again.

All her hopes and dreams were before her and she was settling in but longing to have her own roots. Ideas that stewed and blossomed into plans were poking around in the corners of her mind. She had a task for the day. She would be heading to town.

Her visit to Clive's Mercantile had been quick and painless, she headed immediately over to the second- hand store and purchased the pitcher and washbowl and had it packed carefully and boxed up. Clive joined her at the store as the owner had just finished up the packing.

"I am ready for you. I got the wagon out front. It's not far to go." Clive said all business. Angela had hoped she hadn't been a nuisance to the man today. He would never let on with her. He seemed to be ready and able to drop anything at any time for anyone.

"I appreciate your help, Clive, as always." Angela said and gave him a peck on the cheek.

Clive's satisfied smirk was a joy to see.

He carried her box and placed it in the back. They headed just off the main street to a warehouse. Inside was a myriad of supplies. Bulk items, lots of labeled boxes set about in an organized way. There was order here, and not a cobweb in sight.

"I was thinking that a back room I have recently emptied would work well for you. It has a door, shelves and can be locked. It has two keys. I can give you one and I will keep the spare at the mercantile."

"That would be grand." Angela saw the room was bare and clean. It had only a tiny window but once Clive lit the lantern she saw the room had plenty of space for her current plans.

"This is perfect. I would like a reasonable rate of cost to rent the space, I will not accept it for free." Angela stated with a firm stance. She was getting better about holding her ground.

Clive harrumphed only a slight little bit, way less than she expected. She felt a small twinge of pride that she was beginning to believe in herself.

He made an offer that was very reasonable. Angela agreed and promised to drop by a six-month payment to him later at the mercantile. She would like an official invoice so everything was above board.

Clive laughed and then offered to take her to lunch at the hotel restaurant. She agreed and they enjoyed sharing a meal and many laughs together.

With a quick trip to the bank done soon after lunch she had free reign to do as she wished. Her mother would have started a hope chest for her when she was a young lady. Starting to gather things a woman needed to set up her own home; her own dreams and pretty things, and useful things would have filled its cedar sides. It would be filled with linens, doilies and the hopes and dreams of a girl who would someday have her own legacy to build upon. Angela was starting one herself. But her goal was bigger. She saw her home, her very own home. The walls and staircase and kitchen had a feel to it in her mind. Wood floors she would shine, and her own dishes and dining room table. She would have a lace tablecloth for special guests, and a linen one with embroidery for every day.. She would have a front porch that faced a mountain view and a barn with a cow and chickens clucking away somewhere nearby.

She would grow things, a garden, a fruit tree, perhaps a family. Her dream was big. It had walls and grass and she would live and grow where God had planted her.

Chapter 33

Lucas came through the door and shrugged out of his jacket soaked through with rain. He kicked his boots off and made his way over to the wooden rocking chair near the fire.

The three women in the house all greeted him cheerfully.

"Thank you ladies." Lucas said, the frustration in his voice was evident. Corinne and Violet were in the kitchen. Corinne brought Lucas a hot mug of coffee. Lucas thanked her and took a sip and closed his eyes momentarily enjoying the warmth of it. He knew he should have changed out of his damp clothes but he didn't feel like moving away from the fire just yet.

Angela who was sitting on the love seat crocheting finally spoke up and asked what everyone was wondering.

"How did it go down at the land committee meeting?" Angela blurted out.

Lucas looked at his wife then Angela. "They would not consider my case. Mr. Prince is still on the committee and made a strong stand that since the land we currently owned isn't fully developed yet, then why should we be allowed to have more land." Lucas sighed. "I had several people speak on my behalf but the lobby against was too strong. Mr. Prince and his deals with the building committee are something the town council does not want to lose."

Corrine gave her husband a kiss on his cold cheek. She grabbed a blanket from the back of the sofa and draped it around Lucas's shoulders.

Violet came in with her own cup of coffee and joined the conversation. She was becoming more part of the family than housekeeper as the weeks past. Everyone seemed to prefer it that way.

"I have found in my life that these kinds of obstacles build my faith more than anything else. I am praying that God shows himself in this situation." Violet took a sip and stared at the fire. Everyone turned to her and smiled in that way that they always had to with her. Violet had such a depth within her. She never shared much about her background. But she always made everyone feel better with her words.

"Thank you Violet." Corinne said sincerely. "I will pray more about this myself. The land would be convenient. But we do not know God's plans."

❖ ❖ ❖ ❖ ❖

Angela snuck out of the room a while after Lucas came home. She wanted to move forward with her plans but needed to pray. She had this feeling inside her for months. Her daily walks lately had been past the very land where Lucas was trying to purchase. She had walked the land many times. The small cabin and barn were not in good shape but part of the land had been broken and a small orchard had been started. They looked to be apple trees, but they were small. The land commission had rules about the land, the price was low but you had to have a cabin built within a set time period and then break the land and live in the cabin for two years. The landowners here had been negligent on several occasions. The cabin had only been built after threat of losing the deed, two separate times. The owner had a reputation for laziness and procrastination. Angela scoped out the land and found several favorite places. One spot, near the creek was a pretty hill with some lovely trees and a weeping willow kept beckoning her back to it. When she stood atop that hill she could see the land spread out, she saw the outline of Grant's Grove and further away the big barn of John Harpole. She began imagining the way it would feel to sit on the front porch and watch the way the sun would set to the west. She never said a word to anyone but thoughts hatched inside of her. Owning an orchard would be a pleasant way to live.

When Lucas had said several weeks before how he had his eye on the land across the way, her heart had sunk. He and Corinne had hopes of snatching up nearby land so they could expand their operation when they needed to. Lucas still had nearly half their three hundred acres to break on the west side of the creek but they had hopes of building an orchard too. Corinne had plans for almonds and olives, for the expressing of their oil to expand her business. She was always explaining how well they both worked for the health and benefit to the human body.

Lucas and Russell talked over land plans and schemes for how the property next to them was a good choice for planting an orchard. It is a slow business, waiting for trees to grow, and rotation and pruning to get the best production available was always a challenge.

How could I possible throw a fit about land that isn't even within my grasp when they have a plan, are actually farmers and are men? Angela wondered to herself. She laid aside the idea in her mind. She had foolishly been living in her fictitious house atop that hill and she had to let that dream go. Her heart had been broken worse than this, she reminded herself often. She let God heal the minor words of a hope lost and moved on with her dreams of someday.

Now that Angela had news that the land was no longer being pursued by Lucas, a fresh idea burst into her head and she couldn't shake it. She had sat listening to everyone talk to Lucas about his

257

afternoon full of disappointments and she was shaking on the inside. The house on the hill was renewed in her mind but now it had taken wing and she saw rows of almond trees and an olive grove. Her thoughts were leaping inside her head, as well as the guilt of rejoicing over someone else's loss.

Dear Lord, show me how to move forward. Angela prayed as she sat on her bed. She watched the rainfall and wanted to banish it. How could she leave and get to town when the rain poured and the wind blew? No one in the house would understand why she would leave in this kind of weather. She would have to wait. The one person she needed to see was not to be seen today.

❄ ❄ ❄ ❄ ❄

Angela felt ten times the fool when two hours had passed and the person she had wanted to see knocked on the Grant's door.

Clive bound in with his usual vigor and made his presence known to the house. His comedic actions of shaking the rain free from himself had everyone smiling.

"Just checking in on my girls and see how Lucas was fairin' after his lovely chat with the land council." Clive deposited his hat, coat and muddy boots where they could dry off.

Angela had resumed her spot on the loveseat and Clive felt obligated to join in next to her. She gave him a wink and kept up with her crocheting, even though her heart was pounding in her chest with excitement. She had no idea how she could talk with him privately without raising suspicion but she gladly prayed for her heart to calm and for God to find a way, she added a thank you to God in her mind for already easing her fears. If this dream of hers was God's will, she knew that He could work it out.

The rain outside eventually slowed down. Violet served a hearty stew with her amazing bread pulled fresh from the oven. Everyone decided to let talk of the failed attempt with the land council go and they all spoke of other things. The harvest festival was coming up soon and both Violet and Lucas were going to be performing music for part of the time. All the musicians decided to take turns so they all could have a chance to enjoy dancing with their spouses and families. After dinner Clive and Angela pestered Lucas and Violet to perform a song they had been practicing to play at a Sunday meeting.

Corinne and Angela snuggled together in the loveseat and Clive sat in the rocker as Lucas and Violet shared their musical gifts with them. Corinne whispered in Angela's ear after the song.

"The music is so good for the heart. I just can't explain it."

Angela nodded and whispered back. "I know what you mean."

Lucas tuned his violin and played a slow ballad that had been a favorite of his mother's. Corinne wiped away a tear or two as the sweet notes carried through her home. After the music Clive was ready to get on home. He had a few miles to go to get to his cabin.

"My horse is sure to be wanting his supper." Clive said with a grin.

"Clive can I walk you out. I want to chat with you for a minute." Angela stood and did a quickstep to the door to catch up with Clive.

"I wouldn't mind at all, Red."

Angela grabbed her shawl.

The air smelled of damp earth outside and the rain had stopped but for a few errant drops. The moon was only a half circle but it was trying to peak through hazy clouds.

"What's on your mind little thing?" Clive asked.

"Well, I know I don't have a long stretch to talk to ya but I have an idea I wanted to run by ya." Angela said quickly.

Clive saw her eyebrows were knitted together in a bit of a worry.

"Yer sounded like Corinne with yer ideas lately. What's frettin' ya?"

"The land Lucas tried to buy. I want it." Angela blurted out and then sighed a big breath.

Clive grabbed his chin for a moment.

Angela took that as a sign to just say the remainder of what was on her heart.

"I feel slightly guilty about it, since I never mentioned that I had even been dreaming about the place." She paused only a second and continued. "When Lucas was talking to Corinne and Russell about wanting it, I put all my thoughts aside. I had this perfect hill all picked out for a house, next to the creek and I was going to grow an orchard and sell the produce from it. If I grew almonds and olives I could actually sell to Corinne and Lucas and help them grow their business. I just figured I could afford a good field hand. I turn eighteen in a week."

Clive began to chuckle softly

Angela gave Clive a weak smile, wondering what in the world he was thinking.

"It must be something in the water over here that makes the women ambitious." Clive chuckled again. "Is this hill close by?"

"Just a few minutes walk from here." Angela said with a bigger grin.

"Let's get our boots muddy." Clive offered her his arm.

259

The walk was indeed short and Angela knew she was prattling but could not help herself. She told him about the state of the land, and the existing cabin that would not do for her home at all.

"I want a farmhouse with lots of rooms and a huge front porch." She said with a little emotion in her throat.

They reached the hill and stood atop it the way Angela had done so many times. The valley was showing off with the moon sparkling across the landscape.

"You picked yourself a nice spot. You got a house plan picked already? I know you been looking through the magazines and pamphlets since you been home from San Francisco." Clive asked.

"Yessir." Angie said humbly. She was proud of her choice. She had everything in her hope chest at Corinne's.

"Do you think Lucas will be disappointed in me if I go for the land? I am not sure they will even let me have it being a woman." Angela was worried about this part the most. The what if's.

"Your money spends, you do have a beau. That will help."

"We have no understanding or engagement between myself and Ted." Angela explained.

"He would be considered a prospect, and you do have word that he is coming next spring. I will think on it a spell." Clive gave her a sideways hug and they walked back to the Grant's home.

"I am not sure how to talk about it with the Grant's. I do not want to be secretive or seem like I want to profit from their misfortune with the land council. I will admit to having my eye on the place since I got back from San Francisco. But they don't know that. I would certainly like to have my own place. Since I turn eighteen so soon, I guess I just am hoping that God can work all this out with no hard feelings." Angela was wringing her hands with her worry.

Clive took a moment to consider things and then spoke. "I think I can make a few inquiries, no names, just hypothetical is all and see what comes of it. I know of someone you might want to talk to iffen you do want to run an orchard. He might seem like an odd fit, but he was a brilliant farmer until he ran into some bad luck. He came out west and was trying to earn enough to start over then he lost his left hand in an accident. But he sure is smart as a whip. I hired him on to manage my warehouses, but he longs to be back on the land. If you built yourself a farmhouse, he would probably be glad to fix up the little cabin to live in. His name is Earl Burgess, if all works out I can introduce ya."

Angela smiled and put Earl's name in her memory. She had a lot to pray about.

"Clive, I want to say something and I want you to take me perfectly seriously." Angela stopped walking and waited for Clive to turn to her.

Her looked her in the eye and nodded to affirm that she had his full attention.

"I always had God preached to me as a child, first by my ma, then the work orphanage had us going to service, they used God as a fear tactic a lot. Then I met Corinne and she shared her bible with me and taught me more. But I have to say, I never quite understood how God could be so loving until I met you. You are the best Grandfather a girl could have, you share your heart, your wisdom and your love, even though we aren't blood kin, and you always treat me like I am. I will never, ever forget all the good you have done for me. If God can make a flesh and blood man that can be so much for me here on this earth, I know that God loves me, it proves it."

Clive handed her a handkerchief and she wiped the tears from her pink cheeks.

"I have never been more speechless child." Clive said. His voice was a little thick.

They walked slowly back to the Grant's home, Clive got his horse from the barn and right before he saddled up he gave Angela a big bear hug.

"I would be proud to call you my kin, ya know." He said next to her ear.

He heard her sniffle a little and let her go. He climbed up in the saddle and gave her a wave.

"I will come by soon with news. Once your birthday comes we can see what can be done." Clive said and was off.

❉ ❉ ❉ ❉

Sept 1st 1850

"Happy Birthday, Aunt Angela!" Cooper said in a near yell as he swooped into the house. Violet and Angela were sipping coffee and Corinne was coming from her bedroom.

"Well thank you, Coop!" Angela held her arms open for the big hug that waited for her.

"Are you old now?" He asked with a mischievous grin that was irresistible.

"Yep, so very, very old." Angela laughed and hugged him again.

"What are you going to do for your birthday?" Cooper asked.

261

"Well I am going to town with your big sister and Violet, but I was hoping later me and you could take a walk down by the creek. There is a special spot I wanted to show you." Angela gave Cooper a wink.

"That would be great. I am gonna go help Pa with the horses but I wanted to say happy birthday first." Cooper was out the door with the speed of a wild animal. The door didn't close all the way behind him and Corinne laughed and took care of the swinging door.

"He is so dear to me." Angela sighed and sipped her coffee, her grin stayed for over a minute.

"He is much like my little brothers were. So full of life." Violet said with a sigh.

"I didn't know you have brothers." Corinne said it first but Angela looked up with the same inquisition in her mind.

"I do, but I do not see them. God gave me a fresh start and a new chance at life. I don't think much about that time of my life anymore." Violet said with a smile that seemed the tiniest bit forced.

"I will not pry Violet. You have been a Godsend for Lucas and me. Your privacy is your own. I would never force your confidence." Corinne took Violet's hand and squeezed it. "But I will pray for your brothers, as I am sure you do."

"I do every day." Violet said, her smile was real now.

"God saved me from a life of servitude and loss. I know what it's like to get a new chance at having a family." Angela shared. Her and Violet had a close bond. They didn't have to know the full story of each other's lives to know that hurt was buried down deep. They knew that only God and time could heal those wounds.

"Let's stop being so weepy and go have fun today." Violet stated.

"Who's being weepy?" Lucas made and appearance from the back bedroom. He was wearing his work clothes and his broad hat in his hand. He looked ready to get to work.

"Us girls just being girls." Corinne said with a laugh. She jumped up and got her husband a fresh mug of coffee.

"Actually before we go I would like a chance to talk to everyone." Angela stood.

"Well, you are the birthday girl. You have the floor Miss Fahey." Lucas gave a slight bow and sat at the table. Once Corinne delivered his coffee she sat down as well.

"Today I turn eighteen, and if all goes well I will take action to do something that I hope you will consider wise." Angela took a deep breath.

"You all know that I have been dreaming of making a place of my own for a few months and I had a place in mind but kept it secret.

When Lucas informed me he was trying for the orchard property next to you I set the thoughts aside. I would never want to interfere with your plans and goals."

Lucas sighed and gave a look to his wife. Her face showed the smallest amount of concern.

"I have talked to Clive about trying for the property across from yours, I have house plans, a business plan to grow almonds and olives in hopes of being a client of yours. I know you want to expand your business to express oils from them. I have been paying attention. Clive knows a great farm manager and a farmhand or two to help me run the place. I have the startup money and Clive thinks if he cosigns for me they will allow me to own the land under my own name if I promise to get married within a set amount of time to add a man to the deed."

Angela looked from Lucas's face to Corinne's and saw they both looked pleased.

"I do not in any way want to offend you. I know you wanted the land, but once it was not to be I thought of the chance of knowing I could always live near you and even be a help to your business. It was consuming my thoughts. Please tell me what you think. I you say nay I will drop every plan and proceed no further. I love you both too much to offend you in any way."

Lucas laughed and Corinne jumped up and squeezed Angela in a big hug.

"What a beautiful schemer you are, that is a brilliant plan. You will have the safety of your own income and we get to be ahead of schedule with our plans." Corinne gave Angela a kiss on the cheek.

"I can think of no reason how I would be offended. The plan would make my wife happy, having you live so near her. You have no idea how melancholy she would get when you were away. She tried to hide it, but she could not." Lucas stood and hugged Angela as a sign of his goodwill.

"Have you met the land manager?" Lucas asked.

"I was hoping to meet him today. He currently works as Clive's mercantile manager but longs to be back on the land. He had an accident and lost a hand but Clive says his farming acumen is superb. His name is Earl Burgess."

"I have heard talk of him. Farmers all around seek his advice." Lucas stated. "He is a good Christian man. Lost his family back East in a fever. Very sad. He came west to start over. He is still strong and able. Gets around with only one hand better than some men with two."

Everyone laughed at Lucas's description.

"I give you my full blessing, but will stay clear of any of the council meetings. My presence will do you no good. Mr. Prince is better off not seeing my face near him, it makes him irritable." Lucas said with a hint of sarcasm.

"Well, Clive has a bit of a plan to make Mr. Prince take notice of my offer. It should be a fun spectacle, seeing Mr. Prince have to do our bidding. It will be mutually beneficial." Angela said with a gleam in her eye.

"Well, let's get to town." Corinne said, now eager to hear from Clive all the plans. "A part of me is jumping for joy at the thought of foiling Mr. Prince's schemes to run the land council."

"Please be sure to fill me in later darling. I will get the wagon for you ladies. I will be off to the west fields today." Lucas kissed his wife and waved to Angela and Violet.

"Be safe, my husband!" Corinne said.

"I will, my wife." Lucas said before he shut the door.

The wagon could be heard, as it pulled in front of the cabin, harnesses jangling and horses ready for their duties. Angela and Violet climbed into the back and sat on the side benches.

Corinne put on her leather gloves and drove them to town in safety. The road was only a little muddy from the recent rains but there were no mishaps.

The road in town was a little worse for wear but the ladies were able to get into Clive's store without soiling their skirts. Clive was waiting at the front counter with his son, JQ.

Clive welcomed the ladies and gave Angela a birthday kiss on her hand. He laughed and took the ladies across the street to the Milliners.. He insisted on Angela picking out a new hat.

"A woman must get a new hat at least once a year." Clive said in a high-pitched voice. "It keeps her from swooning."

The women enjoyed Clive's antics and once several hats had been tried on Angela settled for a dark green velvet bonnet with lace and two elegant feathers that wrapped across the top.

"That is so fetching with your red hair." Violet stated emphatically.

Angela made all the girls try on hats with her and made notes mentally to the hats that everyone fussed over. *It was always good to have a gift idea waiting in the back of your mind.* She had been poor for so long, suddenly having her own money to be a blessing to others had its merit. She knew she would be smart with the money her parents left her, but she would also be generous.

The meeting with Earl Burgess went extremely well. He was of medium height but was stocky and seemed strong. He had been informed about the prospect of land management and was excited for it. Clive had filled him in.

"I hope you won't mind working for a woman." Corinne stated once introductions were made. "I know some men get themselves all tied up when they have to do the daily work when a women is the one that pays 'em."

"I know some men like that, I am not one that minds working for any man or woman. My mother ran a thriving farm market when I was a youngin' and she was able to maintain good working relations with all the farm hands. My ma and pa were equals in business. I have no qualms in working for ya, Miss Fahey. Neither iffen you do get married I will gladly show respect to yer husband as well. I am looking forward to getting back to what I love doin'." Earl said. He had a big friendly grin and he used it often.

"I hope you don't mind my asking, why do you not want a farm of yer own. You are still young enough to have your own place." Angela asked, feeling bad for asking but her curiosity was genuine.

"I was saving to get my own place when I lost my hand. It was a long recovery and I nearly lost every dime I had while I laid in bed. Clive was kind in offering me a job to get me back on my feet. Someday I may like to start up a farm of my own again. But the land is a part of me, whether I help you build yours or my own, the joy is the same in seeing a farm take shape. The reaping and sowing is in my blood. I would be honored in helping you get your dream started." Earl's voice was solid and his intelligence showed in his eyes. He was a good man fallen on hard times. Angela could see that he would be loyal and work hard for her.

"We will be in touch. If you would walk the land with Clive and I some day soon we can make a detailed plan to show the land council. We do not want to have any reason for anyone to deny me because of ill preparedness." Angela said calmly, but her resolve to get the land was growing within her.

Earl nodded. "Yes Ma'am. Any night you wish. Just let Clive know and I will be there."

Clive gave Earl a pat on the back and thanked him. The women decided to go do some more shopping. Corinne was trying to convince Angela that she needed her own horse.

Angela said she would look at saddles and think about it. Corinne knew it would take time to convince Angela to trust the large animals but she was determined to someday make a rider out of her friend.

✢ ✢ ✢ ✢ ✢

Clive came by the Grants a week later with the paperwork in his hands. They had settled with Clive as the cosigner. Angela would be able to be the landowner with Clive as a cosigner until a husband was procured.

"You have two years to build a dwelling, and within that time to also break ground on at least two acres of fresh land." Clive read from the paper. "They added an addendum. They want a husband on the deed within four years."

Angela huffed a little at them dictating when she needed a husband.

"Well, I had hopes of starting the house before the winter?" Angela asked Clive with a twinkle in her eye.

"We shall see, Red." Clive said.

Corinne and Angela shared a smile and they both looked to Clive with their eyes wide. They had a few ideas on how things should get started.

— — The End — —

Character List

Corinne Grant - Married to Lucas Grant. Age 19. Started a business making medicinal oils from plants. Also has built a greenhouse for the cultivating of plants and herbs.

Lucas Grant - Graduate of Yale agricultural school, thrives on farming technology and making improvements in the agricultural field. Married to Corinne.

Chelsea Grant - Married to Russell Grant. Granddaughter of Clive Quackenbush

Russell Grant - Lucas Grant's brother, owns a farm nearby. They help each other often on each other's land.

Clive Quackenbush - Mountain man, fur trapper, Hudson Bay store owners, Government liaison for Indian Affairs, hunter and business man.

Jedediah Quackenbush - (nickname JQ) son of Clive, works at Oregon City store.

Millicent Quackenbush - (nickname Millie) married to JQ. Rarely works in the store but is active in her community and church.

Gabriel Quackenbush - Son of JQ and grandson of Clive, runs the Hudson bay store in San Francisco, California territory.

Amber Quackenbush - Married to Gabriel, Irish immigrant, came over as a child with her parents. Helps her husband run the store.

Dolly - (Indian name is Bluebird) half Indian, half white. Mother was Hopi and father was a french fur trapper. She was sent by her tribe to learn from Corinne about plants and medicines to bring back and teach the tribe.

Angela Fahey - Irish immigrant orphaned and sold into a work house at a young age with her brother. She became a maid in Corinne's Aunt's home and they were fast friends. She attempted to cross the Oregon Trail and was wounded early on and had to recover before continuing her journey.

Sean Fahey - Irish Immigrant who ran away from the work orphanage. Older brother to Angela Fahey. Last know whereabouts, fur trapping along the Snake River in the company of Ol' Willie.

Henry & Edith Sparks - Henry is the Captain at Fort Kearney, they took Angela in after an unfortunate accident. Edith and Henry are nursing her back to health.

Wildflower Series

Book 1 – Finding Her Way
(first release named Seeing the Elephant)

Book 2 – Angela's Hope

Coming 2014 … Book 3 – Daughter's of the Valley

Coming 2014 … Book 4 – The Watermill

Also by Leah Banicki

Runner Up – A Contemporary love story,
Set in the world of reality TV.

Connect with me online:

https://www.facebook.com/Leah.Banicki.Novelist

Please share your thoughts with me. leahsvoice@me.com

The self-publishing world is very rewarding but has its
challenges. Please remember to spread the word about my books
if you like them. By using word-of-mouth you help to bless an
author. Thank you, Leah B.

If you find glaring mistakes in this manuscript please let me know. I do my
best and my beta-readers and editors work very hard but we all are human.
Please email me with the mistake and location (at least the chapter), thanks.

If you love to read Christian romance you should check out these authors!

Books by Patricia Strefling
Edwina
Cecelia

Beyond Forgiveness

Ireland Rose
Rose's Legacy

Cadence

Wedgewick Woman

Stowaway Heart

Lacy's Lane
Lacy's Life
Lacy's Legacy

* * * * *

Also Available

By Patty A. Gammons

Hazards on the Hardwood